Out of the B...

Isabel Wolff was born in Warwickshire and read English at Cambridge. Her first novel was the bestselling romantic comedy, *The Trials of Tiffany Trott*, which was followed by her second bestselling novel, *The Making of Minty Malone*. Her freelance articles have appeared in many national newspapers, she writes a column for P-S magazine and reviews the papers for Breakfast News on BBC1. She lives in London.

ACCLAIM FOR *THE MAKING OF MINTY MALONE*

'Wolff's depiction of the up-and-down world of life for a go-getting Londoner is both hilarious and accurate and the plot moves quickly with abundant twists and turns ... truly gripping'   *The Times*

'The author has plenty of energy, a neat turn of phrase and a sense of the ridiculous'   *Telegraph*

'It's effervescent and heartwarming and somehow the pages just turn themselves'   *The Big Issue*

'A witty tale of a nice girl who reinvents herself'   *Elle*

ACCLAIM FOR *THE TRIALS OF TIFFANY TROTT*

'I absolutely, genuinely, loved it ... to be frank, I wish I'd written it myself. It's funny, charming, upbeat and unputdownable. Acutely observed, and so well-written. I was completely diverted and entertained'   MARIAN KEYES

'A very, very funny book'   NANCY ROBERTS, Talk Radio

'A hilarious novel'   JONATHAN SALE, *Independent*

ISABEL WOLFF

OUT OF THE BLUE

HarperCollins*Publishers*

This novel is a work of fiction. The names, characters and incidents portrayed in the story are products of the author's imagination, other than the names of the actors and actresses who appear in fictionalised incidents in the story. Any resemblance to actual persons, living or dead, events or localities is entirely coincidental.

HarperCollins*Publishers*
77–85 Fulham Palace Road,
Hammersmith, London W6 8JB

The HarperCollins website address is:
www.**fire**and**water**.com

A Paperback Original 2001
1 3 5 7 9 8 6 4 2

Copyright © Isabel Wolff 2001

Isabel Wolff asserts the moral right to
be identified as the author of this work

ISBN 0 00 651341 7

Set in Meridien by
Palimpsest Book Production Limited,
Polmont, Stirlingshire.

Printed and bound in Great Britain by
Omnia Books Ltd, Glasgow

For my godchildren

Nadia, Raphael and Laurie

Acknowledgements

Once again I owe a huge debt of gratitude to my agent, Clare Conville – *sine qua non* – and to my editor Rachel Hore. For background information about weather forecasting, I'd like to thank Helen Young, Sarah Wilmshurst, Andrea McLean and Tanya James. For insights into breakfast TV I'm indebted to Andrew Thompson and Michael Metcalfe; for sharing with me a few secrets from the make-up room I'd like to thank Judy Thonger and Marilyn Widdess. For an explanation into the mechanics of divorce I'm grateful to Sarah Anticoni and Emma Arkell. For the lowdown on life as a Private Detective I'd like to thank Ian Terry and Annie Sinclair. I owe a huge debt of gratitude to Colin Maxwell at the Royal Opera House, and to Emily Stubbs of the Wigmore Hall. I'm very grateful, too, to my mother, Ursula, for her memories of her convent days, and, for their many invaluable insights I'd like to thank Catherine O'Sullivan, Kate Williams, Eleana Haworth, Amanda Denning and Jane Cole. Thanks too, to Lucy Ferguson for her hawk-eyed copy-editing and, once again, I'm indebted to my father, Paul, and to Louise Clairmonte for reading the manuscript and giving me such helpful feedback along the way. In addition I'd like to thank everyone at the Battersea Dogs' Home, Marian Covington at the Chelsea and Westminster hospital, Hester Lacey at the Independent and Gareth and Helen Pugh at the Painswick Hotel. I'm also grateful to Peta Heskell for teaching me how to flirt, to Patrick Harris for musical advice, to Julien Hofer for enlightening me about computer games and to Jonathan Dicker for information about financial trading on the net. At HarperCollins I'd like to thank, well, everyone really – but especially Fiona McIntosh, Yvette Cowles, Amanda McElvie, Anne O'Brien, Venetia Butterfield, Tilly Ware and Jennifer Parr, who make it all such fun.

No dogs were harmed in the writing of this book.

January

It's funny how things can suddenly change, isn't it? They can alter in a heartbeat, in a breath. I think that's what happened tonight because, well, I don't really know how to explain it except to say that nothing feels quite the same. The evening started out well. In fact it felt like quite a success. There we were, in the restaurant, enjoying ourselves. Talking and laughing. Eating and drinking. Just eight of us. Just a small party. I wanted to cheer Peter up, because he's got his problems right now. So I'd planned this evening as a surprise. He hadn't suspected a thing. In fact, he'd even forgotten that it was our anniversary, and he's never done that before. But when he came home it was obvious that today's date had passed him by.

'Oh, Faith, I'm sorry,' he sighed as he opened my card. 'It's the sixth today, isn't it?' I nodded. 'I'm afraid I completely . . . forgot.'

'It doesn't matter,' I said brightly. 'Honestly, darling. Because I know you've got a lot on your mind.' He's having a bad time at work, you see. He's publishing director at Fenton & Friend, a job he used to love, but a year ago a new chairwoman called Charmaine arrived and she's been giving him serious grief. She and her creepy sidekick, Oliver. Or rather 'Oiliver' as Peter calls him, though not to his face, of course. But, between the two of them, Charmaine and Oliver are making Peter's life hell.

'How was it today?' I asked him cautiously as he hung up his coat.

'Awful,' he said wearily, running his hand through his sand-coloured hair. 'The old bat was going on at me about the bloody sales figures,' he said as he loosened his tie. 'She went on and on. In front of everyone. It was hideous. And Oliver just stood there, with a smirk on his fat face, oozing sycophancy from every pore. I tell you, Faith,' he added with a sigh, 'I'm for the chop. It can't be long.'

'Well, leave it to Andy,' I said.

A faraway look came into Peter's eyes and he said, 'Yes. I'll put my faith in Andy.' That's Andy Metzler, by the way. He's a headhunter. American. One of the best in town. Peter seems to think the world of him. It's 'Andy this' and 'Andy that', so I really hope Andy delivers the goods. But it'll be hard for Peter if he does have to leave Fenton & Friend, because he's been there for thirteen years. It's been a bit like our marriage, really – a stable and happy relationship, based on affection, loyalty and trust. But now it looks as though it might be coming to an end.

'I suppose nothing stays the same,' Peter added ruefully as he fixed us both a drink. 'I'm not joking, Faith,' he added as I took the last baubles off the Christmas tree. 'I'll be getting the old heave-ho, because *Oil*iver's after my job.'

Peter tries to be philosophical about it all, but I know he's very depressed. For example, he's not quite his normal genial self, and he's finding it hard to sleep. So for the past six months or so, we've been in separate rooms. Which is no bad thing as I have to get up at three thirty a.m. for my job at breakfast TV. I do the weather, at AM-UK! I've been there six years now, and I love it, despite the hideously early start. Normally, I let the alarm pip twice, slip out of bed, and Peter goes straight back to sleep. But at the moment he can't stand being disturbed, so he's in the spare room on the top floor. I don't mind. I understand. And sex isn't everything, you know. And in some ways I quite like it, because it means I can sleep with Graham instead. I love Graham. He's absolutely gorgeous, and he's incredibly bright. He snores a bit, which annoys me, but I poke him in the ribs and say, 'Darling – shhh!' And he opens

2

his eyes, looks at me lovingly, then drops off again – just like that. He's lucky. He sleeps very well, though sometimes he has nightmares and starts twitching violently and kicking his legs. But he doesn't mind being disturbed in the dead of night when I get up to go to work; in fact – and this is really sweet – he likes to get up too. He sits outside the bathroom while I have my shower. Then I hear the cab pull up, I put on my coat, and hug him goodbye.

Some of our friends think that Graham's a slightly odd name for a dog. And I suppose it is compared to Rover, say, or Gnasher, or Shep. But we decided on Graham because I found him in Graham Road, in Chiswick, where we live. That was two years ago. I'd been to the dentist for a filling, and when I came out there was this mongrel – very young, and terribly thin – looking at me expectantly as though we'd known each other for years. And he followed me all the way home, just trotting along gently behind, then sat down outside the front gate and wouldn't move. So eventually I invited him in, gave him a ham sandwich and that was that. We phoned the police, and the dogs' home, but no-one ever claimed him, and I'd have been distraught if they had because, to be honest, it was love at first sight, just like it was with Peter. I adore him. Graham, I mean. We just clicked. We really get on. And I think the reason why I love him so much is because of the sweet way he put his faith in me.

Peter was fine about it – he likes dogs too – and of course the children were thrilled, though Katie, who wants to be a psychiatrist, thinks I 'mother' Graham too much. She says I'm projecting my frustrated maternal desires for another child onto the dog. I know . . . ridiculous! But you have to take teen-agers very seriously, don't you, otherwise they get in a strop. Anyway, Graham's the baby of the family. He's only three. He doesn't have a pedigree, but he's got bucketloads of class. He's a collie cross of some sort, with a feathery red-gold coat, a white blaze on his chest and a foxy, elegant charm. We take him almost everywhere with us, though not to restaurants, of course. So this evening Peter settled him on his beanbag,

3

put on the telly for him – he likes *Food and Drink* – and said, 'Don't worry, old boy, Mummy and I are just going out for a quick bite.'

But Peter had no idea what I'd really planned. He thought we'd just be having an impromptu dinner, *tête à tête*. I'd told him I'd booked a table, but he'd assumed it was just for two. So when we got to the restaurant, and he saw the children sitting there, with his mother, Sarah, he looked so surprised and pleased. And I'd invited Mimi, an old college friend of ours, with her new husband, Mike.

'It's like *This Is Your Life*!' Peter exclaimed with a laugh, as we took off our coats. 'What a great idea, Faith,' he said. To be honest, I didn't do it just for him. I did it for myself, too, because I felt like marking the occasion in some way. I mean, fifteen years. Fifteen years. That's nearly half our lives.

'Fifteen years,' I said with a smile as we sat down. 'And it hasn't been a day too long.'

I've been very happy in my marriage, you see. And believe me, I still am. For example, I'm never, ever bored. There's always loads to do. We don't have much money, of course – we never have had – but we still have lots of fun. Well, we would do if it wasn't for the fact that Peter's working so hard: Charmaine's got him reading manuscripts most nights, and I have to be in bed by half past nine. But at weekends, that's when we catch up and really *enjoy* ourselves. The children come home – they're weekly boarders at a school in Kent – and we do, ooh, all sorts of things. We go for walks along the river, and we garden. We go to Tesco for the weekly shop. Sometimes we pop down to Ikea – the one in Brent Cross, though occasionally, for a bit of a change, we'll try the one in Croydon. And we might take out a video, or watch a bit of TV, and the children go and see their friends. Well, they would do if they had any. They're both what you'd call loners, I'm afraid. It worries me a bit. For example, Matt – he's twelve – just loves being on his computer. He's an addict, always has been; he was mouse-trained very young. I remember when he was five and I'd be putting him to bed, he'd say, 'Please can you wake me up at six o'clock tomorrow, Mummy, so I can go on the computer before I go to school?' And that struck me as rather sad, really, and he's still just like that now. But he's as happy as Larry with all his computer games and his CD Roms, so we don't like to interfere. As I say, he's not what you'd call an all rounder. For example, his written skills are dire. But as well as the computers he's brilliant at maths – in fact we call him 'Mattematics'. And that's why we sent him to Seaworth, because he wasn't coping well where he was. But he wouldn't go without Katie, and it suits her very well too because, look, don't think I'm being disloyal about my children – but they're not quite like other kids. For one thing Katie's far too old for her years. She's only fourteen now, but she's *so* serious-minded. She does nothing but read. I guess she takes after Peter, because for her it's books, not bytes. She's not at all fashion-conscious, like other girls of her age. There's no hint of any teenage rebellion, either; she seems to be just as 'sensible' as me. And because I never kicked over the traces, somehow I wish that she would. I keep hoping that she'll come home one weekend with a lime-green mohican or at the very least with a stud in her nose. But no such luck – all she ever does is read. As I say, she's dead keen on psychology, she's got lots of books on Jung and Freud, and she likes to practise her psychotherapeutic skills on all of us. And when we sat down at the table this evening, that's what she was doing.

'So, Granny, how did you feel about your divorce?' I heard her ask my mother-in-law. I made a sympathetic face at Sarah, but she just looked at me and smiled.

'Well, Katie, I felt fine about it,' she said. 'Because when two people are unhappy together, then it's sometimes better for them to part.'

'What were the chief factors, would you say, in the break-down of your relationship with Grandpa?'

'Well, darling,' she said as she lowered her menu, 'I think we just married too young.'

People sometimes say that about Peter and me. We married at twenty, you see; and so people do sometimes ask me – and to be honest I wish they wouldn't – if I ever have any regrets about that. But I don't. I never, ever wonder, 'What if . . . ?' because I've been happy really, in every way. Peter's a decent and honest man. He's very hard-working, he's *great* with the kids, and he's kind and considerate to his mum. He's quite handsome, too, though he needs to lose a little weight. But then, funnily enough, this evening I noticed that he *is* looking a bit more trim. I expect he's shed a few pounds recently because of all his stress. He's well turned out at the moment, too – I've noticed he's got a couple of lovely new ties. He says he has to be ready to slip out to interviews at the drop of a hat, so he's been dressing very smartly for work. So despite his present anxieties, he's looking pretty good. And after such a long time with Peter I could never fancy anyone else. People sometimes ask me if I *do* fantasy – sorry, *fancy*, anyone else – after fifteen years with the same man, and the answer is absolutely, categorically, definitively hardly ever. I mean, don't get me wrong. I'm made of flesh and blood. I can see when a man's attractive. For example, that chap who came round last week to mend the washing machine. He got my delicates cycle going again. And yes, objectively, I could see that he was a handsome sort of chap. Yes, I admit it – he was a bit of a hunk. And to be honest, I have been having some rather strange dreams about him recently. Quite vivid ones, featuring all sorts of peculiar items like a mobile phone for example, a TV remote control, and – this is *really* odd – a tub of blackcurrant sorbet! God knows what it means. I asked Katie actually, and she gave me this rather peculiar look and said it's just my *id*, running wild. As I say, I always humour her. No doubt my dreams are just the product of my rather fertile imagination. So no, I don't look at anyone else, although I do meet lots of attractive men at work. But I never fancy them, because I'm a very happily married woman, and sex isn't everything, you know. And of course Peter's very preoccupied right now. But yes, to answer your question, my marriage is in great shape, which is why I wanted to celebrate our fifteen happy years. So I booked a table at Snows, just down the road at Brook Green. We don't eat out very often. Peter has to go out to dinner with authors and agents sometimes, he's been doing quite a bit of that of late, but we don't do much ourselves. We can't afford it; what with the school fees – though luckily Matt got a scholarship – and of course publishing doesn't pay well. And my job's only part-time because I'm home by eleven every day. But I thought Peter needed a bit of a treat, so I decided on a party at Snows. It's actually called Snows on the Green, which was rather appropriate because today the snow *was* on the green. More than an inch of it. It started to fall this morning, and by late afternoon it had built into gentle drifts. And I love it when it snows because there's this eerie hush, and the world falls silent as though everyone's dropped off to sleep. And I just want to rush outside, clap my hands and shout, 'Come on! Wake up! Wake *up*!' And snow always reminds me of our wedding, because it snowed on that day too.

So I was sitting there in the restaurant, looking out of the window for a minute, watching the flakes batting gently against the panes and idly wondering what the next fifteen years of my life would bring. And I was feeling the slightly dizzying effects of the champagne. Not real champagne, obviously – just the Italian sparkling, but it's *very* good, and only half the price. I glanced round the table, listening to the low babble of conversation.

'Are your parents coming, Faith?' Sarah asked me as she nibbled on an olive.

'Oh no, they're on holiday again. I think they're scuba diving in St Lucia,' I said vaguely. 'Or maybe they're heli-skiing in Alaska. Or are they bungee-jumping in Botswana . . .' Mum and Dad are pensioners, or rather what you might call Silver Foxes or Glamorous Greys. They seem to stagger from cruise to safari to adventure holiday in a variety of increasingly exotic locations. Well, why not? After all, they've worked hard all their lives and so now's the time to have some fun.

'No, Sarah,' I said, 'I really can't remember *where* they are, they go away so much.'

'That's because they have classic avoidant personalities,' announced Katie with mild contempt. 'The incessant holidays are the means by which they avoid spending any time with us. I mean, the second Grandpa retired from Abbey National, that was it – they were off!'

'Oh, I know darling, but they send us lots of lovely postcards,' I said. 'And they phone up from time to time. And Granny loves chatting to you, doesn't she, Matt?'

'Er . . . yes,' he said slightly nervously as he looked up from his menu. 'Yes, I suppose she does.' Lately I've noticed that my mother often asks to speak to Matt on the phone. She loves chewing the fat with him, even ringing him at school, and I think it's *great* that they're developing such a nice bond.

'I do envy your parents,' said Sarah ruefully. 'I'd love to go away, but it's impossible because I'm tied to the shop.' Sarah owns a second-hand book shop in Dulwich. She bought it twenty years ago with her alimony after her husband, John, left her for an American woman and moved to the States. 'Oh, I've a small anniversary gift,' Sarah added as she handed me a beribboned parcel, inside which – Peter helped me open it – were two beautiful crystal glasses.

'What lovely tumblers, Sarah – thank you!'

'Yes, thanks Mum,' Peter said.

'Well, you see the fifteenth anniversary is the crystal one,' she explained as I noticed the red sticker on the box marked 'Fragile'. 'Anyway, are we all present and correct, now?' she added pleasantly.

'All except for Lily,' I replied. 'She says she's going to be a bit late.' At this I noticed Peter roll his eyes.

'Lily Jago?' said Mimi. 'Wow! I remember her at your wedding, she was your bridesmaid – she's famous now.'

'Yes,' I said proudly, 'she is. But she deserves every bit of it,' I added, 'because she's worked so incredibly hard.'

'What's she like?' asked Mimi.

'Like Lady Macbeth,' said Peter with a hollow laugh. 'But not as nice.'

'Darling!' I said reprovingly. 'Please don't say that – she's my best and oldest friend.'

'She treats staff like disposable knickers,' he added, 'and treads on heads as though they're stepping stones.'

'Peter, that's not fair,' I said. 'And you know it. She's very dedicated and she's brilliant, she deserves her tremendous success.' It used to grieve me that Peter didn't like Lily, but I got used to it years ago. He can't understand why I keep up with her and I've given up trying to explain. The fact is, Lily *matters* to me. I've known her for twenty-five years – since our convent days – so we have an unbreakable bond. But I mean, I'm not blind – I know that Lily's no angel. For example, she's a little bit touchy, and she's got a wicked tongue. She's also a 'bit of a one' with the boys – but then why shouldn't she be? She's single, and she's beautiful. Why shouldn't she play the field? Why shouldn't a gorgeous thirty-five-year-old woman, in her prime, have lots of lovers and lots of fun? Why shouldn't a gorgeous thirty-five-year-old woman be made to feel desirable and loved? Why *shouldn't* a thirty-five-year-old woman have romantic weekends in country house hotels with jacuzzis and fluffy towels? Why *shouldn't any* thirty-five-year-old woman have flowers and champagne and little presents? I mean, once you're married, that's that; romance flies out the window, and you're with the same old body every night. So I don't blame Lily at all, though I don't think her choice of boyfriends is great. Every week, it seems, we see her staring at us out of the pages of *Hello!* or *OK!* with this footballer, or that rock star, or some actor from that new soap on Channel 4. And I think, mmm. Mmmm. Lily could do better, I think. So, no, she hasn't got brilliant taste in men, although at least these days – praise the Lord! – she's stopped going for the married ones. Yes, I'm afraid to say she used to be a little bit naughty like that. And I did once remind her that adultery is forbidden by the seventh commandment.

'I didn't commit adultery,' she said indignantly. 'I'm single, so it was only fornication.' Lily's not interested in marriage herself, by the way; she's totally dedicated to her career. 'I'm footloose and fiancé free!' she always likes to exclaim. I must say, she'd be a bit of a challenge to any man. For a start, she's *very* opinionated, and she bears interminable grudges. Peter thinks she's dangerous, but she's not. She's simply tribal; by which I mean she's loyal to her friends but ruthless to her foes, and I know exactly which category I'm in.

'Lily had twelve other invitations tonight,' I said. 'She knows *so* many people!'

'Yes, Mum,' said Katie matter-of-factly. 'But you're her only friend.'

'Well, maybe that's true, darling,' I said with a tiny stab of pride, 'but I still think it's sweet of her to come.'

'Very gracious,' said Peter wryly. He'd had a couple of drinks by then. 'I can't wait for the dramatic entrance,' he added sarcastically.

'Darling,' I said patiently, 'Lily can't *help* making an entrance. I mean, it's not her fault she's so stunning.' She is. In fact she's jaw-dropping. Everybody stares. She's terribly tall for a start, and whippety thin, and she's always exquisitely dressed. Unlike me. I get a small allowance from work for the things I wear on TV and I tend to spend it in Principles – I've always liked their stuff. Just recently I've started to get quite interested in Next, and Episode. But Lily gets a *huge* clothing allowance, and the designers send her things too, so she always looks amazing – in fact, she's amazing full stop. And even Peter will admit that she has huge talent, and guts and drive. You see, she had a very tough start in life. I remember the day she arrived at St Bede's. I have this vivid picture in my mind of Reverend Mother standing on stage in the main hall one morning after Mass; and next to her was this new girl – we were all *agog* to know who she was.

'Girls,' said Reverend Mother as a hush descended. 'This is Lily. Lily Jago. Now, we must all be kind to Lily,' she went on benignly, 'because Lily is very poor.' I will never forget, to my dying day, the look of fury on Lily's face. And of course the girls weren't kind to her at all. Far from it. They teased her about her accent and they laughed at her lack of finesse; they disparaged her evident poverty and they made terrible fun of her folks. They called her 'Lily White', which she loathed. Then, when they realised how clever she was, they hated her for that as well. But I didn't hate her. I liked her and I felt drawn to her, perhaps because I was an outsider too. I got laughed at a lot at school. My nickname was 'Faith Value', because they all said I was very naïve. I was impossible to tease, apparently, because I could never get the joke. I thought it was obvious that the chicken's reason for crossing the road was to reach the other side. I couldn't see why that was funny, really. I mean, why else *would* the chicken cross the road? And of *course* a bell is necessary on a bicycle – otherwise you could have a very nasty accident. It's obvious. So why's that funny? Do you see what I mean? The other girls all said I was a credulous sap. Ridiculous! I'm not. But I *am* trusting. Oh yes. I want to have faith in people and I do. I give everyone the benefit of the doubt, and I tend to believe what they say. Because that's how I want to be. I decided, a long time ago, that I didn't want to be cynical like Lily. She's the suspicious sort, and though I'm desperately fond of her, I could never be like that myself. That's probably why my purse is full of foreign coins, for example, because I never, ever check my change. Shopkeepers are constantly palming off on me their dimes and their pfennigs and their francs. But I don't care, because I don't want to be the kind of woman who's always on her guard. I guess I'm a natural optimist – I always trust that things will work out. I'm trusting in my marriage, too. I simply don't think that Peter would ever stray. And he hasn't – so I was right. And I believe you can make your own destiny, by the strength of your mental attitude. Anyway, I rather liked the fact that Lily was naughty, because I knew it was something I could never be. I remember, once, when we were thirteen, making a dash for the town. We'd lied to Sister St Wilfred, and said we were going for a walk. But we got the bus to Reading instead – using my pocket money, of course – and we bought sweets and Lily bought cigarettes, and she got talking to some boys. Then, on the way back, she did something awful – she went into a newsagent and nicked a copy of *Harpers and Queen*. I wanted her to return it but she refused, though she promised to mention it in confession. But I remember her poring over it in the dormitory later, utterly entranced; she was fingering it reverentially, as though it were a holy text. Then she swore out loud that one day she'd be the editor of a magazine like that; and the girls all fell about laughing. But now she is.

'Lily's been in New York for a long time, hasn't she?' said Mimi as she broke into her bread roll. 'I've seen lots of stuff about her in the press.'

'Six years,' I said. 'She was working on *Mirabella* and *Vanity Fair*.' And as we ate our anti pasti I told them about her career, and about how single-minded she'd been. Because I'm very proud of my friendship with her. And I told them about the way she'd even left Cambridge early because she was offered some lowly job at *Marie Claire*. But it was the start of her long climb up the greasy pole, or rather shiny cover. She was determined to reach the top – and now she has. Three months ago she became the first black woman to edit *Moi!*

That's *Moi-Même!* magazine, of course, commonly known as *Moi!* Or perhaps 'Mwaaah, mwaaah!' as Peter always likes to say. He's a bit of a snob about magazines, he thinks they're utterly trite. He calls Lily the 'High Priestess of Gloss'. But *chacun à son goût*, I say, and Lily's brilliant at what she does. Mind you, some of the stories are pretty silly. Not my kind of thing at all. It's all this, 'What's Hot What's Not!' kind of stuff, and 'Grey – the new black! Fat – the new thin! Old – the new young!' But the magazine always looks beautiful because the photography's out of this world. And the writing's good too, because Lily says she can sort out 'the wit from the chaff'. Oh yes, Lily's seriously successful. And yes, she's got a wicked tongue. But she would never do anything to hurt me. I know that for a fact.

Anyway, by nine Lily still hadn't arrived, and we'd all finished our starters and were waiting for the main course which in my case was chump of lamb. And the conversation

12

had turned back to marriage, and to Peter and me.

'Fifteen years!' Mimi exclaimed with a laugh. 'I just can't believe it! I remember your wedding day so well. In the university chapel. We all froze to death, it was snowing, just like today.'

'That's because it was a white wedding!' I quipped. Peter laughed.

'But how amazing that this is your fifteenth anniversary,' Mimi added. 'Good God! I haven't even had my first!' We all smiled at that, and she gave her husband, Mike, a gooey look and said, 'I've only just had *my* happy ending!'

'New beginning, you mean,' he replied. And I felt very strange when he said that; very strange indeed. But at the same time I thought, yes, he's right. It *is* a new beginning. That's exactly what it is. They only got married last May. They both peeped at their six-week-old baby, Alice, who was asleep in her car seat on the floor. I looked across the table at my two 'babies', who are fourteen and twelve. And it struck me again, as it has done recently, that Peter and I are completely out of step with our peers. Most of them are like Mimi, they're marrying and having kids now. But we did that fifteen years ago, and it won't be long before our children leave home.

'You two got married when you were still at college, didn't you?' Mike asked.

'In our second year,' I said. 'We just couldn't wait,' I explained. 'Isn't that right, darling?' And Peter looked at me, through the flickering candles, and gave me a little smile. 'We were madly in love,' I went on, emboldened by the sparkling wine. 'And good Catholics don't live in sin!' Actually I'm not a very good Catholic, though I was, then. I'm a sort of Christmas Catholic now. I go to church no more than three or four times a year.

'I remember when you two met,' said Mimi. 'It was in our first term at Durham, at the freshers' ball. You looked at Peter, Faith, and you whispered to me, "That's the man I'm going to marry," – and you did!'

'We were like Superglue,' I giggled. 'We bonded in seconds!' At that Peter's mother, Sarah, smiled. I like Sarah. We've always got on well. And yes, she did have misgivings at the time because she thought we'd end up divorced, like her. But we didn't do that, and I'm sure we won't. As I say, I have faith in the future. Anyway, Sarah was chatting away to the children – she hadn't seen them for a while – and Peter was beginning to unwind a bit as we talked to Mimi and Mike. We'd had a bit to drink by now, and were all feeling mellow and warm, when suddenly there was an icy blast – the door had opened: Lily had finally arrived.

It's always fun watching Lily entering a room. You can almost hear the clunk of jawbones hitting the floor. That's what it was like tonight. She's so used to it, she claims never to notice, but it always makes me smile.

'Darlings, I'm *so* sorry!' she called out as she swept in on a cloud of Obsession, oblivious to the collective male stares. '*So* sorry,' she reiterated as her floor-length arctic fox slid from her shoulders and was quickly gathered up by the *maitre d'*. 'You see Gore's in town – Vidal not Al – so we had a quick drink at the Ritz, then I had to go down Cork Street where there was this *tedious* private view . . .' She removed her fur hat and I could see snowflakes on her shoulder-length, raven-black hair. 'And Chanel were launching their new scent,' she went on, 'so of course I had to show my face there . . .' She handed the waiter an assortment of exquisite little bags. 'But I only stayed ten minutes at Lord Linley's Twelfth Night party because I just wanted to be here with you.' I glanced at Mimi – she was speechless.

'Happy anniversary, Faith, darling!' Lily exclaimed, handing me a Tiffany bag. Inside, in a silk-lined presentation box, was a small cylinder made of sterling silver.

'It's a telescope,' I said wonderingly, holding it up to my left eye. 'Oh! No it isn't, it's a . . . ooh how *lovely*.' As I rotated the end with my right hand, a thousand sequins – red and purple and green – arranged themselves into dazzling patterns, like the fractals of a technicolour snowflake.

'How wonderful,' I murmured. 'A kaleidoscope. I haven't seen one of these for years.'

'I couldn't decide what to get you,' said Lily, 'but I thought this might be fun. It's for Peter as well,' she added, giving him a feline smile.

'Thank you, Lily,' he replied.

'What a fantastic present,' I said, hugging her. 'Hey, great outfit, too!' Today she was wearing a viridian green cashmere twin-set, a knee-length gaberdine skirt, and a pair of what I think were probably Jimmy Choo snakeskin boots.

'The cashmere's only Nicole Farhi,' she said. 'But I'm getting *so* bored of Voyage. Jil Sander sent me the skirt. Wasn't that sweet? The cut's so sharp it ought to be classed as an offensive weapon. When I've finished with it, Faith, it's yours.'

'Thanks, Lily,' I said ruefully. 'But it wouldn't go past my knees.' Lily's a size ten, and I'm a fourteen. She's almost six foot – more in her heels – and I'm only five foot four. Which is funny, because when we were nine we were both exactly the same size. She used to have my cast-offs then, but now she gives me hers. She used to be the one who was penniless, but now it's me. Still, we all make our choices in life, and as I say, I'm quite happy with mine.

The waiter poured Lily a glass of Chablis, and then he looked at the large, Louis Vuitton carrier on her lap and said, 'May I take that for you, madam?'

'Oh, no thank you,' she replied, looking slightly furtive. 'This is my handbag, you see.'

'Really, madam?' he said suspiciously.

'Absolutely,' Lily shot back with a dazzling smile, her refulgent teeth sparkling like frost against the rich, dark bronze of her skin. 'I always hang on to this one,' she explained. I knew why. She's very naughty like that. But then, as I say, Lily has always broken rules. As the waiter retreated she put the bag under the table and quickly undid the zip. Then she looked at me, grinned, and swiped the last bit of meat from my plate.

'Here, darling!' she whispered as her beautifully manicured

15

hand shot down below. 'Auntie Faith wants you to have this.' We could hear snuffling, snorty little sounds, followed by a tinny whine. Katie, Sarah and I lifted the cloth and peered under the table where Lily's Shih Tzu, Jennifer, had just scoffed the last of my lamb. A pink tongue shot out and wrapped itself around her furry little face; then she stared at us blankly with a pair of huge, bulging, black eyes.

'What a sweet hairstyle,' said Sarah with a laugh. Jennifer's flowing locks had been gathered into a top knot and secured with a sparkling clip.

'Oh yes, she's *so* gorgeous,' Lily replied with a sigh. 'Isn't she, Faith? Isn't she just the prettiest little thing in the world?'

'Oh, yes,' I lied, looking at Jennifer's undershot jaw, her crooked teeth, her bearded chin and flat little face. 'Jennifer's just . . . great,' I added with a hypocritical smile. Again, some people might think that Jennifer's an unusual choice of name for a dog. In fact her full name is Jennifer Aniston. This is because of her long, silky blonde hair, and because she's 'worth it'. At least I hope so, because Lily spends half her salary on that pooch. The Louis Vuitton doggy bag, for example – that's at least five hundred pounds' worth. She's also got eight Gucci dog collars, five Chanel leads, two Burberry coats, three Paul Smith bowls, and you should see her bed! It's like an oriental tent, complete with Chinese wall-hangings and a silk rug. The purpose of this, apparently, is to remind Jennifer of her ancient origins in Imperial Peking. Shih Tzus were temple dogs, and Lily worships hers. But between you and me, Jennifer Aniston is simply not my type. She's not Graham's, either. He tends to stare at her, slightly incredulously, as though he's not entirely sure she's a dog.

'How's *mag*land?' I asked brightly, changing the subject.

'Fabulous,' Lily replied. 'Here's the February issue – look! It's just come in from the printers, I'm having them biked all over town.' The magazine felt heavy in my hands, and shone under the spotlights like ice. *Moi!* it proclaimed on the masthead, above a photo of Kate Moss. I glanced at the headlines: 'Pees and Queues – Five Star Loos!' 'Prolier Than Thou – the REAL

16

New Labour!' 'It Girls – Just Lamé Ducks?' and 'Pulling Power – Our Top Ten Tweezers!'

'Hype springs eternal!' muttered Peter, rolling his eyes.

I gave him a discreet kick, then Sarah and I flicked through the magazine, careful to admire, aloud, the wonderful photos, the features, and the fashion. And the ads, of course. There were lots of those. Some of them, I happen to know, cost thirty thousand pounds a page, which is more than I earn in a year. There was one particular ad for an expensive face cream, with a photo of a Persian kitten, and though I'm a doggy sort of person, I just couldn't help going, 'Aaaaah!'

'That's the "classical conditioning" reflex, Mum,' said Katie knowledgeably. 'Extremely effective for selling. It works by establishing an association between a product and a pleasant feeling. Stayman and Batra did a fascinating study in 1991 which proved that emotional states affect consumer choice.' As I say, she's not like other girls. In the meantime Lily had been rattling on about circulation and pagination and subscription rates and God knows what. 'We've got a hundred and twenty advertising pages,' she explained happily, 'and a hundred and thirty editorial. This is our biggest issue yet. We're on a roll.'

At the front was an article about dieting and a profile of Sharon Stone. There was an extract from the new Ian McEwan novel, and the society diary section, 'I Spy'. There were pages on lotions and potions, and a competition to win a car. Now, I love competitions. I do quite a lot of them, though obviously I couldn't enter this one because friends of the editor are barred. But whenever I've got time I send off the forms. I actually won something recently – I was really chuffed – a year's supply of Finish rinse aid. I've never won anything big though, but maybe one day I will.

By now, Mimi, who works at Radio 4, had plucked up her courage and was talking to Lily about her career.

'Other women's magazines have falling circulations,' Mimi said, 'but yours seems to be soaring.'

'It's gone up by twenty per cent since I took over,' said Lily triumphantly. 'They're all quaking in their Manolos at *Vogue*!'

'Would you like to come on *Woman's Hour*?' Mimi asked. 'When I'm back from maternity leave? You'd be talking about *Moi!*, of course, and about your innovatory editing style. But I think the listeners would also like to know about you – your background, and your convent days.' Lily snorted with laughter.

'I wasn't exactly a model pupil. Ask Faith!' I smiled and nodded. It was true. But there are reasons for that. There are very good reasons why Lily, though obviously gifted, was rather difficult at school. For a start, she was just plucked from her home: it was done with the best of intentions, but she was taken away and placed in an environment where she was bound to feel she didn't fit in. At eight, her exceptional brain was spotted by a teacher, who told the local priest, who then contacted the bishop, who wrote to Reverend Mother who agreed to take her on as a scholarship girl. And that was how Lily left the Caribbean to be educated at St Bede's.

'Lily was a brilliant pupil,' I said. 'She wanted to be top in everything, and she was!'

'Except good behaviour,' Lily pointed out with a throaty laugh. This was absolutely true. We had to go to confession every Saturday morning, and she used to spend hours in there. I was convinced she must be making things up, so I remember once telling her that inventing transgressions was, in itself, a mortal sin.

'It's a bit like wasting police time,' I explained, 'so you really shouldn't fabricate sins.'

'I wasn't fabricating anything,' she retorted, rolling her huge brown eyes.

I'm afraid Lily wasn't what you'd call popular. She could be very sharp, for example, and the girls feared her razor tongue. When we were sixteen, Sister St Joseph gave us a career talk and she looked at Dinah Shaw, who was terribly dim, and said, 'Dinah, what are *you* going to be when you leave St Bede's?' And Lily shouted, 'Twenty-five!'

But if, as I say, Lily was naughty, it was because of all the appalling snobbery and spite. Venetia Smedley was the

18

worst. She came from the Channel Islands and was known as the Jersey Cow. At breakfast one morning – I'll never forget it – Venetia announced, in a very loud voice, 'My parents are off to St Kitts next week. They always stay at the Four Winds in Banana Bay. Isn't that a coincidence, Lily? Perhaps your mother will be cleaning their room.' Lily just looked at her, lowered her spoon and said, 'Yes, Venetia. Perhaps she will.' But a few months later she exacted a dreadful revenge. Venetia had had bridgework, having fallen off her pony two years before. She was very embarrassed about this and would never let anyone see her cleaning her teeth. Lily made some toffee; it was unbelievably sticky because – I only learned this afterwards – she'd adulterated it with glue. Then she offered some to Venetia, and the look of triumph on Lily's face when Venetia's three false teeth came out ... 'Oh, I'm *so* sorry, Venetia,' she said sweetly. 'I forgot that you wore dentures.' Afterwards, I found her in the grounds, rocking with laughter. And she looked at me gleefully and whispered, 'Vengeance is mine, saith the Lord. I will repay!' And she did.

She's still calling in her debts to this day.

'I had Camilla Fanshawe on the phone this morning,' she said to me with a snigger as she spooned up her guacamole. 'She's marrying some squitty banker and she was begging me, Faith, *begging* me to cover her wedding in "I Spy". But she was only saying that because Letty Brocklebank got hers into *Tatler*. And Camilla was practically blubbing and saying how she always liked me *so* much at school and how she *knew* I'd be a success because I was *so* clever, and what about it? Old school tie and all that? And I let her go on and on and then I said, very sweetly, "Well I'm *terribly* sorry, Camilla; I'm afraid we don't cover small, provincial weddings in *Moi!*"'

Yes, Lily's had the last laugh, all right. She's outsmarted them all – in every way. Intellectually, of course, though that was easy enough – but she outsmarted them socially, too. Her mind was like a radar, and she quickly cracked the code. Her table manners changed, her deportment improved and within two years her voice was transformed. Gone was her rich, Caribbean inflection and in its place was cut glass. Peter says she has 'irritable vowel syndrome', but, as I say, he's not really a fan.

Mimi, clearly fascinated by Lily, was asking us about St Bede's. So we explained that there was Mass every morning, benediction on Wednesdays, the rosary on Thursdays, confession on Saturdays, and sung Latin Mass on Sundays.

'Was there time for any lessons with all that?' Mike enquired.

'Oh yes,' I said tipsily, 'and Lily was jolly good at them! She got twelve "O" levels, four A-grade A levels, and an exhibition to Cambridge at seventeen.'

'What about sports?'

'We had hockey and netball.'

'I was *useless*,' said Lily with a laugh. 'All that running and jumping – such a bore – I really couldn't be fagged. I was no good at music, either,' she giggled. I kept quiet; it was perfectly true. In fact she had a voice like a corncrake and standing next to her during 'Faith of Our Fathers' was not a musically rewarding experience. 'As for dancing,' she went on. 'I was *appalling* at that! I had two left feet – I still have.'

'There was lots of drama,' I went on enthusiastically. 'It was great. Especially the annual school play . . .' Suddenly I saw the smile slide off Lily's face and she gave me a censuring stare. And then I remembered. Drama's a sore point. We don't talk about that. You see, Lily wasn't very good at acting, and without sounding conceited, I was. The awful thing was that she loved it, but she was always so over the top. I mean, she couldn't even make the sign of the cross without looking as though she was directing traffic. So acting was not her forté and this spoiled our friendship for a while. When we were in the Lower Sixth, Reverend Mother was casting the school play. She decided to do *Othello* and, as the only non-white girl at St Bede's, Lily presumed the title role would be hers. She prepared hard for the part, and I helped her to go through her lines. But when, after auditions, the list went up, the lead had gone not to Lily, but to me. She didn't take it well, I'm afraid. In fact she stormed into Reverend Mother's office – I was there at the time – and shouted, 'It's because I'm *black*, isn't it?'

'No, Lily,' said Reverend Mother calmly. 'It's because you are not a good enough actress. You have many gifts,' she went on calmly. 'I know you are going to be a huge success in life. But I confidently predict that your future triumphs will not take place on the stage.' There was silence. Then Lily left. She wouldn't speak to me for a month. But what was I supposed to do? Refuse the part? It was a wonderful role, and everyone said I did it well; I can still remember those marvellous lines to this day: '*I had been happy . . . so I had nothing known. So now, forever, farewell the tranquil mind!*'

Lily gradually got over her disappointment, though she refused to come to the play; and we never, ever spoke of it again – until tonight. I don't think it was tactless of me to mention it, given that it was eighteen years ago and our roles have long since been reversed. I mean, she's the star now. Not me. She's the celebrated and successful one. She's the one with the huge flat in Chelsea, and the fridge full of champagne and foie gras. I'm the boring suburban housewife with two children and sensible shoes, who thinks a trip to Ikea's a treat. So I appreciate the fact that Lily's kept in touch all this time, when you consider how our lives have diverged.

At this point – it must have been almost ten thirty – we'd gone on to pudding. The candles had almost burned down, and the bottles of wine had been drunk. I thought Peter had had one too many; I could tell that he was quite well oiled. He and Matt were talking about the Internet, and Katie was doing some psychometric tests on Lily – Lily's her godmother, so she claimed not to mind. Meanwhile Mimi, still clearly struck by the novelty of being married, was asking me if I had any wisdom to impart.

'Tell me, Faith,' she whispered, 'what's the secret of a successful marriage?'

'I don't know,' I murmured, lifting a spoonful of poached autumn fruits to my mouth. 'I only know that after fifteen years together Peter and I have this unbreakable bond. We're like the wisteria growing up the front of our house – we're completely intertwined.'

'What quality do you admire in him most?' Mimi added.

'His ability to find my contact lenses whenever I lose one,' I giggled. 'He's brilliant at it.'

'No, seriously,' Mimi pressed me. 'What do you like about him best?'

'His decency,' I replied, 'and his truthfulness. Peter always tells the truth.'

Mike thought that was such a nice thing to say that he said he thought Peter ought to make a little speech.

'Go on,' he said.

'Oh no,' groaned Peter.

'Please,' Mimi insisted. 'This is an occasion, after all.'

'Oh, all right,' Peter conceded after another sip of wine. 'Er . . . I just want to say . . .' he began, getting unsteadily to his feet, 'that Faith was my first love, and that my fifteen years with her feel like a millstone . . .'

'Freudian slip!' said Katie.

'I mean, a *mile*stone,' he corrected himself. 'A milestone. That's what I mean. An incredible achievement, in fact. When you consider. And I just can't believe where the last fifteen years of my life have gone.' That was it. He'd finished. I tried to smile. As I say, he's very preoccupied at work, so he's not quite his usual relaxed and happy self.

'He's rather tired,' I whispered diplomatically to Mimi and Mike.

'He does seem distracted,' Lily agreed.

'Yes,' I said, 'no doubt because, well, he's got a lot on his mind right now.'

'I must say, he's looking good though,' Lily murmured as our coffee arrived. 'Hasn't he lost a bit of weight?'

'Er, yes, he has. He's looking pretty trim, you're right.'

'Nice tie he's wearing,' she whispered appreciatively.

'Yes. Yes,' I agreed. 'Nice tie.'

Then Lily reached into her bag, took out a box of Pandora matches and struck one. It hissed and flared as it ignited, then died down to a steady yellow flame. She lifted a cheroot to her lips, lit it and inhaled deeply, then blew the smoke away. Then she looked at me seriously and said, very, very softly, 'I think you're *marvellous* to trust him.'

This struck me as a very strange remark, because of course I trust Peter – I always have. As I say, he's a truthful man. So I didn't have a clue what Lily meant, and I certainly didn't want to ask her in front of everyone else. In any case, Peter was waving for the bill now – it was late, and the evening was drawing to an end.

'– let's get our coats.'

'– is this inclusive?'

'– no, our treat, Mike.'

'– Katie, can you get Granny's coat?'

'– very kind, Peter. Next time we take you.'

'– who's got the baby?'

'– oh look, there's a cab.'

Before we knew what had happened, we were all standing outside, kissing each other goodbye.

'What a wonderful evening,' said Mimi as the snowflakes fell gently onto her hair. 'I hope *we* make it to fifteen years,' she added as she strapped the baby into the back of the car.

'I hope we make it to thirty,' said Mike gallantly. 'Thanks for a lovely dinner, you two – bye bye.' The children were submitting to being kissed by Lily, though both of them hate her scent, Jennifer had been zipped up, and Sarah had gone to her car. Then I flagged down a passing cab, and climbed in with Peter and the kids.

'What a great evening,' he said as we swished along the wet, sleety road.

'Yes, it was, darling,' I said. 'I really enjoyed it too.' And it's true. I did. But at the same time I was aware, in a way I could not yet define, that somehow, something had changed.

There are three things that people always ask you if you work for breakfast TV. What time do you have to get up? What time do you have to go to bed? And does it wreck your social life? Sometimes I just feel like holding up a banner at parties saying, 'Three thirty, nine thirty, and YES!' You simply never get used to it. Did I say that you do? Well, it's not true – you *never* get used to the early start. It's horrible. It's horrible when the alarm goes off at half past three and your body's still crying out for sleep. And it's even worse if you're feeling unhappy, as I was this morning, and are slightly hungover to boot. Graham grumbled as I lurched out of bed, but declined to stand guard by the bathroom door. I showered, squished on a little Escape – my favourite scent at the moment – put on my navy Principles suit, then went down to the waiting cab. As we pulled out of Elliot Road, I remembered Lily's words again: *I think you're marvellous to trust him . . . trust him . . . I think you're marvellous to trust . . .* I stared out of the window as we drove through the slush-filled streets, turning her comment over and over in my mind; examining it from all angles, as I might study an interesting stone. But however much I thought about it, I still didn't know what she meant. Nor was I at all sure that I really *wanted* to know. I mean, Lily does have a habit of saying things I don't particularly like, but usually I just ignore them. That's what I forced myself to do this morning as I wrenched my thoughts towards work. After all, I told myself firmly, I have an important job to do. People depend on me. I can make or break their day. When I'm about to go on air Terry, the 'star' presenter, looks into the camera and says, 'Well folks, what's the weather going to do today? Let's h-a-v-e- FAITH!' So on I come, and I tell them, and the viewers *do* have faith in me. They rely on me to tell them if they need to take a coat or a brolly, or if the humidity's going to be high. I let them know if it's going to be very windy, and if it's safe to set sail, or drive. So I think the weather forecast's really important, but I'm afraid my colleagues don't feel the same. They just see it as this insignificant little slot that comes on three minutes before the news. To them it's just a buffer, before the junction – they're always trying to cut me down. I'm meant to have two and a half minutes, but often it's less than one. But there's nothing I can do about it because it's all controlled from the technical gallery. For example, I can be in the middle of some fascinating piece about warm fronts when I suddenly hear the director, in my earpiece, shouting at me to stop. They're really rude about it sometimes – I hear them yelling, 'Shut up, Faith! Shut up! SHUT UP!' It's terribly distracting. What they're *meant* to do is to calmly count me down from ten, and I know that by the time I hear them say 'zero', I have to have signed off, with a nice smile. Equally, if they lose a news item, I'll hear someone screaming, 'Fill, Faith! Fill! Fill! *Fill*!' But I'm not fazed, because I can cope; I once filled from thirty seconds right up to *four minutes*! And I pride myself on being able to stay calm in those situations and to come out *exactly* when required. Another thing, because I use open talkback, I can hear them all gossiping in the gallery during my slot. The weather's their down time, you see. That's when they put their feet up because they don't have anything to do. This is because I change the graphics with my clicker, and I ad lib my script, so I don't have an autocue. So while I'm doing my slot I can hear them sorting out what went wrong with the previous item, or telling make-up to fix Terry's hair, or instructing the cameraman to close in on so and so, or boasting about some bird they pulled down at the pub. And they forget that I'm on air, broadcasting live, and that I can hear every word they say. So one way and another, being a weather presenter is a pretty stressful job. But I enjoy it. I really do, especially at this time of year. I love the winter, you see: not just because of my optimistic outlook on life, but because in winter the weather's *great*. In the summer we only get three types: either it's rainy, it's cloudy, or it's fine. But at this time of year we get the works. We get ice, and fog, and frost, and rain, and we get sleet and hail and snow. We get fine, clear weather too if there's an anti-cyclone, and we can get hurricane force winds as well. So if you're in the weather business, like I am, then winter's a thrilling time. And although the hours are pretty dreadful, I enjoy myself once I'm at work. So this morning, despite my worries, and my headache, I felt the usual frisson as we drove through the gates.

It takes about twenty minutes to get to AM-UK! which is based in a converted warehouse in Ealing. It's not a beautiful building, but I rather like it there. The production office on the third floor is open plan, which has its drawbacks, of course, not least seeing the ashen faces of my colleagues every morning when I arrive. They sit there in the green glow of their computer screens like extras from *The Night of the Living Dead*, but that's what comes of spending half the year in almost perpetual dark. I usually get in at four, have a quick espresso from the machine, and then get straight down to work. First I read the faxed briefing from International Weather Productions, which forms the basis of my reports. Then I log on to my computer – with its 'rainbow' screensaver – and study the satellite charts. For although I never trained as a meteorologist I do actually know my stuff, because when AM-UK! took me on, they sent me on a six-week forecasting course. So I'm not just spouting someone else's script, I get to write my own. I'd like to make it clear that I'm not a glamorous type of weather girl. Nicole Kidman in *To Die For*? Well, that's just not me. Blonde and gorgeous? No. In fact I'm a bit mousey to look at, which is why I got the job.

'What we like about *you*,' said our wimpish editor Darryl when he interviewed me, 'is that you're so nice and *ordinary* – you won't threaten the housewives too much. They'll be sitting there and thinking to themselves, "Well, I could do better than that!"'

To be honest, I wasn't quite sure how I felt about that remark, but I gave him the benefit of the doubt. And I can see what he means: he wanted someone who'd look business-like but pleasant, and I do. I'm not the kind of forecaster to hog the limelight, or try to 'twinkle' too much. I just go to work and do my job in a competent, friendly way. I'm very happy standing by the charts, with my clicker, talking about cold snaps and sunny spells, and I don't regard weather presenting as a stepping stone to greater things. I've got just the job I want, thank you very much – unlike our showbiz reporter, Tatiana.

'Hello Tatiana,' I said pleasantly as I passed her desk. Usually she's reasonably friendly, because she knows that I'm no threat. Today, however, she was preoccupied and didn't hear me; this was because she was busy mutilating a publicity shot of Sophie, our new presenter.

'Morning Tatty,' I tried again, and was rewarded with a thin smile. Then she put down her Stanley knife, threw the pieces into the bin and went over to talk to Terry. I try to steer clear of office politics, but those two are clearly in cahoots. They've united recently in a common cause: to make Sophie's life complete hell. Tatiana wanted that job. She's wanted it for years. And when our old presenter, Gaby, went off to present *Blankety Blank* Tatty assumed it would be hers. Terry was desperate for her to have it too, because he knew she wouldn't show him up. He's of the old school, you see. He doesn't regard himself as the programme's 'co-presenter', but as Presenter One. And it is the job of Presenter One – middle aged and male – to do all the serious stuff while Presenter Two – young and blonde – sits there gazing at him admiringly before introducing some item on knitting. That's what it was like with Terry and Gaby, but Sophie's a different case.

'Morning everyone!' Sophie called out cheerfully as I studied my isobars. 'I say, did you see Jeremy Paxman lay into the Russian defence secretary last night?' she said as she took off her coat. 'I thought what he said about Chechnya was absolutely spot on. He said he thinks the Organisation for Security and Cooperation in Europe should be much more involved in the negotiations, and I must say I totally agree.'

'Oh, do you really?' said Terry.

'As for the sneaky way the Russians are flogging their nuclear expertise to Iraq,' she added as she switched on her computer, 'well, it's an international scandal, don't you think?'

'Ra-ther.'

Terry is thirty-nine – or so he claims – and has a third from Wolverhampton poly. He is not adjusting well to having a twenty-four-year-old Oxford graduate with a starred first in Politics, Philosophy and Economics sitting beside him on the studio sofa. Sophie's appointment came as a bit of a shock. As

Terry never tires of saying, she didn't know an autocue from a bus queue when she arrived. This was true. She'd come from radio, she was an editor at London FM, and Darryl had been invited to take part in a phone-in there about the future of digital TV. So impressed was he with Sophie's brilliance that he invited her to audition for AM-UK! The next thing we knew, she'd got the job.

But it's *obvious* that Sophie's much too bright for a programme like ours. I mean – don't think me disloyal – but most days AM-UK! is more of a dog's dinner than a successful breakfast show. The mix of items is bizarre. Take today's running order, for example: celebrity disfigurement – failed face-lifts; heroic hamsters and the lives they've saved; psychic granny predicts the future; Tatiana's profile of Brad Pitt; coping with ovarian cysts; ten new ways with chrysanthemums; and, somewhere in the middle of all that, an interview with Michael Portillo.

'I'm doing the Portillo interview,' said Terry as he leaned back in his swivel chair.

'But I'm down to do that one,' said Sophie as she tucked her short blonde hair behind one ear.

'So I see,' said Terry indolently, 'but it's clearly a mistake. I think you'll find that that one falls to me. I've more experience than you,' he added.

'With respect, Terry,' replied Sophie carefully, 'I've interviewed Michael Portillo twice before.'

'Sophie,' said Terry wearily, 'on this show we all pull together. I'm afraid there's absolutely *no* room for big egos, so *I'll* be doing the Portillo interview – OK?' And that was that. Terry has quite a lot of clout, actually, and he knows it, because he's the housewives' choice. Moreover, he has a cast-iron two-year contract, so Darryl can't push Sophie's cause too far. The atmosphere gets pretty stormy sometimes, but Sophie handles it well. I mean, on breakfast TV the hours are so awful that most disputes tend to be settled with machetes. Things that wouldn't bother you at three in the afternoon induce homicidal rage at five a.m. But so far Sophie has coped with Terry and Tatty's provocations with a sang froid that would chill champagne. She simply pretends she has *no* idea that they've anything against her. She's so polite to them, despite their dirty tricks. For example, Tatiana's recently taken to sidling up to her three seconds before she goes on air and saying, 'Not sure that colour suits you,' or, 'Oh no! Your mascara's run,' or, 'Did you know your hair's sticking up?' But Sophie just smiles at her and says, 'Oh, thanks *so* much for telling me, Tatiana. You look *lovely* by the way.' It's impressive, but as I say Sophie's brilliant at politics and I think she's playing a clever game. She's very business-like about her work, and she's also very discreet. None of us has the slightest clue about her private life. I mean, she *never* makes personal phone calls, but I think she's got a chap. Because after the Christmas party last month, I went back up to the office to get my bag and I heard Sophie talking to someone called Alex in an obviously lovey-dovey way. I coughed to let her know I was there and she suddenly looked up and froze. So I just grabbed my bag and walked straight out, because I didn't want her to think I'd heard. But I had. And that's the downside of working in an open-plan office – there's not much you don't get to know. But my approach is an old-fashioned one: hear no evil; see no evil; and above all, speak no evil.

So I sat there this morning, engrossed in the weather charts, preparing the bulletins that I do every half-hour during the show. My first one's at six thirty, so at ten past six I went down to Make-Up on the second floor. The second floor is where all the exciting stuff goes on. That's where the Studio is, and the Technical Gallery, and Wardrobe and the dressing rooms, and the Green Room, and the Duty Office, where all the complaints and comments are logged. And as I walked down the carpet-tiled corridor, doors were opened and banged shut, and researchers sprinted past me in both directions, clutching clipboards and looking tense. I glanced into the Green Room where various contributors were slumped, comatose, in leather chairs, while Jean, our friendly Guest Greeter, tried to rouse them with cups of Kenco.

'Danish pastry?' I heard her say. 'Or how about a nice scone?' Then someone came flying out of the gallery screaming, 'Where the hell's Phil? Where's Phil? Are you Phil? Right – you're on!' In fact things were pretty noisy all in all.

'– could someone page Tatiana?'

'– would you prefer Earl Grey?'

'– the psychic granny's lost her crystal ball!'

'– I've got some nice Assam.'

'– Sophie's jacket looks a bit creased.'

'– the skateboarding cat's just arrived!'

So to go into the Make-Up room is to enter a haven from all this chaos: inside, Iqbal and Marian quietly transform our sleep-deprived faces for the camera. I sat in a gently reclining chair, while Iqbal – we call him Iqqy – put a flowery nylon gown round my shoulders and clipped back my short brown hair. Laid out on the counter before me were serried ranks of foundation bottles, powder compacts, eye-shadows, lipsticks and combs. Canisters of hairspray gleamed in the theatrical lightbulbs round the mirror.

'Ready with the Polyfilla?' I asked wryly as I surveyed my exhausted-looking face.

'You do look a bit tired,' he said solicitously. 'Were you out on the tiles last night?'

'Yes. It was my wedding anniversary – we went out for supper, *en famille*.'

'How lovely,' he said soothingly.

'It was,' I replied. 'In a way, or it would have been . . .' You see the thing about Iqqy and Marian is that you just want to talk to them. You naturally want to open up. They're so calm and sympathetic and kind. It's as though you're in the psychiatrist's chair, not the make-up chair, and you want to tell them all your troubles. And as they work miracles on your ravaged exterior, you fancy they can repair you on the inside, too. So it was on the tip of my tongue to tell them that actually I hadn't enjoyed myself that much last night because my best friend, Lily, had made this very odd remark about my husband, and I'd been trying ever since to work out what she might have meant, and this – and the fact that I'd drunk too much – had resulted in my getting no sleep.

'How many years have you been married?' asked Marian.

'Fifteen,' I replied.

'Wow,' she said. 'You must have married young.'

'Yes,' I sighed. 'I did.'

'Fifteen years,' she repeated wonderingly. 'But then, I've already been married eight.'

'And Will and I have been together for five,' said Iqqy as he pulled mascara through my pale lashes. 'Although,' he went on ruefully, 'we've had our ups and downs. But fifteen years, that's wonderful. No wonder you felt like celebrating.'

'Well, yes, except, actually, it was a bit strange . . .' I began. 'Because, look, I don't know what you two think about this . . .' Then I immediately stopped, because Terry had just come in. He needed more powder. And as he sat there, bitching about Sophie, I ignored him, in the way I usually do, by pretending to be engrossed in my script. Ten minutes later, primped and preened for the cameras, I slipped into the studio. It's like the soft furnishings department of a provincial department store. There are two large, pink, chequered sofas with squashy cushions, and a smoked-glass coffee table. There are anaemic prints on the walls, a Habitat-style shelf unit with cheesy ornaments and arrangements of faded silk flowers. Behind is a trompe l'oeil backdrop of London, to one side is a small stage, and, next to that, my weather chart. I picked my way towards it, between the four cameras, stepping over the thick coils of electric cable and trying not to bash my head on the perilously low-slung rigging. It was hot. It's always hot in the studio, because of all the lights. We'd just hit the first ad break, and Terry was taking the opportunity to throw one of his little fits.

'Look, Sophie, I've told you before,' he whined, '*I* sit on the lefthand side of the sofa.'

'Oh, but, with respect, Terry,' she said pleasantly, 'why?'

'Why?' he repeated. 'Why? Because I've been sitting on the

lefthand side of this sofa for ten years, so I don't see why I should move for you.'

I knew why he wanted to sit on that side. He's convinced the lighting is better there and that it makes him look younger.

'Well, I really don't see why it matters, Terry,' said Sophie wearily as she got up, 'but if it's so important to you, well, of course.'

The sound engineer attached a microphone to my lapel, and I slipped in my earpiece as I took up my place by the weather chart. I heard the director count us all out of the break, there was a brief burst of signature tune, then Terry leaned into the camera and said, 'Welcome back, everyone; you're watching AM-UK! Now. Has a message from beyond the grave changed *your* life?'

The interview with the psychic granny went quite well, then there was a sports report; that was followed by a piece about Princess Anne and Save the Children, and then it was Sophie's turn. She was doing the interview about ovarian cysts and had only got halfway through, and in fact it was rather interesting as the gynaecologist was very good, and Sophie had just paused for a second, between questions, when to my astonishment, Terry cut in.

'Now, what's the weather doing today?' he asked, beaming at Camera One. I caught the cameraman's surprised expression. 'Let's h-a-v-e FAITH!' He'd done it deliberately, of course, to cut down Sophie's time on air. He doesn't just steal her limelight, he goes in for daylight robbery. Whenever he thinks she's been talking long enough, he just butts right in. Especially if she's doing something remotely 'serious', like a medical interview or current affairs. And when Darryl tries to tell him off at the meeting afterwards he just looks at Sophie, all wounded innocence, and says, 'Oh! Sorry, Sophie, I thought you'd finished.' I really hate it when Terry does that, not just because it's nasty, but because it means I'm thrown on air with no warning. The red light suddenly flashes on top of Camera Two and there I am, live to the nation.

'Good morning!' I said, with a huge smile to cover my

annoyance with Terry, and because I always smile more when the weather's bad. 'And I'm afraid the outlook's not good,' I began as I turned towards the chart. 'The snow that fell across the country yesterday has now turned to sleet and slush, and as temperatures drop again this means a very high chance of black ice, so do be careful if you're driving,' I added as I pressed the clicker, aware, in my earpiece, of the furious babble in the gallery.

'– Terry's a bastard!'

'Wind speeds are picking up in the south and south-east . . .'

'– he cut her interview by two minutes!'

'Those beastly easterlies are at it again . . .'

'– and it was really interesting.'

'Possibly bringing a little sunshine in the north . . .'

'– I had an ovarian cyst once.'

'Elsewhere, an overcast and bitterly cold day . . .'

'– very painful, actually.'

'With a seventy per cent chance of further snowfalls . . .'

'– it was the size of a lemon, apparently . . .'

'And with this frontal system in mid-Atlantic . . .'

'– and full of pus.'

'We're about to enter a prolonged period of low pleasure.'

'– low *pleasure*?'

'I mean, low *pressure*. So, to summarise . . .'

'– God, Faith looks tired.'

'A cold, nasty day for most of us . . .'

'– Terry, sit up straight.'

'But maybe a glimmer of sunshine in the north . . .'

'– and her hair's a mess. Ready when you are, Faith? Ten, nine, eight . . .'

'But temperatures in the south and south-east dropping . . .'

'Seven, six, five . . .'

'To no higher than four degrees . . .'

'Three, two . . .'

'So do remember to wrap up warm . . .'

'One and . . .'

'See you in half an hour.'

'Zero. Cut to the skateboarding cat!'

Once I've done my first forecast, the rest of the morning flashes by. In between 'hits' I check the charts, phone the met office and update my bulletins as required. The nine thirty forecast is my last one, and that's when the programme comes off air. We have a quick meeting in the boardroom, then I take off my make-up, sit at my desk and go through my mail. I get lots of letters. Most of them are from children asking me to help them with their geography homework. They write asking me what clouds are made of, for example, or why frost is white, or what the difference is between snow and sleet, or how rainbows are formed. Then I get letters thanking me for cheering people up. *What I like about you*, wrote Mr Barnes from Tunbridge Wells, *is that, even when you're giving us bad news you do it with a nice smile*. Then – and I hate these ones – there are the letters about my appearance. The slightest change in it – such as a hair trim – produces a sack-load of disapproving mail. Then there are the 'requests' from those viewers who seem to think I'm God. *Dear Faith*, wrote a Mrs McManus from Edinburgh, this morning, *please, please, PLEASE could we have some better weather in Scotland. We've had not a ray of sunshine since Hogmanay*! I write back to everyone, unless they're obviously nuts. Then, when I've done that, I tidy my desk and go home. People often ask me how I spend the rest of the day. The answer is, I potter. I feed Graham, of course, and take him for a walk. I might meet a friend, or go to the shops. I do the housework – I hate it, but we can't afford a cleaner – I fill in competition forms, and I read. In an ideal world I'd do an afternoon job, but I can't because I'm too tired. In any case it would be very awkward, because people know my face from TV. But the first thing I do when I get home is to go to bed and sleep for a couple of hours, so that's what I did today. Or at least I tried to. But I found myself thinking, yet again, about what Lily had said last night. As I've said, she does sometimes say things I don't like – including the odd uncharitable comment about Peter. Usually I just forget them, but this time I found I couldn't. Why on earth had she said what she said and whatever could it mean? She's so shrewd and clever – was it just a casual remark? I tried counting sheep, but that didn't work. I tried remembering all the stations on the shipping forecast, but that didn't help either. I tried recalling the names of all Peter's authors, but still sleep eluded me, chased away by Lily's remark. So I turned on the bedside radio to distract myself but that made no difference either. I opened my book – *Madame Bovary* – but even that didn't help. My mind returned to Lily's comment again and again and again. It was nagging me. Annoying me. Needling me. Gnawing at me. It kept going round and round in my mind like a mosquito in a hotel room. 'Neeeee . . .' it went. *'Neee . . . neeee . . . neeeeeeeeee.'* I tried to swat it away but back it came, so I pulled the duvet over my head. I thought of the children, and Graham, and I thought of the programme and how it had gone. I thought of my parents on their latest trip, and of the man who came to fix the roof. I thought about my Tesco reward card and tried to remember how many points I'd accrued; but still Lily's strange words continued to clang away, like tinnitus. What *was* that remark about? What on *earth* could it mean?

'Stuff it!' I said to Graham as I threw off the duvet. 'I'm going to damn well go and find out.'

'Darling!' said Lily, meeting me at the lift on the forty-ninth floor of Canary Wharf an hour and fifty minutes later. 'What a divine surprise! But what are you doing over here?'

'I was just passing,' I said.

'Really? Well, how lovely. You can share my take-away lunch. And how are you this morning?'

'Not at my best,' I replied. 'Rather hungover, in fact.'

'Oh dear,' she murmured. 'The wrath of grapes! But it was a wonderful evening,' she added as she tucked the dog under her left arm. 'Jennifer *adored* it, didn't you poppet?' Jennifer gave me a vacant stare. 'And how marvellous of you to get up three hours later like that and calmly do the weather,' Lily added as we crossed the editorial floor. 'I watched you from the gym at six thirty. That girl Sophie's rather bright,' she went on, 'perhaps we ought to do something on her in *Moi!* Terry whatshisname's a bore though, isn't he?' she added. 'A clear case of mistaken nonentity. Now,' she said as we swept past a rail of designer clothes, 'where are your lovely kids?'

'They've gone back to school,' I explained as a pink feather boa lifted in the breeze from Lily's scented wake. 'Peter took them to the station this morning. Term starts again today.'

'They're such darlings,' Lily exclaimed as she stroked Jennifer's topknot. 'Isn't Katie a scream with her psychoanalysis? Though I can't help feeling she's a little Jung. We *must* do a makeover on her for the magazine and get her out of those blue-stocking clothes. Now Jasmine . . .' She'd stopped at the desk of a whey-faced girl of about twenty. 'I've told you not to drink coffee at lunchtime, you know it stops you sleeping in the afternoons.'

We passed the picture desk where a photographer was having his portfolio assessed and long-limbed girls leaned over the illuminated lightbox. Then we entered Lily's glass-sided office, with its earthenware pots of splayed orchids, the Magnum shots of pouting models, the framed *Moi!* covers and the shining industry awards. She waved her hand at the wall-sized shelf-unit displaying all her rivals' magazines.

'World of Inferiors,' she quipped. Then she removed a bottle of greenish liquid from the small fridge in the corner.

'Wheatgrass juice?'

'Er, no thanks.' She poured herself a glass, then sat behind her desk and held up a plate.

'Vegetarian sushi?' she enquired.

'Oh, I'm not hungry, thanks.'

'These seaweed rolls are awfully good . . .'

'No thanks.'

'And this shiitake's divine.'

'Look, Lily,' I tried again, 'I just wanted to ask you something. Um . . .'

'Of course, darling,' she said. 'Ask me anything you like.' Suddenly there was a tap at the door and Lily's secretary Polly appeared.

'Lily, here's the February edition of *Vogue*. It's just come in.'

Lily winced. She loathes *Vogue*, in fact it's a minor obsession. This is because in 1994, when she was features editor there, they failed to promote her to deputy editor, a lapse of professional judgement she will neither forget nor forgive. She began to flick the pages of the magazine in an indolent, insolent way.

'God, how boring,' she muttered. 'Tsk . . . that old story . . . seriously *vieux chapeau*. Oh good Lord, what a cliché – at *Moi!* we avoid clichés like the plague. Oh, purleeze, not Catherine Zeta-Jones *again*! Oh, God!' she declared suddenly with an appalled expression on her face. 'They've got Sally Desert working for them – I wouldn't let that crummy little dwarf write my shopping list! Faith,' she announced as she tossed the magazine onto the floor, 'I am going to outsell *Vogue*.'

'Yes, I'm sure you are Lily, but –'

'We're not far off,' she added as she leaned back in her chair, steepled her long fingers and scrutinised the ceiling. 'Lots of their advertisers are coming to us, and who can blame them?' she asked. This was clearly a rhetorical question. 'We make our advertisers feel wonderful,' she went on seamlessly as she fed Jennifer bits of sushi. 'We woo them. We flatter them. We give them very good rates. We –'

'Lily.'

'– look after them. Make them feel special. In short, we do not bite the brand that feeds us.'

'Lily.'

'And in any case they now realise that *Moi!* is *the* fashion magazine of the Millennium.' She went and stood by the window, then raised the Venetian micro-blind. 'Isn't it wonderful?' she said as she gazed down on the Dome. 'Isn't it just wonderful?' she repeated. 'Come here, Faith, and look. Look at all . . . this.' She'd threaded her slender arm through mine. 'Don't you think it's just fantastic?'

'Not really,' I said truthfully as I inhaled the aroma of her Hypnotic Poison. 'To me it's all style and no substance.'

'I was there,' she murmured dreamily, ignoring my remark. 'I was there, Faith, at that party.'

'I know.'

'I was there with the Queen and Tony Blair. Don't you think that's amazing, Faith? That your little schoolfriend was invited to that?' Suddenly I looked at Lily's profile and was transported back twenty-five years. I remembered the awkward girl, standing on stage in her blue gingham dress, and the look of fear and confusion on her face. Now here she was, atop London's tallest building, with the world spread out beneath her feet.

'Don't you think that's amazing?' she pressed me again.

'What? Well, yes, er, no. I mean, not really, Lily – I always knew you'd succeed.'

'Yes,' she said dreamily as we gazed at the boat-speckled river shining below. 'I've succeeded, despite the attempts of a few people to put a spanner in the works.'

'What people?' I said.

'Oh, no-one significant,' she breathed. 'Just nobodies, out to spoil my success. But they know who they are. And *I* know who they are, too,' she went on with an air of slight menace. 'But no-one's going to stop me,' she murmured. 'No-one's going to hold *me* back.'

'Lily,' I interjected, wishing she'd stop talking just for a second and listen.

'I've trounced my enemies, Faith,' she went on calmly, 'by my vision and my hard work. And the reason why *Moi!* is going to be *the* Number One glossy is because we've got so many original ideas. Now,' she added enthusiastically as she returned to her desk, 'I just want your advice on a new feature we're planning – top secret, of course. What do you think of *this*?' She handed me a mock-up page. It was headed 'Your Dog's Beauty Questions Answered'. *I am a Yorkshire terrier*, I read. *I have very fine, fly-away fur. I can never get it to stay in one place. What should I do? I am a white miniature poodle*, wrote another. *But at the moment my coat looks slightly discoloured and stained. This is causing me considerable distress. What grooming products can I use to restore it to its former glory?*

'The readers are going to love it,' said Lily with an excited smile. 'I'd like to do a dog special at some point, a pull-out supplement, maybe for the July edition, yes,' she went on distractedly. 'I could call it *Chienne*. We could get it sponsored by Winalot.'

'Lily!' I stood up. It was the only way to attract her attention. 'Lily,' I repeated. 'I wasn't just passing.'

'*Weren't* you, darling?'

'No,' I said as I sat down again. 'I'm afraid that was a lie.'

'*Was* it?' she said, her eyes round. 'Really, Faith, that's not like you.'

'I came here for a reason,' I went on, my heart now banging like a drum. 'Because there's something I need to ask you.'

'Faith, darling,' said Lily seriously, 'Jennifer and I are all ears.'

'Well,' I began nervously, 'I know this will sound silly, but last night you said something that disturbed me.'

'Oh, Faith,' she said before taking a sip of wheatgrass juice, 'I'm *always* saying things that disturb you, we both know that.'

'Yes, but this wasn't in the usual category of your flippant off-the-cuff remarks. It was not only what you said, but the way you said it.'

'And what was it, then?' she enquired.

'Well, you said,' I said, 'you said . . . You said that you thought I was "marvellous" to "trust" Peter.' Lily's arched eyebrows lifted an inch up her high, domed brow.

'Well I *do*, darling!'

'Why?'

'Because I think *any* woman who trusts *any* man is a complete and utter marvel, given that the species are such beasts. I mean, why do you think I dump them at such a rate?'

'Oh, I see. So it was just a general observation, was it?'

'Yes!' she said gaily. 'Of course it was! You are silly to let that worry you, Faith. I thought you always prided yourself on never believing anything I say.'

'Oh, I do!' I exclaimed. 'I mean, I know that you're usually being funny. You like to pull my leg. I don't mind – I never have done – and I know it's still easy to do.'

'Faith Value,' she said with an indulgent shake of her head.

'Yes,' I said, 'I suppose I am. And you're still Lily White.'

'I know,' said Lily with a smile. 'I'm sorry if I worried you,' she went on as she chewed delicately on her seaweed roll. 'It's just my sense of humour, darling. You know that.'

'I know,' I agreed. 'But last night I couldn't help wondering, if what you said was a joke or not.'

'Of course it was,' she said, 'don't give it a second thought.'

'Oh, good,' I said, vastly relieved, and I allowed myself to smile.

'I was just joking, Faith.'

'Oh, great.'

'Because I'm good at badinage.'

'Oh yes.'

'I was just pulling your leg . . .' She was flicking through a copy of *Moi!*

'I know . . .'

'I was just winding you up, like I do.'

'Yup. Got that,' I said as I stood up to go. 'Great to get it sorted out.'

'Al*though* . . .' Lily added softly, without looking up.

'Although what?' I said.

'Well . . .' She sighed as she lifted her gaze to mine. 'Now we're on the subject, I must say that Peter didn't exactly seem relaxed. In fact I thought he was decidedly sharp. Mind you,' she continued judiciously, 'Peter's often sharp with me. I know he doesn't really like me,' she went on philosophically. 'I'm his *bête noire*,' she added with a throaty laugh.

'It's a personality thing,' I said diplomatically. 'It's just one of those little clashes one sometimes gets. But he has huge professional respect for you,' I said.

'*Does* he?' she said with a sceptical smile.

'In any case,' I went on quickly, 'between you and me, Peter's got a lot of hassle at work so he's a little bit anxious at the moment.'

'Anxious? Darling,' she added, 'he was jumpier than the Royal Ballet.'

'Well . . .'

'And I couldn't help noticing how trim he looked. And did you see he was wearing a Hermès tie?'

'Was he? I wouldn't know. I don't really notice labels.'

'Yes, Hermès. They're seventy pounds a throw. Now, I knew *you* hadn't bought it for him,' she went on. 'So I couldn't help wondering who had?' I stared at her.

'He bought it himself.'

'Really?'

'Yes. As an investment. He said his headhunter has advised him to smarten up a bit. Peter's looking for a new job, you see – I didn't tell you this, but we think he's about to be kicked out.'

'Really?' said Lily. 'Oh! How *awful*.'

'Well, yes, because he's been happy at Fenton & Friend.'

'I'll say he has,' she said.

'Sorry?'

'All I mean is that *any* man would be happy working at Fenton & Friend.'

'What do you mean?'

'Well,' she said as she adjusted Jennifer's butterfly barrette, 'it's stuffed with gorgeous girls.'

'Oh. Is it?'

'And I *thought* I heard someone say, the other day, that they'd seen Peter having lunch with an attractive blonde. But I could have been wrong,' she added softly.

'Yes,' I said, 'you were. Or rather you were mistaken. Because Peter has to take authors and agents out to dinner sometimes. It's all part of his job.'

'Of course it is, Faith, I know. But . . .'

'But *what*?'

'Well, he *is* a publisher, and so . . .'

'Yes?'

'I really *hate* to say this, darling, but maybe he's making someone an *advance*?' I gazed into Lily's liquid brown eyes.

41

They're huge and hypnotic, slanting in shape, with interminable thick, curling lashes.

'An advance?' I repeated. I could hear the beating of my heart.

'Maybe he's looking for a new chapter,' she went on softly, then took another sip of wheatgrass juice.

'Lily, what are you talking about?'

'Maybe, in the bookshop of life, he's been picking up more than a Penguin . . .'

'Look, I –'

'And the *only* reason I say this is because his speech last night was so odd. Katie spotted the Freudian slip, Faith, didn't you?'

'Well, I . . .'

'And after all, you have been married for a very long time.'

'But . . .'

'All I'm suggesting is that in your situation, well, I'd be just a *little* on my guard.'

'On my guard?'

'Vigilant. Now, I'm only saying this as your friend.'

'I know . . .'

'Because I have only your best interests at heart.'

'Yes. Thanks . . .'

'But I think you ought to do a Christine . . .' I looked at her. 'What? *Hamilton*?' I said aghast. 'You mean, search his pockets?' Lily was fiddling with the Buddhist power beads at her slender wrist.

'That's what many women would do, Faith,' she said reasonably. 'But don't worry, darling. I'm sure there's absolutely *nothing* to be concerned about.'

'Well, I don't know,' I said, suddenly panicking. 'Maybe there *is*.'

'No, no, I'm sure it's *fine*,' she said soothingly. 'But all I'm saying, as your best and oldest friend, is that maybe you should, well, sharpen up a bit.'

'What?'

'Learn to spot the signs.'

'I wouldn't know how,' I groaned.

'Of course you wouldn't, you're so trusting. But that's something I can help you with, darling, because as luck would have it, *Moi!* did a big feature on this only last month.' She stood up and began to sort through a pile of back issues on the floor.

'Now, where is it?' she said. 'Oh, here we are!' she exclaimed happily. 'You're in luck. "Is Your Man a Love-Rodent?"' she read. '*Seven classic signs: one, he's distracted and distant. Two, he's "working late"; three, he's looking fit; four, his wardrobe's improved. Five, he's not interested in sex; six, he's bought a mobile phone and seven* – and I gather that this is the clincher, Faith . . .' Suddenly there was a sharp rap on the door.

'Lily . . .' It was Polly again. 'Lily, I'm sorry, but I've got Madonna for you on line one.'

'Oh God,' said Lily rolling her eyes, 'I've told her not to call me in my lunchbreak. Still . . .' She sighed. 'We do want her on the cover in June. Sorry, Faith darling. Must go.' She blew me a kiss as I stood at the door, then waved Jennifer's little paw up and down.

'Now, I don't want you to worry,' she called out as I opened the door. 'In any case I'm sure it's all going to work out for the best, as you always like to say.'

I journeyed back to west London as if in a trance. I'd got what I wanted, all right. I'd had my nagging doubts dispelled, and replaced with naked fear. Peter was having an affair. Lily hadn't said it in so many words, but she clearly thought something was up and she's, well, a woman of the world. My morale was so low it was practically underground, and as I left Turnham Green tube and walked home I began to entertain all kinds of mad ideas: that Peter was in love with another woman; that he would up and leave; that I had been a bad wife; that he had been driven to find solace elsewhere; that our house would have to be sold; that our children would suffer and fail; that our dog would become a delinquent; that we'd never go to Ikea again; that – as I placed my hand on the garden gate, my heart suddenly skipped a beat. For there, on the doorstep, was an enormous bouquet of white and yellow flowers. I gathered it up in one hand and unlocked the door with the other, and as Graham leaped up to greet me with a joyful bark, I peeled off the envelope. The phone started to ring, but I ignored it as my eyes scanned the message on the small white card.

Happy Anniversary, Faith, it read. *So sorry I forgot. All my love, Peter.* Relief knocked me over, like a wave. I sank gratefully onto the hall chair.

'Of *course* he's *not* having an affair!' I said to Graham as my hand reached for the phone. 'Peter loves me,' I said, 'and I love him, and that's all there is to it. Hello?'

'Faith, darling, it's Lily. Sorry we got cut off there.'

'Oh, don't worry,' I said cheerfully. 'I'd said everything I wanted to say and in fact Lily, although it's *very* kind of you to give me advice, and I do appreciate it, I really don't think you're quite right, and to be honest I think I just really overreacted and I'd been in a silly sort of mood you see, and I was very tired too from work, so –'

'No, but Faith, there was one thing I meant to tell you,' she said. 'Something *really* important – the seventh sign. Apparently it's the absolutely copper-bottomed-it-simply-never-fails-dead-cert-surefire-sign that one's husband is up to no good.'

'Er, yes?' I said faintly. 'What is it?'

'It's if he's sending you flowers!'

'What are *you* getting up to?' Terry enquired saucily as he leaned into the camera a few days later. 'Why not get up to AM-UK! where there's lots of snap, crackle and pop! It's coming up to . . .' He glanced at the clock. 'Seven fifty. And later in the show, Internet dating – how to "click" on-line; women with beards – why they prefer the rough to the smooth; and our Phobia of the Week – griddle pans. Plus all the news, weather and sport.'

'But first,' said Sophie as she read her autocue, 'we ask that old question, what's in a name? Well, quite a lot according to sociologist Ed McCall, who's just written a book about names, about what they mean, and how they can influence our lives. Ed, a warm welcome to the show.' I was standing by the weather chart, listening to this, and I must say it was great. Interesting items are rare, as one of the TV critics noted ironically, 'AM-UK!'s healthy breakfast menu is virtually fact-free!' But this interview was riveting, and Sophie handled it well.

'Looking at surnames,' Ed McCall began, 'I've concluded that people are often drawn to careers which reflect their second names. For example there's a man called James Judge, who's a judge; then there's Sir Hugh Fish, who was head of Thames Water; there's a newly ordained vicar called Linda Church, and I discovered a Tasmanian police woman called Lauren Order. *Gardener's Question Time* has Bob Flowerdew *and* Pippa Greenwood, and there's another well-known horticulturalist called Michael Bloom.'

'I believe the medical profession has some intriguing examples,' Sophie prompted him.

'Oh, yes. I uncovered an allergist called Dr Aikenhead,' he said, 'and dermatologists Doctors Whitehead and Pitts; I found a urologist called Dr Weedon, and a paediatrician called Dr Kidd.'

'This is great, Sophie,' I heard Darryl say in my earpiece.

'Any others?' she said with a smile.

'There's a surgeon called Frank Slaughter, a police officer called Andy Sergeant, several bankers with the surname Cash, and a convicted criminal called Tony Lawless. There are many other instances of this type,' he went on, 'so I've concluded that these people were drawn to their professions, whether consciously or not, because of their family names.'

'I suppose you could call it nominative determinism,' suggested Sophie in her academic way.

'Er, certainly,' he said uncertainly, 'though that's a very technical way of putting it. But yes, I believe that names do determine our lives in some way; that they're not just labels but form an inherent part of our identity.'

'And is this as true of Christian names as it is of surnames?' Sophie asked.

'Oh, definitely,' he said.

'So what does Sophie mean?' Terry interjected with a smirk. 'Smug little show-off?'

'Sorry?'

'Sycophantic show-stealer?'

'Shut up, Terry!' I heard Darryl hiss in my earpiece.

'Er, no,' said Ed McCall, clearly shocked by Terry's shameless on-screen slurs. 'Erm, the name Sophie actually means wisdom, and may I say,' he added gallantly, 'that it's a name that obviously suits this Sophie well.'

'And what does Terry mean?' asked Sophie pleasantly.

'Terry is either the diminutive of Terence,' Ed replied, 'or it could be derived from the French name, Thierry, from Norman times.'

'It's not a very popular name any more, is it?' Sophie went on sweetly. Ah. She'd obviously read the book. 'In fact you point out that Terry's rather a *dated* name these days.'

'That's right,' Ed agreed, 'it was especially popular in the 1950s.'

'The 1950s!' she exclaimed. 'Oh, I'm sure Terry wasn't born as long ago as that, were you?' she enquired innocently.

'Oh, no no no,' Terry said, 'much later.'

'Of course you were,' said Sophie benignly as the cameraman sadistically lingered on Terry's reddening face. 'I'm sure you were born much, much later than that, Terry.'

'Yes, yes, that's right. I was.'

'I'm sure no-one would believe you could possibly have been born in – ooh – 1955?' she concluded with a smile. Touché. He deserved it. For once he was lost for words. 'And what about our weather forecaster, Faith?' Sophie went on smoothly as Terry seethed; she indicated me with an elegant sweep of her left hand as the light on 'my' camera flashed red.

'Faith is one of those abstract virtue names which the Puritans invented,' Ed explained. 'It's like Charity, Verity or Grace. And these names were given mostly to women, of course, as a means of social control; so that baby girls given these "virtuous" names would develop those desirable characteristics.

46

There were some really awful names of this kind,' he added, 'but thankfully they haven't survived. Can you imagine calling your child Abstinence, Humility or Meek?'

'How dreadful!' Sophie exclaimed with a laugh.

'But the more attractive names of this type have stayed with us and I think they do have an influence on character. I mean, if you're called Patience or Verity, then people expect certain things. How can you be called Grace and be clumsy, for example, or be a miserable Joy, or a promiscuous Virginia, or a depressive Hope?'

'Or an adulterous Faith,' said Terry, trying to get back in the show. 'Are you faithful, Faith?' he asked me, very cheekily I thought.

'Only to my husband,' I said with a smile.

'There's a fashion for naming children after places, isn't there, Ed?' Sophie went on.

'Oh yes,' he replied, 'we've got just about every American state now – Atlanta, Georgia, Savannah etc – though Nebraska and Kentucky don't have quite the same ring. Then there's Chelsea, of course, and India. And people often name their children after the place in which they were conceived. Like Posh Spice and David Beckham calling their baby Brooklyn after a trip to New York.'

'Well, it could have been worse,' said Sophie judiciously. 'At least they didn't call him Queens.' Ed laughed at her witticism as she thanked him for coming on the show. 'It's been fascinating,' she concluded warmly. 'And Ed's book, *The Game of the Name*, is published today by Thorsons and costs six pounds ninety-nine.'

'And now,' Terry intervened, 'it's time for a look at the weather. So let's see if Faith lives up to *her* name today!'

As the programme ended an hour later, Terry and Sophie sat there beaming at each other amiably while the credits rolled. Then, the split-second they were off air, he stood up, towered over her and shouted, 'Don't you *ever* do that to me again!'

'I'm sorry, do what?' said Sophie sweetly as she removed her microphone pack from the back of her skirt.

'Don't you *ever* discuss my age on screen again,' he hissed.

'Well, for my part I'd be grateful if you didn't insult me on screen,' she replied as she took out her earpiece.

'I am thirty-nine!' he shouted after her as she made her way towards Make-Up to get her slap removed. 'Thirty-nine! Not forty-six. Got that, you superior little cow?'

'Of course I know you're thirty-nine, Terry,' she flung over her shoulder. 'I don't know how I could have got that wrong. After all, everyone here tells me you've been thirty-nine for *years*.' His face went white with anger. It was as though Sophie had made a declaration of war. And though I was glad to see her start to get her own back, I hoped she wouldn't come to regret what she'd done. Still, as I say, I always keep out of office disputes. As I picked up my bag I saw that there were two copies of *The Game of the Name* lying on the planning desk. No-one seemed to want them, so I put a pound in the charity box and took one of them home. There was an index at the back, and I looked up Peter; it said that Peter means a rock, which I knew. I thought how Peter always has been my rock, really – steady and unswerving and strong. I pondered my own name, and wondered, not for the first time, to what extent it has shaped who I am. Would I have turned out differently if I'd been called something racy, like Scarlett or Carmen or Sky? But I was christened Faith, so I guess I couldn't be racy if I tried. And I decided I might as well be true to the name I have and I resolved not to have doubts about Peter. So when I opened the front door and saw that Lily had sent me the December edition of *Moi!* I simply felt like throwing it away. But then, on the other hand, I knew she could only mean well.

I'm sure there's absolutely nothing to worry about, she had written in her large round hand. *But just to be on the safe side, do read this as it's full of handy hints. PS, why not check out the IsHeCheating.com website?*

'How ridiculous,' I said to Graham as I flicked through the magazine again. 'Peter *isn't* having an affair.' Even so, I couldn't resist reading the article. Just out of interest, of course.

How to Tell If Your Man's Playing Away:
1. He's distracted and distant.
2. He's looking fit.
3. He's working late.
4. His wardrobe's improved.
5. He's not interested in sex.
6. He's bought a mobile phone.
7. He's sending you flowers.

Now, the scary thing was that I knew I could answer a resounding 'yes' to all of these. But I decided to remain quite calm, because there's a rational explanation in every case. Peter is distracted and distant because he has many worries, and has lost weight, ditto. He's working late because his boss is vile; he's improved his wardrobe because he has to look smart for job interviews. He's not interested in sex because his libido is low due to his depression about work. He bought a mobile phone so that his headhunter can contact him at the drop of a hat; and he sent me flowers for the simple reason that he forgot our anniversary and felt bad.

'So there we have it,' I said to Graham as I read and reread the piece. 'He's in the clear. We have nothing to worry about.' I looked into his eyes – they're the colour of demerara – and I stroked his velvety nose. Graham's been anxious too, you see. He's very sensitive to my moods and over the last couple of days he's been feeling a bit insecure. I know this because he's been sitting closer to me than normal – preferably on my lap. Also, he's following me around more than he usually does. So this afternoon I said to him, 'It's OK, Graham, you don't have to get up every time I leave my chair.' But he does. He came with me as I climbed the stairs to the spare room on the top floor. As I say, I didn't really think that Peter was having an affair, but in order to put all my fears to rest, I'd decided to check his pockets. Peter's fairly tidy, and he doesn't have huge numbers of clothes, so I knew my investigations wouldn't take long. I found that my pulse was beginning to race as I consulted the magazine again. *You must leave everything exactly as you found it*, it advised. *If he suspects you're onto him he may stop what he's doing, which means you'll never get to the truth*. So, feeling like a thief, which evoked in me a curious mixture of tremendous excitement and deep dread, I carefully went through his clothes. First I looked in the pockets of his sports jackets. But all I found was an old bus ticket, a hanky and some coins.

'Nothing suspicious there,' I said to Graham. He looked at me with what I can only describe as an expression of enormous relief. In the laundry basket in the corner were some shirts. Graham and I both sniffed them. But there was no whiff of alien scent, no tell-tale lipstick marks, just the familiar aroma of Peter's sweat.

'We're doing well,' I said to Graham. His ears pricked up and he wagged his tail. Then I took Peter's corduroy trousers off the dumb valet and turned out the pockets of those. All I came up with was a packet of chewing gum – unopened – and some lint.

'No condoms or billets-doux – my husband is innocent,' I declared. By now I was rather enjoying myself. Relief was flooding in. I'd already checked the glove compartment for foreign knickers but found not so much as a thong. I'd done 1471 on the telephone, and it had read back to me Sarah's number. I couldn't check his briefcase, of course, because he'd taken that to work.

'Ah – his mobile phone statement,' I said as I spotted an envelope marked One-2-One lying on the window sill. It had been opened, so I just slipped it out and read the bill. There was one 0207 number on it which appeared over thirty times. So I went downstairs, cunningly pressed 141 to conceal my number (as advised by *Moi!*) then dialled it with a thumping heart.

'Andy Metzler Associates,' said a female voice. I immediately put the phone down.

'It's just his headhunter,' I said to Graham. 'Peter's blameless. Gimme five!' He held up his right paw and I shook it, then looked at the magazine again. *Most love cheats are caught out either by unfamiliar numbers on their phone bill, or by suspicious entries on their credit card statements*. Now, I didn't actually know where our credit card statement was, as I don't get to see it. This is not because Peter's hiding it from me, but because it comes in a brown envelope and I never, ever open brown envelopes. It's a kind of phobia, I suppose. I'll open any number of white ones, but brown ones I avoid. So Peter always deals with our credit card, and I've never ever seen the bill. In any case, I hardly use my card as it's so easy to over-spend. I rummaged in the bureau in the sitting room and found a small black folder labelled 'Credit Card'.

'So far Peter has passed the fidelity test with flying colours,' I said to Graham. 'This, my darling doggo, is the final stage.' I examined the top statement, which was dated January the fourth. As I expected, there were very few entries; we'd used the card to book theatre tickets at Christmas, we'd bought Katie some books from Borders, and there was a sixty-pound entry for WH Smith for a new computer game for Matt. Then there was a fourth entry, for some flowers. My flowers, obviously. They'd cost forty pounds and had been ordered from a place called Floribunda. I know where that is – it's in Covent Garden, near Peter's office. So that was that then. No unexplained restaurant bills. No references to country house hotels. No suspicious mentions of Knickerbox or La Perla. My investigations were at an end. But as I snapped the folder shut and went to put it back, I suddenly felt my heart contract as though squeezed by an alien hand. Those flowers on the bill weren't *my* flowers. How could they be? My bouquet had only been sent yesterday. The bill for my ones wouldn't appear until the February statement in three weeks' time. I could hear my breathing increase as I lowered myself onto a nearby chair. I went into the hall, looked up Floribunda in the phone book and dialled the number with a trembling hand. What would I say when they answered? What on earth would I say? Please could you tell me who my husband ordered flowers for on December eighteenth as I'm suspicious that he's having an affair. Perhaps I could pretend to be the recipient and claim that they'd never turned up? I'm so sorry, but you know the flowers my husband Peter Smith ordered on the eighteenth of December? Yes, that's right. Well I'm afraid they never arrived; there seems to have been a mix-up, could you just confirm which address you sent them to . . .'

'Hello, Floribunda, can I help you?' said a pleasant-sounding female voice.

'I – I –' I put the phone down, aware that the handset was wet with sweat. I just couldn't do it. I didn't want to know. I could feel the urgent banging of my heart as I sat on the foot of the stairs. Peter was having an affair. *I had been happy so I had nothing known*, I remembered as my hands sprang up to my face. *So now, forever, Farewell, the tranquil mind* . . . I sat there, gazing at the gold sunburst mirror Lily had given us for our wedding. I stared at it for a minute or two, too shocked to know what to do. Then suddenly I gasped, and smiled, then smacked my forehead, hard, with the palm of my hand.

'You IDIOT, Faith!' I shouted. 'You STUPID IDIOT!' I'd suddenly remembered, you see. His mother's birthday's on December the eighteenth. I'd organised the birthday card, and signed it, and we'd given her a silver photo frame. And now it was obvious that Peter had decided to send her flowers as well. Of course. That was it! I flung my arms round the startled dog.

'I'm a very silly Mummy,' I said as Graham nervously licked my ear, 'and I got it completely wrong.' I felt so mean for having suspected Peter, especially when he's got so much on his mind. I felt mean, and low, and somehow tarnished. Now, I resolved as I picked up the credit card folder, I'd never distrust him again. Then I went into the kitchen and made myself a cup of coffee – real coffee by way of celebration. And the heady aroma of arabica had filled the air and I was feeling quite mellow again, calmly flicking through the rest of *Moi!* when I heard the trill of the telephone.

'Hello, Faith,' said Sarah. 'I just wanted to thank you for organising that lovely party last week. I did enjoy myself,' she added warmly, 'and it was wonderful to see the children – they're so grown up.'

'Oh, they are,' I said with a wistful smile.

'And I thought it was so sweet the way you arranged it as a surprise for Peter.'

'I wanted to cheer him up,' I explained. 'I expect he's told you that he's got a few worries at work.'

'Well yes,' she said. 'He phoned me last night. I'm sure it will all work out, but I must say he *is* a bit distracted at the moment.'

'Yes,' I agreed. 'He is. In fact,' I went on enthusiastically, in a way I was shortly to regret, 'he'd even forgotten that it was our anniversary and he's never done that before.'

'Well,' Sarah exclaimed with a little laugh, 'he actually forgot my birthday!'

'*Sorry*?' It was like falling down a mineshaft. 'I'm sorry, Sarah, what did you say?'

'He forgot my birthday,' she repeated. 'And he's normally so thoughtful like that. I mean, I got your card of course, and that lovely frame, but Peter usually gives me a little something extra, just from him, but for the first time ever, he didn't. Not a thing. But please *don't* mention it to him,' she added quickly. 'He's got enough on his plate right now.'

'So you didn't get . . . ?' I began faintly.

'Get what?'

'You didn't get any . . . ?' I heard the sudden, sharp ring of her doorbell.

'Oh, I've got to go,' she said, 'my bridge partners have just turned up. Let's chat another time soon, Faith. Bye.'

I replaced the receiver very slowly. 'Oh God,' I said to Graham. 'Oh God,' I repeated, breathing more quickly. 'Who the hell did he send those flowers to, and what on earth shall I do?' I consulted the magazine again. Under the box headed, 'Action Stations!' was the following advice: *On no account let your husband know that you have doubts about his fidelity. However hard it is you MUST carry on as though absolutely nothing is amiss.*

'So how was it today, darling?' I enquired with phoney brightness as Peter arrived back from work.

'Godawful,' he said wearily. 'Do you know what the old bat's doing now?'

'What?'

'She's trying to fob Amber Dane off onto me.'

'I thought Amber Dane had given up writing those awful novels,' I said.

'We all hoped so,' he replied with a grim smile. 'But she's written another one which she claims is "satire" if you please. Satire? From what I've read so far it's about as satirical as a box of Milk Tray. We really shouldn't be publishing it – in fact that's what I said. But Charmaine's given me the manuscript and wants a full report. Talk about getting the short bloody straw,' he added as he loosened his tie.

'Oh dear.'

'And that creep,' he said exasperatedly as he fixed himself a drink, 'that fat Old Etonian creep got all hoity toity with me because I called him Olly.'

'What's wrong with that?'

'Exactly! Nothing. I mean, lots of people call him Olly. Charmaine calls him Olly. And today, in a meeting, I called him Olly too, and afterwards he took me to one side, and he'd gone puce in the face, and all sweaty, and he said, very crossly, as though he was my bloody boss, "Peter. Kindly *don't* call me Olly. My name is *Oliver*." Pompous git! You know, Faith, I used to love Fenton & Friend, but now I just can't wait to get out.'

'Any news from Andy?' I asked. At this Peter blushed slightly, I guessed because he was embarrassed to admit that there wasn't any news.

'Er . . . no,' he said with a sigh as he sank into an easy chair. 'There's nothing. Nothing yet. But I'm . . . hopeful.'

I managed to remain all breezy and 'normal' as the magazine article advised, and I couldn't help congratulating myself for keeping up this pleasant façade when my mind was in such turmoil. As we sat down to supper I looked at Peter across the kitchen table, and it was as though I was seeing him in a whole new light. He looked different to me now, in some undefinable way, because for the first time in fifteen years I couldn't read his face. It was like looking at one of those smart clocks with no numerals – they can be rather hard to read. All I knew was that I didn't instinctively trust him in the way I had before. I mean, before trust just wasn't an issue between Peter and me. That may sound naïve, but it's true. I never ever gave it a thought, and I felt sorry for wives who did. But now, I found myself, like thousands of other women, consciously wondering if my husband was having an affair. And it was a very peculiar feeling after being married to him for so long. As we sat there chatting over the lasagne – reduced by a pound in Tesco actually, and double points on the loyalty card – I thought about Peter's name again, and about how he's always been my rock. Strong and steady and reliable – until now, that is. In the Bible it was Peter upon whom Christ built his church. That's what we were taught at school. But it was also Peter whose resolve cracked in the garden of Gethsemane, and who denied Jesus, three times. So Peter the Apostle had feet of clay and I thought, my Peter does too.

'Are you all right, Faith?' said Peter suddenly. He'd put down his knife and fork.

'What?'

'You're staring at me,' he said.

'Am I?'

'Yes.'

'Oh. Sorry.'

'Is everything all right?' he asked. 'I mean, have you had a good day?'

'Er . . .'

'You seem a little bit tense.'

'Oooh no, I'm not tense at all no, no, no, no. No.'

'How was the programme?' he asked. 'I'm sorry I missed you this morning. You know I always try to watch.'

'Well, it was quite good,' I replied. 'There was this really interesting interview about names and what they mean. Yours means a rock,' I added.

'I know.'

'Mine means – well it's obvious,' I said. 'And I always have been faithful, as you know.'

'Yes. Yes, I do know that,' he said rather quietly, I thought. And now there was a silence, during which I could hear the ticking of the kitchen clock. 'So how was the weather today?' he added.

'Um . . . well, the weather was fine,' I said. 'I mean, it wasn't fine. In fact the outlook is rather unsettled,' I went on thoughtfully. 'Temperatures are dropping quite a bit, and then there's the chill factor.'

'Of course,' he said. 'The chill factor.' We looked at each other again.

'Gorgeous flowers,' I said brightly, indicating the bouquet of creamy jonquils and narcissi, pale anemones and golden mimosa. 'They smell heavenly. That was so sweet of you, Peter.'

'You deserve them,' he replied. Then another silence enveloped us both. And in that silence I suddenly decided – don't ask me why – to ignore what the magazine advised.

'Don't you normally buy your mother something for her birthday?' I asked innocently as I put down my knife and fork.

'Oh Christ!' he slapped his forehead. 'I completely forgot.'

'Well, we all gave her that silver frame, don't you remember, and you did sign the card.'

'I know. But I usually send her some flowers or get her a box of chocs. You know, something that's just from me. I'm not remembering anything at the moment, Faith,' he sighed as he picked up our plates. 'I guess it's all the stress at work.'

'But you're remembering . . . *some* things,' I suggested tentatively as I opened the freezer door.

'Am I?'

'Yes.'

'Like what?'

'Well, I don't know,' I said as I took out a box of ice-cream. 'To be honest, Pete, I was going to ask you.'

'Faith, what are you talking about?' he asked as he got down two bowls.

'Well, nothing really,' I replied nonchalantly as I flipped open the lid, 'except that you seem to have remembered someone else recently – someone I don't know.'

'Faith,' he said edgily, 'I haven't got time for this. I'm very tired. And I've got an excruciating evening ahead of me because I've got to start the Amber Dane. So if you've got something to say to me, please would you be direct?'

'OK,' I said, 'I will.' I inhaled deeply, and then spoke. 'Peter,' I began, 'I looked at our credit card bill today, and I found an entry on it for some flowers. I knew they weren't for your mother's birthday, because she told me you'd forgotten, so I just couldn't help wondering who on earth they *were* for?' Peter took his ice-cream, then stared at me as though I were mad.

'Flowers?' he said incredulously. 'Flowers? I sent someone flowers? Who would I have sent flowers to apart from you or my mum?'

'Well, that's just what I was wondering,' I said as I put the ice-cream away.

'When was this exactly?' he asked calmly as I got the chocolate sauce. If he was lying, he was very convincing.

'December the eighteenth,' I replied.

'December the eighteenth? December the eighteenth . . .' He chewed his lower lip thoughtfully, theatrically almost, then he suddenly said, 'Clare Barry.'

'Who?'

'She's one of my authors. That's who those flowers were for. They were for her book launch, I always send her flowers.'

'Oh, I see,' I said. 'But –'

'But what?'

'But I thought you had a different credit card that you use just for your work expenditure.'

'Yes, I do. It's American Express.'

'But sending Clare Barry congratulatory flowers, well, that would have been for work, wouldn't it?'

'Ye-es.'

'So why would you have ordered flowers for one of your authors using your personal credit card?'

'Oh, I don't know,' he said irritably. 'Maybe it was a simple mistake. Or perhaps I mislaid my American Express card and was in a hurry, so I used my other card instead. Does it really matter?' he said.

'No,' I said airily. 'It doesn't. I'm . . . satisfied.'

'Satisfied?' he said wonderingly. '*Satisfied*? Oh!' he suddenly exclaimed. 'Oh! I get it. You think I'm carrying on with someone.' I glanced at Graham. His shoulder muscles had stiffened and his ears were down.

'Ooh, no, no, no, no,' I said. 'No. Well, maybe.' I took a deep breath. 'Are you?'

'No I'm not,' he said with what struck me as a slightly regretful air. 'I'm not carrying on with anyone. That's the truth. In any case, Faith, don't you think I've got enough to worry me right now without getting involved with some chick?' Chick? 'So please, will you give me a break?' A *break*?

'A break?' I repeated. Ah. 'You want me to give you a break?'

'Yes,' he replied firmly, 'I *do*. And I hope you believe me when I say that those flowers were for an author? Do you believe me, Faith? Do you?'

'Yes. I believe you,' I lied.

February

'I'm getting good at this,' I said to Graham as I went through Peter's clothes again this morning. You see I'm used to it now, so the second time wasn't so bad. My heart wasn't in my mouth as it had been when I'd done it the first time. My nerve endings didn't feel as though they were attached to twitching wires. In fact I was quite business-like about it, and I told myself that I was perfectly entitled to go through my husband's things.

'Other women do this all the time,' I said to Graham briskly. 'In any case, I *need* to go through them to see if any of them want dry cleaning.' I found nothing untoward this time, except, well, one very odd thing actually – in his grey trouser pockets – a packet of Lucky Strike cigarettes. I showed it to Graham and we exchanged a meaningful glance.

'I think I'll go to the gym this evening,' Peter said when he got home. 'I haven't been for over a week.'

'Oh,' I said. And whereas before I'd have thought nothing of it and gaily waved him off, now I was instantly on the alert. *Why* did he want to go to the gym all of a sudden? *Who* was he meeting there? Perhaps he had a rendezvous. Right. Let's nip this in the bud.

'Can I come too?' I asked. 'I'd like to have a swim.'

'Yes. Yes, of course,' he said, so we put on *Ready Steady Cook* for Graham, got our sports bags and left.

'Any news from Andy?' I enquired as we drove along.

'No,' he sighed, 'not yet.' He changed up a gear.

'And did you manage to finish the Amber Dane?'

'Yes,' he said wearily. 'At long last. Satire!' he expostulated again. 'It's not so much Juvenal as juven*ile*. I mean, why Charmaine wants to keep her on, I really don't know. God, that woman gives me stress.'

'Is that why you've started smoking?' I asked innocently as we loitered at a red light.

'Sorry?'

'Is that why you've started smoking?' I repeated. I wanted to see how well he could lie.

'I don't smoke,' he said indignantly. 'You know that.'

'In that case, darling, why, when I emptied your grey trouser pockets at the dry cleaners today, did I find a packet of cigarettes?'

'Cigarettes?' he said. And I could see, even in the semi-darkness, that his face had flushed bright red. 'What cigarettes?'

'Lucky Strike,' I replied.

'Oh. Oh. Those cigarettes,' he said as the car nosed forward again. 'Yes, well, I didn't want you to know this, but actually . . . I do smoke, just occasionally, when I'm stressed.'

'I've never seen you do it,' I said as the sign for the Hogarth Health Club came into view.

'Well, I didn't think you'd approve,' he replied. 'In any case, you've never seen me with serious stress before. But when I'm stressed, then just now and again, yes, I do like to have a quick fag.'

'Ah,' I said. 'I see.' And then I suddenly remembered another thing that didn't quite fit.

'You don't like chewing gum, do you?' I asked as he parked the car.

'No,' he agreed. 'I hate it.'

'So you'd never buy it, then?'

'No. Of course not. Why on earth would I?'

'Well, exactly,' I said.

'Look, Faith, I hope that's the end of today's inquisition,' he said as he pulled up the handbrake.

'No further questions,' I said with a grim little smile.

'And in future, Faith,' he added as he turned off the ignition,

'I'd rather you didn't go through my pockets. You've never done it before and I don't want you to start now.' Of course he didn't. Because then I'd find out for certain what at present I only suspected.

'Don't worry,' I said breezily. 'I won't do it again.' When we got home at nine thirty I pretended I was going to bed, but instead I crept into Matt's room to use his computer. I knew he wouldn't mind. There was a pile of CD Roms on the chair, and dozens of computer games on the bed. He seemed to be in the middle of reorganising his vast collection. I picked them up and looked at them – they've got the weirdest names: *Zombie Revenge, Strider, Super Pang* and *Chu-Chu Rocket*. Oh well, I thought, they keep him happy. Then I sat at his desk, turned on the computer and hit 'Connect'. Eeeeeeeeeekkkk. Berddinnnnnggg. Chingggg. Bonggggggg. Pinggggggg. Beeeep. Beeeep. Beeeep. Blooooop. Krrrrrkkkkkkk. Krrrrrrkkkkkk. And I was in. I clicked onto Yahoo, did a search for the www.IsHeCheating.com website, then click, click, click . . . And there it was. As the page downloaded I quickly got the gist. It was one of these interactive sites. American. You could log on pseudonymously, e-mail your suspicions, and ask other people for advice. It was riveting to read. Sherry from Iowa was worried because she'd found a stocking in her husband's car; Brandy from North Carolina was in despair because her boyfriend kept talking about a woman at work; and Chuck from Utah was upset because he'd intercepted his wife talking to her lover on the phone.

I'm almost certain he's cheating, said Sherry. *But although I want to know in one way, in another I don't, because I'm scared of what I may find out.*

Go with your guts, girl, advised Mary-Ann from Maine. *A woman's intuition is NEVER wrong.*

Maybe it's HIS stocking? suggested Frank from New Jersey. *Maybe your husband's a cross-dresser, and is too embarrassed to say.*

Follow him to work, said Cathy from Milwaukee. *But make sure you wear a wig.*

I can't. He's a long-distance lorry-driver, Sherry had e-mailed back. I decided to log on as 'Emily' because that's my middle name.

I think my husband may be having an affair, I typed. *Or it could just be that I'm paranoid and insecure. But he has been behaving strangely, and I'm not sure it's all due to pressure at work. He's a publisher,* I went on. *So he gets to meet all sorts of glamorous people in the book world. And though I know he's never strayed before, I think he may be doing so now. Firstly, he ordered flowers for someone in December, using our joint credit card. And when I challenged him about this he claimed – not very convincingly – that they were congratulatory flowers for an author. Secondly, I've been finding some odd things in his pockets – chewing gum, which he hates; and today I found a packet of cigarettes. But in fifteen years of marriage I have never, ever, seen him smoke. So I simply don't trust him in the way I've always done before. And it's making me feel terrible, so I'd be grateful for your thoughts.*

The next afternoon I phoned Lily. 'I need your advice,' I said.

'Of course, darling,' she replied. 'Whatever I can do to help.'

'Well,' I said, 'it's about Peter.'

'*Is* it?' she breathed. 'Oh dear. What's happened?'

I sat down on the hall chair. 'I've found out a few things.'

'Really?'

'Yes. But I don't know what they mean.'

'They probably mean *nothing*,' she said confidently. 'But I'll tell you what I think.'

'Right . . .' I began nervously. 'He sent me flowers.'

'I see,' she said thoughtfully. 'Mmm,' she added with a regretful sigh. 'You know what they say about that.'

'Yes, but the thing is,' I said miserably, 'that he sent someone else flowers, too.'

'No!' she gasped.

'He claims they were for an author, Lily, but I'm just not sure. And then . . .'

'Yes?'

'Oh Lily, I feel so disloyal telling you this,' I said as I twisted my wedding ring back and forth.

'Darling, you're not being disloyal,' she said quietly. 'All you're doing is protecting yourself.'

'Protecting myself?'

'Yes. Because if it *is* serious – though I'm absolutely *sure* it's not – you don't want to be taken by surprise. So tell me, what else have you found?'

'Well . . .' I began again. And then stopped. 'Oh God, I can't go on, Lily. I feel so treacherous. I mean, I don't want to hurt your feelings, but you see, you've never had a husband.'

'Oh, don't be silly, Faith,' she said with a giggle. 'You know perfectly well I've had *lots*. Now, what were you going to say?'

I heaved a huge sigh. 'I've found some pretty strange things in his pockets. For example, a packet of chewing gum, but Lily, he *hates* the stuff. And yesterday I discovered a packet of Lucky Strike. But the point is, Peter doesn't smoke.'

'Mmm. How very strange.'

'And then this morning when I got back from work I went through his pockets again . . .'

'Naturally . . .'

'And I found this note in his jacket.'

'A *note*? What does it say?'

'It says: *Peter, Jean has already phoned three times this morning and is absolutely desperate to talk to you*, desperate is underlined. Twice,' I added anxiously.

'Jean,' she said. 'Well . . . that could mean nothing, really. It could be quite innocent.'

'Do you really think so?'

'Yes. I do. And if it *is* innocent – which I'm *quite* sure it is – then he'll be perfectly happy to tell you exactly who this "Jean" is. So my advice is to ask him outright, and watch how he reacts. Now, don't worry about all this, Faith,' Lily added. 'I'm praying for you, by the way.'

'Oh. Thanks.'

'I said five Hail Marys for you last night and I chanted for twenty minutes, too.'

'Great.' Lily has a slightly promiscuous approach to religion.

'I also looked at your horoscope this morning,' she went on seriously. 'There's a lot of tension in your sign at the moment between Saturn and Mars, so this is leading to adverse celestial activity on the relationship front.'

'I see.'

'But you're doing the right thing.'

'Am I? You know, Lily, I think I'd rather bury my head in the sand and let life jog along like before.'

'Well, of course, ignorance is bliss, they say. But . . .' She sighed.

'But I've got to see it through,' I concluded as Lily murmured her assent. 'And now I've started it's becoming an obsession. I feel I've just *got* to find out the truth.'

'Well, you're going about it the right way,' she said encouragingly. 'And although of course I don't want to interfere, it seems to me that you're sleuthing away quite nicely there. I mean, your investigations are getting results.'

'My investigations *are* going well,' I agreed, 'but now I've got a bit stuck.'

'Well, Faith,' she added, softly, 'privately I'd say that your detection work has been very good.' Privately? Detection? Eureka!

'I need a private detective,' I said.

'Have you seen this?' said Peter last night. He waved the *Guardian* at me. 'It's about AM-UK!'

'What? Oh, I missed it.'

'The TV critic's had a go.' I looked at the piece. It was headlined 'CEREAL KILLERS!' Oh dear. *AM-UK! normally serves up a load of waffle for breakfast*, began Nancy Banks-Smith, *with the odd Poptart. But with the arrival of brilliant bluestocking Sophie Walsh, it's a clear case of Frosties all round. The on-screen chemistry between 'husband and wife' team Walsh and old-timer Doyle, is about as warm as liquid nitrogen. But young Sophie handles Doyle's sadistic joshing with rare aplomb. His crude attempts to wrest back the limelight are mesmerising to watch. But it's Sophie who's winning this breakfast battle – so-fa.*

'Gosh,' I said. 'They've all noticed. Mind you, it's impossible to miss.'

'It's probably good for the ratings,' said Peter. 'Maybe that's why Terry does it.'

'I don't think so,' I said.

'I'm going upstairs,' he went on, opening his briefcase. 'I've got another manuscript to read.'

'Before you do that,' I said carefully, 'please could you just tell me one thing?'

'If I can,' he said warily. I took a deep breath.

'Please could you tell me who Jean is.'

'Jean? *Jean*?' He looked totally confused. I was almost convinced.

'So you don't know anyone called Jean, then?' I said.

'Jean?' he repeated with a frown.

'Yes, Jean. As in the girl's name.'

'No,' he said firmly. 'I don't.' I had no idea he was such a good actor. 'Why do you want to know?'

'No particular reason,' I said. Peter gave me an odd look, then he snapped his briefcase shut and repeated, very slowly, 'I do not know *anyone* called Jean.'

'OK.'

'But I know why you're asking,' he added wearily. 'And it's really getting me down. Faith, I am not enjoying being the object of your crude and unfounded suspicions. So to allay them, I'm now going to tell you the names of all the women I *do* know.'

'Really, there's no need,' I said.

'Oh, but I want to,' he went on, 'because maybe that way you'll actually believe me, and these constant inquisitions will stop. Because, to be honest, I'm at the end of my tether, with everything that's going on at work. So I hope you don't think me unreasonable, Faith, but I can't cope with any hassle at home.'

'I'm not hassling you,' I said.

'Yes you are,' he shot back. 'You've been hassling me for three weeks. You've never done it before, but – and I really don't know why – you seem to have got this bee in your bonnet. So just to convince you, darling, that I'm not fooling around, I'm now going to list, from memory, all the women I know. Let's see. Right, at work there's Charmaine, Phillipa and Kate in Editorial, um, Daisy and Jo in Publicity; Rosanna, Flora, and Emma in Marketing, and Mary and Leanne in Sales. Now, I talk to these women on a regular basis, Faith, and I'm not involved with any of them.'

'OK, OK,' I said.

'Then of course there are all my women authors. There's Clare Barry, to whom I sent flowers, Francesca Leigh and Lucy Watt; then there's Janet Strong, J.L. Wyatt, Anna Jones, and um . . . Oh yes, Lorraine Liddel and Natalie Waugh.'

'I'm not interested,' I said in a bored sort of way.

'Who else?' he said, folding his arms and gazing at the ceiling for inspiration. 'Well, there are a number of female literary agents with whom I converse on a regular basis. There's Betsy and Valerie at Rogers, Green; Joanna and Sue at Blake Hart; Alice, Jane and Emma at A.P. Trott, and Celia at Ed McPhail.'

'All right,' I said.

'No Faith, it isn't all right,' he said. 'So let me tell you some more. Oh yes, on that silly Family Ethics Committee on which I sit four times a year, there is Baroness Warner, who's sixty-three; the sociologist, Dame Barbara Brown, and two very married and rather boring women MPs, both of whom are called Anne.'

'This is unnecessary,' I said.

'Other females of my acquaintance include Andy Metzler's colleagues, Theresa and Clare, and then of course there are a number of women I know socially, but then you know them all too – there's Samantha at number nine, and we know Jackie at number fifteen, and that nice woman – whatshername – who we occasionally bump into at the health club. Add to that our old college friends like Mimi and I'd say that pretty well completes the list. Oh, and Lily of course. But if you thought for a second I was having it off with her, Faith, I'd take you down to the head doctor like a shot.'

'OK, OK, OK,' I said weakly. 'Look, I didn't ask for all this.'

'Oh yes you did,' he said. 'By your suspicious behaviour. But let me assure you that the only person who's strayed around here is *Graham*!'

'Look,' I said, beginning to feel upset, 'I only asked you if you know someone called Jean.'

'No,' he said emphatically. 'I can honestly say that I *don't*.'

But I knew this was a lie. Not even a white lie, but a flashing fluorescent pink and green one. And this was very significant, because Peter's usually so truthful, but now he was being barefaced. But I couldn't admit that I'd seen the note about Jean, because then he'd know I'd been snooping again. I really *would* like to have *him* followed, I thought. But then I reminded myself that it was out of the question, because private detectives don't come cheap.

'Are you all right now, Faith?' Peter asked me as he stood by the door.

'All right?'

'Are you feeling convinced? Can we just kick all this nonsense of yours into touch? Because I'd just like our marriage to be . . .'

'What?'

'Well, normal.'

'I guess it *is* normal,' I said.

Work is a refuge these days, from my current marital distress. There's something about staring at the satellite charts, with their masses of Turneresque cloud swirling above the blue planet, which makes me forget my concerns. And of course the cold snaps in the studio are pretty distracting. Sophie had a very bad morning. Gremlins in the autocue. Funny that, I thought. I mean, normally Sophie reads it very fluently and I've never ever seen her fluff. She makes it all look so natural, as though she's ad libbing, not reading a script. But of course it's not like that at all. Up in the Gallery, Lisa the autocue operator works the machine by hand, scrolling the script down at a pace to suit the presenter. If the presenter slows down – she slows down. If they pick up – she picks up. But this morning something went wrong.

'Welcome back . . . to . . . the show,' Sophie said awkwardly after the break. 'And . . . now,' she went on at thirty-three rpm and I could suddenly see confusion in her face, '. . . a . . . report . . . on . . . sexual equality . . . in . . . the . . . boardroom . . . . . . concludes . . . that ambitious . . . young . . . women . . . are . . . spearheading . . . Britain's . . . drive . . . into . . . the twenty-first . . . century.'

It was agonising to watch. Once or twice she glanced down at her script, but it was clear that she'd lost her place. Then she looked up at the autocue again, but it was still crawling along the hard shoulder. It was like watching her being tortured, but she bravely battled on.

'Nearly four . . . in . . . ten . . .'

'What's going on, Lisa?' I heard Darryl bark into my earpiece.

'Ooh, I don't know,' she whined. 'I just can't get it to work.'

'Boardroom bosses . . . are now . . . female,' Sophie continued. 'The . . . highest figure . . . since data was . . .' I heard her sigh. '. . . collected. Women are also . . .'

'Oh, come on, Sophie!' interrupted Terry suddenly. 'We haven't got all day. Sorry folks,' he said into his autocue with a regretful smile, 'but Sophie seems to have lost the gift of the gab. So we'll skip that item and go straight to Tatiana's report from the Old Vic. Yes, the lovely Tatiana's been talking to Andrew Lloyd-Webber about his plans for this much-loved London landmark where Laurence Olivier and John Gielgud first trod the boards.'

'What's going *on*?' I heard Sophie say into her microphone as Tatiana's filmed report went out. 'What happened to the autocue?'

'There were problems with it, apparently,' Darryl said.

'Well, it worked perfectly OK for Terry,' she pointed out. I could see that she was close to tears. 'Lisa,' she said carefully as she swallowed hard, 'kindly don't do that again.'

'I didn't "do" anything,' I heard Lisa whine. To be honest, I've never liked that girl. 'It just seemed to get, I don't know . . . *stuck*,' she concluded feebly.

'Well, kindly *un*stick it for my next item,' Sophie said crisply. I didn't blame her. There is nothing worse than broadcasting live to the nation with a dodgy autocue. I've done it once or twice and believe me, you look a total prat. Worse, people remember it for years. They say, 'Oh! I saw you on breakfast TV.' And you think you're about to get some lavish compliment, instead of which they say, 'Yeah. Two years ago. It was really funny – the autocue broke down!' And you have to go, 'Oh yes – that *was* funny. Oh, yes – ha ha ha!'

'You *poor* thing,' said Terry to Sophie with phony concern. 'That must have been *awful* for you. So *humiliating*. And at *peak time* too. When *everyone's* watching. Five *million* people. Oh *dear* – what a shame.' She pretended not to hear him as she looked down at her script.

'But that's the thrills and spills of live TV for you,' Terry went on philosophically. 'Don't take this the wrong way, love, but I'm not sure you've got what it takes.'

At the meeting afterwards, Darryl was livid.

'Lisa, I think you should apologise to Sophie,' he said, crossing his arms.

'I'm very sorry, but I'm not going to apologise,' she whined. 'It was a technical hitch.' She remained adamant that it wasn't her fault. But as I was leaving I spotted Terry and Tatiana having breakfast in the canteen. They looked rather pleased with themselves. Then Lisa sat down with them too. And you don't need to be a brain surgeon to guess what had happened, though I wonder what she'd been paid.

When I got home I took Graham for a walk along the river – he loves it there – then I checked out the IsHeCheating.com website again. I'd asked for advice, and I'd got it.

Emily, give your husband a break! said Barbara from New York. *You don't have ANY hard facts that he's playing around so why go looking for trouble?*

If you feel your man's being evasive, then he IS, said Sally from Wichita.

Why don't you cheat on HIM? suggested Mike from Alabama. *Just to even the score.*

Sneak into his office and bug his phone! advised someone else.

Call an attorney right now!

Go back home to your mom!

Just have the bastard trailed!

I was mulling over all these options tonight in the kitchen as I chopped up vegetables for supper. I wasn't going to have an affair myself – that would be cheap and low; there was no way I could gain access to his office even if I had surveillance equipment; I couldn't afford a lawyer, so that was out of the question, and I couldn't go back to my mum because she was always away. As for having Peter followed, I'd decided I hadn't the heart. Nor did I have the cash. I'd made a couple of calls and ascertained that it would cost at least two grand. I just didn't know *what* to do.

'Mum, are you all right?' Katie enquired. She was cleaning out her goldfish, Sigmund.

'What?' I said.

'I said, are you all right?'

'Yes, of course I'm all right, darling,' I replied. 'What on *earth* makes you think I'm not?'

'The gratuitously vicious way in which you're chopping up those carrots.'

'Am I?' I said wonderingly, sword-sized Sabatier poised in mid-air.

'Yes. You remind me of Jack Nicholson in *The Shining*. In fact ever since Matt and I came home this evening, I've been picking up a lot of stress.' Oh God. I had that shrinking feeling. I knew what was coming next.

'I've been detecting a lot of tension,' Katie went on, 'and a lot of suppressed anger. You're feeling pretty hostile, aren't you Mum?'

'I am *not* hostile!' I spat.

70

'Is there anything you want to tell me?' she continued calmly. 'There you are, Siggy. Nice and clean.'

'Tell you?' I repeated wonderingly.

'What I really mean is, Mum, is there anything you need to talk through?'

'No thank you,' I said as I got down the salt.

'Because I'm getting a lot of anxiety here.'

'Are you?'

'Yes. Have you been having many negative thoughts?'

'Negative? No.'

'Are you in denial?'

'Certainly not!'

'Disturbing dreams?'

'Of course not. What a ridiculous suggestion. No.'

'You see, I'm worried about your super-ego,' she added matter-of-factly as she laid the kitchen table. 'I think there are some repressed conflicts here, so we need to work through them to take some of the pressure off your subconscious. Now,' she said as she got out the spoons, 'how about a little free association?'

'No thanks.'

'I think it would help your ego really open up.'

'My ego's busy cooking supper, darling. Sorry.'

'Really Mum, there's absolutely nothing to it.'

'I know,' I said as I strained the beans. 'That's precisely why I'm not keen.'

'All you have to do, Mum, is just sit down, close your eyes, and say whatever comes to mind.'

'Oh Katie, please don't turn me into one of your human guinea pigs,' I said irritably. 'Can't you do that at school?'

'No,' she said regretfully.

'Why not?'

'Because they're all in therapy already. Honestly Mum, free association's easy,' she persisted as I opened the oven and checked the shepherd's pie. She took a notebook out of her pocket. 'You just say whatever pops into your head, no matter how frivolous it might be.'

71

'Oh God . . .'

'No matter how trivial,' she went on reassuringly. 'No matter how disgusting or depraved.'

'Katie!' I said crossly. 'I object to being psychoanalysed by someone who, until relatively recently, was playing with Barbie dolls!'

'Yes, but I was only ever interested in Barbies as a paradigm of US cultural imperialism. Please, Mum,' she said persuasively, 'just for five minutes – that's all.'

'Oh, all right,' I conceded. 'I'm prepared to humour you. But let me assure you young lady, that I find all this psychobabble very silly.'

'That's absolutely fine, Mum,' she said soothingly. 'Go with your anger. Don't hold back. Just let it out. Whatever you say is OK. Right,' she went on briskly. 'Sit down. Close your eyes. That's good. Relax. Breathe deeply. Let your mind wander. Now, what word springs into your mind?'

'Um . . .'

'No, don't think about it, Mum. Just say it. Straight out. OK? *Go*.'

'Er, carrot.'

'Yes.'

'Chop . . .'

'Carry on.'

'Knife . . . sharp . . . er . . . stick . . . beat . . . time. Fifteen. Happy. Not. Over. Yet. Maybe. Wrigley. Wriggly. Lucky. Strike. Hit. Hurt. Wound. Heart. Flowers. Betrayal. Lying. Cheating. Philandering *bastard*. OK, that's it!' I suddenly got to my feet. 'I don't want to play this game any more.'

'You're exhibiting classic resistance, Mum,' said Katie benignly. 'It's quite natural, don't worry, because it means we're getting close to the source of the problem.'

'I don't have any problems. Oh, hello Matt. You're down.'

'What we saw *there*,' said Katie cheerfully as she snapped shut her notebook, 'was your unconscious struggling to avoid giving up its dark secrets.'

'Look, Katie,' I said patiently as I wiped my brow. 'I haven't got any dark secrets, and all this Freudian mumbo-jumbo is simply *ridiculous*. Now, supper's ready, so just do me a favour and go and kill your dad.'

Who is Jean? I keep on wondering. My rival. And what does she look like? Is she blonde or dark? Tall or short? Is she younger than me? Is she prettier? Probably is. Is she slimmer? That wouldn't be hard. Is she wittier, and brighter? How – and when – did they meet? Did she make a beeline for Peter, or did he chat her up? Does he imagine he's in love with her, or is it just a physical thing? Oh God. Oh God. I'm torturing myself, but I just can't stop. You see I found another note in his pocket about Jean this morning, and I was doubly upset about it because the weekend had gone quite well. We were perfectly 'normal' together, as a family. We walked the dog. We got out a video – 'Analyze This' – and the children enjoyed themselves. Matt was closeted in his room most of the time, as usual, although curiously he went out to the post box several times. But all in all, it went well. And I was just beginning to relax and to think that maybe I'd got it all wrong. After all, I still have not a shred of hard evidence that Peter's up to no good, just these horrible, uneasy feelings which refuse to go away. But this morning, when I got back from work, I saw that he'd left his briefcase at home. So I opened it – it wasn't locked – and I know you'll all disapprove, but all I can say in my own defence is that it was something I just . . . *had* to do. I feel so tormented, you see. I've lost my peace of mind. My life's in limbo until I've found out one way or the other for sure. So I opened it. And I'm glad I did, because there it was. Tucked into the pocket. A note from Peter's secretary Iris, which said, *Peter, Jean called again – sounded rather anxious. Says you're a very 'naughty boy', not to have called back, and 'please, please, PLEASE to ring*. A 'naughty boy'? Good God! She was probably into S and M. And I felt really annoyed with Iris, who I'd always thought was nice, for helping my husband to pursue his sordid little *liaison dangereuse*. Then I looked at the manuscript he was working on and there was Jean's name again. It appeared several times. Peter had doodled it in the margin as though he was quite obsessed. *Jean*, he'd written, and sometimes just a simple *J*. And the point is that if Jean was purely a professional contact, then Peter would happily have said. But the fact that he vehemently denied that he knew her makes me feel certain that he's involved.

'I'm in agonies,' I said miserably to Lily this evening. 'I just don't know what to do.' We were sitting at the bar of the Blue-bird Café in the King's Road, not far from where she lives.

'Have some Laurent Perrier, darling,' she said above the babble. 'That'll cheer you up.'

'No thanks,' I replied. 'I have nothing to celebrate. The opposite, in fact. It's like living with a stranger,' I added as I sipped my virgin Mary. 'Out of the blue, somehow, every-thing's changed. I feel as though I don't really know him at all.'

'Well,' she said firmly as she slipped Jennifer Aniston a crisp. 'Are you sure you've done everything you can on the investigation front? You must snoop to conquer.'

'I have been snooping,' I said.

'But . . .'

'It's not working.'

'No,' she said, 'it's not, because you haven't looked under every stone. You poor darling,' she added sympathetically as she lit a cheroot. 'It must be *horrible* having all these doubts. It must affect your peace of mind.'

'Yes, it does,' I agreed. 'That's *exactly* it. I've lost my peace of mind.'

'Well then,' she said reasonably, 'you've just got to get it back. Now,' she went on briskly, 'I know someone whose husband was up to no good and she used a decoy duck.'

'What, one of those women who chat up your husband and see if he takes the bait?' She nodded. 'Oh God, I'd never do that. It's entrapment. I will not lead Peter into tempta-tion,' I said.

'But Faith, it looks as though he may have led *himself* there.'

'Well, yes,' I conceded mournfully. 'It does. I'd follow him to work, Lily, if I didn't know that he'd spot me in a flash.'

'Yes,' she said thoughtfully. 'He would.'

'You know, I'm *very* tempted to get a private detective.'

'Oh yes,' she said vaguely. 'I seem to remember you mentioning that the other day.' We looked at each other as we sipped our drinks. 'Well, why *don't* you then?'

'Because they cost far too much,' I replied. I glanced round the restaurant at all the happy couples having dinner. 'Look at all these lucky people,' I moaned. 'They're all happy with their partners.'

'Actually Faith, I'm not sure that's true. In fact,' she went on as she expelled a twin plume of pale blue smoke, 'I know for sure that it's not. Do you see that couple over there, by the window?' she went on. I followed her gaze. A man in a pin-stripe suit was having supper with an attractive brunette. They were both talking and smiling, gazing deeply into each other's eyes. In short, they looked as though they were in love.

'He's a banker,' Lily explained. 'I've met him socially once or twice.'

'So what?'

'The woman who he's having such a nice dinner with is *not* his wife.'

'Oh,' I sighed. 'Oh, I see.'

'Where's Peter tonight?' she asked in a voice that was zephyr soft.

'He's at a book launch,' I replied blankly.

'Well, that could be true I suppose. I must say,' she went on, 'a private detective sounds like a *very* good idea to me. But I'm not going to say any more,' she added, 'because you're my best friend and I don't want to meddle.'

'Oh God, Lily,' I went on, 'this is such a *nightmare*. It's like struggling in wet concrete. It's like trying to run up an escalator that's going down. You know, I really do want to have him trailed. I just wish it didn't cost so much.'

'Poor Faith,' Lily said as she lifted her champagne glass to her sculpted lips. 'But hey! I've just had an idea. *I'll* pay.'

'Sorry?'

'I'll pay for you to hire someone,' she repeated as she opened her bag. 'In fact, Faith, I'm going to write you a cheque right now.'

'Lily!' I said. 'Don't be silly, I couldn't possibly let you do that.'

'But I want to,' she protested.

'Why?'

'Why?'

'Yes, why?' She placed her hand on my knee.

'Because you're my dearest friend in the world. That's why. But that's not the real reason,' she suddenly added with a guilty little giggle. 'I have an ulterior motive, you know.'

'You do?'

'Yes. You see for some time I've been planning an infidelity special for *Moi!* I want to publish it in June, to counteract all those *nauseating* weddings. I'm going to call it *Rogue*.'

'Oh yes?'

'I could interview you!'

'Oh no, I couldn't do that.'

'Totally pseudonymously,' she said reassuringly. 'So I could pay for your private detective and put it through as an expense. We have a budget for this kind of thing, Faith, and anyway, I'm the boss.'

'You'd pay?'

'Yes. I would. It would be perfect for the magazine. I'll interview you myself, of course, as I know you trust me, and I'll protect your identity. It would be a First Person piece – *Why I had My Husband Trailed*. I'd let you see it before it goes in, and don't worry, both you and Peter will be completely disguised. So what about it?' she said.

'Well . . .'

'It's a good offer, isn't it?'

'Well, yes. Yes it is. But to be honest, Lily, I'm really not sure.'

'Look, Faith,' she said patiently, 'it's very simple. Do you want your peace of mind back? Or don't you?'

'Yes,' I said suddenly, 'I *do*.'

February Continued

So that was how I came to find myself sitting in the offices of Personal Quest. I'd found them by sticking a pin in the Private Investigators section of the *Yellow Pages*. My appointment was for three o'clock. So at ten to I climbed the rickety stairs of a narrow house in Marylebone. I experienced a frisson of excitement as I knocked on the semi-glazed door. But there was no sign of a trenchcoat, or a trilby; no glamorous secretary filing her nails. Just a harassed looking man of about forty-five with short brown hair and a beard.

'Now, I've had a busy day,' said the private detective, Ian Sharp, Dip., P.I., as he rummaged through some files on his desk. 'So remind me again will you, is your case industrial, financial, political, medical, insurance fraud, nanny check, neighbour check, child abduction, missing persons, adoption search, or good old matrimonial?'

'Er, matrimonial,' I replied, looking at a framed sign which read, 'No Mission Impossible'!

'Well, if it's matrimonial,' he went on, 'let me save you a lot of money right now by telling you that it's either his secretary or your best friend.'

'Actually it's neither,' I said as I lowered myself into a cheap, green vinyl chair.

'How do you know?' he asked.

'Because his secretary, Iris, is fifty-nine, and he can't stand my closest friend.'

'So who might this other woman be,' Ian Sharp enquired, 'and what makes you think your husband has strayed?'

'Her name's Jean,' I explained, 'and, well, my husband's been acting suspiciously for weeks.'

'Jean?' he repeated thoughtfully. 'Jean. Mmmm. With that name she's probably Scottish.' This thought hadn't occurred to me, but now, somehow, it seemed to ring true. So I told him about the two notes I'd found, and the flowers Peter had sent, and the mystery gum and cigarettes.

'I see,' he said thoughtfully. 'Anything else?'

'Yes. He's distracted and distant, he's working late, he's looking fit, he's bought a mobile phone, he's not interested in sex, he's improved his wardrobe, and he's started sending me flowers.'

'Ah,' he said, sitting back and steepling his fingers. 'All the classic signs.'

'Yes, exactly,' I replied.

'But no hard evidence?'

'Not yet.'

'So at the moment it's simply a hunch,' he added, bouncing his fingertips against each other. 'Alarm bells have been ringing.' I nodded. 'Your antennae are twitching.'

'Like mad.'

'In fact it's becoming an obsession,' he said matter-of-factly.

'It certainly is,' I agreed.

'So what you're seeking, by coming here, is peace of mind?'

'Yes. Yes, that's it,' I said enthusiastically. 'I want to have my peace of mind restored.'

'Well, I may not be able to do that,' he said seriously. He leaned forward, placed his elbows on his desk and clasped his hands as if in prayer. 'I may be able to provide you with the facts,' he went on judiciously, 'but as for restoring your peace of mind – I might well do the opposite. Because the truth is that women's instincts about their husbands' misbehaviour are proved right ninety per cent of the time.'

'Oh,' I said faintly. 'I see.'

'So you have to consider the consequences, Mrs Smith, if I were to find evidence of your husband's . . . indiscretions. For if I take on this case, I will present you with a written report of my findings, which may well include compromising photos of your husband with the other woman.'

'Yes,' I whispered, 'I know.'

'You must prepare yourself emotionally, Mrs Smith, for what may lie ahead. You may, in a week's time, say, find yourself back in this office staring at a photograph of your husband holding another woman by the hand . . .'

'Oh.'

'Or kissing her.'

'Oh dear.'

'Or entering a hotel with her.'

'Oh God.' I felt sick.

'Or seeing his car parked outside her house. So I ask you, as I ask all my matrimonial clients, to give that serious thought. Will you be prepared for such . . . unpalatable images, Mrs Smith?' he enquired. I heaved a sigh.

'Yes. I think I will.'

'In that case my fees are forty pounds an hour exclusive of VAT, fifty-five pounds for evening work, with any expenses on top, plus petrol which I charge at a very reasonable eighty-five pence a mile. Now,' he went on, 'do you just want the basic?'

'What does that involve?' I enquired.

'I trail your husband to work and wait in my car, with my small but powerful camera at the ready. Wherever he goes, I won't be far behind, going snap, snap, snap!'

'Isn't there a danger that he'll spot you?'

'Mrs Smith,' said Ian Sharp patiently, 'what do you notice about me?'

'Notice?' I said, dumbfounded. 'Well, nothing, I don't know what you mean.'

'What distinguishing features do I have?'

'Well, none that I can see, really.'

'How tall am I?'

'Er . . . medium.'

'What sort of frame do I have?'

'Well, you know . . . normal. Not fat, not thin.'

'Pre*cisely*!' he exclaimed triumphantly. 'Mrs Smith, I am

totally nondescript!' he went on proudly. 'I am very ordinary. I can pass undetected in a crowd. People do not clock me. They do not remember me. I am invisible in my averageness.'

'Well, I wouldn't put it quite like that.'

'I would not be picked out in a line-up.'

'Wouldn't you?'

'My appearance is dull and hum-drum.'

'Well . . .'

'Which means, Mrs Smith,' he went on confidently, 'that your husband will be oblivious to my presence. May I add that in fifteen years as a private investigator, I have not been spotted once. Mind you,' he added, 'these men are usually so wrapped up in their assignations that they don't notice me trotting along behind. But there I am, Mrs Smith. There I am.'

'Right. Well, good.'

'So that's the basic search. What we call the Bronze Service. However, you can have a more sophisticated service, the Silver Service, in which I wear . . .' He suddenly opened his jacket with both hands, revealing what looked like a bullet-proof waistcoat. 'This!'

'Er . . .'

'This is a body-worn harness in which there is a concealed video camera. Can you see the camera, Mrs Smith? Can you? If so, kindly tell me where it is.'

'Er, no,' I said truthfully, 'I can't.'

'It's here,' he said, pointing to a tiny pin on the lapel. 'There is a lens hidden in this pin, which is mere microns thick.'

'Good Lord!' I said.

'Now, if you want video footage, this is what I'll use, but surveillance equipment of this kind is pricey so that'll add another ninety-five pounds a day.'

'I see.'

'We could also use this.' He picked up a briefcase and slapped it on the desk. 'This is a recording briefcase, Mrs Smith. I could have it placed in a cupboard in your husband's office; inside is a powerful radio mike – extremely sensitive – which would pick up any sweet nothings he cared to murmur down the phone.'

'I see.'

'And if you want the Full Monty Five Star No Holds Barred Gold Service – well, then that's going to involve four of my colleagues following your husband full-time, detailing his every move. Mrs Smith, he would not be able to scratch his backside without me and my lads knowing about it.'

'Oh, I don't think that will be necessary.'

'Nor do I, Mrs Smith, nor do I. I think the Bronze Service will be more than adequate for your purposes. Now,' he added, 'do you have any idea what this other woman looks like?'

'No,' I said. 'Not a clue. And I can't find out surreptitiously, from Peter, because he denies that he even knows her.'

'I see. Have you got a photo of your husband?'

'Yes,' I said. I produced a recent snap.

'How tall is he?' he asked. 'It's hard to tell from this.'

'About five foot eleven, and he weighs thirteen stone. No, he's lost weight recently, so I guess he might be only twelve. His hair is sandy, as you can see, and he has a fair, lightly freckled complexion.'

'And what time does he leave for work?'

'He goes at about eight fifteen and gets the District line to Embankment; then he walks to his office in Villiers Street, where he works on the seventh floor.'

'Make of car and registration?' I told him. 'Right,' he said. 'I'm on the case. But first, I need the usual deposit of five hundred pounds up front.'

'Oh, of course,' I said as I opened my bag. 'I can give you a cheque right now.' As I wrote it out I mentally thanked Lily for her wonderful help.

'Mrs Smith,' said Sharp as I reached for the door handle. 'One last question. Have you decided what you'll do if your suspicions do prove to be correct?'

'What I'll do?'

'Yes. What course of action you'll take.'

'Action? Oh, I don't know,' I replied. 'I hadn't thought that far ahead.'

'Well, with respect, Mrs Smith, I think you should try and work out what your attitude to his adultery would be.'

'To his adultery?' I repeated. What a *horrible* word. 'It would be totally unacceptable,' I said.

'So to recap,' I said with professional brightness, 'a typical February day . . .'

'Terry, don't pick your nose . . . four, three . . .'

'With a thick bank of heavy cloud . . .'

'Tory leadership next . . .'

'Sitting over most of the country . . .'

'Two, one . . .'

'And this is known, rather depressingly . . .'

'Oh Christ! Where's the piece about William Hague?'

'As anti-cyclonic gloom.'

'I don't know – who's got the tape?'

'So not the slightest chance of sunshine at the moment, I'm afraid.'

'Find it!'

'Especially in Chiswick.'

'*What?*'

'And there may be wintry showers in the south-east later on.'

'I can't.'

'So have your brollies handy – just in case.'

'Oh God, fill, Faith! Fill, fill FILL!'

'And talking about brollies,' I went on, 'we all know that it can rain cats and dogs . . .'

'A minute and a half please, Faith.'

'But did you know it can sometimes rain frogs and fishes, too?'

'Well done.'

'Yes, here's a little-known Freak Weather Fact for you. Everyone knows that those great big cumulonimbus clouds bring thunderstorms.'

'Do we?'

'Well, sometimes you get tornadoes forming out of the bottom of them.'

'God, I think I've got a tornado in *my* bottom! I had a *nuclear* curry last night.'

'And if these little tornadoes go over a pond, they actually suck up the frogs and fish.'

'Get away!'

'Then, when the storm moves away, the tornado dies and the frogs and fish drop out of the sky.'

'Streuth!'

'There have even been instances of it raining Dover sole along the Thames.'

'You don't say. OK Faith, in three, two . . .'

'But fortunately this is a rare occurrence.'

'And zero. Thanks.'

'See you in half an hour.'

As I made my way back to the office, I saw a copy of *Bella* magazine on the planning desk. 'Is Your Husband Playing Away?' screamed the headline. As usual these days, when I see anything about infidelity I grab it and read it right through. There were some dreadful stories about women finding alien suspenders in the laundry basket, or coming home to find their husbands *in flagrante* with the au pair. Then there were accounts of the nightmare scenario in which the Other Woman decides to spill the beans. Shirley from Kent found a note on her windscreen from her husband's mistress, and Sandra from Penge had the Other Woman phoning her up to confess. I was immediately filled with horror at the thought that Jean might do that to me. In my mind's ear I could hear her, threatening me in an accent which for some reason I'd decided was not so much Miss Jean Brodie as Irvine Welsh: 'Noo, yew listen to me, lassie,' she was saying menacingly, 'I'm in love with your husband!'

'Oh no!'

'Dinna kid yoursel' woman – he's in love wi' me tew!'

'Don't say that!'

'We've been seein' each other foor six months.'

'Oh God!'

'And he's gonna leave yew and come and live wi' *me*!'

I was so horrified I wanted to phone Ian Sharp straight away and ask him what I should do. But I couldn't, because he instructs clients not to ring him until his investigations are through. And he's right because a) there's no way I can make a call to him from our open-plan office at work, and b) if I rang him from home then the number would appear on our phone bill, which means that Peter could check it out. So I have to be patient, and wait, but I feel so upset at the moment that I can scarcely function. Which is why I was rather touched when Sophie spoke to me today, in the ladies' loo, during the third commercial break.

'Are you all right, Faith?' she said as I checked my appearance. And I thought that was nice of her, as we've never really chatted before.

'Oh, I'm fine,' I said. 'Fine. Thanks. Fine. Fine. Really. Yes. I am.'

'Oh, good,' she said. 'It's just that usually you're so cheerful, and I thought you seemed a little . . . down.'

'Oh. No. No.'

'A little distracted.'

'No. Not at all. What makes you think that?'

'Well, because you've just sprayed deodorant all over your hair.'

'Have I? Oh, yes. Silly me. Er . . . I'm just tired,' I explained with casual brightness. 'It's the awful hours, that's all. You know how it is. Buggered biorhythms and all that. But you're doing well,' I added by way of changing the subject. 'You're a brilliant broadcaster and you cope so well with Terry. If it was me I'd be in constant tears. Anyway,' I went on as she washed her hands, 'I think you've got a fantastic future at AM-UK!' And when I said that she looked rather startled, then pulled a funny face and I thought that was a little bit odd.

The next few days passed agonisingly slowly. My nerves were jangling and I could hardly sleep. Worse, the name

Jean seemed to jump out at me from all sides. The actress Jean Tripplehorn was in a new film, I noticed in the *Mail*, and Jean Marsh from *Upstairs Downstairs* was buying a new house according to *Hello!* According to *TV Quick!* there was going to be a new drama based on a Jean Plaidy novel, and a season of Jean Simmonds' old films on Channel 4. I even jumped when I heard someone talking about gene therapy on Radio 4. It was an enormous struggle to keep myself occupied as the week crawled by. I finished *Madame Bovary* – she paid a high price for wrecking her marriage – I went to the health club and swam. I entered a few competitions, and I spent quality time with Graham. And somehow I managed to resist the burning urge to phone Ian Sharp every ten seconds. But I imagined him, all the time, following Peter down the street. Poor Peter, I thought. I felt so treacherous, and I felt sorry for him too. In fact I didn't know how I'd be able to look him in the face, but thankfully he was having a very busy week, so we hardly saw each other. He told me he had three lunches, two launches, and meetings with Andy, of course. I wondered if any of those lunches were with Jean, and which restaurant they'd choose; and what they'd say to each other, and if they'd be playing footsie or worse, and if, being Scottish, she had a kilt complex about the fact that she was seeing a married man. I kept a detailed diary of how I was feeling, so that I'd give Lily good quotes for her piece. Then, finally, finally, the dreadful day dawned, and I went back to see Ian Sharp.

My heart was beating wildly as I knocked on his semi-glazed door. I felt as though I were awaiting the results of some terrifying medical tests. I inhaled deeply through my nose and braced myself for the worst.

'Tell me,' I said imploringly, 'I've simply got to know.'

'Mrs Smith,' he began deliberately, 'there is absolutely nothing to tell.'

'Nothing?' I said faintly. 'Oh!'

'I found no evidence whatsoever that your husband is having an affair.'

'None?' I said, and, curiously, I realised that my main emotion was not so much relief as surprise.

'Not a thing,' he reiterated with a shrug. 'Zero. Nada. Zilch.'

'Are you sure?' I said, feeling vaguely indignant by now. After all, this meant I'd been wrong.

'I'm ninety-nine per cent certain,' he said.

'But what about those three lunches he was having?' I said. 'I thought he might be meeting *her* then.'

'Well, if it *was* "her" he was meeting, Mrs Smith, I can assure you there is no affair. In each case his conduct was proper. He chatted to his lunch partner, paid the bill, said goodbye and returned to work. Here,' he opened his battered folder, 'I'll show you. Now, he had lunch with this lady . . .'

'That's Lucy Watt,' I said as I studied the black-and-white photo. 'She's an author.' He pulled out another shot.

'What about this one?'

'Ah. She's an agent. I met her once. I think she works at A.P. Trott.'

'I sat at the next table to your husband, Mrs Smith, and on neither occasion could his behaviour be said to be even mildly flirtatious. Now,' he said, handing me another photo, 'he had lunch with this man in Charlotte Street.'

'Oh,' I said, 'I don't know who that is. It's probably his headhunter, Andy Metzler.'

'He also had an early evening drink at Quaglino's with this woman.' I looked. The shot was slightly grainy. Sitting at a table with Peter was an attractive blonde of about my age, whom I'd never seen before. And though Peter was smiling at her, he wasn't doing anything wrong. In fact he looked slightly uptight.

'Do you know this woman, Mrs Smith?'

'No,' I said with a shrug. 'I don't. She looks quite tough, doesn't she? She's probably an agent driving a hard bargain about some author.'

Lastly, there were six photos of Peter at his book launches, one of which took place at the Groucho and the other at Soho House.

'You crashed those?' I said. 'I'm impressed.'

'They were both very crowded, Mrs Smith,' said Ian. 'I was able to blend right in. I'm a chameleon,' he added with pride.

'But how did you manage to take photos without using a flash?'

'Tricks of the trade,' he replied, tapping the side of his nose. I studied the pictures. In each of them Peter was talking to the authors in question, Robert Knight and Natalie Waugh, and to his colleagues in Editorial. In one he was even managing to chat politely to Charmaine.

'After both those events your husband got a cab and went straight home,' said Ian Sharp. 'And I know he went straight home, because I followed him all the way. So on the basis of what I've seen this week, Mrs Smith, I believe you were mistaken. May I suggest that it was paranoia which fuelled your suspicions, rather than hard facts?'

'Yes, yes I *was* paranoid,' I said. And by now I was so relieved I wanted to kiss him. 'I just – I don't know – I began to get carried away. My imagination was running riot,' I said with a smile. 'But now my peace of mind has been restored.'

'However, it is my duty to tell you, Mrs Smith, that it is perfectly possible that this woman, Jean, might not have been in London this week. For example, she might have had to go away . . .'

'Oh, I see. To Scotland, perhaps.'

'Making it impossible for her to have a rendezvous with your husband.'

'Yes,' I said, 'I suppose so.' My euphoria had sunk like a stone.

'So I'm simply saying that although I believe your husband is blameless, I can't be entirely sure. If you wanted to be one hundred per cent certain, then we'd have to trail him for a longer period.'

'Yes,' I said, 'I understand.'

'So my advice to you, Mrs Smith, is to assume the best and carry on as though everything is normal. Which it probably is.

But should your suspicions be aroused again, then we can take further action.'

'Of course,' I said. 'That's fine. I'd like to leave it like that. I'll assume the best, because that's what I always did before. And if I feel the need, I can always come back. Yes. That's just what I'll do. Thanks.' Then I wrote him a cheque for fifteen hundred pounds – mentally giving thanks to Lily again – and got the tube home. But although I was relieved that he'd found nothing, there were still lingering doubts in my mind. What was I to make of those notes about Jean? And what about the flowers, the cigarettes and gum? I still had these uneasy feelings, which refused to go away. I left a message for Lily to phone me, then made myself a cup of tea. Half an hour later the phone rang. 'That'll be Lily,' I said to Graham. And I was just about to tell her that Peter was the innocent victim of my unfounded suspicions when I heard an unfamiliar male voice.

''Allo,' it said, 'eez zat Madame Smeeth?'

'Yes,' I said, surprised. 'It is.'

'Ah. Well I am trying to make contact with your 'usband, Peter. And 'is secretary, I 'ope you don' mind, she give me ze house number.'

'Er, yes?'

'Because I need to talk to 'eem.'

'OK. Erm . . . who is this, please?'

'My name is John.'

'John who?'

'No, not John – *Jean*. Jean Dupont. I am calling from Paris.'

'*Jean?*' I repeated.

'Yes,' he said. 'Zat's right. *Jean.*'

'*Jean,*' I said again.

'Yes. Yes. Zat's right. *Jean.* Eet eez spelt –'

'It's perfectly all right,' I said quickly. 'I know how to spell it. I've just remembered. It's spelt J, E, A, N. *Jean!*'

'Er . . . *exactement*, Madame Smeeth.'

'*Jean!*'

'Correct.' I could feel laughter rising up in my throat like bubbles in a glass of champagne. 'I am phoning from ze French publishers, Hachette,' he went on. 'Peter knows me, we are working togezer on a book.'

'Ah,' I said. 'I see.'

'And I need to talk to 'eem again today, but 'is secretary she say she donno where he eez. You know, your 'usband is a very naughty boy, Madame Smeeth,' he added with a laugh. 'Because 'e don' always return my calls.'

'Oh. Oh. Yes, that *is* naughty,' I agreed.

'So I ask you please to ask 'eem to call me at my 'ome, *çe soir*. You have a pen? I give you ze number.'

'Oh yes,' I said as I now suppressed the urge to shout with joy. 'Yes, of course I have a pen,' I added happily. 'OK. Let me write it down. Got that. And thank you *very* much.'

'No, sank you,' he said, clearly taken aback by my enthusiasm.

'It's so nice of you to call,' I added warmly, 'I'm very, very glad that you did. And the minute Peter's home, I'll get the "naughty boy" to phone you right back. *Au revoir*, Jean, *au revoir*!' I slammed the phone down with an exultant cry; and I was just about to phone Lily and tell her about my *ridiculous* mistake, when Graham suddenly barked and I heard the key turning in the lock. It was Peter; back early.

'Darling!' I exclaimed joyfully. 'Listen, I've got something to say!'

'No,' he said as Graham leaped up to greet him, 'I've got something to say to you.'

'But I just want to tell you that I've made this stupid, *stupid* mistake, you see . . .'

'Faith, whatever it is – it can wait. Graham, look, will you please get down. Faith,' he said. 'Faith . . .' His profile was reflected in the sunburst mirror.

'Yes?'

'Look, there's something you've got to know.' My pulse was racing.

'Yes?' I said again. Peter took a deep breath.

'I'm leaving.'

'Sorry?'

'I'm leaving,' he repeated as we faced each other in the hall.

'You're leaving what?' I said, faintly. 'Me?'

'No, you twit – Fenton & Friend. I'm out!'

'My God!' I said with a gasp. 'She's done it! She's finally sacked you, the cow!' Peter's face was still a mask of seriousness; but then he suddenly grinned.

'No, Faith, she didn't sack me,' he explained. 'Because I resigned first. And I told her that I was resigning . . .'

'Yes?'

'Because I've been offered another job!'

'You've got another job!' I yelled. 'Oh, how marvellous!' I threw my arms round him. I was having a *very* good day. 'How fantastic! Oh, Peter! Where?'

'Faith,' he said, and now his face was wreathed in smiles, 'I'm going to be the new managing director of Bishopsgate!'

'Bishopsgate,' I gasped. 'Bishopsgate? My God! But they're huge!'

'Yes, I know,' he said wonderingly as he took off his coat. 'And because they've expanded so much in the last couple of years they were looking for a new MD. So I was interviewed twice.'

'But why didn't you tell me?' I said as we went into the sitting room.

'Because I was scared I wouldn't get it, and I wanted it so much. But they did one final interview with me at lunchtime, then Andy phoned to say I'd got the job.'

'Oh, darling!' I said and I hugged him again.

'And Faith,' he went on, wonderingly, as he fixed himself a drink. 'The money. The money's going to be three times what I get now. We won't have to struggle so much.'

'God, how fantastic! But what did Charmaine say?'

'She was livid,' he said as he sat down and loosened his tie. 'She was spitting fire. Especially when I told her about my new job. She kept telling me that it was "outrageous" – it's her favourite word, silly old bat. She had the nerve to accuse me of being disloyal. So I pointed out that I'd worked for Fenton & Friend very happily for thirteen years, and that the only reason I'd been looking elsewhere was because she's such a nightmare.'

'Oh, darling, that was really brave of you – and typically truthful, too.'

'I had nothing to lose at that stage,' he explained with a shrug. 'Anyway, she tried to kick me out, on the spot. But I wasn't having that. I informed her that I was on three months' notice, as stipulated in my contract. Then I got a call from Personnel, who are going to pay me off to leave by the fourteenth. Now I've got to call all my authors,' he said as he rummaged in his briefcase. 'I feel bad for them, but there's nothing I can do. I suspect half of them are going to end up with ghastly Oiliver, poor things. But, Faith,' he said as he flicked through his address book, 'I feel bad about leaving, but I really had no choice. Charmaine and Oliver were out to destroy me, but now, thanks to Andy, I'm safe. I'm going to take Andy for lunch at the Ritz,' he added as he reached for the phone.

'Oh, yes,' I said, 'you must. He deserves it.' But Peter was busy dialling a number and didn't seem to hear what I'd said.

'I'll call Clare Barry first,' he said.

'You've got to call *Jean*, too. And darling that's what I meant to tell you,' I added. 'I've got a confession to make.'

'You have?'

'Yes. The reason why I've been behaving so . . . stupidly. I'm really sorry. You see, I'd got this silly idea that you were seeing someone called Jean. But now I know that "Jean", isn't "Jean". She's *Jean*. Or rather *he* is. And I only realised that when *Jean* rang up today.'

'*Jean*?' Peter repeated. 'Yes, *Jean* and I have been working on a deal. It was a really boring instant book about some minor French film star which Charmaine fobbed off on me. We were going to publish it simultaneously in Britain and France, so I've been talking to him quite a lot. But it's so tedious, Faith, and I've been so preoccupied, I kept forgetting to phone him back. Oh hello, is that Clare?' he said. 'Clare, look, it's Peter here . . .'

'Nothing?' said Lily when I phoned to report. She sounded vaguely affronted. 'Darling – are you quite sure?'

'Yes,' I said happily. 'I'm sure.'

'Nothing?' she said again. 'Zero?'

'Not a thing,' I confirmed.

'Oh,' she said. 'I see. So it was a case of trail and error.'

'Yes,' I said with a giggle. 'It was. And I'm sorry about your article, Lily . . .'

'Well, yes . . .' She sounded a little depressed.

'But the simple fact of the matter is that Peter hasn't strayed.'

'Mmm.'

'I can't believe I could have been so stupid,' I went on. 'I mean, why did I automatically assume that *Jean* was a woman?'

'Because you're still Faith Value,' she sighed.

'I know. Instead of thinking rationally, or doing a little lateral thinking, I became totally paranoid and insecure. I didn't just jump to conclusions, Lily, I leaped to them with a pole-vault!'

'Oh well,' she added philosophically, 'we can still interview you as a woman whose suspicions were proven groundless.'

'So it's not a complete waste of time and money?'

'No, though obviously it would have been much better – I mean, better copy, obviously – if he'd been up to no good.'

'Well, I'm glad he wasn't,' I said with a laugh. 'Oh Lily, thank you so much for paying for it,' I added. 'And you did me a double favour there, because now my trust in Peter is even greater than it was before!'

There was a sudden silence, broken only by the sound of Jennifer's background grunting, and then I heard Lily say, 'Faith, I'm *so* pleased it's all worked out like this. And you know the *last* thing I'd want is to rain on your parade, but . . .'

'But what?'

'There are still some unanswered questions.'

'Are there?' I said. 'Like what?'

'Well, those flowers,' she said. 'Were they *really* for that author?'

'Yes,' I said, 'I'm sure they were.'

'And what about the chewing gum and cigarettes?'

'Oh, I don't know,' I said airily. 'To be honest I don't really care. I'm sure there's some perfectly innocent explanation, just as there was with Jean.'

'Well, the only thing I'd say,' she went on, 'is that not many British people smoke Lucky Strike. In fact that's an American brand.'

'Then they must have been for Andy, his head hunter.'

'Of course they must. But then why didn't he say so outright? Look, Faith, would you do me one favour, darling? This is purely for the article, of course.'

'Yes. OK. If I can.'

'Would you just ask Peter about those other things?' I sighed. 'Just to tie up those annoying little loose ends?'

'Oh, OK,' I said slightly reluctantly. 'Now that I feel so confident in Peter, I will. But I won't do it until Wednesday.'

'Why? What's happening then?'

'I'm taking him out to dinner,' I explained. 'A very special dinner, actually. I've just booked a table at Le Caprice!'

'I say, that's a bit rash!'

'I know, but Peter deserves it after all the stresses of the last few months. And because I was so mean and suspicious and nasty I'm going to foot the bill myself. In any case,' I went on, 'we've got so much to celebrate. His new job. Our future . . .'

'And what else?'

'It's Valentine's Day!'

On the evening of February the fourteenth I took the Underground to Green Park. London was in love, and so was I. On every platform I spotted young men sheepishly clutching flowers. And I thought of the two dozen red roses that I'd received from Peter earlier in the day. I gasped when I saw them – they're so beautiful. Long-stemmed, velvet-petalled and with a delicious, heady scent. As I walked down Piccadilly, I had to weave through all the couples strolling arm in arm. The early evening air seemed to throb with romance as I passed the Ritz, and despite the fact that I've been married for so long, my heart was thumping as I turned down Arlington Street and saw Le Caprice. I'd been here once, with Peter, years ago, but I knew it was his favourite place. I glanced round the monochrome interior and saw that Peter was already at the table, having his usual gin and tonic. He stood up to greet me, and I was just thinking that he looked very smart, but also slightly subdued in a funny sort of way, when his mobile phone rang out. Or rather it didn't ring, it played 'For He's a Jolly Good Fellow', because that's what it does.

'I guess that's Andy,' I said as Peter fumbled to turn it off. 'And let me say,' I added with a laugh, 'that Andy *is* a jolly good fellow!'

'Oh, yes,' said Peter with a faint smile. 'That's right.'

'He must be thrilled about what he's pulled off for you,' I said as we perused the menu. 'I hope he gets a whopping great bonus for all his hard work.'

'Yes. Yes. Definitely,' Peter said with a funny little laugh. 'Oh, by the way my appointment's in *Publishing News*.' He showed me a copy of the magazine and there, on page three, Peter was profiled with a photo under the headline: 'Peter Smith's Smart Move to Bishopsgate'. I read it through with tremendous pride: *respected publishing director . . . very distinguished list . . . rumoured conflicts with Charmaine Duval . . . Bishopsgate set to expand*. We ordered champagne – real champagne this time – and then our starters arrived. I had Bang Bang chicken, and Peter had creamed fennel soup. The restaurant was full of couples like us having a romantic Valentine's dinner, *tête à tête*. I was feeling quite mellow and calm, although, as I say, I couldn't help noticing that Peter seemed a little bit quiet. But I knew why – he'd just had his last day at Fenton & Friend, which must have been an enormous wrench.

'Did they give you a good send off?' I asked.

'I had a small gathering in my office,' he said. 'Iris cried. I felt quite cut up, too.'

'Well, it's a huge change, darling – especially after so long. But like most changes it's going to be for the best. What a hellish time you've had,' I added as the waiter removed our plates. 'And Peter, I just want to apologise again for being so mean and low. I just don't know what got into me.' He squeezed my hand.

'Faith, don't worry. That's in the past.'

'Anyway,' I said as I raised my glass, 'here's to happy endings.'

'Yes. To happy endings,' he agreed. 'And to new beginnings, too.'

'To a new chapter,' I went on happily. 'With no nasty twists in the tale.'

'I'll drink to that.'

'Even the weather's improved,' I added with a laugh. 'The anti-cyclonic gloom has lifted and there are blue skies ahead.' Peter smiled. 'And did you take Andy to the Ritz?' I enquired as our main course arrived – swordfish for me and breast of chicken for him.

'Er . . . yes,' he replied. 'I did. We went there on, um, Tuesday.'

'Well,' I said as I picked up my knife and fork, 'personally I think Andy's just *fab*.' We chatted away like this as we ate, and at last Peter began to relax. I glanced at the black-and-white photo on the wall beside us and realised that it was Marianne Faithfull. And somehow that made me remember Lily's request. I didn't want to ask Peter directly, so I just said, 'Darling, I'm so sorry I ever doubted you. It was horrid of me. Obviously those flowers were for Clare Barry.' He looked at me. 'Weren't they?'

'Yes,' he replied. 'They were.'

'And as for those cigarettes – well, so what? – why shouldn't you have the occasional fag? It was so silly of me to over-react like that, Peter. I've trusted you for fifteen years, darling, and I've no intention of stopping now. I know you've never had an affair,' I went on with a tipsy giggle, 'and I don't believe you would.' He was silent. 'Because I know you always tell the truth.' I had a sip of wine. 'Don't you, darling? Because the simple fact is that you're a very decent and honourable man. And you're so truthful, too, in fact that's what I love about you *most* and I just want to say how –'

'Faith,' said Peter suddenly. 'Please *stop*.' He was fiddling with his knife and he had this peculiar expression on his face. 'There's something I want to tell you,' he said.

'Darling, whatever it is, it doesn't matter.'

'It does matter, Faith. It matters to me.'

'Peter,' I said, then took another large sip of Bordeaux, 'whatever it is it's not important tonight.'

'It is,' he corrected me. 'It *is*. It's very important, actually. Because you're sitting here telling me what a great guy I am, and quite frankly I can't stand it.'

'Oh darling, I'm sorry,' I said. 'I didn't mean to embarrass you. It's just that I'm feeling *so* happy and I've probably had a bit too much to drink, and I'm just trying to make it up to you for being such a suspicious cow.'

'But that's the whole point,' he said. 'That's precisely what I can't stand.'

'Why?'

'Faith,' he said, fiddling with his glass, 'I've done something rather . . . silly.'

'You've done something silly?' I echoed. 'Oh Peter, I'm sure it's nothing.'

'It isn't nothing,' he said.

'Really, Peter –'

'No, darling, listen to me,' he said as he locked his gaze in mine. I saw him breathe in. Then out. 'Faith,' he murmured. 'I've been unfaithful.' My wine-glass stopped in mid-air.

'Sorry?'

'No,' he said, '*I'm* sorry – because I've slept with someone else.'

'Oh,' I said, aware that my face was suddenly aflame.

'But it was only once,' he added, 'and it doesn't matter.'

'Oh,' I said again.

'But the reason I'm telling you is because, well, we are about to enter a new era, yes, a new chapter; and I knew I just couldn't live with myself unless I'd made a clean breast.'

'Oh,' I said again. For some reason it seemed to be the only word I knew.

'You see, Faith,' he went on as he stared at his uneaten chicken, 'you've been going on at me all evening about how "honest" and "truthful" I am. So I can't bear to conceal from you the fact that . . .'

'What?'

'Well, that I've had this little . . . fling.'

'A fling?' I echoed. 'With whom?'

'Look,' he said wearily, 'that's not important. It's over now. It was a stupid mistake, and it's not going to happen again.'

'I'm sorry, darling,' I said, struggling to remain composed. 'But I don't think it's fair of you to tell me you've had a – fling, and then refuse to say who it was with, because . . . Oh God, Peter,' I added, my throat suddenly constricting. 'You've been unfaithful to me.'

'Yes,' he said, quietly, 'I have. But it's not important,' he repeated. 'I was put under pressure. I – I'd had a few drinks, it was just . . . one of those things.'

'Please tell me who it was with?' I said again, aware that my palms felt damp.

'I –'

'Please, Peter. I'd like to know.'

'Well . . .'

'Just give me her name, will you?'

'No.'

'Go on, *tell* me!'

'I can't.'

'Yes you can!'

'Look, I –'.

'Give me her name, Peter.'

'OK,' he sighed. 'It's Andy Metzler.' My hands flew up to my mouth.

'You've had sex with a *man*?!' Peter was staring at me. He looked shocked.

'No, it's all right,' he said. 'You don't understand.'

'It's *not* all right,' I shot back. 'It is absolutely NOT all right, Peter!'

'Yes it *is*,' he insisted.

'No, it damn well *isn't* –'

'Yes it *is*, Faith, because, you see – Andy's a woman.'

'*What?*'

'Andy Metzler's a woman,' he repeated. I gasped.

'You never told me that.'

'You never asked.'

'But you never *said*. It's been "Andy this, and Andy that" – I had *no* idea he was a she.'

'Well,' he said quietly, 'she is. I agree it's a funny sort of name for a woman. But she's American, and, well, that's what she's called – it's spelled A-N-D-I-E.'

'I see,' I said slowly. 'Like Andie McDowell.'

'Yes,' he agreed. 'Like that.'

'And you had an affair with her?' He nodded. 'When?' He fiddled with the salt pot.

'When, Peter?'

'On Tuesday.'

'On Tuesday? Yesterday? Oh yes, of course,' I said, nodding my head. 'You were going to take her for lunch at the Ritz. To celebrate. Well, it certainly sounds like you did.'

'Look, one thing led to another,' he said sheepishly. 'She was coming on to me, Faith. She's been coming on to me for months. Ever since she met me, in fact. And you were behaving so suspiciously, I was fed up and I felt so grateful to her for getting me the job that, somehow, I couldn't . . . refuse.'

'Oh, I see,' I said sarcastically. 'In order not to hurt her feelings, you slept with her. What a gent. I'm so proud of you, Peter. You took a room, I suppose?'

'Yes,' he said quietly. 'We did.' And suddenly, in that moment, in that terrible moment when he said 'we', I realised that truthfulness was Peter's *least* endearing quality.

'So she *did* get her bonus, then,' I said darkly, aware of a lemon-sized lump in my throat. 'How ironic,' I murmured as I gripped and ungripped my napkin. 'How very ironic. For the past two weeks I've been obsessing about some Scottish woman called Jean, who turns out to be a Frenchman called *Jean*; and now you tell me you've had an affair with an American woman called Andie, who I was quite convinced was a bloke!'

'Er . . . yes.' I shook my head.

'Well,' I whispered bitterly. 'Well, well, well.' Then I looked at him and said, 'This hurts.'

'I'm sorry,' he said. 'I didn't mean to hurt you. But she pushed me into it.'

'Don't be ridiculous,' I said.

'She did,' he insisted wearily. 'I'd made it quite clear that I was – married. But now our professional relationship was at an end and she just . . .'

'Decided to make it personal.'

'Yes. Oh, I don't know – she put me under all this . . . *pressure*.'

'I don't *believe* you,' I hissed. 'I think you slept with her because you wanted to.'

'No I did not.'

'Liar!'

'Keep your voice down.'

'Admit it!'

'OK, then, yes, I *did*!'

'You did!'

'Yes. Since you've forced me to admit it, yes I bloody well *did*!'

'You *bastard*!' I spat. And I was terribly shocked to hear myself say that, because I've never called him that in my life.

'I've been under such stress, Faith,' he groaned. He leaned his head on his right hand. 'These last six months have been hell. And then you started going on at me. You wouldn't leave me alone. You were like a terrier with a rat, banging on about this woman or that chewing gum or those cigarettes.'

'That gum!' I exclaimed. 'That chewing gum was for her.' He was silent. 'Wasn't it?' I said. 'You don't like it – you never have. And those cigarettes, they were for her as well, weren't they?' Peter nodded miserably. 'You had gum and cigarettes at the ready for her. How gallant. Lucky Strike!' I spat. 'So you've had an affair,' I repeated, my voice rising, 'with a – what was it you said – "chick"? Oh. My. God.'

'Look, it was completely spontaneous,' he said. 'It just happened on the spur of the moment.'

'That's not true!' I said.

'Shhhh! Don't shout.'

'You'd wanted to shag her for weeks.'

'No.'

'Oh yes you had. And the reason I know is because of Katie.'

'Katie? What's *she* got to do with this?'

'Her psychoanalytic stuff. She's always going on about Freudian slips, isn't she? Well, she goes on about the Freudian "telling omission" too. And I think it's very, *very* telling, Peter, that you've never let on that Andie was a woman.'

'It wasn't relevant,' he said.

'Oh yes it was,' I shot back. 'Because the other night you recited that great list of all the women you know – every single one. So how *very* strange, Peter,' I added, emphatically, 'that you didn't mention her!' By now his face and neck were blotched with red. 'In fact you even told me the names of Andie's two female colleagues, but you carefully left her out. Now I know why!' I concluded triumphantly. 'Because you didn't want me to know. And the reason why you didn't was because you already knew you wanted to get her into bed.'

'I . . . I . . .'

'Don't deny it,' I said contemptuously.

'I . . . OK,' he said. 'OK, I admit it. She's very attractive. She's single. She fancies me. And yes, I fancied *her*.'

100

'She's got short blonde hair,' I said suddenly. It had come to me in a flash. What the French call an *éclaircissement*. Andie was that unknown blonde photographed with Peter in Quaglino's. 'She's got short blonde hair,' I said again.

'Yes,' he said. 'She has. But how the hell do you know?'

'Because . . .' Oh God, I couldn't tell him. 'Because . . . Oh, female intuition,' I explained. 'I feel sick,' I announced as I fiddled with my pudding spoon. 'You've had an affair. How *could* you?'

'I'll tell you how,' he said, and by now his voice was rising as well. 'Because you'd accused me of having one, and then the opportunity was there and I thought damn it, why not go ahead and do it!' I was aware by now that we were beginning to attract strange looks.

'Any dessert?' enquired the waiter. 'And, er, I'd be grateful sir and madam if you could keep your voices down.'

'No,' I said, 'I will not keep my voice down, because my husband has just been unfaithful!' I was aware of eyes swivelling in our direction, and of the sound of breath being sharply inhaled.

'Well, madam,' said the waiter, 'I just feel that . . .'

'I don't care what you feel!' I hissed. 'We are having marital difficulties here.' By now all conversation in the restaurant had stopped and everyone was staring, but I couldn't have cared less. 'After fifteen years of marriage,' I informed the waiter, 'my husband tells me that he's strayed.'

'– poor woman,' I heard someone say.

'– isn't she the weather girl on that morning TV show?'

'– faithful for fifteen years? The man must be a saint.'

'– of course *you* were unfaithful after five.'

'– no need to bring that up!'

'Now madam,' said the waiter, 'I am very sorry that you have this, er, problem.'

'It's not a problem,' I corrected him, 'it's a crisis.'

'And actually I'm divorced myself.'

'Oh, well, I'm sorry.'

'My wife left me.'

'Oh, bad luck,' said Peter.

'So although I am sympathetic, I must nevertheless ask you to keep your voices down.'

'Yes, Faith,' Peter whispered hoarsely. 'Please would you keep it down!'

'That's right, keep it down,' I said with a hollow laugh. 'Don't rock the boat. Be a big girl. Don't make a fuss. Don't cry. And above all, above all – don't mind. Well, I *do* mind!' I wailed. 'I mind terribly. How *could* you, Peter?' I added, aware that the table had begun to blur.

'Yes, how could you?' said a woman at the next table.

'How could I?' repeated Peter, turning in his seat. 'I've already explained how I could. One, I had the opportunity, and two, I'd had so much stress, three, I'd had too much to drink, four, I was put under pressure and five, my wife had driven me mad with her horrible – and quite unfounded – suspicions.'

'They *weren't* unfounded,' I said as I pressed a tissue to my eyes.

'They were then!' he shot back.

'I don't blame him!' said a man to our left.

'Don't take sides, Rodney.'

'I think she brought it on herself.'

'What an idiot,' said someone else.

'Don't you ever do that to me, Henry.'

'Well, what about you?'

'What do you mean, what about me?'

'I've seen the way you look at Torquil.'

'Torquil? Don't make me laugh!'

'My wife left me for our doctor,' said the waiter.

'Oh dear,' said Peter. 'What a betrayal of trust.'

'Look,' I said to the waiter, 'I'm *very* sorry about your divorce. But to be perfectly honest it has absolutely nothing to do with us. Oh God,' I wailed, 'this is terrible! I just don't know what to *do*.'

'Don't make a mountain out of a molehill!' said a man in a dark grey suit.

'Take him to the cleaners,' said his wife.

'Get yourselves some counselling!' said a man three tables to our right.

'Get yourselves a life, more like!'

'Infidelity isn't the end of the world, I heard.'

'Yes, people can forgive and forget.'

'Forgive and forget?' I echoed, aware of the tang of tears in my mouth. 'Forgive and forget? No! Oh Peter,' I wept as I reached for my bag. 'Oh Peter, I was *so*, *so* happy tonight – but now everything's ruined.'

'I don't like to crow,' said Lily on Saturday morning. 'I really *don't* like to crow, but I was right!'

'Yes,' I croaked, 'you were.' We were side by side on leather benches, in a clinic in Knightsbridge, covered in thick, green slime. While we lay there, naked but for a pair of voluminous paper knickers, a white-coated therapist slapped some more bottle-green paste on our legs. Then she wrapped us in heated blankets and dimmed the overhead lights.

'Now, ladies,' she said pleasantly, 'I'm going to leave you for twenty minutes, to let the marine algae get to work, purifying your system, toning your skin and eliminating the toxins from the body.' I found myself wishing it could eliminate the toxins from my mind. 'I'd like you to relax,' she crooned, 'close your eyes, and concentrate on having lovely, serene thoughts.'

'What a bastard!' Lily said viciously as the door closed and we could talk. 'How could he *do* that to you!'

'I don't know,' I whispered as I stared at the ceiling. 'All I know is, it hurts.' The initial shock of Peter's confession had worn off, leaving a searing pain.

'When we first discussed all this,' Lily went on, 'I never thought for a *second* it might be true. I just wanted you to be a little more on your guard, darling, because you're such a trusting soul.'

'Not any more.'

'But at the same time,' she went on, 'I began to be aware that things simply didn't add up. But now they do. My God, this stuff's fishy,' she added, wrinkling her nose. 'We're going to smell like Billingsgate. Headhunter!' she exclaimed indignantly. 'Headhunter! I ask you! She was after more than his head.'

'Well, she seems to have got it,' I said.

'And *that's* why Peter sent you those fabulous roses on the fourteenth.'

'I've thrown them away,' I wept.

'They weren't really Valentine's flowers,' she went on, 'they were because he felt guilty about his fling.'

'Oh well,' I went on with a bitter sigh, 'you've got a good interview with me after all. It's a nightmare,' I groaned, feeling my throat constrict. 'How I wish I could turn the clock back.'

'You can't,' said Lily briskly. 'It's too serious for that. This is the kind of thing that breaks people up.' I twisted my head sideways and looked at her.

'But I don't want to break up,' I whispered. 'I'm not thinking that far ahead.'

'Faith, darling, I think you should. Because the sad fact is that Peter's infidelity is grievous – you'll never forget it.' I felt physically sick when she said that. 'And of course it would only happen again.'

'Would it?' I said. 'I mean, I'm not letting him off the hook, Lily, but maybe it *was* just one slip. I mean, he has been under a lot of stress lately.'

'Don't be such an idiot, Faith!' she said. 'Infidelity is a slippery slope. Once men stray, that's it. They can behave themselves for a while,' she went on, 'but then they resent being kept on a rope. Oh yes,' she went on authoritatively, 'the first affair is always the beginning of the end. Now, do you have a good lawyer?'

'Well, our family solicitor, Karen. But Lily, the cost of a divorce would break us.'

'Darling,' she went on patiently, as though explaining something to a dim-witted child, 'Peter's got this wonderful new job, so he can afford it.'

'But he's not going to be rich,' I said. 'He'll simply be earning more than he was before. Look, I'm not making any decisions yet about getting divorced,' I said. 'All I know is that I'm not ready to forgive.'

'How have things been at home?' she enquired.

'We're avoiding each other,' I sighed. 'I've hardly seen him since Valentine's Day. Luckily the kids aren't around this weekend because they've got things on at school. Oh God, Lily,' I said as my eyes filled again. 'I just don't know what to do.'

'Faith,' said Lily. 'How long have we known each other?'

'Twenty-five years.'

'Exactly,' she said. 'Since we were nine. So I think I know you better than anyone else. I know you better even than Peter. And I really believe that this will turn out to be the best thing that ever happened to you.'

'How?' I croaked.

'Because what doesn't kill you makes you stronger,' she replied. She reached out and squeezed my hand and gave me a comforting smile. 'This will strengthen you, Faith. This will be the means by which you finally break out of your suburban shell and become a strong, independent woman at last. I popped into Harvey Nicks, by the way, and got you some amethyst power beads to give you courage.'

'Oh, thanks.'

'And I phoned the Samaritans, too.'

'You did what?'

'I phoned the Samaritans last night and pretended to be you. Now, don't worry,' she said, catching my appalled expression. 'I didn't give them your name. I just said my husband had admitted to an affair and I talked about the pain, the humiliation and the fear etc etc. And they started blathering on about counselling and mediation and reconciliation and all that guff, but everyone knows it's a complete waste of time.'

'Is it?' I said faintly.

'Yes, of course it is. Because infidelity is ineradicable. It does *irreparable* harm. You can try and glue the pieces of your marriage back together, but the fact is you'll always see the joins.'

'All right, ladies?' The therapist had returned. We changed the subject while she removed our blankets; then we showered off the green slime. And I was just getting dressed when Lily suddenly said, 'I think my colon could do with a quick clean. How about yours, Faith?'

'What?'

'Colonic irrigation,' she said. 'Fancy it?'

'No thanks,' I said. The thought of having my backside dyno-rodded was more than I could bear.

'I swear by it,' she said happily. 'I like to be clean inside *and* out. If it was good enough for the Ancient Egyptians, it's good enough for me. Give me forty-five minutes for a quick sloosh and then we'll go to lunch.'

I sat outside in the waiting room, trying not to imagine Lily lying on the table with a hosepipe up her bum, and attempting to ignore the voices filtering through the door.

'Ooh, Miss Jago,' I heard the therapist say, 'you really should chew your food more – I've just seen an olive go by!'

To distract myself from visualising the contents of Lily's colon, I flicked through the magazines. A huge range was laid out on the low glass table like a deck of cards. There was *Moi!* and *Tatler* and *Marie Claire*, and a selection of cheaper magazines as well. To be honest, I prefer the more downmarket titles. The models aren't quite so depressingly gorgeous, and they have more competitions, too. So I flicked through *Woman's Own* and *Woman's Weekly*, then I picked up *Bella*, *That's Life* and *Best*. Then my eye caught the cover of *Chat* magazine, and I caught my breath. I stared at the provocative headline, aware of a small voice whispering in my head. Then, almost involuntarily, my hand reached out and picked it up. 'WIN A DIVORCE!' it said.

March

When you get married you say 'I do'. Now I find myself constantly saying, *what* do I do? I repeat it over and over, like a mantra, in the hope that enlightenment will come.

'Do nothing,' said our friendly family solicitor, Karen. She had been sitting there, in her office, scribbling notes on a pad while I tearfully told her the story. 'My advice is to do absolutely nothing,' she said again.

'Nothing?' I repeated.

'Nothing,' she confirmed. 'Because you haven't had enough time to reflect.'

'But it hurts,' I said. I tapped my chest with my left hand. 'It's as though there's this open wound. Here. Right here. Oh God, Karen, I'm in such *pain*.'

'Which is all the more reason to wait.'

'I can hardly function,' I croaked. 'All I know is that something terribly serious has happened.'

'Well, infidelity *is* serious,' she said, handing me a tissue. 'So you must let the emotional shock subside before you decide on any course of action.'

'I feel so *angry*,' I said. 'So humiliated.'

'Well, you're likely to feel considerably more angry and more humiliated if you go ahead and get divorced. Divorce is horrible,' she carried on simply. 'It's painful, humiliating, messy and extremely expensive. For some people it can be a catastrophe, emotionally and financially, from which they never fully recover. It's only two weeks since Peter's confession,' she added. 'You ought to give yourself more time.'

'I just don't know how I can . . . *be*, with Peter again,' I wept. 'I can't bear the thought of him having slept with another woman. I feel my future is lying in splinters.'

'Faith,' said Karen gently, 'you don't yet know *what* your future holds. So I say again, as I say to all my clients, don't do anything rash. Especially as you have kids. But if, after long and careful consideration, you do decide to go ahead,' she went on, 'then, yes, you can start proceedings. But you have to be absolutely certain that you really want a divorce,' she added seriously, 'and that you aren't just using divorce to punish Peter. Because once the wheels are set in motion, Faith, it's very, very hard to go back. So please wait,' she repeated as I stood up to leave.

'OK,' I sighed, 'I will.' I went outside and untied Graham, who had been sitting there looking dejected in the hope that someone would give him something to eat. But when he saw me he leaped up, radioactive with excitement, and emitted a joyful bark. And seeing not just Graham's tail, but his entire rear end wagging with delight, lifted my spirits a little.

'Hello darling,' I said. 'Did you miss me?'

'Woof!'

'You love me, don't you?'

'*Woof!*'

As we walked home in the bright spring sunshine, Graham bouncing along by my side, I thought hard about what Karen had said. I mentally reviewed my marriage, year by year, and remembered how happy Peter and I had been. And I thought of it all coming to an end, and of how devastating this would be. I had a sudden vision of the children and me, standing on the pavement outside the house with our suitcases and carrier bags. 'Divorce can be a catastrophe,' Karen had warned. 'Emotionally and financially . . . never fully recover . . . very, very hard to go back.' At this, a tiny shiver convulsed my frame.

'Karen's right,' I said to Graham as we entered the park. I bent down and unclipped his lead. 'She's absolutely right,' I repeated as he shot away like a flying rug. He came back thirty seconds later with a red frisbee in his mouth.

'Hey!' I heard in the distance. 'That's ours!'

'Graham,' I admonished him gently, 'thou shalt not steal. Would you kindly take this back?' As he sped away I walked under an avenue of plane trees and looked at the primulas and the late crocuses, their petals now pecked by the birds, and at the clumps of pale green spears which would soon be daffodils. Then I sat down on a bench and shut my eyes and asked God to help me through all this. I said a little prayer. At that precise moment the sun came out – I felt its warmth suffuse my face – and I had a kind of epiphany, a sort of vision I suppose, and I knew that Peter and I would come through. We *weren't* going to throw away fifteen happy years, I resolved. We *weren't* going to destroy our life together. After all, I told myself as Graham and I made our way home. Worse things happen. Far worse things. *Terrible* things. You read about them every day. And Peter had only been unfaithful once, and he was very sorry about it.

'That's why he confessed,' I said to Graham as I opened the front door. 'He confessed because he has a conscience, and because he's a decent man.' It was wrong of me, I realised now, to have thrown it back in his face. It was mean-minded, and it was stupid too, because think of all the men who cheat on their wives repeatedly, routinely even, without a shred of remorse. I picked up our wedding photo in its slightly tarnished silver frame, and felt my eyes begin to fill. 'From this day forward,' I remembered. That had been the deal. 'For better, for worse,' I had promised. We'd had plenty of better really, and now we were having a bit of worse. That's what marriage was about. I looked at Peter's open, handsome face and thought, this is the man I love. This is the man of my life. Yes, he's made a mistake, but we all make mistakes, so I have to forgive him and let it go. And I *will* forgive him, I thought, almost rapturously, as I turned on the TV. Because to err is human, to forgive, divine. Now I imagined the scene in which Peter and I would be reconciled again, and the thought of it filled me with a warm glow which rose up from my toes to my head.

'Darling,' I would say to him, 'you made a very serious error of judgement there. You nearly threw away our marriage for a moment of unbridled lust. You allowed yourself to be led into temptation. And you fell. But, Peter, I want you to know that I forgive you.' He was smiling at me hesitantly at first, as though he couldn't quite believe what he was hearing, and then joyfully as the happy news sank in. 'Yes, darling,' I murmured as he enveloped me in his arms. 'We're going to start all over again. We'll use this unfortunate episode to strengthen our marriage, to go forward into the future. And do you know what, Peter, we'll be even happier than we were before.' Now I imagined us in church, renewing our vows in front of a small but select group who all knew what we'd been through. Our parents would be there, and the children, of course, and one or two of our closest friends. They'd all be blinking back the tears as Peter and I looked at each other and said, once again, 'I will.' And Peter and I would be crying as well, barely able to utter our vows with the huge emotion of the occasion. By now tears were indeed streaming down my face as I idly channel-hopped. And as I dabbed at my eyes with my right hand and scratched Graham's chin with my left, the opening credits for the magazine programme, *Loose Women*, started to roll down the screen.

'We're going to be OK, Graham,' I added between little sobs. 'Mummy and Daddy *aren't* going to split up, darling. Don't worry.' Suddenly he barked. Not so much in agreement, but because the second post had just arrived. He leaped off the sofa and went to the front door, where five envelopes were lying on the mat. Two brown ones – bills, presumably, which as usual I left for Peter – a postcard from my mum in Guadeloupe – *We're having such a WONDERFUL time!* – two letters for Matt – oh, I wonder who *they're* from? And a slim white envelope addressed to me. I ran my thumb under the flap, then suddenly stopped, distracted by something on the TV.

'Headhunting is a relatively new but booming industry,' I heard the presenter say. 'Because these days big-hitters don't apply for their jobs. They're lured to them by clever middlemen –

or rather women. For some of the most successful headhunters in the business are female, and we're joined by one of them now. So would you please give a very warm welcome to Andie Metzler!' I heard the polite applause of the studio audience, then walked, as though hypnotised, into the sitting room. And now I stared, blank-eyed, at the screen. It was *her*. Andie Metzler. The emotional shock hit me like an axe to the knees, and I sank onto a chair. There she was. Talking. The Other Woman. The woman who had slept with my husband. The woman who smoked Lucky Strike. The woman who had saved Peter's professional bacon, but who had destroyed my peace of mind.

'Women make wonderful headhunters,' she was saying. 'More intuitive . . . subtle approach . . . better organised . . . Ffion Jenkins is a successful headhunter, and Michael Portillo's wife, of course.' I suddenly realised that Ian Sharp's photo hadn't done her justice. Her short blonde hair shone like spun gold. Her face was heart-shaped and wrinkle-free. She looked elegantly leggy as she reclined in a studio chair, her exquisite suit falling in gentle drapes. She was gorgeous. There was no denying it, though her voice was rasping and harsh.

'A woman headhunter recruited Greg Dyke to be director-general of the BBC,' I heard her say. 'ICI uses a woman headhunter to fill its top posts, and I myself have placed managing directors in merchant banks, in telecoms companies, and more recently in a top publishing house, too.'

At this a wave of nausea arose in my throat, and now I looked at her with a deep, deep hatred, of a kind I had never felt before. I imagined her at the Ritz with Peter. I imagined them having lunch. I imagined them drinking champagne. Now I imagined them having sex. And I wanted to plunge a knife into the television set and kill her there and then. I wanted the rigging to fall and crush her to death. I wanted the studio floor to open and swallow her up. My thumb was still hooked under the edge of the white envelope and I absently drew it along. I pulled out the letter, still staring, with a visceral loathing, at my rival.

'Another quality that women bring to the headhunting business is that we're very tenacious,' she said in her raspy, transatlantic drawl. 'We're ambitious for our clients, and we find them the very, *very* best person. We never give up until we've got the head we want.'

'I bet you don't,' I hissed.

'We go right after them,' she added with a soft laugh, 'and believe me, we get them in the end.'

Out of the corner of my eye I registered the word 'CON-GRATULATIONS!' Involuntarily, I lowered my gaze. *Dear Mrs Smith*, I read as Andie's voice droned away.

'Yes, headhunting is a *very* rewarding career . . .'

On behalf of IPC magazines I am delighted to inform you . . .

'In all sorts of ways . . .'

That you have won first prize . . .

'– it's also one which goes well . . .'

. . . in our Win a Divorce competition!

'With marriage and motherhood . . .'

Mrs Smith, you answered our tie-breaker correctly . . .

'Which is something I find very appealing . . .'

So an all expenses paid divorce is yours . . .

'As I'm planning on settling down quite soon . . .'

With TOP celebrity divorce lawyer, Rory Cheetham-Stabb!

I didn't do anything with the letter straight away. I was too shocked. I sat staring at it for quite some time, turning it over in my hands. Then I went upstairs and hid it in my knicker drawer. I'd never expected to win, I'd just posted the form off very quickly before I could have second thoughts. It was a prize draw, with a qualifier which required you to answer the following questions: a) How big was Princess Diana's divorce settlement? b) Was Jerry Hall legally married to Mick Jagger? and c) How long is it before a decree nisi becomes absolute? They weren't hard to answer: a) Seventeen million; b) No and c) Six weeks and one day. As you know I can never resist doing competitions, but I never actually thought I would *win*. Now I found myself unwilling to ring the organisers and claim my prize. Here I was, being offered what many, many women would envy – a divorce, on a plate, free of charge – but far from feeling euphoric I felt as though I were staring into an abyss. 'Wait,' Karen had said. 'Wait.' So I did. I waited for the shock of seeing Andie Metzler to subside. And it did, little by little, and by the end of that day I was fairly calm and thinking quite rationally once more, and by then I'd decided that, no, I *definitely didn't* want a divorce. After all, I reasoned, it wasn't as though Peter was involved with her. All he'd done was to sleep with her once, under pressure, on the spur of the moment. It wasn't a longterm thing, just a temporary lapse of self-control. Andie wasn't his mistress. She presented no threat to me. She was just a flash in the pan, that was all. So over the next couple of days I tried to mend bridges with Peter – we'd hardly exchanged a word since Valentine's Day. We'd been avoiding each other, which isn't difficult because of the hours I work. I'd been so angry I hadn't even asked him how the new job was going, but now I broke the ice. We talked, awkwardly at first, about his work, and then mine, and about the kids, and soon we relaxed and found ourselves discussing all the things we normally discuss. And we went for a walk along the river with Graham. But neither Peter nor I mentioned his fling. It lay like an undetonated bomb between us. We walked round it, and carefully stepped over it, and pretended that it wasn't there. And I reasoned that if we just ignored it, somehow it would naturally defuse and then disappear. I'd decided that Andie was no more than a nasty blip on the otherwise healthy cardiogram of our marriage. We would come through this, I resolved. Other couples did, and so would we. We would be the way we were. So I made an effort to be warm and friendly to him, but at the same time not *too* much. I needed Peter to know that I was still suffering, and that he could expect a slight touch of frost for a while. However I knew that in the end I'd come round, because I'd decided to stick with my marriage, so I didn't look at the letter from *Chat* again. Four days later someone from the magazine phoned up to arrange for me to collect my prize, but I stalled and told them that I was too busy to do anything about it for at least a week. Because by then I knew that Peter and I would be reconciled, and they could give the prize to someone else. The children came home for the weekend, and we did all our usual weekend things. Though Matt kept going out to the post box – I really don't know why.

I was in the kitchen on Sunday afternoon, and Peter was outside, packing the car, ready to drive the kids back to school, when the telephone rang. Katie picked it up. I heard her chatting for a minute and assumed it must be someone she knew. Then I heard her call out.

'Da-ad! Pho-one!'

'Who is it?' I heard him shout.

'I dunno, some American woman, called Candy, or Randy, or Mandy or something. Says she wants to speak to you.' I sprang out of the kitchen like a tarantula out of its trap. The bitch! The brazen cow! Phoning *my* house to speak to *my* husband, *my* husband of fifteen years, the father of *my* two children, I'd bloody well tell her where to go. But Peter had got there first.

'No, no,' he was saying, slightly breathlessly from his sudden sprint to the phone. 'No. No,' he said, more casually now, though his face had flushed bright red. 'Oh. Yes. Mmm,' he said evasively. 'Well, thanks for calling. Bye.' Then he put the receiver down and looked at me with a guilty expression on his face. My lips were pressed together so hard they hurt. Then the children appeared with their bags, I kissed them goodbye and went upstairs.

When Peter came back three hours later, I was in the kitchen. He came in, wordlessly, and sat down. Then he cradled his head in his hands.

'Have you seen her again?' I asked. No reply. My mouth was as dry as sandpaper and I could hear the pounding of my heart. 'Have you seen her again?' I repeated. He inhaled, then shook his head.

'Not really.'

'Not really?' I said. 'Not really? What on earth does *that* mean?'

114

'All right then,' he conceded, looking at me now. 'I have seen her. We had a drink.'

'A drink? How nice.'

'That's all it was, Faith. A drink.'

'Then what the *hell* is she doing ringing our home?'

'She . . .' He put his head in his hands again. 'She – just needed to speak to me, and my mobile phone was switched off. But you're right, Faith. She shouldn't have done that.'

'She certainly shouldn't,' I said, and I was amazed at how calm and self-possessed I managed to sound. It was as though I was listening to someone else. 'Does she know that I know?' I asked.

'Yes, she does,' he said with a sigh. 'I explained that it can't happen again, but . . .'

'But what?'

'But she won't –'

'Take no for an answer?' He blushed.

'No.'

'So she's after you, then,' I said in a voice as hard and sharp as flint. 'Is that it?'

'I don't know. She says she doesn't see it as a fling. She says she's . . .'

'What?'

'In love with me.'

'Oh! How romantic!' I exclaimed. 'But, Peter,' I said, 'are you . . .' My anger turned to anguish and my voice began to crack. 'Are you . . .' I tried again, then stopped. And there was a silence, during which we heard only the rhythmic ticking of the kitchen clock. 'Peter, are you in love with her?' I managed to ask at last.

'No. I'm not. But . . .'

'*What*?' By now my throat was aching and my contact lenses had slipped.

'But . . . Oh, I don't know,' he said desperately. His eyes were shining with tears. 'I feel so confused, Faith. Don't *ask* me what I feel. All I know is, this is hell. I mean, on the one

115

hand sleeping with her was nothing,' he said. 'Nothing.'

'Well if it was nothing, why *do* it?'

'Because at the same time I felt it wasn't just nothing. How could it be nothing when I'd never been unfaithful before? So no, actually, it wasn't just nothing, and I knew that. In my heart of hearts I knew that. And I know that now.'

'Oh. Well,' I said. I felt sick. 'I see. Do you intend to do it again?' I asked. I knew he wouldn't lie.

'I don't know,' he said miserably. 'I don't know.'

That was it. That was the moment, when I felt something inside me break. Something which I knew could never be fixed.

To my surprise, I didn't get hysterical, or angry; instead I remained quite calm. I took Graham round the block, then I went upstairs to bed. I just lay there, with the dog at my feet, staring into the dark, watching the lights from passing cars spin across the walls like tracer fire. I lay like that until half past three, then I got up and went to work. And when I got home I phoned the magazine and finally accepted my prize.

A week later I found myself sitting in Rory Cheetham-Stabb's office in Belgravia. As he entered my details in a new file I discreetly surveyed the room. It was in the starkest possible contrast to Karen's spartan office in Chiswick. It was the size of a small ballroom, furnished with beeswax-scented antiques, lined with thick leather-bound books, and carpeted in sumptuous, velvet pile. On the walls were darkly gleaming oils of Scottish landscapes and dignified portraits of horses and dogs. I looked at Rory Cheetham-Stabb sitting behind his vast, mahogany desk. He was tall, with jet black hair, an aquiline nose, and very pale-blue eyes. His suit was exquisitely tailored, with discreet hand-stitching on the lapels. A pair of diamond cufflinks flashed in the refracted light from the chandelier.

'Now, Mrs Smith,' he began smoothly, 'you must place yourself entirely in my care. I shall look after you. And you mustn't worry,' he went on with a wolfish grin, 'because

116

I always get my wives just what they want. Oh yes,' he reiterated as he lit a large cigar, 'my wives always get what they want!' He seemed to talk about 'his' wives a good deal, I noticed. I imagined myself in a large harem.

'Now, you do definitely want a divorce, don't you?' he asked.

'Yes,' I said quietly. 'I do.'

'Jolly good,' he said, clapping his hands. 'Jolly good. Because you know an awful lot of rot is talked these days about mediation and conciliation and counselling and all that touchy-feely tripe, Mrs Smith, when the simple fact is that a divorce is a battle. A bloody battle. But a battle which I invariably win! Now, what we've got to do is build our case. Reason for divorce?'

'My husband's . . . infidelity.'

'Right,' he said, scribbling furiously. 'A serial philanderer.'

'No,' I corrected him, aghast. 'That's not true. He's only had one affair.'

'Details, Mrs Smith. Details. Now, does your husband drink?'

'Well, he likes to have a gin and tonic when he gets in from work, and yes, when we're out he'll have a glass or two of wine.'

'Mmm. Serious . . . drink . . . problem,' muttered Cheetham-Stabb as he scribbled away. 'No wife can be expected to live with that. Right, so far we've got a philandering alcoholic on our hands. How ghastly for you, Mrs Smith. How *ghastly*. The judge will be entirely on your side.'

'Mr Cheetham-Stabb,' I said. 'With respect, I think you've got the wrong end of the stick. I don't want to hurt my husband or tell lies about him. He's basically a decent man. But because he's been unfaithful I feel I can't live with him any more. So I just want to end my marriage, that's all.' An expression of non-comprehension mingled with disappointment passed across his handsome face. Then he sat back in his Louis Seize chair and tapped his Mont Blanc pen against his teeth.

'So you don't mind if your husband keeps the house, then?' he asked casually.

'Oh. Well, I wouldn't say that.'

'And you have no objections if he gets care and control of the kids?'

'Well, yes of course I do.'

'And you'd be quite happy, I take it, for him to pay you a pittance in alimony.'

'No, no, I'm not saying that.'

'Nor do you mind if you end up in a squalid bedsit somewhere on the wrong side of the river while he's in the marital home with his new totty?' I was too shocked to reply. 'So you don't mind, then?' he repeated, raising his eyebrows with an insolent smile. I sat there dumbstruck, contemplating the nightmare which had been conjured up before my eyes.

'As I say, Mrs Smith,' he went on smoothly, 'a divorce is a battle. It can be a very vicious one. And when you go into battle you try and frighten the oppo by making a bloody big noise. That's all I'm doing, Mrs Smith. Preparing to make a big noise. Now, do you want a divorce or not?' I stared at him.

'Yes,' I sighed. 'I do.'

'Good. We'll slap a petition on him tomorrow.'

I decided to warn Peter, of course. The thought of him opening the mail and finding a divorce petition was not an indignity I wished to inflict on him. So that night, as I prepared supper, I told him I'd started proceedings. He was so shocked he dropped a plate.

'You're *divorcing* me?' he said faintly.

'Yes. I suppose I am.'

'Oh.' He looked dumbfounded. 'Oh,' he said again. And then he said, 'Is that really necessary?'

'Was it really necessary to have an affair?' I countered. 'Was it really necessary to tell me you're not sure it won't happen again? I've decided I can't live with that insecurity, Peter. So I'm going to protect myself.'

'Faith,' he said as he got out the dustpan and brush, 'I know we've got our problems right now, but this is *crazy*. You've got to give it more thought.'

'I've given it a lot of thought,' I replied bleakly. 'I've thought about the fact that I don't trust you any more, and that I feel differently about you now. I also feel differently about us. I feel that your infidelity has somehow – I don't know – changed the way we're together. I guess that must sound simple-minded, Peter, but I'm afraid it's true.'

'But divorce will ruin us,' he said as he threw the shattered pieces into the bin. 'For God's sake, Faith, I've just got this fantastic new job . . .'

'Your job's got nothing to do with it.'

'At last things were going well. We were about to enter a happier phase.'

'Then what a pity you had an affair.'

'Things were really looking up,' he added desperately.

'Yes, they were. Until you confessed.'

'But now it's all going to go in legal fees.'

'It won't cost a penny,' I said, and I told him about my prize.

'A competition!' he exclaimed. 'Good God, Faith, how absurd! And I don't want any damn publicity!' he said. 'Least of all with my new job!'

'It's OK,' I explained. 'You don't have to worry, I ticked the no-publicity box. Anyway, you should be pleased I've won the divorce because without it, it would be you shelling out, and Rory Cheetham-Stabb doesn't come cheap.'

'Rory Cheetham-Stabb!' he gasped. 'For God's sake, the man's a velociraptor – he'll utterly ruin me! Rory Cheetham-Stabb!' he yelled. 'Christ, Faith. Rory Cheetham-Stabb! So is this what you're planning to do – hit the button marked alimony and watch the cash roll in?'

'Don't be so unfair!' I said. 'I'm not going to clean you out. I simply feel I have to end our marriage, for the reasons I've just explained. And you don't have to contest it. But if you do, then, yes, you'll need a solicitor, but you can't use Karen because she knows us both, so you'll have to get someone else.'

'Thanks for the tip,' he spat. 'So you're divorcing me,' he repeated incredulously. 'Christ!' he expostulated as he took down one of his mother's crystal tumblers and poured himself a large gin.

'Well, what did you think would happen when you told me about Andie?' I said.

'Not this!' he exclaimed, running his left hand through his hair. 'Not this. I thought – my God, how mistaken I was – that you'd appreciate my honesty.'

'Oh really!' I said with a hollow laugh. 'And I thought *I* was naïve.'

'I thought you'd understand,' he said bleakly, then he raised the crystal glass to his lips.

'Well, I suppose I do understand,' I replied. 'I understand what it's like to lose your trust in someone. And now, after fifteen years, I've lost my trust in you. And if we don't have trust any more, Peter, then we really don't have anything.'

'We've got lots of things, Faith,' he said as I began to scrape some carrots. 'We've got our children, and our careers, our home and our dog.'

'Let's not bring Graham into this,' I said wearily. 'The point is, everything has changed.'

'Faith,' Peter went on quietly. 'I realise you're angry, and I deserve it. And I know I've got myself in a . . . *mess*. But that doesn't mean we have to make an immediate decision to get divorced. Can't we just cool off?'

'I have cooled off,' I replied. 'I'm deep frozen.' Peter was staring at me incredulously. I felt like Gary Cooper in *High Noon*.

'Do you want a divorce, Faith?' he said. I was silent. 'Do you really want a divorce? Do you want a divorce, Faith?' he repeated. I stared at him. 'Is that what you really want, a *divorce*? Do. You. Want. A. DIVORCE?' he enunciated desperately.

'Yes,' I said quietly. 'I do.'

Suddenly he turned, raised his arm and hurled the crystal tumbler through the kitchen door where it struck Lily's sunburst mirror.

'Ah!' I gasped as it splintered. 'Ah,' I gasped again. And I was going to shout at him. I was going to scream blue murder. I was going to tell him just what I thought of that. But I couldn't, because Peter had already left the house, slamming the door violently behind him.

The next day he apologised. He looked awful, and truly contrite. I stared at the broken sunburst, which I'd taken off its hook and which was now leaning forlornly against the wall. It had amazed me, for never, ever, in fifteen years had Peter done anything like that.

'I'm sorry,' he murmured. 'I lost control.' I accepted his apology, of course. But now, shocked by what had happened, I asked him if he'd be prepared to move out. He looked out of the window into the garden for a few seconds, then nodded his head. And I appreciated that because Rory Cheetham-Stabb told me that some men stay put in the marital home because they're terrified that they'll lose it if they leave. But I knew that Peter would do the decent thing. In any case, how could we remain together while our marriage began to unwind? I wondered whether he'd move in with Andie – I was sure she'd welcome him with open arms. But a few days later he told me he'd found a small flat in Pimlico, near the Tate. It belonged to a friend of someone who was going abroad for a year, and the rent wouldn't be too high. So I helped him to pack up his things, which was strange, because it was as though I was helping him pack for the Frankfurt book fair or a business trip of that kind. As I took his shirts out of the cupboard, I looked at his two new Hermès ties.

'She gave you these, didn't she?' I said.

'Yes,' he said guiltily. 'She did.'

'You shouldn't have accepted them,' I pointed out.

'No,' he agreed, 'you're right.'

Soon we'd filled two cases, and the spare room in which he'd been sleeping was bare, the wire coat-hangers clinking gently against each other in the slight breeze. While we packed, Graham lay on the bed, his head between his paws, his eyebrows twitching anxiously up and down. Then Peter went into the kitchen and made a last cup of coffee while he waited for his cab to arrive. I sat down with him, and through the open door I could see his luggage standing in the hall. This is unbelievable, I thought. This is surreal. But this is what happens to a hundred and fifty thousand couples every year.

'I'll tell the children at the weekend,' I said. I was dreading how they would react. 'You can spend as much time with them as you like – and with Graham. But I don't want them meeting Andie, OK?'

'Look, I don't even know if I'll be seeing her,' he said as Graham laid his head on his lap. 'Oh God, Faith,' he said, 'oh God.' He reached across the table and grabbed my hands in both of his. 'This is a mess,' he went on miserably. 'Please, please – change your mind.' At that point, feeling the pressure of his hands upon mine, seeing tears standing in his brown eyes, and catching the sharp note of painful appeal in his voice, I almost did. We seemed to stare at each other across a deep chasm, but I knew there was no bridge. And now we heard the sudden urgent honking of a car. Peter went to the door, shouted something, then carried one of the cases outside. And I was about to run after him down the path and say, 'I'm sorry – I've changed my mind! I've made such a stupid mistake. But you see I couldn't cope with my feelings and I didn't know what else to do. I just wanted to show you how much you'd hurt me, and I needed to hurt you back, but I think I've hurt you enough now, so please Peter, please Peter, don't go!' And I'd actually got to my feet and I was about to run outside when his mobile phone suddenly rang out. He'd left it on the table. It was playing 'For He's A Jolly Good Fellow'. I looked at the tiny screen where, to my great surprise, two small intertwined hearts had appeared and were pulsing in time to the music. Then a red light flashed on as a message was left, and I knew who that message was from. Peter had come into the house to collect his other case, and as he went back out, with Graham following forlornly at his heels, I pressed the button marked 'Play'.

'Sweetie,' I heard Andie Metzler say. 'Hope you're OK. Can't wait to see you. Come round later. I'll have champagne on ice. Love ya! Bye!'

'Faith . . .' Peter said as he stood on the step. 'Faith . . . I . . .'

'Goodbye, Peter,' I said, very simply. And then I shut the door.

Some women fight for their man, don't they? If they have a rival, their fists go up, their claws come out, and they hit back with everything they've got. They defend their territory as ferociously as Mrs Thatcher defending the Falklands. But I'm not one of those women. I knew that now. Because when I heard Andie's message I wasn't roused into battle – I was demoralised beyond belief. And, as I listened to her voice I was aware of a profound physiological change: that my heart rate had trebled, that my breath was coming in ragged little gasps and that goosebumps covered my arms. Hearing her call him 'Sweetie' was like a knife to the heart. The insolent intimacy of 'Love ya!' The thought of the chilling champagne in her bedroom conjured images that made my stomach churn. Yet, masochistically, I indulged them. I visualised Andie in her La Perla, slowly undressing Peter. I saw her rubbing a piece of ice over his chest. I imagined her manicured hands stroking his sandy hair. I imagined her kissing him, and pulling him down. As I imagined them making love, I could almost hear her groans and sighs. And now I imagined myself, storming into her bedroom with my biggest Sabatier and plunging it into her heart. My loathing for her was so primitive, so violent, that I was profoundly shocked. I had never believed myself capable of such savage hatred, but now I knew that I was. Peter's affair had shown me a dark part of myself I had never known was there. But Peter belonged to *me*, I reasoned. He was my husband of fifteen years. And this wretched, *wretched* woman had come into our lives and was going to take him away. So, naturally, I wanted to kill her. But I knew I wouldn't. I'd deal with the crisis in my own way. For I knew, too, that my pride would prevent me from fighting for Peter to stay. In any case, it's too risky. I mean, look at Della Bovey – feisty Della – poor girl. The girl who bravely struck back against Anthea

Turner, but who won only a temporary reprieve. And I knew that Andie would get Peter, too. After all, she was a ruthless headhunter. Oh no, I wasn't going to put up a fight.

'You're quite right, darling,' said Lily as we arrived at the Mind Body Spirit festival in Greycoat Square at lunchtime the following day. 'Too undignified, and too risky,' she added as we went up the steps. 'The press would have a ball.'

'Why?' I said miserably. 'Peter and I aren't famous.'

'Well, you're a little bit famous, Faith. Five million people watch you doing the weather every day. And then of course Peter's on that Family Ethics Committee of his.'

'Oh yes, I'd forgotten that.'

'So it would be very embarrassing for him, personally, if there was anything in the papers about his divorce. Oh no,' she added as we showed the security guard our tickets, 'it really wouldn't look good at all – especially as Bishopsgate publish all those how-not-to-get-divorced books.'

'Do they?'

'Yes. That's how they made their money. There's a whole imprint devoted to them.'

'How do you know?'

'Because they're always sending review copies to *Moi!* No, a dignified retreat is much better, Faith, but it's going to be hell for a while.'

'It's hell right now,' I said weakly, feeling the familiar tightening in my throat. 'It's hell, Lily,' I whispered as I groped for a tissue. 'I had no idea anything could hurt so much.'

'Don't worry, Faith,' she said, giving my arm a comforting squeeze, 'you're my best, best friend, I love you, and I'm going to help you in every way I can. Now, you must have some therapies while you're here.'

'Must I?' I said desolately as we made our way into the hall. I hadn't even wanted to come to this thing, but Lily had persuaded me. There were so many people that we could only shuffle slowly between the stands. In the background we could hear the plangent hum of Tibetan initiation bowls; the smell of patchouli and sandalwood hung heavily on the air.

'Maybe you should have your aura cleansed,' she said thoughtfully. 'Or perhaps you should get your biomagnetic field checked out – it's brilliant for emotional stress. Anyway, you've done very well to stay married so long,' she added as we paused by the Paraguayan rainsticks. 'You were trapped in holy wedlock without a key. You won't see it like this yet,' she went on, 'but this is a new beginning, Faith. A new start. The doors of life are opening at last.'

'They weren't shut,' I retorted bleakly as we moved through the milling crowd. 'I call being married and having children life!'

'Yes, but it's not life as we know it, Faith. When I came back from the States last year I looked at you and I thought, Faith is in a time-warp. Still in the same, boring old rut –'

'I liked my rut –'

'Still in dull old suburbia.'

'I *am* suburban,' I said.

'But now you're going to blossom and shine. You're thirty-five, Faith. Halfway through life's journey, but there've been some speed bumps on your bit of road. Believe me, darling,' she said cheerfully, 'divorce is going to be the best thing that ever happened to you. What are you going to have?' she added. I hadn't a clue. Should I have my karma healed, or become a cosmic thinker? Should I have an Ayurvedic face-lift, or discover the goddess within? We passed a stand selling rainbow crystals and Native American dream-catchers. To our right a recumbent woman was having the unlit end of a flaming candle inserted into her ear.

'They're Hopi candles,' said Lily knowledgeably. 'Jolly good for migraines. Did you know your ears are the gateway to your past lives?'

'DNA Restructuring!' announced a sign on the stand to my right. Intrigued, I stopped and looked.

'We restructure your DNA for you,' said a man helpfully.

'That's fantastic,' I replied.

'It's quite a simple procedure,' he explained. 'What we do is, realign and restrand your chromosomes, thereby allowing you to regain your total connection to the God Force.' It sounded so radical I was rather tempted, but Lily grabbed my arm and dragged me away.

'Faith, don't be so credulous,' she hissed. 'Everyone knows that's a load of tosh. Now, I'm just off to have my angels accessed,' she added. 'I'll see you back here in half an hour.'

'Toe-reading!' I heard a woman shout as Lily headed upstairs. *Let me tell you what your toes say about your personality,* announced a slogan on the stand. *Special limited offer today – only ten pounds! Accurate personality analysis and future prospects revealed.* Now, don't ask me why, but somehow the idea appealed. So I paid the money, took off my shoes and rolled up the legs of my jeans.

'Ah, very interesting,' said the therapist as I sat back in the reclining chair and offered up my feet for her inspection. She looked at them through narrowed eyes as she began to prod and tweak. 'Now, your toes are quite spaced out,' she said, 'so this indicates an adventurous personality. You've obviously led an unconventional life. Is that true?'

'No,' I said, disappointed. 'The opposite.'

'Oh. Well, these toes here are very impulsive,' she went on as she wiggled the third toe on my right foot. 'They're very spontaneous. Very Latin. You're a slightly reckless kind of person, aren't you?'

'No,' I said. 'I'm very sensible and cautious.' Then she gave my big toe a squeeze.

'You've got very nice squashy big toes.'

'Have I?'

'Yes, they're really big and *juicy*, which means you've got an artistic nature. You are very artistic, aren't you? You're brilliant at painting.'

'No,' I replied as my enthusiasm dwindled. 'I'm useless at it.'

'You're very musical too, aren't you?' she added desperately.

'Not in the least,' I said.

'You play the flute.'

'I don't.'

'Grade six. With distinction.' She was talking tripe.

'You know, I don't want to appear rude,' I said wearily, 'but I think this is a waste of time.'

'Look,' she said guiltily as I reached for my shoes. 'I'm quite new to toe-reading and my technique's still a bit shaky. But I feel bad about taking your money, and I'm an amateur psychic, so would you like a free crystal ball reading instead?' This was clearly going to be a load of baloney as well, but as she wasn't going to charge I agreed. So I put on my shoes, then sat there while she placed her hands on either side of a large crystal ball.

'You're having *terrible* problems in your marriage,' she declared after a few seconds.

'Yes,' I said, startled. 'That's true.'

'After a long period of domestic stability your life is under-going radical change. You've had a huge emotional shock,' she added.

'Yes. Yes I have.'

'Your husband's confessed to an affair.'

'That's true.'

'But it's his first one, and he feels very bad about it. He's confused and unsure what to do.'

'My God,' I breathed, 'that's *right*. But what's going to happen?' I asked her desperately. 'Please tell me what the future holds?'

'Well, you're going to get divorced,' she said quietly. At that I felt a shiver run down my spine. 'But you *will* be happy again,' she added. 'And sooner than you think. You're going to come through this difficult time,' she concluded. 'God will heal your pain.' God will heal my pain?

'Fa-aith!' It was Lily. She looked enraptured as she rushed up to me. 'Oh Faith, I saw so many angels!' she said excitedly as she dragged me away. 'I saw the fantastic light of the angelic chorus. I was sort of engulfed in it. It was just like, really, really white. And what was so wonderful was that the angels took all my problems away.'

'Did they?'

'Yes, they ascended to heaven with them. All my worries about our cover price and subscription rates. The seraphim and cherubim just took them *all* away. And the Archangel Michael told me that I'm definitely going to beat *Vogue* in the circulation stakes. Isn't that wonderful?'

'It's incredible,' I said.

'And what did you have?'

'Toe-reading.'

'Any good?'

'No. But then I had a crystal ball reading, and that was very accurate. But the woman said I'm going to be OK. She said that God will heal my pain, Lily. But I don't know how.'

'God will heal your pain?' she repeated thoughtfully. 'Well, that can mean only one thing, Faith – you're going to meet someone else!'

'Don't be silly, Lily,' I groaned, 'it's much too soon. Look, I'm not even divorced.'

'Yes, but Peter's not divorced either, is he,' she said, 'and he's got someone else.' And when Lily said that I felt a pain in my chest as though someone had stamped on my heart. 'Peter's got someone else,' she repeated softly, 'so why on earth shouldn't *you*?'

'You're going too fast,' I muttered tetchily. 'I can't think that far ahead.'

'Well, darling,' said Lily, 'you mustn't let the grass grow under your feet. So there's only one thing for it. You've got to get out there again.'

'I wouldn't know how to "get out there",' I said with a grim little laugh. 'I've never been "out there" as you like to say.'

'Mmm,' she said. 'That's true. I can't imagine you chatting anyone up.'

'I wouldn't want to,' I said.

'Really?'

'No. Of course not,' I said indignantly.

'Why not?'

'Well, I suppose I'd want *them* to chat up *me*.'

'Ah,' Lily said. 'Well, in that case you've got to learn how to flirt. And I'm going to help you do it.'

I don't know why I go along with Lily's schemes. I really *don't* know why. But she can always persuade me to do anything, and that's how it's always been. With her in the driving seat and me strapped in by her side. I guess it must be the sheer force of her personality. She's like an avalanche – she sweeps me along. I can't otherwise explain how I found myself attending a flirting workshop with her four days later.

'I only agreed to this because I'm still semi-deranged from shock,' I said as we arrived at the Sloane Hotel in Earls Court.

'No, Faith,' she corrected me as we went through the swing doors. 'You're doing it because you secretly want to, because you know it will do you good. You've *got* to learn how to deal with men again,' she said bossily as we took off our coats. 'You've got to learn how to interact with them in a positive, healthy way. And flirting will make men more interested in you, which will boost your self-esteem. You've been betrayed, Faith,' she said seriously as we found the conference suite. 'So you feel small and unloved.'

'Thanks.'

'You feel unwanted, and undesirable. Insignificant and plain. In fact you feel a total failure.'

'OK, OK.'

'But learning to flirt will make you feel alluring again, gorgeous and sexy.'

'I very much doubt it.'

'And then, when you're ready, you'll be well-equipped to go for it with some stunning new man.'

'I don't want to go for it with any man,' I pointed out bitterly, 'new or old.'

'Not now, darling. But you will,' she said. 'And of course that would really hurt Peter.'

'What?'

'Well, it would hurt Peter like mad if you found someone new.'

'Even though he's the one who had the affair?'

'Yes.'

And when Lily said that I felt something inside me jump, and I realised, for the first time, that I didn't mind at all if I hurt Peter. In fact I *wanted* to hurt him. After all, he'd hurt *me*. He'd betrayed *me*. He'd wounded *me*. This situation was entirely *his* fault. *I* hadn't had an affair. And as I sat there waiting for the class to start, I entertained fantasies of revenge. I no longer wanted to murder Andie, I wanted to murder *him*. I'd like to run him down, I thought calmly. Or push him off a cliff, or slip something nasty in his coffee or . . .

'Hello everyone!' My violent reveries had been interrupted by the arrival of our 'teacher', Brigitte, a pneumatic-looking brunette of about forty-five. Her eyes raked the room like a blowtorch.

'What a great turn-out,' she said. It was true. There were over thirty of us, split fairly evenly between men and women. We were all smiling sheepishly, all except Lily that is. She was winking at a rather attractive man sitting across the aisle from her.

'So you want to learn to flirt?' said Brigitte with a beatific smile. Lily was fingering the hem of her skirt. 'You want to become more attractive to the opposite sex,' she went on benignly. Lily had undone her top button. 'It's just as well that people do flirt,' Brigitte continued as Lily flicked her tongue over her lips, 'otherwise the human race would die out! I flirt a lot,' she confided, 'and believe me, it's a lot of fun. Now,' she said, clapping her hands, 'let's do the first exercise. Get into groups of six, and throw these tennis balls at each other whilst at the same time introducing yourselves in a sexy, flirtatious way.' We all giggled and shuffled our feet, then reluctantly stood up and arranged ourselves into groups.

'Hello, er, ha ha ha, er, I'm Brian.'

'Hello, I'm Sue.'

'Hi there. I'm Mike.'

130

'Er, hello. I'm Faith.'

'Good morning, my name's Dave.'

'Well hell-o-o-o, Dave, you *sexy* love-bucket. I'm Lily.' Dave dropped the ball. Man over-awed, I thought.

'Very good, everyone,' said Brigitte after three or four minutes of this. 'Now, the next exercise is all about eye-contact and how to make it. Most of us feel embarrassed to look deeply into someone's eyes. But making proper eye-contact is extremely sexy and can have a powerful effect. So that's what we're going to do now. We're all going to walk round the room, and we're going to look each other up and down in a flagrantly predatory and provocative way.' This was *bizarre*, I reflected as we all wandered around eyeballing each other, though it was hard eyeing up any of the men as most of them were gawping at Lily.

'That's it,' said Brigitte enthusiastically. 'Let your eyes roam. Up and down. Look *deep* into everyone's pupils. That's right – hold their gaze. Let your eyes speak to that person. Let your eyes say, "Well . . . hel-lo!"'

This was nauseating. My face was on fire. Next we had to get into pairs and pay each other lavish compliments. I was paired up with a Chinese medical student called Ting.

'Now, *really* compliment each other!' said Brigitte. 'And when you receive your compliment just say "thank you" and smile. Got that?'

'Um, you've got nice shiny hair,' I said.

'Tank you. An' you 'ave rubbery ice.'

'Er, thanks. You've got nice teeth.'

'You 'ave goo' eggs.'

'Oh, right. I like your nose.'

'Your skir' is smar'.' Brigitte clapped her hands again.

'The real clue to flirting,' she explained, 'is that people like people who like *them*. This is why imitation really is the sincerest form of flattery. So what we're going to do now is body-mirroring, or what's technically known as Postural Echo. So copy each other's movements as closely as you can. See if you can mirror their breathing patterns too . . . And now,' said

Brigitte excitedly after fifteen minutes of this, 'the next flirting challenge – to find the Animal Within! Yes, you're going to find an animal that suits your personality, and take that animal feeling up and down your body, OK? Right, Lily, what animal are you?'

'I'm a panther,' she purred.

'What animal are you, Faith?'

'Er, I don't know – er, an armadillo.'

'Don't be an armadillo,' said Brigitte, 'they've got armour plating.'

'OK, then I'll be a dog.'

'I'm a lion!'

'I'm an eagle!'

'I'm an ardvaark!'

'I'm a ferret!'

'I'm a budgie!'

By this stage it was so farcical that my inhibitions had vanished and I began to relax. By the time the workshop came to an end I was almost enjoying myself.

'You've all done very well,' said Brigitte warmly. 'But I'm going to give you one more task. A very important task. Which is to give everyone you meet as you go home today a lovely, welcoming smile.'

'I got a lot out of that,' said Lily as we left the hotel. 'I really learned *a lot*.'

'*Did* you?' I said sceptically as she opened the doors of her navy-blue Porsche.

'Oh yes,' she said enthusiastically as the roof descended with an electronic whine. 'And don't forget, Faith,' she added as we pulled out into the Earls Court Road, 'we've got to smile at everyone we meet.'

'Don't worry,' I said confidently, 'I will.' After all, the sun was shining. The cherry trees were in bloom. And, for the first time in several weeks, I'd had a really good laugh. Oh yes, I felt like smiling today, despite all my problems at home. We drew up at a traffic light in the Brompton Road and were sitting there, with the engine idling, when an MGF with its roof down pulled up alongside. Suddenly I became aware that the driver was looking at us. I turned my head to the left and found myself face to face with a smiling man. But who on earth was he smiling at? Lily, I presumed. I looked. But no. He wasn't smiling at Lily. He was smiling at me. He was looking at me. And smiling. Just like that. What a bloody *nerve*! I glared at him but he didn't stop. He only seemed to smile more. By now I was spitting fire. This had got to stop.

'What are you looking at?' I snapped.

'You,' he said with a grin.

'Well that's very *rude*!' I shot back. And at that he began to laugh. He was laughing at me. Imagine the impertinence! So I gave him an evil stare. But still he sat there, just looking at me and laughing. At which point, provoked beyond belief, I had no option but to give him the two-fingered treatment with both hands.

'Faith!' exclaimed Lily. 'What the hell are you doing? You're supposed to smile at him, you fool!'

'I'm not going to smile at him – he's annoying me!' I hissed. 'Just staring like that. Bloody cheek! Who the hell does he think he is? I mean, Christ, Lily! I've been through enough. This is the *last* thing I need. How *dare* you!' I said, turning to him again. 'How dare you just sit there in your pathetic sports car ogling us like this. There's a policeman over there,' I added angrily, 'and I've half a mind to call him over and have you arrested because this is sexual harassment, you know. Officer!' I shouted theatrically. 'Officer!' By now the man in the sports car was convulsed with mirth.

'Stop it right now,' I snapped.

'Faith!' said Lily. 'Shut *up*!'

'No!' I said. 'I won't. I won't have this!' I yelled at him again. 'I'm going to take your numberplate down. And I'm going to report you to the police, do you hear me? I'm going to write to Scotland Yard.'

'Yes!' He roared with laughter. 'Do. But there's no need to check my numberplate – here!' At this he reached into his jacket pocket and now, as the lights changed to amber, he

133

tossed a small white card into my lap. And by the time I'd caught my breath, the lights were green and he'd gone.

'What a . . . How outrageous!' I expostulated. 'God, did you see that, Lily? What a bloody cheek!'

'Didn't you learn anything today?' said Lily crossly. 'The man fancied you, you fool!'

'What? *Oh*.'

'And the only reason you were shouting at him like that is because you're so furious with Peter.'

'No.'

'Yes! It's displaced anger, that's all. But what a performance, Faith,' she said, shaking her head. 'God, you've got a lot to learn!'

I looked at the card. There was a tiny paintbrush in one corner and it said, *Josiah Cartwright – Artist At Large*. And I was very tempted to throw it away; to throw it away right there and then. But I didn't do that; because it's not nice to drop litter. So I tucked it carefully into my bag.

March Continued

On Friday evening the children came home. Breaking the news to them wasn't easy, but I did it as gently as I could.

'You see,' I said carefully as we sat in the kitchen, 'when a mummy and a daddy don't love each other in that special way any more, what happens is that they decide to – Matt, please could you put the newspaper down? I'm trying to talk to you.'

'Oh, sorry,' he said vaguely, looking up from his *Financial Times*. 'But there's been an insurrection in Bolivia.'

'Well, that's very unfortunate, but I have something important to say. You see,' I tried again. 'When a mummy and a daddy don't really ... sort of ... you know ... then they decide to ...'

'Get divorced?' interjected Katie. 'Come on, Mum, cut to the chase. You and Dad are splitting up.'

'Well ... no, I wouldn't put it *quite* like that. But on the other hand,' I said, fiddling with my wedding ring, 'we're not getting on very well.'

'I could have told you that.'

'So we've decided to – separate.'

'Thank God!' Matt exclaimed.

'Sorry?' He looked up from his paper.

'The government have regained control.'

'Matt,' I said irritably, 'I am very pleased to see that you are starting to take such an interest in current affairs, but I'm trying to tell you something serious – something very serious, actually – and I'd appreciate it if you'd listen. As I was saying,

135

your father and I have taken this difficult and very painful decision. But you'll still see him a lot. Matt,' I said crossly, 'I'm not going to say it again. Will you *please* put that away?'

'What? Oh, sorry, Mum,' he said absently. 'But there's been an earthquake in Japan. What's all this about?'

'Mum said that she and Dad are getting divorced,' Katie explained patiently. There was an ominous silence as they both took this in. 'Which means, Matt,' Katie went on, 'that you and I will no longer bear the stigma of having happily married parents.' I stared at her, dumbfounded. 'At Seaworth all the kids' parents are divorced,' she went on matter-of-factly. 'We were the only ones whose folks weren't. It was very embarrassing.'

'Oh,' I said faintly. 'I see.'

'In fact most of them are on their third marriages by now.'

'Really?'

'So don't worry about us. We'll be fine.'

'Oh. Well. Good. That's great.'

'Complex family relationships are the norm.'

'Right.'

'The nuclear family is dead. But we'll have to be very careful with Graham,' she added seriously. 'It could be traumatic for him. I mean, he comes from a broken home as it is.'

'Broken kennel,' said Matt.

'So he'll be feeling pretty insecure. We'll have to give him a lot of emotional support,' she went on as she stroked his ears. 'And we'll have to reassure him that there are lots of *different* kinds of families these days.' I nodded. She was absolutely right. I'd never ever thought it would happen to us, but we were going to become a 'different' kind of family now. This is just awful. *Awful*, I thought. Suddenly the phone rang and Katie ran to pick it up.

'Hello, Dad,' I heard her say. 'Oh, we're fine. Yes, we know. So it's Splitsville Tennessee. You want to take us out? Sure. Matt!' she yelled. 'Dad's going to take us out.'

So at two p.m. the next day the doorbell rang and there was Peter, standing on the step, for all the world like some polite

136

visitor. Graham threw himself at him, barking and whimpering with joy.

'Hello darling,' said Peter as he crouched down to let Graham lick his ear.

'You could have used your key,' I said quietly. 'This is still your house, you know.'

'For the time being,' he said dryly. 'Until Rory Cheetham-Stabb starts on me.'

'Let's not quarrel, Peter. Where are you taking the kids?'

'To the Science Museum – they've got a new gallery there. Then for a spin on the Ferris Wheel. After that I thought we'd go and have a burger at the Hard Rock Café.'

'That sounds lovely,' I said brightly. 'Lovely.' I was determined to be civilised.

'You can come too if you like,' he added.

'Can I? Oh. *Great.* I'd love to, I'll just go and get my coat . . .' Hang on. What was I *saying*? Of course I couldn't go. We're splitting up. 'Um, it's all right, thanks,' I backtracked. 'I'll take Graham out. And then I'll go for a swim. Come on, kids – don't keep Dad waiting!'

'Just a min-ute!'

While they got their coats Peter and I stood there in the hall, smiling awkwardly at each other as though we were strangers making smalltalk at some boring drinks do.

'Faith,' said Peter suddenly. He took a step towards me. 'Faith,' he repeated. 'Please don't do anything drastic yet. I want us to go to counselling.'

'Counselling?' I repeated.

'Yes. I've been thinking about it. I think we should go to Resolve.'

'Resolve?' I said with a grim little laugh. 'Commonly known as *Dis*solve.'

'They might be able to help,' he insisted.

'I doubt it,' I replied. 'In any case I don't want to discuss our marriage with a total stranger.'

'They might enable us to get things in perspective before everything gets out of hand. The Taylors got help,' he added.

'Yes, and she's on Prozac,' I replied.

'Please, Faith,' he added beseechingly. 'Please, Faith, we've got to try.'

'Oh, I don't know,' I said reluctantly. Suddenly Graham jumped up, placed his paws on my chest and looked at me imploringly with his soft brown eyes.

'Please, Faith,' said Peter. I stroked Graham's ears.

'Well . . . all right,' I sighed. 'If you want.'

'You're looking good,' said Marian warmly when I went into Make-Up on Monday morning.

'Yeah,' said Iqbal. 'You're looking *great*. Haven't you lost a few pounds?'

'Have I?' I said wonderingly. 'Yes. Maybe I have. A few.'

'You've lost a bit from your face,' said Marian as she sponged foundation across my cheeks. 'You're looking lovely,' she added generously. 'Not so . . .'

'Dumpy?' I said with a smile.

'Well, I wouldn't say that.'

'What she means,' said Iqbal with a grin, 'is that whatever diet you're on – it works.'

I was longing to tell them that I was actually on the Divorce Diet – great for shifting extra pounds. But I couldn't. Because then it might get out, and I didn't want my marital difficulties being discussed at work. I could imagine the gossip. *Poor Faith . . . another woman . . . American, you know . . . oh no, he's a decent guy . . . just married too young . . . it happens.* No, I did not intend to make myself an object of sympathetic concern. People got divorced every day of the week, I reflected, I'd just have to cope and be strong. But I'd promised Peter that I'd go to Resolve with him, even if it was unlikely to help. So after the programme came off air I discreetly phoned them and booked us both in.

'Who will the appointment be with?' I enquired as I jotted down the date.

'With our principal counsellor,' said the receptionist. 'She's called Zillah Strindberg. She's *awfully* good.'

Later that day I went swimming. The house feels horribly empty now, without Peter. I loathe it. I feel bereft. I miss his familiar presence – our sudden conversations – and the way he knows what I'm thinking without even having to ask. And I hate not hearing the familiar click of his key in the door every night. So I'm making a conscious effort to try and fill the early evenings because otherwise I'd get in a state. So I settled Graham in front of *Ready, Steady, Cook!* and went up to the health club and did my usual thirty lengths. I found the water therapeutic – the way it supported me, and lifted me up. And I was sitting in the bar afterwards, reading *The Times* and having a cup of herbal tea, mentally congratulating myself on at least *trying* to save my marriage, as I idly scanned the lonely hearts ads. Do you know, I've never really read them before but these days I find I'm hooked. All those single men! Today the paper was heaving with 'sporty thirty-somethings', 'tall professionals' and 'eligible bachelors, forty-three'. And I began to think about what Lily had said, that a time would come when I would want to date other men. But it was inconceivable that I should do so now because of course it was much too soon. And I thought of that silly man in his stupid sports car who'd impudently chucked me his card. What a *nerve*, I thought as I opened my bag and took it out. What a cheek, I reflected as I read the telephone number again. What a sauce, I said to myself. Did he seriously think I'd ring? My dating experience might be chronically limited, but blatant pick-ups are just *not* my style.

'Excuse me, is this chair taken?' I looked up, momentarily startled. A man was standing there, smiling hesitantly. 'Is this chair taken?' he enquired again.

'Er, yes,' I replied, feeling my face begin to flush. 'I mean, no. No, it's not taken. It's free. That's what I mean, it's . . .' My voice trailed away. 'Help yourself,' I said feebly. Then I turned back to my paper, feeling slightly flustered, whilst discreetly surveying from behind lowered lids this decidedly attractive man. He was tall, and quite well built. His hair was still damp from the shower. He sat down, smiled at me, and now I noticed his nice blue eyes.

'I'm Stanley,' he said, suddenly. I lowered the paper, surprised that he wanted to talk. 'I'm Stanley,' he repeated. 'Stan Plunkett.'

'Oh. Well. Hello,' I said. 'I'm Faith.'

'I know,' he replied with a smile. 'I've seen you. You do the weather, on the BBC.'

'That's half right,' I said with a little laugh, feeling myself blush with pride. 'I'm on the other side actually, AM-UK!'

'Do you come here often?'

'Quite often. I like to swim.' I assumed that he was only talking to me out of politeness, as we were sharing a table. I thought he'd drink his coffee and then go. But he didn't go. He kept talking. We sat there for ten minutes or so while he told me about his work – it's something quite unusual, actually, involving nuclear arms – and he was just getting into it, and telling me all about it, when I suddenly glanced at the clock and saw that it was half past nine.

'I'm afraid I've got to go,' I said. 'I'm awfully sorry, but it's the curse of breakfast TV.'

'What a pity,' he replied. 'I was really enjoying myself.'

'Well, I have to get my head down by ten, you see.'

'Why don't we meet again?' he suggested brightly as I picked up my bag.

'Er . . . yes,' I said uncertainly. 'I'm sure we'll meet again here.'

'No, I mean, let's get together,' he said warmly. Oh. 'Let's have a drink. Are you free on . . .' He whipped out his diary. 'Thursday?'

Gosh. I suddenly twigged. He was asking me out. He was asking me out on a date. And I was just about to say, 'Well I'm awfully sorry, and of course I'm terribly flattered, but actually, I'm married you know,' when I suddenly remembered. I remembered that everything has changed. I remembered that I'm separated; I remembered that Peter now lives elsewhere; and I remembered that, as from today, I no longer wear my wedding ring.

'We could go to Café Rouge,' he went on. 'The one down by

the river.' I looked at him and I thought to myself, why not? Yes – why ever not?

'Are you free, then?' he repeated as I picked up my bag.

'Yes,' I said. 'I am.'

So on Thursday I got myself ready for my first date in fifteen years. It was an historic occasion for me. I'd never really been courted, or wined or dined. I mean, don't get me wrong, Peter and I were very happily married – at least we were until his fling. Oh yes, until Andie Metzler came along our marriage was like a picnic without the wasps. We were so compatible. So harmonious. We'd never really quarrelled – until this year. We'd just bumped along optimistically, happy and trusting, seeing only the best in each other. We'd had a lovely marriage really, which I'd always believed only death would end. But in the end it wasn't death which was going to part us. I've read that some people, when their relationship ends, want to destroy their past, deny that they've ever been happy – as though the affair has wiped out all the good things. It's a coping mechanism, I suppose. But I didn't feel like that. Even though Peter had strayed and I was angry with him I still knew our marriage had been a happy one. At the same time, we'd been so young when we got together that I knew there were things we'd missed. Oh yes, I realised, there certainly were. Because Peter was my first love. I'd never really dated before, but now, at thirty-five, I was about to start. I was terrified, of course, and I was very depressed, but at the same time, yes – I was a tiny bit thrilled. I admit it. I was slightly excited. Because I could hear a door creaking open in my mind. I mean, take Mimi, for example. She'd had a few boyfriends before she met Mike, and although I was happy with Peter I used to envy her going on dates. I thought of her, as I thought of Lily and all single women, as independent and brave and strong. But now I was going to be an independent woman, too. A woman going on dates. And as I checked my appearance in the mirror, I realised that Marian was right – I *had* lost weight. I'd been too preoccupied with my problems to notice, but now it was quite clear. The waistband of my skirt was loose, and my bust seemed to have shrunk a bit. My little double chin had disappeared – thank God – and my features looked more defined. I'd lost that 'puddingy', 'mumsy' look I'd been getting, and my hair had grown a bit too. As I surveyed my reflection one last time I felt my heart give a little jump. For I knew that I was capable of attracting men – without even trying, I had pulled! So I felt the stirrings of a new confidence beneath my nervousness as I ventured out to meet Stan. As I walked to Café Rouge I mentally rehearsed a few amusing anecdotes about my work, which I was sure he'd want to hear. He wasn't there when I arrived so I sat at a table by the window, and I was glad I'd brought the paper with me because he was almost half an hour late.

'So sorry,' he said as he rushed up to my table, 'but I was delayed because of work. I was at the House of Commons, actually.'

'Oh. Gosh,' I said, impressed. So of course I asked him what he'd been doing there, and he said he'd been lobbying some Labour MP. Then he told me some more about his organis-ation Start Again, which exists to pressurise governments into giving up their nuclear arms. Suddenly he opened his bag and produced a thick, A4-sized document.

'This is our annual report,' he said. 'It's for you.'

'Oh,' I said, surprised, 'thanks.'

'I want you to read it.'

'Er, well, sure.' I flicked it open and on the inside front cover was a large photo of Stan, looking very serious. *Stanley Plunkett, Founder-Director*, it announced. Founder-director! Wow!

'What an interesting job,' I said.

'It's more than interesting,' he said seriously as the waiter arrived. 'It's vital. It's essential. Because the world could blow up at any time. Oh, a bottle of Chilean chardonnay, please. Don't you ever worry about global security?' he said to me.

'To be honest, I don't think I do.'

'Well you should, Faith,' he said emphatically, 'because the fact is the world is *very* unsafe.'

'Is it? Oh dear. I thought the Cold War was over.'

'It is,' he said, 'but the nuclear threat is much greater now than it was then. In fact,' he went on confidentially as he dipped his ciabatta in olive oil, 'we're on the brink of Armageddon.'

'Oh, no.' He nodded his head with a regretful air.

'It could happen at any time, Faith. Most of the world's nuclear submarines are on twenty-four-hour, hair-trigger alert, so all it would take is one false move.' And then he carried on talking, non-stop, about nuclear warfare for the next forty-five minutes. 'Cruise and Pershing . . . ballistic missile defences . . . Warsaw Pact . . . Pakistan's a real menace of course . . . threat to Taiwan . . . Start 2 Treaty . . . Vladimir Putin . . . Polaris. Do you know, there are thousands of old SS24s knocking about,' he went on knowledgeably. 'And of course Britain is still expanding its nuclear capability with its ongoing commitment to Trident.' He leaned forward. 'Did you know that each Trident warhead can cause *eight times* as much destruction as *one* Hiroshima bomb?' By now I was beginning to feel depressed. 'Quite frankly,' he said crossly, 'Trident makes a mockery of Britain's supposed commitment to non-proliferation.'

'Oh dear.'

'I want Britain to give up Trident!' he announced, giving the table a thump.

'I see.'

'That's what I'm trying to achieve – a world without nuclear arms.'

'Well, that would be nice.'

'I can't sleep, Faith,' he went on with missionary zeal, 'knowing that those weapons of mass destruction are – *out* there.' I discreetly stifled a yawn. Suddenly he reached into his bag again and produced four A3-sized sheets of paper. They were copies of assorted newspaper articles he'd written.

'These are for you too,' he said.

'Oh, well, thanks very much,' I replied. I glanced at them briefly, then put them in my bag. There was a sudden lull in the conversation, and I thought at last he'd ask me something about myself. But he didn't. He simply poured us both another drink, then started talking about a recent trip to Washington.

'I was at a press conference in the State Defence department,' he explained. 'And you know, it was *very* funny, Faith,' – he gave a faux-modest little laugh – 'because the press secretary suddenly said, "But we want to know what Stan Plunkett thinks about this issue!"'

'Gosh. Well – wow!' I said. He shook his head and grinned. And as he rattled on again I looked at him across the table and thought, he isn't attractive at all. I could see now that his jaw receded badly, and that when he smiled he had three or four chins. He had thin lips too, and small, yellowing teeth, and he talked in this excitable kind of way. He was as boring as hell, I thought crossly. And he wasn't even that bright. Yet he was so boastful – he talked only about himself. Peter had never bored on about his career. He'd always been so modest about what he'd achieved. He'd think this guy was a plonker, I thought as he rattled away. I realised now that this was the only reason he'd asked me out. I was no more than a human mirror in which he could admire his heroic reflection. I glanced discreetly at my watch and saw that it was nearly nine.

'I'm afraid I'll have to go now,' I said. 'I have an appointment with my pillow. But it was great to meet you,' I added with hypocritical politeness. 'Good luck with saving the world!' Then I went home and dropped his report, and his articles, into the bin.

'What a bore!' said Lily when I phoned to tell her about my date.

'He seemed to have a Superman complex,' I said. 'I half expected him to dash into a phonebox and emerge wearing pants over his tights.'

'What an egomaniac!' she said contemptuously. 'And as though anyone's going to be impressed, when these days the nuclear threat is, quite frankly, *vieux chapeau*. Mind you . . .' she went on suddenly. 'Maybe . . . yes . . . maybe it's due for a revival!'

'What?'

'Yes,' she said. 'It is. I've just hit on something – the Cold

144

War is due for a comeback. *Moi!* should do a special. Yes,' she said animatedly, 'we could call it *Nucleaire*, or rather, *New-Cleaire*. We could do fashion shoots with those lovely Russian greatcoats and Brezhnev hats,' she went on enthusiastically, 'and of course those absolutely *fabulous* furs. We could get it sponsored by La Maison de la Fausse Fourrure,' she went on excitedly. 'We could do an interior design section on converted bunkers –'

'Lily –'

'And we could have a competition to win a cruise. We'll do it in November. What a *brilliant* idea, Faith. I'd never have thought of it without you. But, Faith darling,' she added carefully, 'you really mustn't date second-rate creeps like that again. Now, have you got anyone else lined up?'

'No,' I said. 'I haven't.'

'What about that man you two-fingered in the Brompton Road? Now, he *really* liked you,' she said.

'Well, I didn't like him,' I replied, as I absent-mindedly opened my bag and took out his business card.

'I thought he was rather tasty,' she added. 'I think you should give him a chance.'

'I have absolutely, categorically, not the slightest intention of doing so at all whatso*ever*,' I said as I read his name again. Josiah Cartwright, I mused as I put the phone down. Josiah – that's unusual these days. So, just out of curiosity, I reached down that book about names and looked it up. And when I saw what it meant I caught my breath and felt the hairs rise up on the back of my neck. Josiah is a Hebrew name, I read, meaning 'God heals'. God heals? God *heals*. My pulse was suddenly racing and my skin was covered in tiny bumps. 'God will heal your pain,' the psychic had said to me. 'God will heal your pain.' This was a *sign*. That's what it was – a sign! It was a sign that I was meant to move on. I looked at the card again, read the address and telephone number, then went straight to the phone and dialled. It rang twice, then picked up and I heard this rather nice voice: 'I'm very sorry I'm not here,' it said, 'but *please* do leave me a message after the beeps, and I absolutely *promise* I'll ring you straight back.' He sounded so straightforward, and normal, and kind. I blushed to think of how I'd screamed at him. And now I heard the tone beeping quite a few times – lots of messages – then it suddenly stopped and I spoke.

'Look,' I said, 'I know this will sound funny. But a week ago you gave me your card – we were at traffic lights in the Brompton Road. And I wasn't very polite to you. In fact I was extremely rude – you see I was a bit taken aback. Erm, my name's Faith, by the way. Anyway, as I say, I know this probably sounds very silly, and you probably think I'm an awful woman, but if you wanted to give me a ring sometime, well, that would be fine.' Then I read out my phone number and hung up.

Within twenty-four hours I was regretting my spontaneity with all my heart. I hadn't heard back. Not that day. Or the next. Or the next. 'I'm a fool,' I said to myself between weather forecasts as I sat at my desk at work. I was in agonies of insecurity, mingled with a kind of shame. 'What a stupid, naïve thing to do,' I breathed as I began to flick through the *Independent*. 'I have given a totally strange man my home telephone number – I must be absolutely round the twist. But then it's hardly surprising,' I told myself as I turned the pages of the newspaper. 'After all, I'm in the middle of a major marital crisis so I feel vulnerable and obviously I'm not thinking straight, and I –' My heart stopped dead in its tracks. Oh God. Oh God. This was beyond mere coincidence. This was *spooky*. I had entered the Twilight Zone. For now I found myself staring at a large black-and-white photo captioned *Josiah Cartwright*. I was so shocked my contact lenses nearly fell out. There was an interview with him, on the arts pages, headlined, 'Cartwright Brings Magic to the Royal Exchange'. I could hear my heart drumming as my eyes devoured the page. *Stunning design for* The Tempest . . . *Cartwright's striking visual imagination . . . dense, rich, surrealist . . . hottest young designer of his day*.

The piece explained that he was thirty-seven, born in Coventry, studied at the Slade, and that in addition to being an accomplished fine artist, he was much in demand in the theatre. In the photo he looked casually handsome, wearing a sports jacket and open shirt. His hair was dark blond and fairly long, and he had large, expressive grey eyes. He was smiling sheepishly at the camera, as though slightly surprised by the attention. *I guess I've been very lucky* . . . he was quoted as saying. *I'm passionate about what I do* . . . *The director's wishes always come first*, he added. Oh, *that* was a nice thing to say. He was also generous about other designers. *Carl Toms was a genius* . . . *I'm a huge admirer of William Dudley. Stephanos Lazaridis' work is just wonderful.* I thought that that was great. I photocopied the article and tucked it into my bag, feeling more than a little disturbed. Then I went back down to the studio and forced myself to concentrate, trying to ignore, as usual, Terry's persecution of Sophie. Darryl really ought to put his foot down, but he never does. Today Terry hijacked another of her interviews and criticised her, yet again, on screen. Then a news item went down, so I had to fill, and the white-water rafting labrador was late. And Iqbal needed jollying along because he's having trouble with his boyfriend, Wilf, so it was a pretty stressful morning all in all, which enabled me to banish Josiah from my mind.

By the time we came off air I was glad to get home and rest. I went to bed, knowing now that he wouldn't ring. When I woke at one, I mooched around the house in my nightie, feeling mournful again about Peter and gazing at things he'd left behind. There were two old sports jackets hanging in the hall – I inhaled their familiar musty smell. Beneath them were his gumboots – he takes a size ten – I put my foot in one. The house still reverberated with his presence. I kept imagining him coming through the door. I'd think of things during the day that I wanted to tell him, and then remember that he wasn't here. I felt hollow and empty – not just bereft, but *bereaved* – it was almost as though he was dead. To distract myself from my bleakness I watched some cretinous daytime show. As I sat there gawping at the screen I absent-mindedly put my hand down the side of the sofa, felt something soft, and up came one of his socks. And now, as I held it in both hands, I felt my eyes brim with tears. The dynamic of our marriage had been changed for ever, and we would never get back what we'd had. My mother always says that action is the best antidote to despair, so I forced myself to get dressed and I went into the garden to do a little hard pruning. And as I clipped away at the clematis and the ceanothus I gave myself a good talking to. I am going to recover from this, I vowed. I am going to endure the pain. I have made the right decision to end our marriage, but before long I *will* move on. After all, I told myself, I have a lot of life still to live. Now, feeling stronger and more cheerful I planted the Stargazer lilies, while Graham did his Sphinx impression on the lawn. And as I stood back to admire my work, the phone suddenly rang out.

'Is that Faith?' said a cultivated male voice.

'Yes,' I said. 'It is.'

'Well.' He began to laugh. 'I, er . . . Well . . .' he tried again. By now my cheeks felt warm and I was smiling too. 'Look,' he said, 'oh dear, this is a bit difficult, but, well, it's Josiah Cartwright here.'

'Yes,' I said. 'I know it's you. Hello!' I said with a laugh.

'Hello,' he chuckled back. 'I've just got your message, Faith. Of *course* I remember. How could I forget? And yes . . . I'd *love* to meet up!'

April

I hardly ever go to church. Perhaps I'm making up for all those years of going to Mass every day at St Bede's. Oh yes, we had masses of Masses – enough to last for the rest of our lives. But though I'm more or less lapsed these days, I can never quite give it up. Once a Catholic, they say, and it's true. Though I haven't been to confession for over ten years; I'm not really sure what I'd say. When I was young, I rather enjoyed it. I liked coming out of that little wooden box feeling spiritually squeaky clean. The nuns taught us that our souls were like pure white shirts which got besmirched with daily wear. They explained that venial sins made little spots – like felt-tip, or fried egg or tea. But mortal sins, they said, made nasty big stains, like ketchup or black paint, or oil. They said that going to confession was just like putting our souls in the washing machine. And when Lily asked which cycle they should go on – sixty degrees or forty – they made her write out 'I will not be facetious' two hundred times. But the rest of us believed that after confession our souls would be shiny and new. I still like to think that it's true. Sometimes I'm tempted to do something really sinful, then confess just to have that smug feeling of being absolved. But no, I'm not a great Catholic. As I say, I rarely go to Mass, but at Christmas and at Easter, I do. And as Peter was having the children and Graham for Easter Day, I phoned Lily to see if she'd come.

'We could go to Westminster Cathedral,' I suggested.

'Thanks but no thanks,' she replied, 'I've already booked to go to Holy Trinity Brompton.'

'That's C of E,' I said, surprised.

'Ye-es,' she replied judiciously. 'But I think I'm an Anglican waiting to happen.'

'I know the real reason,' I added with a knowing laugh. 'You think there'll be some nice men there.'

'Faith!' She sounded shocked. 'What a suspicious creature you are these days. Mind you,' she added, audibly drawing on a cheroot, 'there is *rather* a tasty vicar. But the point is they've got a very nice crèche there where I can leave Jennifer Aniston.'

So on Easter Sunday I went to church alone. I decided to go to my local one, St Edward's, in the Chiswick High Road. At ten thirty I sat there in a pew halfway down on the right, inhaling the pungent but familiar Catholic aroma of incense and beeswax and dust. I looked at the huge crucifix, and the statuary, and at the flames of the votive candles bending in the breeze. And I began to think about what had happened to me in the past three months.

'Lord have mercy,' said the priest. I mean, in January I was a perfectly happily married woman. *Christ have mercy*. Three months on I find I'm a betrayed wife, several steps down the road to divorce. *Lord have mercy*. With my husband residing elsewhere. *Let us pray*. As we bowed our heads to ponder the miracle of the Resurrection, I wondered if my marriage could be resurrected, though I still didn't think that it could. Because Andie was somehow *there* now, in our marriage, making it, to quote, 'a bit crowded'. In any case, the toe-reading psychic had told me that I would definitely get divorced. What a mess it all was. What a mess. I forced myself to concentrate on the service as we stood up to say the Creed.

We believe in one God . . . I mean, what's the point of going to church if you're just going to think about other things? *The Father, the Almighty* . . . Though I found myself wondering how often Peter sees that American cow. *Maker of heaven and earth* . . . I never ask him because quite frankly I don't want to know. *Of all that is, seen and unseen* . . . But one thing's for sure – if he is seeing her, then *I'm* entitled to see people too. *We believe in one Lord, Jesus Christ, the only Son of God* . . . And I thought about how much I was looking forward to seeing Josiah. *Eternally begotten of the father.* He's working in Manchester at the moment. *God from God, Light from Light* . . . Which is why he didn't return my call . . . *True God from true God* . . . But then he heard my message on his answerphone and phoned me up from there. *Of one being with the Father* . . . I know – amazing! *And through him all things were made.* He obviously makes brilliant sets. *For us men and for our salvation he came down from heaven* . . . He's heavenly looking. *And was made man* . . . Yes, he's a *very* attractive man. *For our sake he was crucified under Pontius Pilate.* Wonder if he's ever been married? *He suffered death and was buried.* Probably has. *Together with the Father* . . . Wonder if he's got any kids? *He is worshipped and glorified.* I bet he'd be a *great* dad. *We believe in one Holy Catholic and Apostolic Church* . . . He's got such lovely grey eyes. *We profess one baptism for the remission of sins* . . . Gorgeous smile, too. *We look for the resurrection of the dead* . . . I feel *so* much better since he phoned me. *And the life of the world to come.* Ah. Men.

'And now a reading from the Old Testament,' the priest continued as we all sat down. Suddenly I sat bolt upright. I couldn't believe my ears – it was all about Josiah.

'Josiah reigned thirty-one years in Jerusalem,' said the reader. This is another sign, I thought breathlessly as I sat forward on the edge of my pew. 'And Josiah did what was right in the eyes of the Lord . . . And he did not turn aside either to the right hand or to the left.' The passage was all about what a great king Josiah was, and about how he destroyed the idols and graven images that the Israelites had set up and about how he unfortunately had to slay quite a few people too. And in the sermon the priest took up this theme and explained that Josiah was a force for renewal, and how he turned people from spiritual infidelity to faithfulness. And I thought, God is *definitely* trying to tell me something here. I'd been the victim of infidelity, and now Josiah had arrived to heal my pain. But then, before Communion, as we all offered each other the Sign of Peace, I found my thoughts turning to Peter once more. 'Peace be with you . . .' we said to each other. That's what it's like these days. I have this kind of Janus vision, in which I'm looking both forwards and back. 'Peace be with you,' we all mumbled as we sheepishly shook hands. 'Peace be with you.' Could our marriage be saved? I wondered. I don't know. I don't know.

By seven o'clock that evening I had a pretty good idea. The children had come back clutching smart carrier bags, inside which were the most enormous Easter eggs I'd ever seen. They were from Godiva and must have cost a bomb. Moreover Graham had a huge pack of Good Boy! doggy chocs.

'That was nice of Dad to buy you those,' I said as I began to prepare their supper.

'Oh, they're not from Dad, Mum,' said Katie.

'Aren't they?' I said, surprised.

'No,' said Matt as he pulled the velvet ribbon off his. 'Andie gave them to us.'

'Andie?' I said. My mouth was so pinched I could hardly pronounce her name.

'Yes,' said Katie. 'Andie. We met her today.'

'Oh!' I said viciously. 'I *see*! And where, pray, did you meet her?'

'At Dad's flat,' Matt explained. 'If you think these eggs are good, Mum, then you should have seen the one she gave *him*!'

'At his flat?' I spat. The harlot was trying to corrupt my children. I had visions of her disporting herself semi-naked in front of the kids.

'Don't worry, Mum,' said Katie. 'They weren't doing anything. She wasn't even invited. She just dropped round to give us the goods.'

'Why would she do that if she's never even met you before?'

'Because they're sweeteners of course,' Katie explained with weary patience. 'Bribes, if you prefer. It's classic aspirant step-parental behaviour,' she went on knowledgeably as she broke off a large chunk of chocolate. 'Potential partners try to ingratiate themselves with their romantic target's offspring in order

152

to conquer their natural hostility and to gain acceptance. But don't worry, Mum,' she added brightly, 'it won't cut any ice with Matt or me.'

'And it especially won't cut any ice with Graham,' said Matt contemptuously. 'She didn't even give him *real* chocolate.'

'I will not have Andie having anything to do with the children!' I hissed as Peter and I arrived at Resolve three days later. It was in a tall, narrow, mid-house halfway down Wimpole Street. 'Don't you dare involve them again!'

'Hello, may I help you?' said the receptionist pleasantly as we stood by the desk.

'Look, she just turned up unexpectedly,' Peter explained wearily. 'I didn't know she was going to do that.'

'It's bad enough that you're seeing that ... *bitch*,' I spat, 'without dragging in the children – and Graham.'

'Do you have an appointment?'

'I didn't drag them in,' he groaned.

'Exposing them to her like that!'

'She's not a disease, you know.'

'Can I help you?'

'Allowing them to get emotionally confused.'

'They're *not* confused,' he said.

'They bloody well are,' I lied. 'They were ... traumatised when they got home.'

'No they damn well weren't!'

'What name is it, please?'

'I don't like you seeing her,' I snarled.

'Why *shouldn't* I see her?' he shot back. 'After all, you've thrown me out.'

'OK. OK. That's true. But why then, as you evidently *are* still seeing her, did you want me to come to Resolve? Mmm?'

'Because ... because ... oh, because I don't know what's going to happen,' he said, running his left hand through his hair.

'Oh, I see,' I said sarcastically, 'just hedging your bets, are you? Well, Peter, let me tell you right now that you can't have your crumpet and eat it!'

'Er, sir, madam . . .'

'Yes, what *is* it?' we both snapped.

'May I take your names?'

'Oh. We're Mr and Mrs Smith.'

'Is that your real name?'

'Yes.'

'And you're here to try and save your marriage?'

'Correct.'

'Well, Ms Strindberg will see you in ten minutes,' she crooned, 'so please take a seat next door.' The large waiting room was furnished with reproduction antiques and vases full of faded dried flowers. On the chairs arranged against the walls sat six couples, purse-lipped and hatchet-faced in an atmosphere of furtiveness and mild shame. To distract myself I flicked through the magazines, most of which were long out of date. There was the *Chat* magazine win-a-divorce issue, and the December issue of *Moi!* I reached for *Marie Claire* and as I did so I suddenly looked up and – oh my *God*! – Samantha and Ed from number nine. Good Lord! I always thought they were the perfect couple, we'd been to their parties once or twice. I felt my face flush red. How embarrassing for them, I reflected, being spotted like that at Resolve! Samantha gave me a tight little smile which I returned with as much warmth as the situation would allow; and I was just wondering whether I should add, 'Nice to see you,' or something of that kind when suddenly I heard voices. They were coming from the door to our left, marked 'Ms Zillah Strindberg'. Inside, things were clearly hotting up. At first we could only catch certain words, 'reconciliation . . . rubbish! . . . get over it . . . quite ridiculous! . . . try again . . . don't bother! . . .' Oh dear, oh dear. The couple clearly weren't getting on at all. And now, as everyone stiffened into silence, we could hear what they were saying quite distinctly.

'We've really been working it all out.'

'Oh yes?'

'And we've decided we don't want to get divorced.'

'What?'

'Yes, we've decided to stay together,' said a male voice now.

'Well, I really don't think you should.'

'No, really Ms Strindberg, we've taken a long, hard look at ourselves.'

'You don't know what you're saying.'

'And we've decided to make a go of it.'

'I've heard *that* before.'

'You see, we'd let the *little* issues get in the way.'

'They're not that little, you know.'

'Of the larger fact?'

'What larger fact?'

'Well, that we're still in love.'

'That's got *nothing* to do with it!'

'So thanks very much for your help, but we're going to stay together after all.'

'No, I'm sorry,' we heard Zillah Strindberg say, more stridently now, 'but I think you *should* get divorced.'

'No, we really don't want to.'

'Because it's crystal clear to me . . .'

'Honestly, we've just decided.'

'That you're *totally* incompatible.'

'No, we're not.'

'Yes you are.'

'No we're not. We get on terribly well.'

'I'm sorry!' we heard her almost shout. 'But I really *don't* think you do. In fact I'm confident that you should split up.'

'But we don't *want* to split up any more. We did. But now we don't.'

'Look,' we heard her say, 'in my view –' Suddenly the door flew open and the couple left at a brisk trot. Then Zillah Strindberg emerged looking visibly flustered, her bony cheeks flushed with red. She smoothed down her hair, consulted her clipboard, then delicately cleared her throat. 'Mr and Mrs Smith, please,' she enunciated with a tight little smile. Peter and I looked at each other, and fled.

*   *   *

155

'There's a really good band of rain coming in,' I said as I pressed the clicker on Monday.

'God, Faith's lost a bit of weight. Ten . . .'

'So a rather dismal start to the day.'

'She looks almost shaggable these days. Eight . . .'

'If we take a look at the radar picture now.'

'You know why she's thin, of course. Seven . . .'

'We can see those April showers pushing through.'

'*Big* problems with her marriage. Six . . .'

'So it's looking rather unsettled.'

'He's been bonking an American. In five . . .'

'Especially in London W4.'

'Three. So she chucked him out. And two . . .'

'Though there might just be a chink of sunshine.'

'My sister spotted them at Resolve. One . . .'

'But don't hold your breath.'

'She lives in the same road.'

'So there we have it. See you at nine.'

'Any chance they'll stay together?'

'Zero.'

'Thank you, Faith,' said Sophie with a lovely smile. 'You're watching AM-UK! And now, at eight thirty, here are the national headlines . . .'

I felt sick and shaky as I unplugged my mike. Oh God, oh God, they all knew. They knew everything. And I'd tried so hard to be *discreet*. I went up to the office and made myself look busy by tidying my desk. In any case it needed it – there were piles of faxes and memos and three old coffee cups, and my piece of seaweed had fallen off its hook, and my weather house was covered with dust. Peter bought it for me when I first got the job at AM-UK! I had been temping there for three months when the vacancy came up. And the children were at school by then so I was thrilled to get the job. And Peter bought me the weather house. It's like a tiny Swiss chalet, and inside is a little man in lederhosen and a little woman in a dirndl skirt. And the little man is holding up an umbrella. And when he comes out, and the woman stays in, that means it's going to rain. When the little woman comes out, and the man stays in, then that means it's going to be fine. But sometimes, when the weather's a nice mix, then they both come out together. Today the little man was right out, all alone with his brolly aloft. There's a metaphor in that, I thought bleakly as I opened my pile of mail.

The first letter was hard to read as the writing was a mess. But I soon got the gist. *You think you're so marvelus don't you?* wrote the sender, Mark from Solihull. *But beleeve me, yore not.* Oh God, this was all I needed – an illiterate prat. *I don't 'have Faith' in you*, he went on with ignorant contempt. *Nor does anyone else I no. Everywear i go i hear peeple saying how useless you are at the weather and you all ways get it rong. i hear them slagging you off in the bus queues, in the queue for the chekout, at the pictures, and down the pub.* I hear it at work. All day. That Faith's no good, they all say – For God's sake! I tore it up and threw it into the bin. The other letters at least were quite flattering, most of them commenting on my recent loss of weight. *Don't lose too much*, advised Mrs Brown from Stafford. *We don't want you looking like Posh Spice. Frankly I preferred you fat*, said Mr Stephenson from Stoke. *The longer hair's nice*, opined Mrs Daft from Derby, *but I should grow out the layers if I were you. How are rainbows formed please?* asked ten-year-old Alfie from Hove. *So sorry to hear about your marital problems*, wrote Mrs Davenport from Kent. WHAT? *I've just read about it in* Hello! her letter went on. *So I felt I had to drop you a line. I got myself divorced last July. It's hell, Faith, but I know you'll come through.* I ran, heart pounding, to the planning desk and got out this week's *Hello!* There, in the celebrity news section, was a small photo of me, with the caption, *Storm Clouds Gathering for Weather Girl.* But who the *hell* had told them? *AM-UK!'s Faith Smith is set to divorce her publisher husband Peter after he confessed to a fling. Our source tells us that a distraught Faith holds out no hope for her marriage, despite attempts at counselling. Peter Smith's new job as head of Bishopsgate may now be in jeopardy as the firm is owned by Bible Belt Americans with strict views about their workers' private lives.*

I threw it in the bin, then went back to my desk and cradled my head in my hands. Here it was, in the public domain, for everyone to see. But who could have told them, I wondered, and *why*? *Hello!* don't pay for tips. In any case it's not as though I'm a real celebrity, so why would anyone care? I mean . . . Oh. *Oh*. Of course. How slow of me. It must have been Andie – the cow! She's trying to make damn sure that Peter and I do split up. No question of her just leaving us to sort it out between ourselves; just giving it a little helpful push in the media. That American spinster was spinning, because of course it wasn't really *Hello!* she wanted for Peter and me – it was *Goodbye*! I read the piece again. *A distraught Faith* . . . I am *not* distraught I thought, as a hot tear splashed onto my cheek. *Holds out no hope* . . . I am not hopeless, I said to myself as my contact lenses slipped down. In fact I am coping *very* well with this horrible situation, I reflected as I ran, head down, to the ladies' loo. Thank God. No-one here. I went into a cubicle, lowered the seat, then sat there and wept like a child. My breath came in shuddering gasps and my face felt hot and wet. Then I pulled the flush and came out, only to see someone standing there. I pushed my lenses back into place, and the badly blurred figure became clear. 'Faith!' Sophie exclaimed softly. 'It's you. I heard you crying. But what on earth's wrong?'

'Nothing's wrong,' I wept.

'Yes it is,' she said as I walked to the basin. 'What's the problem?' she asked. Oh God, I didn't want to tell her, it was far too personal. 'You can tell me,' she said as I splashed cold water onto my face. 'Please tell me what's happened,' she repeated as I lifted my swollen face to the glass. I sighed.

'I've just had some nasty fan mail, that's all.'

'Oh. Well, at least you *get* fan mail,' she exclaimed cheerfully. 'All mine seems to have stopped. But I really don't think it's worth crying about,' she added. 'Are you sure there isn't anything else?'

'No, no, no,' I said as I pulled down a green paper towel. 'It's just, well, you know how it is here with the awful hours. If things go wrong, you get more upset.'

'Yes, but what's gone wrong, Faith?' she asked. 'Perhaps I

can help.' She laid a hand on my arm and I stared at her, my throat aching with a suppressed sob. She was swimming out of focus again as my eyes began to fill.

'I'm getting divorced,' I croaked. Through my tears I could see that Sophie's face registered sympathy but not the slightest trace of surprise. She already knew. That was clear. It was obvious that everyone at work knew. 'But the reason I'm crying,' I went on, 'is because I just saw a piece about it in *Hello!* And seeing it like that, in black and white, made it suddenly *real*. It was in the papers!' I groaned. 'You can't imagine how awful that feels.'

'I can imagine,' said Sophie, flinching. 'I'd be *terrified* of having *my* private life exposed. I mean, my God!' she added with an appalled little laugh. 'The tabloids would have a field day with me!'

'I'm getting divorced,' I sobbed as fresh tears snaked down my face.

'Faith,' said Sophie softly. She put her arm round my shaking shoulders. 'Faith, do you really have to?' I stared at the floor. Did I *have* to?

'Yes,' I gasped. 'I do.'

'Why?' *Why*?

'Because my husband's had an . . . affair,' I wept. 'And I can't get over it. I just can't forget it. I feel that everything is *spoiled*.'

'I know we don't know each other very well,' said Sophie as she handed me a tissue, 'but can I give you some advice?'

'OK,' I croaked, aware at the same time, with a degree of embarrassment, that she was more than ten years younger than me.

'I've been in the situation that your husband's in,' she explained. Oh. It must have been with that chap, Alex. 'I was recently unfaithful to someone. I was completely in the wrong, and I'm afraid that someone found out. And,' she hesitated now – this was obviously hard, 'that someone can't forgive and forget. Now, I'm not married so there's no divorce, but it's still –' She sighed bitterly. '– a *mess*.' I looked at her as my sobs subsided, grateful for her confession, especially as she was normally so private about her affairs. Sharing a confidence like that can't have been easy, and she only did it to help.

'If you are able to forgive him, then do,' she advised me, 'because I believe you'll be happier if you can.'

'Well, maybe,' I murmured. 'I don't know. But you've been very kind, Sophie, thanks.'

Suddenly we heard the flush of a cistern, one of the cubicles opened and to our surprise Tatiana emerged.

'Yes, Sophie,' she said with a smirk. 'Thanks *very* much indeed.'

There's one thing we weather forecasters always do when we leave the house. We look up at the sky. We can always tell what's going to happen, you see, by the shape of the clouds. For example, if there are cirrus, then we know it's going to be fine. They're long and wispy, and very high, and made of ice, and we sometimes call them mares' tails. If we see cumulonimbus then we know stormy weather is on the way. Those are great barrelling black clouds, and they give thunder and lightning and rain. Then there are stratus, which are flat blanketing layers of grey producing drizzle or fog. But today, as I made my way to Rory Cheetham-Stabb's office, the sky was filled with puffy white cumulus. I love cumulus clouds because they produce my favourite weather – a mixture of sunshine and showers. At this time of year you look up and you see big clouds, like billowing cushions, with clear blue sky between; and the clouds can be grey or white, and sometimes they're tinged with gold. And the gusting spring winds make them rip through the sky, giving sudden bursts of rain. Then, when the shower passes and the sun comes out, that's when rainbows appear. So I always love to see cumulus, and that's what I saw today. I like being able to look up like that and see at a glance what's on the cards. If only it were that easy when it comes to my private life. I'm not making any forecasts there. Oh no, the satellite picture is not at all clear. On the one hand the wheels are turning towards divorce, and I can hear them creak and grind. But on the other hand it's just so *terrible* that I'm tempted to try and go back. I thought about what Sophie had said. I thought about all that's at stake. And Peter is clearly hesitating, too. But things have changed so much between us that I just don't know what to do. It's as though our marriage has crash-landed and now we're both trying to find the black box.

'The only reason your husband is hesitating,' said Rory Cheetham-Stabb as I sat in his office an hour later, 'is because he knows what it's going to cost him.'

'Oh,' I said with a pang. 'I thought it might be because he loves me and hopes to be reconciled.'

'Mrs Smith,' said Rory Cheetham-Stabb patiently. 'I don't wish to sound cynical, but that's what happens to husbands when the chips go down – they start to squeal like stuck pigs. What they'd all like, of course, is to be able to have it both ways. They'd like to hang on to their marriages while keeping their totty in tow. Tell me, would you find that acceptable?' I shook my head. 'And the other reason he may be hesitating is because he knows that divorce might affect his new job.'

'So you saw the piece in *Hello!*' I said, dismally.

'Yes,' he said. 'I did.'

'Well, he's on six months' probation so the timing of all this just couldn't be worse. Believe me,' I added, 'we've got our problems, but I don't want him to get fired.'

'Nor do I,' said Cheetham-Stabb. 'I mean, he's our golden goose. After all, Mrs Smith, you've been a devoted wife. For fifteen years you've been flashing your loyalty card and now you're hoping for a little . . . cashback.' I found myself wondering what sort of card Andie has. An Unfair Advantage card, no doubt.

'As it happens, I know quite a bit about Bishopsgate,' I heard Rory Cheetham-Stabb say. 'They're a bloody irritating bunch. They publish all these absurd books about how-to-save-your-marriage. That's how they got started. They're owned by an American newspaper consortium from Georgia. The chairman, Jack Price, is a bit of Puritan – he doesn't like his staff having messy private lives. He maintains that it's at odds with Bishopsgate's image, and it probably is. So he certainly won't like the fact that his brand new managing director is up Separation Creek. Your husband doesn't want any personal trouble until his probationary period is up. But I wonder who fed it to the press?'

'I think it's Andie Metzler,' I said.

'Mmm. But who else knows?'

'Well, it could have been someone who saw us at Resolve. And we did have this awful row in Le Caprice on Valentine's Day. But on the other hand, we're not famous so it's not a big story. And the point is that whoever fed this stuff to the press would have had some motive, so I think it *must* be Andie.'

'Why?'

'Because she's desperate for Peter to get divorced.' Cheetham-Stabb steepled his fingertips and narrowed his pale-blue eyes.

'I doubt it's her, Mrs Smith. Remember, your husband is not just her lover – he's her client. If he gets fired before the end of his probationary period, she'll have to refund her huge fee. No, that theory just doesn't make sense.'

'You're probably right,' I sighed. 'In any case, she's clearly mad about him so she wouldn't want him to get sacked.' But Cheetham-Stabb wasn't listening to me. He had a faraway look in his eyes.

'Actually – I think you're right!' he suddenly exclaimed. 'Yes!' he said. 'I've just worked it out. It *is* her, Mrs Smith. But what a very cunning woman she must be.'

'What do you mean?'

'She wants Peter to divorce you, but at the same time she doesn't want him to lose his job. So what she'll be doing is quietly assuring Bishopsgate, with whom she'll still be in touch, that Peter's private life will be normalised quite soon when he . . .'

'Marries her?'

'Exactly.' I thought I was going to throw up. 'That way,' Cheetham-Stabb went on, 'it gives her an additional hold over your husband. It means she can subtly put pressure on him to make things official whilst ensuring that his divorce stays firmly on track.'

'What a brilliant scheme,' I said wearily. 'But then she set out to get Peter and she's not going to stop at anything. She's on probation herself,' I added, 'and she knows it. She's after a permanent contract, too. But how do you know all this about Bishopsgate?'

'Because Jack Price's ex-wife is British – I did her divorce last year.'

'He's divorced!'

'Oh yes, Mrs Smith. She'd endured his womanising for thirty years and felt that was quite long enough.'

'But if he's divorced, why is he so puritanical about what his staff do?'

'Because hypocrisy is a luxury he can easily afford. Yes, I got rather a nice result there,' he added as he lit a cigar. 'I got Mrs Price eight million. That's pounds, not dollars, by the way. Now,' he said, 'let's press on, shall we, with stage two of *your* divorce! This is the Statement of Arrangements,' he explained as he pushed a white form towards me. 'Just sign it there, at the bottom, would you, Mrs Smith? That's it. That's it. Splendid!'

'Take him for everything you can get,' said Lily when I went round to her flat last night feeling downcast and confused. She'd insisted on kitting me out for my date with Josiah. She reached into her gleaming Smeg fridge and pulled out a bottle of champagne and some canapés while Jennifer grunted at her feet.

'Don't beg, darling,' she said as she slipped the dog a piece of foie gras. 'I mean, I really don't want to comment negatively on Peter's *appalling* behaviour,' she added as she got down two glasses. 'But this situation is entirely his fault.'

'Yes,' I said dismally. 'I know. But I don't want to be one of these grasping wives, Lily. I just want, you know, *enough*.'

'Oh, don't be ridiculous,' she said contemptuously. 'Peter should be made to pay! Let Rory Cheetham-Stabb get what he can,' she added.

'Maybe,' I said. 'I don't know.'

'Has Peter got a solicitor?'

'Yes, he has.'

'Oh well, let them fight it out.'

As Lily cracked open the bottle of Laurent Perrier I surveyed the hand-distressed kitchen with its blond wooden floors and gleaming granite worktops and its shining juice-squeezers and espresso machines. The flat could double as a shoot for *Ideal Home*. We went through to the huge sitting room, with its expanse of white carpet and its towering arrangements of scarlet amaryllis, and its Damien Hirst spin painting and the Elisabeth Frink horse on its marble plinth. And magazines, of course. Everywhere. They shone on every available surface and spilled casually onto the floor; their covers glinted like glass under the downlighters which spangled the ceiling like stars. We picked our way carefully over them, clutching our flutes of champagne.

'You've been married for fifteen years,' Lily said as she produced three large bags of designer clothes. 'So you deserve *lots* of lovely maintenance, Faith – and then we can have some fun!'

'Can we?' I said doubtfully as she opened up the first bag.

'Oh yes,' she said. 'You're going to do all the things you never did before. Proper shopping, for a start,' she said with a laugh. 'No more looking in Oxfam for you!'

'But I like Oxfam,' I said. 'Ooh, is that a Clements Ribeiro shirt?'

'No more Principles, either.'

'But I love Principles,' I replied as I pounced on a pair of Cerruti jeans.

'We can go to parties, and nightclubs,' she went on happily. 'We can be girls about town. We can do all the things we said we'd do when we were young – things you've so tragically missed out on all these years.'

'I'm not sure I've been missing out on anything,' I said as I tried on a Prada silk top. 'Anyway, nightclubs aren't really me,' I added, 'I'm all for a quiet sort of life.'

'But look at *my* life!' said Lily zealously as she passed me an Agnès B shirt. 'Just look at my mantelpiece!' I looked. It was white with invitations. They were stacked up like tiny billboards, advertising the success, oh yes, the huge success, of Lily's social life. She picked her way over the gleaming magazines and began to read them out.

'Monday – book launch at The Ivy; Tuesday – drinks do at Home House for Tibet; Wednesday – a fashion show in aid of Dolls Against Addiction; Thursday – *three* private views; Friday – dinner with Tom and Nicole; Saturday, a bash for Marie Helvin at Tramp.'

'I get the picture,' I said.

'But Faith, this could be your life, too,' she said warmly.

'No – I'm not glamorous enough. In any case, do you really enjoy it, Lily? Do you really *know* any of these people?'

'No. I only stay a few minutes at each one.'

'Then what on earth's the point?'

'The point *is* that I was *there*.'

'But doesn't it ever wear thin, Lily, staggering from one party to another? Don't you ever just want to settle down?'

'Settle down?' She looked stupefied. 'I'd rather go to my own autopsy.'

'But are you really *happy*, Lily?' I added.

'Oh, *yes*. I'm as happy as a bulimic at a buffet. Screw Peter for every penny you can get,' she added firmly.

'Oh, I don't know, Lily. In any case I'm not sure how much money there's going to be because there's a chance Peter could lose his job.' I hadn't meant to tell Lily about that, but I guess the champagne had loosened my tongue. 'He might get fired,' I explained.

'Really?' said Lily, with calm surprise. 'That would be terrible. Now, why don't you try on this Miu Miu coat?'

'You see, there was a piece in *Hello!*' I went on as I took off my Laura Ashley skirt.

'*Was* there?' she said. 'What did it say?'

'It said we were having problems and that Peter's job might be on the line.'

'Why?'

'Because Bishopsgate don't like their staff getting in a marital mess. Peter's only on a twelve-month contract,' I explained. 'If there's anything more in the press about our split, his job might not be confirmed.'

'Well, that would be *awful*,' she said sympathetically. 'But surely his transatlantic totty could find him a new job,' she said with a sip of champagne.

'Possibly,' I said. 'But it wouldn't be nearly as good. His value in the market place would be that much lower, having been dumped by Bishopsgate.'

'Yes,' she said, thoughtfully, 'of course. This is a worrying time for you, Faith, but Jennifer and I have lit some candles for you – look!' The Buddhist shrine in the alcove by the fire was aglow with flickering votive lights. 'And we're going to say five decades of the rosary for you. Aren't we, Jen?' Jennifer momentarily lifted her furry face from the sofa, then emitted a porcine snore.

'Aaah!' sighed Lily. 'The poor little darling's exhausted. But then she had a very busy time at the office today.'

'Really?'

'Yes. I've made her contributing editor to *Chienne*. It's a very tough brief. Oh Faith, that looks *lovely*,' she added warmly as she appraised my appearance. 'You know, there really was *quite* a nice figure lurking under all that fat. So Peter might lose his job?' she added.

'Yes. And if he does, then things could get tough for me.'

'Yes,' she said thoughtfully, 'I see. But on the other hand, Faith,' she went on animatedly, 'Andie earns a fortune so she'll be subsidising you in a way – which would only be poetic justice.'

'Mmm . . .'

'And with this change in your life, Faith, you really ought to have more ambition.'

'Like what?'

'To become a regular presenter.'

'I don't want to,' I said. 'I like my little weather bulletins.'

'But, Faith, nothing stays the same,' she said. 'That's the only

166

constant in life. I mean, look how your private life is changing – it's high time you branched out at work as well. Take Ulrika Johnsson, for instance – she was just a weather girl, and now she's a household name.'

'Oh really?'

'And whatshername – Tracey Sunshine – Tanya Bryer – she started out pushing weather symbols about. Look at her now.'

'Mmm.'

'Then there's Gaby Roslin – she was a forecaster, and she's had a fabulous career. And so could you,' she added benignly. 'No, I say it again,' she said as she nibbled on a canapé. 'This divorce is a marvellous chance for you to change your life at *last*!'

'Well, yes, maybe,' I said. 'Maybe you're right.'

'I am right. And I'm going to help you Faith, because I always do.'

'Yes, you do,' I said doubtfully.

'I'm going to get you some really nice coverage in the gossip columns! I'm going to talk you *up*! I'll have you photographed in our society pages – I'll be your unofficial PR. Your life will be transformed,' she went on messianically. 'It will be a new start for you.'

'Ye-es.'

She poured us both another glass of champagne and then lifted hers up. 'To your brilliant, new life, Faith!' she said happily. 'Here's to Faith in the Future!'

'You know, I'm very fond of Lily,' I said to Graham this evening. 'But I do think it's ridiculous the way she anthropomorphises that dog. I mean anyone would think Jennifer Aniston's a human *being*!' I added with a snort. 'I suppose it's because she lives on her own,' I went on, 'so the dog's a substitute person. Now, Graham,' I said as I held up two videos: 'Do you want Gary Rhodes or Keith Floyd?'

Ten minutes later I was on the tube heading towards Tottenham Court Road to meet Josiah. He'd suggested we have a drink at Bertorelli's in Charlotte Street. I felt pretty nervous, but at least I knew I looked good. I was wearing a Versace skirt which skimmed my knees, a pure-white Prada shirt and a gorgeous houndstooth Galliano jacket. I'd hardly recognised myself – was that really me?

'I suppose it is me,' I said wonderingly as I appraised my reflection. 'Now that I've discarded my Principles.' Lily had told me to turn up a little late, so it was just after ten past seven when I walked up the steps and was shown to the bar. There was Josiah, reading *The Week*. Suddenly he looked up, saw me and jumped to his feet. I said hello and held out my hand. And then – and this was lovely – he lifted it to his lips!

'That's to make up for my very ungallant behaviour in the car,' he said with a smile. 'You must have thought I was a terrible spiv.'

'Er, no,' I said, 'not exactly,' and now I was laughing. 'But I was a little bit taken aback.'

'It was very forward of me, I admit it. I don't normally smile at strange women, but you see I thought I *knew* you because I recognised you from the TV. I'm sure that happens to you a lot?' he said.

'Well . . . you know, sometimes,' I replied. I was thrilled.

'And then you reacted so furiously,' he went on, 'and that's what made me laugh. By the time you'd given me the two-fingered treatment I'm afraid I was prostrate before you. I love spirited women,' he added as we sat down.

'Do you?' I said. That was good.

'Oh yes. They present the most wonderful challenge.' He smiled again and his large grey eyes seemed to twinkle and shine. 'Now, I don't know about you, Faith,' he said, 'but I fancy a glass of champagne.'

'I'd like that too,' I replied. And do you know what he asked for – a bottle of Krug!

'Sorry it's only the non-vintage,' he grinned as the ice-bucket arrived. 'But I'm trying to economise.' We sat there for an hour or so, chatting like long-lost friends. I found him so easy to talk to – I felt as though I'd known him for years. He had such lovely manners, too, because every time I started asking him about himself, he'd turn the conversation back to me. And now I noticed, with a quiet thrill, that he was flirting. I could tell because he was mirroring my body language. We both sat, turned in towards each other, with our legs crossed in exactly the same way. When I lifted my glass to my lips, he did the same. When I leaned forward a little, so did he. That woman from the flirting course was right. Having someone unconsciously echoing your movements makes you feel just *great*. What was it she'd said? Oh yes. 'People like people who like *them*.' And now Josiah was smiling at me again, and asking me all about AM-UK!

'I love the way you do the weather,' he said.

'Well, I'm only on for a couple of minutes.'

'Yes, but you do it so well. I especially love the way you smile at us more when you know the weather's going to be vile. May I also say,' he went on, slightly shyly, 'that you're a *lot* prettier in real life. You're a bit slimmer too,' he added thoughtfully. 'But then they say that TV adds a stone.' I didn't explain that the real reason I looked slimmer was because I'd just *lost* a stone. 'You were married, weren't you?' he asked hesitantly. 'I'm sure I read somewhere that you were.'

'Yes. I was,' I replied. 'I still am, but I'm separated,' I explained with a tiny sigh, 'and it looks like we're getting divorced.'

'I'm sorry,' he said tactfully. 'Do you mind very much if I ask you why?'

'No, I don't mind,' I said. And I didn't. 'It's because my husband had an affair.'

'Oh,' he said. 'How awful. That must be very painful for you.'

'It has been,' I agreed. 'It's been hideous. It just happened out of the blue. But I'm coping all right – I think.'

'Now, are you hungry, Faith?' he asked. 'Would you like to have dinner with me?' He held my gaze for a second and I felt a strange warmth suffuse my insides. 'Have dinner with me,' he repeated gently.

'Well, I'd love to,' I smiled. 'You mean here?'

'No, there's an amusing little place just round the corner,' he explained. 'But you'd have to be in an adventurous mood. Are you feeling adventurous tonight?' he added with a grin.

'Yes,' I smiled. 'I am.' So we walked up Charlotte Street, then turned right into Howland Street, then came to Whitfield Street off Fitzroy Square.

'Here it is!' he said. We'd stopped outside a tiny restaurant called The Birdcage. As we walked in, I caught my breath. The interior was tiny – and totally bizarre. Diners sat on richly embroidered armchairs, surrounded by golden Buddhas and Tibetan prayer wheels. On the blood-red walls were stuffed turtles and erotic paintings of naked men. Antique birdcages hung from the walls, while vases of peacock feathers stirred in the slight breeze from the bronze ceiling fan.

'It's fun, isn't it?' he said. 'It's what's known as Oriental fusion. And just wait until you see the food!'

A black waitress in a bright blue wig seated us at a table near the window, upon which was an odd assortment of things – an Indonesian flute, a magnifying glass, and a wind-up plastic bird.

'The theme here is playful,' Josiah explained. 'They like to joke.'

'So I see,' I laughed. Now the waitress brought us two old hardbacks, in the front of which were the folded menus.

'I've got *The Magic Mountain*,' he said, looking at his book. 'How about you?'

'Mine's *The Faerie Queene*,' I replied. And now, as I scanned the menu I thought my eyes would start from my head. 'Juniper-smoked reindeer carpaccio . . . goat consommé with Irish moss . . . whitefish in paperbark with lavender-drenched potato . . . kaballah healing salad.'

I chose the coconut, gold leaf and foie gras soup, while Josiah had the bitter cactus rice knapsacks. The waitress brought us two Iguazu beers, which she proudly informed us contained extract of lizard, and some boiled peacock eggs as a canapé.

'Are these *real* peacock eggs?' I asked. She nodded.

'This is magical,' I breathed.

170

'Magical,' Josiah echoed. 'Magical. That's the word.' And at this he held my gaze again and I felt my face begin to burn. As we ate our strange starters, I got him to talk about himself. He told me about his production of *The Tempest* at the Royal Exchange in Manchester, and about some work he'd done in Milan. He also told me about his commission to design the Royal Opera's new production of *Madame Butterfly*.

'So you're in demand,' I said as I toyed with my square of gold leaf.

'Yes,' he said, 'I guess I am. I know that I'm very lucky. But do you know, Faith, what really makes me happy is just to paint.'

'What kind of painting do you do?'

'I specialise in trompe l'oeil,' he explained as our main courses arrived. 'I do murals to commission. There's nothing I love more than to put a gorgeous Tuscan landscape on the wall of a British bathroom, or to paint a piece of Morocco into someone's dining room. I can give them a whole new perspective,' he said. 'I can really open their eyes.'

'And you?' I added with sudden boldness as I toyed with my seaweed and hemp risotto. 'What about *your* private life?'

'What about it?' he said with a shrug.

'Have you ever been married?' He shook his head. 'Did you ever come close?' He smiled.

'I've had relationships, of course, though I'm no playboy. But I guess I've never met anyone who I felt I could commit myself to. It's such a huge thing, isn't it, Faith? From this day forward, and all that. "Until death do us part." The question of who we choose to spend the rest of our lives with. For you, it seems to have been easy, you just married your college sweetheart.'

'Yes. I did.'

'Did you never regret marrying so young?' he asked me as he spooned purple potato onto his plate.

'Well, I . . . not really. Sometimes, maybe. But then again . . . no.'

'But you missed out on a lot of fun.'

'That's true.' I sighed.

'So perhaps now you can catch up a bit?'

'Yes. Perhaps I can.'

'Maybe you could catch up on some fun with me?'

'Maybe,' I replied with a smile.

At this he smiled back and held my gaze, and I felt so exhilarated, as though I were skiing downhill. And I was going so fast that I thought I was actually flying through the air. Or maybe I was falling. I didn't know. I only knew that I didn't want the evening to come to an end.

'Would you like a glass of pudding wine?' he enquired as he looked at the menu again. 'With a chocolate-covered scorpion?'

'That sounds absolutely delicious,' I said, 'but I don't think I've got room.'

'I think I will,' he said. And so it was brought to his table on a marble slab. A small scorpion, covered in dark chocolate, leaning, almost casually, on a stem of lemon grass. I hadn't believed it would be real, but it was. You could even see the sting in its lifeless tail.

'Are you *really* going to eat that?' I giggled.

'Well, I will,' he said carefully, 'but only on one condition.'

'Yes?'

'That you'll agree to see me again very soon.' I looked at him, then smiled and nodded. He lifted the scorpion to his mouth, and with two crunchy bites it had gone.

'I've had the most wonderful time,' he said as we stood outside on the pavement waiting for our cabs. He lifted my hand to his lips once more. 'I'm so glad we met.'

'So am I.'

My cab arrived, and I stepped inside and wound down the window.

'Thank you so much,' I said.

'It was all my pleasure,' he replied. 'And, Faith, do you know what I'm going to do tomorrow morning?'

'No.'

'I'm going to turn you on.'

May

I tend to forget. I forget that I can be recognised in the street. I never really think about it, because to me, doing the weather's just a job. But at the same time it's a job that puts me in front of more than five million people every day. So although I'm certainly not a household name, I do get spotted sometimes. That's why Josiah – I call him Jos now – smiled at me that day. Usually I'm blissfully unaware of any stares, but then I get pulled up short. I can be walking down the street, and I hear someone singing 'Stormy Weather', or whistling 'Raindrops Keep Fallin' On My Head'. Or I can be in a shop, minding my own business, when I suddenly catch someone looking. And I automatically think, why the *hell*'s that person staring at me? Have I got ink all over my face? Then I remember – it's because of my work. Sometimes people come up to me and say, 'I'm sure I *know* you – haven't we met?' And I tell them I don't think we have. But they keep on insisting, until they're blue in the face, that we've *definitely* met somewhere before. But it would be so arrogant to say, 'Honestly, you *don't* know me, you simply think you do because you recognise me from the TV.' So I just have to stand there, smiling, while they try and work it out. It happened only yesterday, in Tesco's. I was at the deli counter, in a kind of happy daze, absently wondering whether Jos likes potted shrimp or not, when this man came up to me. And he stood there staring at me, quite blatantly, not hiding the fact at all, and then he said, 'I *know* you, don't I?' I shook my head. 'I *do* know you,' he insisted.

'I don't think so,' I replied.

So he stared at me for a bit longer and then he suddenly blurted out: 'I've got it! You're that girl on the telly, aren't you? You're that girl on the telly!' I just nodded and gave him a feeble smile and hoped he'd go away.

'I just want to tell you something,' he said excitedly. 'I just want to tell you . . .'

'Yes?' I said as I braced myself for some embarrassing but complimentary remark.

'That I don't like you much.'

'Oh,' I said, crestfallen.

'Nor does my mum.'

'Right. Well, it's a free country,' I said with a shrug. Now, normally an incident like that would seriously get me down. I'd probably go home feeling mortified and mope for the rest of the day. But at the moment I feel unassailable, because the truth is I'm nuts about Jos. I've seen him twice more since our date at The Birdcage, and I think I've fallen under his spell. This is what love does – I'd forgotten. It gives you emotional armour plating; it's a natural anaesthetic against pain; love fills you with confidence and restores your self-esteem. Which is why I managed to laugh gaily about my encounter in Tesco's when Jos called me the next day.

'Well, *my* mum thinks you're wonderful,' he said loyally, 'and so do I by the way. You looked lovely this morning,' he added warmly. 'Scrumptiously pretty, in fact. I felt so proud of you,' he added softly, and I felt my cheeks begin to burn.

'It's not difficult,' I said. 'I've been doing it a long time.'

'But you do it so well,' he insisted. Then he began to sing that song, 'Nobody does it better'. '"Nobody does it . . . half as good as you,"' he crooned as I stifled my giggles, '"B-a-by, you're the best." Now,' he added briskly, 'when can I see you again?'

'Again?' I said with a laugh. 'You've already seen me three times in ten days!'

'Yes, and I'm coming back for more. I mean it, Faith,' he added softly, 'when can I see you again?'

'Well, when would you like to see me?'

'Immediately!' he said. 'If not sooner. How about tonight?' he suggested.

'I'm afraid I can't,' I lied.

'How about tomorrow, then?'

'Ditto.'

'Right, Miss In-Demand and Playing-*Slightly*-Hard-To-Get, I guess it'll have to be Thursday.'

'Yes, I *think* I can manage Thursday,' I conceded with a smile. 'Where?' I added.

'At my place.' Oh. 'This will be our fourth date, Faith, so I think it's time that you . . .'

'Yes?'

'. . . got to see where I live. I'll cook supper for you. Would you like that?'

'That would be lovely,' I said.

I felt like an infatuated schoolgirl as I put down the telephone. Here I was, just an ordinary, pre-middle-aged, suburban mother of two being pursued by a man of huge talent and charm. Who needs drugs, I thought? I was high on happiness. I was intoxicated, I realised happily as I emptied the washing machine. I was exhilarated, I was elated, I was ecstatic, I was – suddenly Graham barked. The second post had arrived. On the mat were three letters for Matt – he gets *so* many these days – and one addressed to me. To my surprise it was from Peter.

Dear Faith, I read. *I thought this would be easier to write than to say. It's just to let you know that after a lot of soul-searching I've decided not to contest the divorce. I think you're right. Too much has happened in the last three months for us to be able to go back. So I've signed the Acknowledgement of Service and sent the original back to the court. To make it all easier, I've admitted adultery, which in any case, of course, is true. I can't explain what's happened to us. It all seems so unreal. But I guess we should be thankful that we were happy for as long as we were. And although it's all gone so wrong for us now, I'll always be glad that I married you. Peter. x*

My euphoria had taken a headlong dive and was drowning

in my tears. My forehead dropped to the kitchen table as I clutched the letter in my hand. I felt Graham lay his head on my lap and I absently stroked his left ear. We stayed like that for quite a long time, then I reached for the phone and dialled Lily.

'It's *terribly* sad,' she said softly. 'I feel very sad about it myself. And of course you're bound to be upset because this letter makes the end of your marriage more certain.'

'Yes,' I sobbed. 'I know. Oh, Lily,' I wept, 'it's just so . . . *awful*. I wish Peter and I could go back.'

'Faith,' she said, more firmly now. 'I'm afraid you can't.'

'Can't we?' I said. I ripped off a piece of Fiesta kitchen roll and pressed it to my eyes.

'No,' said Lily, 'you can't. And though naturally I don't want to be negative about Peter's *terrible* betrayal, you really have to face facts. And the cruel fact is that, well, he's got someone . . .'

'*Else*,' I wailed. 'But now I wish he only had *me*.'

'Faith, darling,' said Lily carefully, 'I'm afraid you're being a little hysterical. Just stop and think about this. Maybe the reason Peter's pressing on with the divorce is because he wants to be with . . . ?'

'*Her*,' I wept. 'Yes, of course, he does,' I gasped, 'he wants to be with that – uh-uh – bitch. That brazen cow. She just – uh, uh – stole my – uh, uh – husband.'

'Faith,' said Lily, her voice becoming sterner. 'She didn't just steal your husband. Your husband offered himself up for theft.' Oh God. Yes. That was true. 'So you certainly can't go back to him now,' she concluded firmly.

'Why not?' I said. 'After all, we're not divorced. I – uh, uh – *want* to go back.'

'Faith,' she said, 'you *can't*. Because even if he gave Andie up, and promised never, ever to see her again, the fact of his infidelity would always be there.'

'Would it?' I croaked dismally.

'Yes,' she said. 'It would be like some lingering odour, which no amount of Jo Malone cologne could ever dispel.'

'Oh. Ye-e-e-s,' I sobbed. It was true. Lily was right. She was right. Though I do wish she didn't spell things out in quite such a brutal way. But now her tone of voice had changed again and was positive, encouraging and kind.

'You're moving on, Faith,' she said brightly. 'Just like you said you would. You're going forward, and you're being brave . . .'

'Yes. I *am* being brave,' I blubbed as a slick of snot slithered down my top lip.

'Very brave,' she repeated, 'when you consider, well, let's face it, what Peter's put you through.'

'Ye-e-e-s,' I gasped, 'he's put me through – uh-uh – hell!'

'Exactly, Faith. He has. He doesn't deserve you,' she said. 'But now you've got out there again and you've met some-one else.'

'Yes,' I sobbed. 'I have.'

'You've met someone great. Someone who seems to be mad about you.'

'Well – uh-uh – ye-es,' I said, suddenly recovering now. 'He does seem rather – uh-uh – keen.'

'He's handsome, and he's very talented . . .'

'Oh yes, yes, he is.'

'He's eligible, and he's kind.'

'Oh he's *really* kind,' I said, sniffing.

'In fact, Faith, he seems perfect.'

'Well . . . yes,' I said, swallowing my tears. 'I think he *is* perfect, in every way.'

'*Exactly*. So aren't you lucky, then, to have found someone like that?'

'Oh, yes.'

'Just think of all the dumped wives who take *ages* to find anyone new.'

'Do they?' I said.

'Oh, yes. It can be a *nightmare*. Don't you realise that? There are *so* many lonely divorced women out there. But you've managed to find a lovely new boyfriend almost straight away.'

'Yes,' I sighed. 'That's true.' By now my sobs had subsided and ebbed far away, like the waves of a retreating tide.

'So just be grateful,' I heard Lily say, 'for the good fortune that's come your way. And look ahead, Faith, into the future, because I really believe that it's bright. Now,' she added briskly. 'When are you seeing Jos again?'

'On Thursday,' I said as I threw the piece of sodden Fiesta into the bin. 'He wants to cook me supper.'

'Cook you supper?' said Lily excitedly. 'Oh – I *say*. Well there's only one thing that can mean! Have you got something nice to wear? I've got loads of spare La Perla, you know. Stockings, suspenders . . .'

'Lily!' I exclaimed. 'You're going much too fast. I'm not ready for, you know – that.'

'Yes, darling, but maybe *he is*.' Oh. My stomach was suddenly aflutter with a thousand butterflies. 'Now, Faith, are you feeling all right again?' said Lily solicitously.

'Yes,' I said quietly. 'I am. And Lily, thanks for being such a wonderful friend.'

'Oh, not at all,' she replied.

'Then add two tablespoons of milk,' said Delia on Thursday as I checked my appearance in the hall mirror one last time, 'and give it a jolly good stir. Add two twists of black pepper,' she went on as I squished on a little more CK Contradiction. 'And, this is very important, a *really big* pinch of salt . . .'

'Bye Graham,' I called out. 'I won't be too late.' He looked at me slightly reproachfully, I thought, then returned his gaze to the screen.

I shut the front door quietly behind me and walked to Turnham Green tube. Jos lived at World's End, so it would take me less than half an hour. World's End, I mused as the tube train rattled along. World's End – that was funny. I thought my world *had* ended, but now a new one had begun. I walked down Lots Road, then turned left into Burnaby Street and found number eighty-six at the end. It was a flat-fronted terraced house, painted a creamy white. A lovely wisteria, in full flower, clambered up the front. I stood there for a moment inhaling its scent, then lifted my hand to the bell.

'Faith!' Jos exclaimed. He flung his arms round me.

'What a lovely welcome,' I said. 'I like the flowery apron,' I added. 'Have you been slaving away?'

'I certainly have,' he replied. 'You are about to have the best chicken tikka this side of Bombay. Now, what would you like to drink? Faith, did you hear me? What would you like to drink?'

'What?' I was staring, dumbstruck, at the walls and ceiling. It was as though the wisteria had crept in from outside and was growing all the way down the hall. Huge purple racemes hung down, like enormous bunches of grapes; I wanted to sink my nose into the pendant flowers and stroke their papery petals. I wanted to run my finger along the gnarled and twisted trunk. There were even bees, their legs laden with pollen, resting on the feathery leaves.

'How amazing,' I whispered. 'This is magic, too.'

'No, Faith. It's just illusion.'

'Well, it's a lovely illusion,' I breathed.

'I suppose it's not bad,' said Jos judiciously, 'even if I say so myself. And of course this is the best time of year to see it. My wisteria often produces hysteria,' he added with a laugh. 'Now, Faith, come with me.' He took my hand and led me through to the kitchen, where a gasp escaped me again. For the whitewashed walls were hung with pink hams, strings of garlic and a brace of coppery pheasants; curling sprigs of rosemary and sage dried out over the stove.

'It's just . . . incredible,' I said. 'No, I mean the *opposite* – it's credible. It's utterly believable. My eye was completely tricked.'

'That's what trompe l'oeil means,' Jos explained. 'To fool the eye. Artists have been duping people in this way since Classical times. Zeuxis painted grapes so realistic that it's said the birds came to peck at them. Now, how about a glass of champagne?'

'I'd love some,' I replied as he reached into the fridge. 'I say – more Krug! What a treat.'

179

'It's my one extravagance,' he explained with a guilty grin. 'But I'm afraid it's non-vintage again.'

'I think I'll manage,' I said. We smiled and chinked glasses, then went through to the small conservatory where humming birds and tropical butterflies seemed to flit and pirouette amongst the plants. He'd even painted a few translucent geckos onto the glass. If you looked very closely, you could even see their tiny hearts.

'What a brilliant deception,' I murmured.

'That's what all painting is,' Jos explained. 'It's just a confidence trick in which two dimensions pass themselves off as three. Now,' he went on as we sipped our champagne. 'Shall I show you how artful I've been elsewhere?' Like an entranced child I nodded, and let him lead me through the rest of the house.

At first glance the dining room looked quite conventional. It was painted ox-blood red, with a mahogany sideboard and table, but one wall was lined – or so it appeared – with beautiful antique books. Some were packed in tight rows, while others were stacked more casually in horizontal piles. Gibbon's *Decline and Fall*, I read in deeply tooled gold lettering. Alongside were *War and Peace*, *David Copperfield*, and *The Gathering Storm*. I wanted to pull them down and sniff the leather, and feel their weight in my hands. Now we climbed the stairs, and as we did so I peered, bewitched, through the carved pillars of a medieval courtyard onto a plunging Italian hillside far below. The sunburned grass was punctuated with spiky cypresses and dusty olives with twisted trunks. Upstairs, one wall of the drawing room had been transformed into a French orchard, the low evening sunlight radiating through the branching apple trees. Now Jos opened the bathroom door and I found myself staring out through the whitewashed walls of a Moorish palace onto an azure sea. I wanted to shield my eyes from the stinging sunlight and pluck the dates from their palms.

'It's Morocco,' he explained. 'I love it. Have you been there?' I shook my head. 'Well, we'll go there together one day.' At this I felt my face redden and my head began to spin. 'Now,' he added with a knowing grin, 'would you like to see my bedroom?' He took my hand again and led me down the corridor, and I felt my pulse begin to race. He opened the door and I peered in. Everything was white – the carpet, the cupboards and the embroidered white duvet cover on the enormous bed. Then I looked at the far wall. Flat-topped umbrella thorn trees dotted the scrubby landscape; on the horizon two giraffes entwined their necks against a darkening sky. In the foreground was a watering hole where a solitary lion crouched to drink. I could almost hear it lap the water.

'How wonderful,' I breathed, laughing and shaking my head in disbelief. 'So you just lie in bed and look at this, and think you're in Africa.'

'Well, it beats wallpaper!' he said. 'But enough of my painting,' he added, 'it's my cooking I'm really hoping to impress you with.' We went back down to the kitchen where a delicious aroma filled the air.

'How clever of you to make curry,' I said as he checked the pan of bubbling rice.

'It's not hard,' he replied. 'The trick is in the way you combine the spices. I make my own garam masala by combining cumin, fennel, turmeric, cardamom, peppercorns and cloves. It's a bit like mixing oil paints on a palette,' he explained expertly.

'Well, it smells divine,' I said. 'It tastes divine,' I added ten minutes later as he dished it up. And as we sat in his kitchen chatting happily, I realised that Jos was no longer a stranger – I knew so much about him now. I knew about his family – he's very close to his mother – and I knew a lot about his work. He'd told me the names of one or two of his friends, but so far hadn't mentioned any exes. And to be honest I hoped he wouldn't, because I didn't want to know. After all, it was still early days and he might say something I didn't like. So I'd made a conscious decision to contain my curiosity about his past, and to care only about the here and now. As we chatted I felt replete, happy and slightly tipsy.

Suddenly Jos reached across the table and placed his hand on mine.

'Faith,' he began gently, 'Faith, I . . .' Suddenly we heard the sharp trill of the telephone.

'Fuck!' he said. 'Sorry,' he added as he stood up. But instead of answering it in the kitchen he picked it up in the hall; I didn't want him to think I was listening, so I busied myself by clearing the plates. I placed my foot on the chrome pedal bin and flipped up the lid, and I was just about to scrape in the remains of our rice, when something caught my eye. Lying on top of the rubbish was a large, colourful packet labelled *Tandoori Tonite!* I peered at it, dumbfounded. *Just pour on and serve*! it announced. *No preparation required*! I was totally taken aback. All that guff about cumin and turmeric and he'd just used a packet mix! My first instinct was to feel very indignant, but then I began to laugh. Of *course*. How sweet. It was quite funny, really. Well, he'd said he was trying to impress. And as he came back into the kitchen, I gave him an indulgent smile.

'Sorry about that,' he said, running his left hand through his thick hair. 'Er, it was my mum. She likes to chat.' I glanced at my watch. It was ten past ten.

'That was utterly delicious,' I said. 'Thank you, but I think I'll have to go home.'

'Oh,' he said, crestfallen. 'Must you?'

'Well, yes,' I said. 'Because of Graham.'

'Doesn't he trust you with strange men, then?' Jos asked with a meaningful smile.

'That's never been tested,' I replied. 'I wonder how he'd react to you?' I went on. 'I'm sure he'd like you, because I do.'

'Do you?' said Jos. He was standing right next to me. '*Do* you like me?' he said again, almost childishly. 'How much do you like me?' he asked, and now I was aware of his breath, warm and sweet, on my face.

'I like you . . . very much,' I replied shyly.

'Do you, Faith?' he repeated as I felt his arm go round my waist.

182

'Yes,' I whispered. 'I do.'

'Do you like me very, very much?'

'Yes,' I murmured as his lips found mine. 'I like you very, very, *very* much.' And now he was kissing my throat.

'Is that very, very, very much or even very, very, very, *very* much?'

'It's very, very, very, very, *very* much, actually,' I said as he began to unbutton my shirt.

'Is that very to the power of six?' he said.

'No, it's very to the power of ten.'

'So you really, really like me then?'

'Mmm. I really, really do.'

'So, would you go to Africa with me?'

'Africa? Ah. Oh. Er . . . yes,' I said. 'OK.'

'But we mustn't disturb the lion,' he said as he led me up the stairs.

'No, no, we mustn't,' I said. 'We must be really, really quiet.'

'Yes, shhh!'

'Shhhhhhh!'

'Sssshhhhhhhhhhhhhhhh! Oh look, you've frightened it!' We were both giggling now as we kicked off our shoes and removed each other's clothes. I pulled his shirt down over his shoulders, while he unzipped my skirt. Then he slowly unbuttoned my silk shirt and let it slither off my shoulders to the floor. Then we fell, laughing and kissing, onto the white expanse of his bed. I looked at the ceiling, and now I saw that he'd painted it pale blue, with streaks of white. A solitary swift, in search of gnats, wheeled and dived through the air.

'Those are cirrus clouds,' I murmured. 'That means fine weather.'

'I know,' he said. 'And do you know what *I* forecast?' he added as he slowly slipped down the strap of my bra. 'I forecast,' he whispered as he kissed my left shoulder, 'that you and I are going to make love.'

'Mmmm,' I said, and a wave of desire convulsed my frame.

'You're very beautiful, you know.'

183

'Am I?' I said, as if in a trance. 'I really don't think I am.'

'Oh yes, you are,' he murmured. 'Trust me,' he added softly. 'I'm an artist. I should know.' And now, maybe it was the effect of the wine, but suddenly I felt very strange. I looked up into Jos's large grey eyes and imagined that they were brown. I stroked his dark-blond hair, and suddenly wished it was sandy-red. I looked at his perfect, six-pack body, and longed for Peter's chubby frame instead. Jos was a gorgeous, gorgeous man, but my desire had evaporated like the dew.

'What's the matter, Faith?' he asked.

'Nothing,' I said. 'Nothing. Except . . .'

'What?' I paused. I could feel his breath in my ear. 'What is it?' he asked again.

'Well,' I sighed. 'Well . . . this is the first time I've . . . since Peter.'

'Ah,' he said. 'I see. Don't you want to?' he added gently.

'Yes. Yes. I do. I mean, no. I don't think so. I'm not sure. I don't know. You see . . .' My voice trailed away. 'You see . . .' I tried again, but my throat was aching and I found it hard to speak. 'You see, I've never, ever, ever slept with anyone other than my husband. We married so young,' I explained miserably, 'and there was never anyone before. And even though he was unfaithful to me, this just feels all . . . wrong. So, well . . . I'm just . . . sorry, Jos,' I finished lamely. I sat up and reached for my shirt.

'Well, never mind,' he said with a philosophical shrug.

'I didn't mean to mislead you,' I croaked as a tear snaked down my cheek. 'I thought I wanted to go to bed with you, and I did. But now that we're here, I just . . . *can't*. I'm sorry,' I murmured again. I thought he'd be angry, but he wasn't. He just put his arm round me and gave me a gentle hug.

And then he said, 'Don't worry about it, Faith. It really doesn't matter. How about a quick game of Scrabble instead?'

'Now,' said Sophie at nine fifteen this morning as she looked into camera Two, 'do you tend to take things too fast? Particularly

184

when you're behind-the-wheel? Well, in futureyou may find-thatyourspeed is controlledbyglobalsatellite.' I saw confusion register on Sophie's face as she tried to keep up with the racing autocue. 'If the Intelligent Speed Adaptation System isintroduced,' she said as she struggled to remain calm, 'then-electronicspeedlimiterscouldbecome a legal requirement. Sup-porters ofthe systemsaythatmorethantwothousand livesayear-couldbe saved.' Oh God, poor girl. 'Linked to a navigation-satellite, thiswouldpinpointeveryvehicle'sposition andautoma-ticallyrestrictitsspeed to thelegal limit. Itssupporterswant the-systemtobephasedinbylawover the nexttwoyearsandby2005 –'

'Oh dear, oh dear, Sophie,' interjected Terry irritably. 'You're clearly well over the limit yourself. Sorry about that everyone,' he said smoothly as he turned to Camera Three. 'Let's wait for Sophie to get back in the slow lane, where she belongs. I suggest we go straight to Tatiana's report from the Stephen Joseph theatre in Scarborough where a new Alan Ayckbourn play opens tonight.' Sophie sat there muttering into her microphone as Tatiana's piece went out.

'You said it wouldn't happen again!' she hissed to Lisa in the Gallery.

'Oh, sorry Sophie,' Lisa whined. 'Technical hitch, I'm afraid.'

'Well, Terry never seems to have any technical hitches!' Sophie spat.

'Leave me out of this,' said Terry. 'It's not my fault you're incapable of reading a simple autocue.'

Sophie remained composed, but despite the thick stage make-up I could see that her face had flushed red. The studio lights cruelly highlighted the tears shining in her eyes, and as we came off air and the credits rolled, she walked smartly to the ladies' loo.

'Sophie,' I called out a minute later. 'Sophie. It's only me, Faith.' She emerged, swollen-faced from the end cubicle. Nor-mally so calm and self-controlled, it was shocking to see her cry.

'Those two won't be happy until I've left,' she wept as she clutched the side of the sink.

'Which is precisely why you mustn't leave,' I said as I handed her a tissue.

'But I can't *stand* it,' she said as huge sobs racked her slender frame. 'It's bad enough coping with the hideous, *hideous* hours without being victimised as well. And I get no support from Darryl.'

'Darryl's just a wimp. In any case there's not much he *can* do because he knows Terry's contract's cast iron.'

'I'm just trying to do my job,' she added as fresh tears streamed down her face.

'And you're doing it terribly well,' I said. 'Which is why those two are so cross.'

'It was so humiliating,' she wailed as her face crumpled like an empty crisp packet. 'Five *million* people saw me cock up. Five *million*! I was a laughing stock.'

'Well, I'm prepared to predict right now that it'll be you who'll have the last laugh.'

'Do you really think so?' she said as her sobs subsided.

'Yes,' I said, 'I do.'

'But how?' she said bleakly. I shrugged.

'I don't really know. But all I *do* know is that you're clearly going places, and Terry and Tatiana aren't.'

'Thanks, Faith,' Sophie said with a sniff. She heaved a teary sigh. 'Thanks very much. I feel fine now.' She gave me a thin smile, then washed her mascara-stained face.

'So how are things with you?' she asked as she peered into the mirror.

'Well, I'm definitely getting divorced,' I replied.

'Oh. I'm sorry,' she said quietly. She pulled down a thick green paper towel.

'But the amazing thing is that I've already met someone else.'

'Wow! Gosh!' she said. 'That's good.' And I wasn't going to say any more about Jos, and I wouldn't have done, had Sophie not suddenly said, 'So tell me, what's he like?'

'He's really nice,' I confided warmly as she chucked the towel away. 'In fact, Sophie, he's absolutely great.' And now,

186

fired up by my enthusiasm for Jos, I got a bit carried away. 'He's kind and he's decent,' I added happily as she repaired her make-up. 'He's terribly talented, too. He's a successful theatre designer and he's incredibly attractive – he's got lovely dark blond, curly hair.' Suddenly Sophie caught my eye in the mirror.

'What's his name?' she asked.

'Jos Cartwright.' Her lipstick had stopped in mid-air. 'Have you heard of him?' I added. There was a momentary silence.

'Er . . . yes,' she said. 'I have.'

'Oh, do you know him socially then?' I went on, aware that my heart had just skipped several beats.

'Not really,' she said judiciously. 'I mean, I've never actually met him.'

'You just know of him?'

'Yes,' she said, reddening. 'I do.'

'Because of his reputation?'

'Yes. Yes. That's right.'

'Well, that doesn't surprise me,' I went on, 'because he's becoming quite well known. I only met him a few weeks ago, Sophie, so it's very early days. But I like him *so* much,' I added, 'and he seems keen on me.' By now Sophie had this rather strange expression on her face.

'Faith –' she began, but I'd already charged straight on.

'I'm incredibly glad I met him,' I said. 'I was so depressed before. But Jos makes me feel happy and wanted. He makes me feel . . . desired. I thought I'd never feel like that again after the misery of the past few months.' There was silence, then Sophie just nodded and gave me an odd little smile.

'I'm very glad for you, Faith,' she said as she closed her bag. 'I – I really hope it goes well.'

And it is going well. No doubt about it. I do feel happy with Jos. I mean, he's witty and attractive and talented. And he's gentlemanly, too. He proved that the other night. I thought what happened might put him off; that he'd write me off as neurotic and baggage-laden, which I guess I *am*. But he didn't do that at all. He understood that I needed more time. And so we're taking things slowly, enjoying each other's company, and today he asked me if I'd like to have lunch. So we met in Covent Garden, because he'd just had a *Madame Butterfly* meeting at the opera house. He showed me his sketches for the costumes as we sat outside Tuttons wine bar in the sun.

'These are Butterfly's kimonos,' he explained.

'They're exquisite,' I murmured. 'There's so much movement in them. I'd love to frame them and hang them on my wall.' Then he showed me the designs for the set, which is almost ready to be built.

'We make a model of it first,' he said, 'a miniature version which is accurate in every detail. Then, when the director's happy with that, we build the set for real. My design's quite traditional,' he said, 'with this simple tea-house, here, centre stage, but I've added this slightly sinister-looking tenement building behind. Essentially the opera's a simple one and doesn't lend itself to anything too *avant-garde*. Mind you,' he went on thoughtfully, 'there was an interesting production at Glyndebourne about ten years ago.'

'Was there?' I said absently as I studied the sketches.

'Shall we go?' he said suddenly.

'Where?'

'To Glyndebourne. The new season opens on May the twenty-fifth.' My heart leaped. Glyndebourne? I'd never been before.

'I'd love to,' I said. 'But isn't it hard to get tickets?'

'Not with my contacts!' he exclaimed. He grinned, then tapped the side of his nose. 'Insider dealing, Faith. I'm sure I can swing it. *Cosi Fan Tutte*!' he exclaimed.

'What?'

'*Cosi Fan Tutte* – that's what they're opening with. I absolutely love it, don't you?'

'Oh, yes. Well, I think I do. I haven't seen it for years – in fact I've forgotten what it's about.'

'It's about infidelity,' he explained. 'Oh dear, Faith – do you think you could cope?'

'Yes,' I said with a laugh. 'It's only in real life that I can't.'

'And unlike real life,' he added, 'the opera has a happy ending. But maybe you'll have a happy ending too, Faith.'

'I do hope so,' I said.

'Maybe I'll have one, too,' he said ruefully, and then he grinned. 'Maybe . . .' he added meaningfully as he reached for my hand, '. . . we'll *both* have a happy ending.' I smiled and hoped my face didn't betray the joyful clamour in my heart.

'Right,' he said, clapping his hands together. 'That's settled, then. To Glyndebourne we shall go. And we'll take the most scrumptious picnic, and of course *lashings* of Krug.'

'Will that be vintage or non-vintage?' I enquired.

'Don't ask difficult questions,' he said. 'Now,' he added, leaning across the table and drawing my face to his, 'what have you got on this afternoon?'

'Er, nothing,' I said.

'Oh, good,' he whispered, his grey eyes laughing. 'I was hoping you'd say that. Because I've finished for the day and I thought it would be nice to go back to my place . . .'

'Yes?'

'And . . .'

'What?'

'Make passionate love to you, actually,' he said. 'What do you think about that?' There was a moment's silence. Then I stood up. 'Oh dear, have I shocked you?' he said ruefully.

I held out my hand and said, 'Let's go.'

I rang Peter at work the next day to ask him if he'd look after the kids. Now that my new relationship is really getting off the ground, I find I can talk to him without too much pain. I am communicating with my ex, I reflected happily as his extension rang. Is this what's known as an ex-communication? I wondered wryly. Peter seemed glad to hear me – he always does, which is touching, though he seemed to be in a frivolous mood.

'Why do you want me to babysit?' he said suspiciously.

'Because it's half-term and the kids will be home.'

'No, I mean *why* do you *need* me to look after them? Where are you going?'

'Why do you ask?' I said.

'Don't answer a question with a question,' he said. 'You're still my wife, I'd like to know.'

'I'm going to Glyndebourne,' I replied. He emitted a long, low whistle.

'Glyndebourne. Wow. I say!'

'Well, I've never been,' I added pointedly.

'Is that a rebuke?' he said. 'Faith, you know perfectly well that I would have taken you there, but quite simply, we never had the cash.'

'Well, you should have borrowed it,' I said unreasonably. 'If our marriage had really been important to you, Peter, you would have borrowed the money so that I could have occasional life-enhancing treats of that kind.'

'You reckon?' he said with a hollow laugh. 'And just who, might I ask, *is* taking you to Glyndebourne?'

'What's it to you?' I replied.

'Well, as I say, I'm still your husband and I believe I have a right to know.'

'Peter,' I said crossly, 'you forfeited your right to know when you left me.'

'Don't rewrite history, you kicked me out. Come on, Faith, who is this blighter? Is he anyone I know?'

'Peter,' I said stiffly. 'I do not ask you about your association with . . . her. So kindly be so good as to extend to me the same respect for my privacy.'

'Don't be so hoity-toity. Anyway I'll get the kids to tell me,' he said, 'or Graham. He'd spill the beans. Come on – who is it? He must be loaded if he's taking you to that palace of operatic and sybaritic delights.'

'He is not loaded,' I said indignantly. 'But he's doing quite nicely. He's an artist,' I explained.

'How can an artist afford to take you to Glyndebourne, Faith? Are you sure he's not a drug-dealer on the side?'

'Quite sure, thank you,' I replied. 'He's very successful. He's an opera and theatre designer. And he's a brilliant painter, too. He specialises in trompe l'oeil, actually.'

'Is he heterosexual, Faith?' he said suddenly. 'You've got me a bit worried now.'

'Of course he is,' I said impatiently. '*Very*,' I added meaningfully. 'He's also extremely attractive.'

'Oh, really?'

'Yes,' I said. 'He is. Added to which he's an *extremely* talented cook.'

'Ooooooh!' said Peter. 'Definitely gay.'

'He is most definitely *not* gay,' I retorted. And now Peter's voice seemed to fade as I remembered the glorious afternoon we'd spent in bed the day before. It was bliss. It was heaven. I'd forgotten how wonderful sex could be.

'No, Jos is a raging heterosexual,' I announced facetiously.

'Oh, Faith,' Peter said. 'Have you? You haven't? That's not like you. And before we're even divorced. No, that's not very *nisi* of you. Still, you convent girls . . .'

'Peter, as *you* have, why shouldn't I?' I retorted.

'Honestly, Faith, answer the question. Have you been to bed with him?'

'All right, then. Since you ask, yes.' And when I said that I felt a stab of sadistic pleasure and something very close to revenge. 'I have been to bed with him,' I reiterated. 'And it was brilliant, since you ask.' There was silence.

'I didn't.'

'Now,' I went on briskly. 'Will you kindly confirm that you are prepared to look after your children next Thursday?'

'No,' he said. 'I can't.'

'What do you mean, you can't?'

'I mean I can't. As in, I am unable. Indisposed. Otherwise engaged. In short, I'm busy.'

'Doing *what*?'

'The Bishopsgate sales conference, Faith. That's what. I shall be holed up in a hotel in Warwickshire rallying the troops. It's rather important, as I'm sure you'll understand. Not least because I'm on a probationary contract and I'm under considerable scrutiny at the moment. So I'm sorry,' he added. 'I really am, but it's just not feasible. And even if you'd given me three months' notice – which you wouldn't have done because three months ago we were still happily married and you had *no* intention of going to Glyndebourne let alone bonking other men – but even if you had then I'm afraid I would still have had to say no. I'm sorry, Faith,' he added. 'But no can do. Can't you listen to the CD instead?'

'Don't be beastly, please, Peter. I'd like to be able to go.'

'Well then, you'll just have to pay someone to babysit,' he said. 'Have you asked my mother?'

'No, because of the shop.'

'What about your parents?' he suggested. 'Now that the children are practically grown up perhaps they won't mind doing the odd shift – if you can get hold of them, that is.'

I couldn't of course. I never can. I tried, but there was no reply. I had a vague idea they were birdspotting in Tobago. Or were they canoeing in Colorado? Or perhaps they were sailing round the Seychelles on their 'Indian Ocean Odyssey'. I really couldn't be sure, and I was just about to try them again when, to my amazement, Mum rang me.

'How's it all going, darling?' she enquired breathlessly.

'Well, it's been rather interesting,' I began. 'In fact I'm glad you rang because I was wondering if you and Dad would come and . . .'

'Hang on, Faith, the money's running out – Gerald! I need another fifty pence! Thanks. Sorry darling, we're at Heathrow, the flight's about to board so I can't talk long.'

'Where are you off to now?' I said wearily. 'I thought you'd only just come back.'

'Wales,' she said.

'Wales? Why on earth are you flying to Wales?'

'No, darling. We're going to *watch* whales. In Norway,' she explained.

'But I thought you did whale-watching last year in Cape Cod?'

'Different whales, darling. Apparently Norwegian ones jump

right out of the sea with the most enormous splosh. After that we go up to Lapland for a fortnight's reindeer-herding.'

'Well, how lovely,' I said.

'Yes, and what's *so* nice is that it's not radioactive any more.'

'Great.'

'Now, we haven't spoken for ages, Faith. Any particular news?'

'Yes,' I said. 'Since you ask. Peter and I are getting divorced.'

'*Are* you darling? Gerald, *do* watch our bags!'

'In fact he's already moved out and lives in Pimlico, not far from his new job as managing director of Bishopsgate. But I've got a new boyfriend called Jos . . .'

'Oh yes?'

'. . . who's a successful theatre designer.'

'How *super*!'

'In fact he's taking me to Glyndebourne next week.'

'You lucky thing.'

'And Peter's gone off with his headhunter, Andie.' My mother let out a gasp.

'No, it's all right, Mum, Andie's a woman.'

'Well, that's a relief,' she observed.

'Anyway, the children are being very phlegmatic about the whole situation.'

'Lovely. Matt's such a bright boy, isn't he?' she added proudly. 'I think he's doing *awfully* well.'

'Oh yes,' I said. 'And so's Katie. But I'm a little bit worried about Graham.' *Bing-bong*!

'Oh darling, the flight's being called, I've got to dash. Sorry, did you say you're worried about Graham?'

'Yes. I am. He's not taking the divorce very well.'

It's true. He isn't. In fact he's a little disturbed, not his normal jolly self. I've been noticing it in all sorts of ways. For example, you know how when dogs are about to lie down, they first go round in circles? Don't ask me why, but they do. Well, Graham spends *ages* going round and round in circles, and then he lies down with a big, grumbly sigh. Also, he's been spending a lot of

193

time staring out of the window. I know this because he leaves nose-prints all over the panes. Another thing, he's snapping at flies an awful lot, which makes him look vaguely moronic, and nor is he quite his usual relaxed and easygoing self. In the eight days since I spoke to Mum I've seen him getting worse. I noticed it again on Thursday afternoon as I waited for Jos to arrive. Lily had very sweetly offered to look after the kids and she was due to arrive at two. Jos was coming at two fifteen, to pick me up in his car. The drive down to Glyndebourne takes two hours, then we'd have drinks on the lawn, with the opera starting promptly at five. Lily was thrilled to bits about it all and has been an enormous help. Not only did she immediately offer to babysit when I told her about my childcare problem – even offering to take the afternoon off work – she also lent me a wonderful ankle-length Armani silk dress, in pale pink, with a matching stole. And I was so excited about it all I'd got ready too early, like I used to do when I was small. So to pass the time I thought I'd take Graham through a few obedience tests.

'Sit,' I said to him in the kitchen. To my surprise he gave me a defiant stare. 'Sit,' I said again. Nothing. 'Graham,' I repeated patiently, 'sit. Down.' He stifled a yawn. 'Sit!' I snapped. Still he remained upstanding. Matt looked up from his copy of *Time*.

'Graham,' he said seriously, 'sit.' Nothing. 'Sit,' Matt said again. 'Sit. *Please*,' he added. Graham slowly lowered his seat to the ground.

'We've never had to say please before,' I observed. 'Usually he's very biddable. He's being rather wilful at the moment.'

'He's just testing the parameters of your authority, Mum,' said Katie as she sprinkled fish food onto Siggy's tank. 'It's classic behaviour in juveniles during a divorce. With only one parent in charge the offspring start pushing out boundaries, basically, trying their luck. Fortunately it's just a phase.'

'I don't agree with that analysis,' said Matt. 'I'd say he's simply depressed because he knows Jennifer Aniston's coming. He thinks she's a bit of a bitch.'

'I don't know what's the matter with him,' I said. 'I just wish he'd buck up. Graham, darling,' I added as I ruffled his silky ears, 'you don't want Jos to think you're a naughty puppy, do you? You're a big boy now, you're three.'

'Mummy, don't infantilise him,' said Katie wearily. 'He's a dog, not a child.'

'Did you hear that, Graham?' I said with a smirk. 'Your big sister thinks you're a dog.'

'He is a dog,' she said.

'He is not . . . a dog,' I said. 'I do feel that's unfair.'

'He *is* a dog, Mum,' said Katie. 'That's exactly what he is. How*ever*,' she went on smoothly, 'he's a dog with special, almost human understanding and insight, so you're quite right to be concerned about his mental health. It's the divorce,' she repeated matter-of-factly. 'It's making him feel vulnerable. He may also be feeling guilty,' she added, 'as though he feels the break-up is somehow his fault. Basically, he's confused,' she concluded. 'Perhaps we should get canine counselling.' Suddenly the letterbox rattled and we heard Lily's crystalline vowels.

'Hellooooo – open up!' she shouted. 'We're here! The babysitters. Darling, you look divine!' she said as she swept inside. 'Oh yes, that dress is a *dream*. Faith, what are you staring at?'

'Er, nothing,' I lied. In fact I was staring at Jennifer, who was wearing a tiny red T-shirt emblazoned with *So Pretty!* and a stars and stripes baseball cap. Her floor-length ears had been pulled through the specially cut gaps on either side.

'Isn't this outfit sweeeeeet!' Lily raved. 'We got it at Crufts and Jennifer specially wanted to wear it today, didn't 'oo darling? I thought we could all go to the park,' she breathed. 'As long as Graham isn't too rough.'

'Oh no, he's a little subdued in fact. Not his normal cheery self. We think he's depressed about the divorce.'

'Well I'm certainly not!' said Lily. 'I mean, I'm dealing with it,' she corrected herself. 'Of course it's *very* sad,' she went on hastily, 'but, well, life goes on! Now where's this delicious new man of yours?' she added. 'I'm simply dying to meet him.' Two minutes later her wish was granted. We heard a car pull up, there was the click of heels on the path, then suddenly Jos was standing in the hall, looking like an absolute God. No, not a God – an angel. That's what he looked like. His blond hair curled gently over the collar of his dinner jacket. He radiated a kind of magnetic warmth, like a distant fire on a freezing night. He looked so utterly gorgeous, I thought I'd faint with desire.

'Thank you God,' I prayed. 'Thank you *so* much for sending me Jos.' Lily was almost beside herself as the two shook hands.

'How *lovely* to meet you,' she said. 'I've heard so much about you, all of it terribly nice! You must let me interview you for *Moi!*' she added enthusiastically. 'Our arts pages are the best.'

'Thanks, Lily,' Jos said. 'I've heard lots of wonderful things about you too, and I *love* the magazine – it's so much better than *Vogue*.' By now Lily was holding up two cards saying '10'.

'And you're Katie, aren't you?' Jos went on, giving her a lovely smile.

'Yes,' she replied with a sophisticated air of indifference.

'So I guess you're the boy genius, Matt.' At this Matt blushed and said, 'Hi.' Jos stood there smiling at us all benignly as we basked in his male beauty and charm. And then he said, 'Where's Graham?' Oh. That was funny. Where *was* Graham? He'd disappeared. Matt went to find him and returned a minute later, dragging Graham by the collar. On Graham's face was the mixture of fear and contempt he normally reserves for the vet.

'Graham, do say hello to Jos,' I said brightly. Jos's hand went out to pat him, but in a flash Graham had bared his teeth and given his fingers a tiny nip.

'Ouch!' said Jos, shaking his hand. He looked appalled, then sort of irritated; but then he suddenly laughed. 'My fault,' he said. 'I must have startled him.'

'No, you didn't,' I said. 'Graham!' I exclaimed. 'That was very, *very* naughty, and Mummy's very *very* cross!' Graham slunk away. 'I'm so sorry, Jos,' I said soothingly. 'Do you need a plaster for that?' He shook his head. 'Graham's normally terribly friendly,' I went on, 'but at the moment he's a little . . . confused.'

'No he isn't, Mum,' said Katie authoritatively. 'He's just jealous.'

'Jealous?' I repeated.

'Of Jos.'

'Ha ha ha – darling, really!' I said. 'What a silly idea! Katie loves to psychoanalyse everything and everyone,' I explained. 'She'll be starting on you, Jos, if you don't watch out. Won't you, Katie?'

'Yes,' she replied flatly. 'I will.' There was one of those rather awkward moments, when no-one says anything.

Then Jos smiled and said, 'Well, I'm very interested in psychiatry myself, in fact I'm a friend of Anthony Clare.'

'Wow!' said Katie. She'd lit up like a firework. 'I think he's great, though I don't agree with his views on Freud.'

'Would you like to meet him?' said Jos. 'I could arrange it.' I thought her eyes would pop out of her head.

'I'd love to,' she said.

'Well, Jos'll fix it,' he replied with a smile. Then he picked up my picnic hamper, we said our goodbyes and left.

'You look gorgeous,' he said as we drove away from Chiswick in his MGF with the roof down. He reached out and stroked my right knee with his left hand.

'So do you,' I said. 'Divinely handsome, in fact.' I looked at the broken skin on his middle finger. Thank God he hadn't drawn blood. 'I'm really sorry about Graham,' I said.

'It's OK,' he replied wryly. 'I'm just glad he didn't have a gun.'

'You see, he's not quite his normal, happy little self,' I explained. 'I don't know what it is.'

'I do,' said Jos. 'Katie's right. He's jealous. And it's understandable,' he added. 'Because he loves you, and he knows I love you too.' It was as though my heart had done a somersault, three handsprings and a backflip. I felt breathless, dizzy and ecstatic. For Jos has this habit of suddenly saying something which takes my breath away. Peter never did that, I reflected, but then he's not really the romantic kind. Though now I began to wonder whether he was romantic with Andie. Perhaps he was . . . But then I banished such unwelcome thoughts, because I knew I'd moved on. Lily was right when she'd said I was going to go forward. And here I was, going forward with Jos. As we drove down to Sussex I felt as though I were in a dream. As we'd idle in the traffic I'd catch myself looking at his handsome profile, and then he'd turn towards me, and reach out and hold my hand. I didn't care if we never got to Glyndebourne, just sitting in the car with him was bliss. Soon we had left behind the fume-filled arteries of south-east London and were driving down narrow Sussex lanes. The countryside was as green as salad. The cow parsley was high in the hedgerows and the trees were dressed in pale lime. The towering chestnuts waved their pink and white candles in the light summer breeze. We passed beneath a tunnel of beech, their leaves a translucent, coppery green; and now we were suddenly nose to tail with Bentleys and Mercedes and Rolls.

'Welcome to Glyndebourne,' said Jos as we turned into the long tree-lined drive, then nosed into a space and parked. I looked around as he flipped up the boot and removed the picnic things. It was as though we'd stepped onto the set of a Merchant-Ivory film. Men in dinner jackets and cummerbunds strutted like glossy black crows; women proud in their haute couture or billowing silk tripped elegantly across the lawn. In the distance sheep were dotted white against the rolling, hillocky fields.

'What we do,' he said, 'is claim our picnic spot, have a few drinks, then have dinner in the long interval at half past six.' We carried our hamper and rug through the garden, past the rose beds and the lily pond. I caught my breath at the beauty of the Elizabethan house, with its wisteria-clad casements and warm red brick which glowed bronze in the late afternoon sun. The sheep grazed on with nonchalant disdain as we spread out the soft rug by the sunken wall.

'This is the ha-ha,' Jos explained as he twisted open the Krug. 'And the point of the ha-ha is to protect the sheep from the opera-goers.'

'Ha ha!' I said.

'I'm sorry the Krug's only non-vintage!' he added as I held up my glass. 'I only ever have vintage on very, very special occasions.' I smiled. This was special enough.

'Now, what's the weather going to do?' he asked. I glanced up at the sky.

'It's set fair,' I replied happily. 'With blissfully long, sunny intervals.' We sipped our champagne and nibbled smoked salmon canapés, then a distant bell summoned us in.

'This is another world,' I whispered as we walked hand in hand towards the house.

'It certainly is,' Jos replied.

'– no, I'm with Rothschilds, actually.'

'– are you doing Ascot this year?'

'– our two youngest are at Radley.'

'– yes . . . yes . . . Mozart's *super*.'

'Most of these people have affluenza,' Jos whispered with a grin as we found our seats. Then the orchestra tuned up, the house lights dimmed and a reverential hush came down.

I love this, I thought to myself as the safety curtain rose. Jos was holding my right hand in both of his, and I could feel his body gently rise and fall with each breath. The opera was in Italian but I'd read the synopsis in Peter's *Kobbé*. I'd found it a pretty silly sort of story, full of trickery and deceit. Two men, in disguise, woo each other's girlfriends to test the women's fidelity. They do this to win a bet with their cynical friend, Don Alfonso. And you really have to suspend your disbelief, because the two girls completely fail to recognise their own boyfriends, who they've spoken to only five minutes before, just because they've come on dressed as Albanians! The women faithfully hold out against their romantic advances, but then the men resort to low tricks. They pretend they've taken poison and can only be saved from death if the women relent.

199

So they do. But it's so unfair because the men have really deceived their partners into being unfaithful, and then they have the nerve to be cross. But the character who interested me the most was the girls' maid, Despina. She's really dubious, because although she seems friendly and loyal on the surface, in reality she isn't. Because she's busily manipulating the action, from the sidelines, as if she were a puppeteer. And I thought, how could she do that to the two women? What hidden motive did she have? So to be honest I found the opera disquieting rather than funny. Then I decided that the plot doesn't really matter because the music is so sublime. The curtain came down for the interval in a shower of applause, and we all trooped out into the grounds.

'– better than Birtwhistle, eh?'

'– oh, I like modern opera, as long as it *behaves* itself.'

'– isn't that the Duke of Norfolk?'

'– Cap Ferrat for us again this year.'

'– service was appalling. *Appalling*!'

'– no, I'm with Merril Lynch.'

'Josiah?' Jos suddenly stopped dead in his tracks. An attractive young woman in her mid-twenties had stepped right in front of him, blocking our way. 'Long time no see,' she said. She had an oddly defiant expression on her face.

'Yes,' he said, 'it is.' And although he smiled politely, he didn't look at all pleased.

'How are you?' the girl enquired as she pulled her velvet stole round her slim shoulders.

'Oh, I'm fine,' he replied. 'I'm fine. And, er, how are you?'

'I'm *very* well,' she said rather pointedly. 'I've been working at Opera North.'

'Right. Well, that's great,' he said. And I kept thinking he'd introduce me, but he didn't. 'Anyway, it's nice to bump into you again,' he added, 'but we really mustn't keep you from your picnic.' At this he put his arm through mine and began to lead me away.

As we stepped onto the lawn she called out: 'I hear you've been involved in some *very* exciting productions!' Jos stopped, then turned back to face her, and I noticed a small muscle flexing at the corner of his mouth.

'Yes,' he said. 'That's right. Well, nice to see you again, Debbie. Goodbye.'

We made our way back to our picnic rug and sat sipping champagne in the evening sun. But somehow, after that strange encounter, the Krug seemed to taste a little flat.

'Jos,' I said as I opened the hamper and got out the plates. 'I know it's none of my business, but that girl – who was she? She seemed a bit . . . hostile.'

'She was,' he said, sighing irritably. He paused for a moment before he continued. He clearly didn't want to talk about it and perhaps it was wrong of me to have asked.

'I'm sorry,' I said. 'I didn't mean to pry.'

'No, it's OK,' he said with another, slightly fretful sigh. 'I don't mind telling you. She's a young designer,' he explained as I handed him some smoked chicken. 'I once gave her some work. It was set-painting, really,' he added as I helped him to some salad. 'But she's very ambitious and wants to get on. And . . . when she heard I was to do *Madame Butterfly* at the opera house she wrote asking me to make her my assistant. But I . . . didn't think she was up to it, so . . . I told her that I'd filled the job. I thought no more about it,' he added wearily, 'but it's obvious that she hasn't forgiven me.'

'Never mind, darling,' I said as I passed him a paper napkin. And I was relieved by his explanation because I'm beginning to feel a bit possessive about Jos, and I was worried that she might be an ex. But this was just a professional fracas. I could cope with that.

'My world's a very bitchy one, Faith,' Jos added as we ate our supper. 'I do like to bring on young talent, but I'm not going to give work to someone unless they're really first rate.'

'I understand,' I said. 'Anyway,' I added brightly as I passed him some potato salad, 'let's just forget it, shall we?' And though on the surface we had, I felt that a slight shadow had been cast over the rest of the night. I glanced at Jos's face once or twice as we sat in the auditorium for the second half, and

I thought he still looked a bit tense. But then I turned my attention back to the opera, and I was so surprised by what happened at the end. In the synopsis it had suggested there was a happy denouement, in which the two men 'forgive' their fiancées for accepting the advances of the 'Albanians', and all ends happily with the peal of wedding bells. But it wasn't like that at all. When they discovered that they'd been duped, the two women were absolutely livid. They gave the men a filthy look, flung down their engagement rings, then stormed off-stage in tears.

'Not quite a happy ending, then,' I said to Jos as we walked to the car.

'No,' he said. 'It wasn't. I guess real life was allowed to intrude.' He seemed subdued as we drove back to town.

'Are you still thinking about that girl?' I asked him softly. I tried to read his expression, but his face was strobing amber and grey in the lights. 'I hope you're not worried,' I said.

'A bit,' he said as he changed gear. 'I'm wondering whether she'll try and cause trouble for me.'

'Of course she won't,' I said. 'Anyway, how could she? Your reputation is secure. You're a brilliant designer, Jos, everyone knows that.' He turned to me in the semi-darkness and gave me a grateful smile. 'People who are as talented as you are often the target of resentment and jealousy. You're a tall lily, Jos, so people will want to cut you down.'

'Thanks. I wonder how *your* tall Lily is?' he added as we turned into Elliot Road. We found her slumped asleep in front of a *Friends* video, Jennifer Aniston clasped, snoring, to her breast.

'Beauty and the beast,' said Jos with a smile. 'It was nice of her to babysit.'

'Yes,' I whispered, 'it was. I'm sorry you can't stay,' I added. I glanced at Graham, lying on the bottom step.

'I know I can't,' said Jos. 'Because a) there's no way Graham is going to let me upstairs, and b) you've got to get up in three hours and go to work.' He kissed me. 'Poor darling,' he said and he gave me an enveloping hug. 'You're going to be very tired tomorrow.'

'But very happy, too!'

'I'll watch you,' he added, then he kissed me and then stepped out into the inky night.

By now Lily was awake and yawning, and gathering her things, and I thanked her before climbing the stairs. The children had long since gone to bed, but to my surprise I saw a whiteish glow coming from under Matt's door.

'Matt!' I exclaimed softly. He was sitting at his desk in his pyjamas. 'You'll go blind if you don't stop that.'

'What?' He squinted at me wearily, then returned his gaze to the screen.

'What are you doing?' I said. 'It's a quarter to one. You're only twelve, young man.' I peered over his shoulder as his fingers tapped away.

'It's nothing,' he said. 'It's just my chat room.'

'Chat room?' I repeated. 'I don't want you going into chat rooms; you could meet all sorts of creeps.'

'No, this is a special chat room,' he explained.

'What do you chat about?'

'Well, current affairs mostly. You know, China and Taiwan, Opec, the future direction of British industry. That kind of thing.'

'Oh,' I said, 'I see. Well, that all sounds very commendable, but I want you to stop chatting right now.' As I straightened up I glanced at his walls. To my surprise the shelves were bare. 'Where are all your computer games?' I asked.

'Oh, I, er, got rid of them,' he replied as he switched off the machine.

'What, all of them? But you had nearly a hundred.'

'I know. I just got . . . bored of them,' he shrugged as he climbed into bed.

'What, even *Zombie Revenge*, and *Chu-Chu Rocket*?'

'Oh yeah, Mum, absolutely. I'd played them all millions of times.'

'I see. So you gave them away, did you?'

'Yes. Yes. I did.'

'What, to a charity shop?'

'Yup. That's right.'

'Oh. Well, they were very expensive, darling. We spent a lot of money getting you those. And you just gave them away?' I added.

'Yes,' he said. 'I did.'

'Well, I'm a bit annoyed about that. Because you could have taken them to a second hand shop and got quite a bit of money for them.' He shrugged. 'Yes, I'm a bit cross about that, darling,' I said. Then I realised that I couldn't be cross any more. I'd had a lovely evening. All was well with my world, and in any case Matt's motives were pure.

'That was *very* generous of you,' I said as I kissed him goodnight, 'because they'd be worth quite a lot.'

'Yes,' he said meaningfully, 'I know.' I switched off his bedside light and turned to leave.

'Mum?' he suddenly called out from the darkness as I gently pulled the door shut.

'Yes?'

'Was the opera nice?'

'Oh yes, thanks darling. The opera was lovely, though I thought the story was a bit strange.'

'And do you like Jos, Mum?' he added quietly.

'Do I like Jos? Well, yes. I do. And did *you* like him, Matt?' I enquired. There was a moment's silence.

'I don't know,' he whispered. 'I suppose so. Um . . . he seems very charming,' he said.

June

Matt's absolutely right. Jos *is* charming. He's an incredibly charming man, in an age when real charm is rare. He's attractive and friendly and a great talker, always ready with some witty quip. He's just one of these people you want to be with, because he makes you feel so *good*. That's why he seems to draw people to him like moths to a flame. And I can't believe my luck in having met him, because before I was in a mess. I only have to read this month's edition of *Moi!* to realise that. In it is the *Rogue* supplement on infidelity, with Lily's interview with me. Lily's disguised us as 'Fiona' and 'Rick' so no-one will know that it's us. It was as though I was reading about someone else, because it's almost hard to remember, now I've met Jos, just how anguished I was. *I began to suspect my husband . . . felt sick . . . started to go through his things . . . my relief when the detective found nothing . . . then the dreadful shock when Rick confessed . . . where on earth do I go from here? . . . I feel my whole world has caved in.*

That was only three months ago, but now my life has been transformed, because Jos has been my Faith healer – that's what he is. As his name suggests. And with just a few deft strokes of his magical paintbrush, the pewtery skies have turned blue.

The children seem to like him, which is an enormous relief. I mean, it's a big thing, a *really* big thing, introducing your new man to the kids. But they've been fine about Jos, it's only Graham who's less than keen. But then that's understandable because he's only a dog, so he can't rationalise what's going on. And of course he doesn't like the fact that I have to close

205

the bedroom door on him sometimes. Jos doesn't stay over at weekends, because that's when the children are here. But during the week now, once or twice, he does. And he doesn't mind when the alarm goes off at three thirty, he just drops straight back to sleep. Then he quietly lets himself out of the house at about half past eight and goes to work. So our relationship is progressing quite nicely, except that Graham is giving him grief. But the really sweet thing is that Jos seems quite upset about it. We were discussing it in bed last night.

'It's not easy,' he said with an exasperated sigh. 'I mean, when you're around, Faith, he's perfectly civil. But the *second* you're out of sight, then it's Snapsville Tennessee.'

'He hasn't bitten you again, has he?' I asked, horrified.

'No,' Jos replied. 'Not exactly. But he likes to give me a little nip from time to time, just to keep me on my toes. It's like being followed around by a piranha.'

'That'll be the sheepdog in him,' I explained. 'Don't take it personally. He's just rounding you up. He wants to keep his eye on you,' I added, giving him a kiss, 'and so, may I say, do I!'

'Well, I *do* take it personally, Faith,' Jos replied with a wounded air. 'I resent the fact that he continues to be so hostile when *I'm* making such an effort!' This is true, Jos makes an enormous effort with Graham. He brings him Scooby Snacks and bits of meat, and he chucks balls for him in the garden. He got him the new Delia Smith video, and a lovely new collar, too. It's really rather touching and I just hope that Graham will come round. I was discussing it with Katie as we watched *Frasier* on Friday night.

'I suppose,' I began as we sat on the sofa with Graham sprawled across both our laps, 'that Graham sees Jos as an interloper, challenging his place as Top Dog.'

Hello, Seattle, this is Dr Frasier Crane.

'I mean, he's definitely exhibiting neurotic behaviour,' I added. 'The constant snapping at flies, for example, is classic obsessive-compulsive.'

Yes, I'm listening, Russell.

'No, Mum, that's what dogs do.'

'Graham has a lot of anger,' I continued as he heaved a contented sigh. 'He probably has a lot of unresolved issues from his past as well. Now, if you add to that his natural fear, as a stray, of rejection and abandonment, then it's clear that Jos's presence will be a challenge to his fragile self-esteem.'

Thank you Russell, and who's our next caller?

'Also,' I went on as I stroked his ears, 'I think he may have an unresolved oedipal complex in which he wants to replace the "father" figure, in this case Jos, and marry me.'

Katie gave me a sceptical look. 'He never wanted to replace Dad.'

'Mmm. True,' I agreed. 'You know, I used to find all this psychoanalytic stuff rather tedious, but now I'm quite fascinated. And it's clear to me that Graham's displaying signs of incipient paranoia.'

'Nice try, Mum,' said Katie. 'But there's a much simpler explanation.'

'Is there?' I said.

'Yes. Graham just doesn't *like* Jos.'

'Oh,' I said, crestfallen, 'I see.'

'It happens,' she said with a shrug. She waved her hand at the TV. 'I mean, Eddie can't stand Lilith – he always knows when she's within two blocks. It's a personality clash, that's all. I don't think it helps to over-analyse too much. Because the simple fact is,' she concluded cheerfully, 'that Graham just hates Jos's guts.' Oh. 'Now, what I find much more interesting,' she added, 'is why Jos should *mind*.' Hmmmmmm.

'Well, he minds because Graham snaps at him.'

'No, Mum,' said Katie firmly. 'He minds not being *liked*.'

'But we all want to be liked,' I pointed out. 'It's natural.'

'True, but most of us don't really care whether or not we're liked by a *dog*.'

Now, as you know I always humour Katie, however crazy her ideas. But it's *obvious* why Jos minds. He minds because he sees Graham, quite rightly, as a member of my family, so he wants to get on with us *all*. And he does, by and large. I mean I'm mad about him, and the children clearly like him, and Lily absolutely adores him and thinks I've really landed on my feet.

'He's completely gorgeous!' she declared, yet again, at the Cobden club a few days later as Jos went to get us both a drink. She'd got us invitations to the launch of a new cook book, *Nosh Kosh*, by society chef Nutella Prince.

'I mean, he's an absolute wow,' Lily reiterated above the animated babble. 'He's divinely handsome, he's terribly sociable, he's fashionable, and he's fun.' I looked at Jos as he retreated into the throng in search of more champagne. Lily was right. He really stood out, even in this glamorous crowd. I felt my heart swell with pride that this delicious-looking man was with me.

'He's the one for you, Faith,' she said. 'Jennifer and I are just thrilled.'

'Where is Jennifer?'

'At home. I thought it would be too exciting for her this evening, she's had a very busy week.'

'What? Sitting around? Eating foie gras?'

'No, Faith!' said Lily with an indulgent snort. 'Coming up with *ideas*. Oh look, there's the famous fertility specialist, Godfrey Barnes. That reminds me,' she added, 'you know, Jennifer was thinking of having puppies – because of course her pedigree's *superb*. Well, sadly the vet's decided she's just not strong enough.'

'Oh dear.'

'So I'm going to have her cloned instead.'

'What?'

'Well, we've had Dolly the sheep and Dolly the cow, so I don't see why we shouldn't have Dolly the dog. There's a firm in the States researching it; it's called "Puplicity" – I've just put her name down. Don't you think that would be lovely, Faith, *lots* of little Jennifer Anistons?'

'Mmm,' I nodded enthusiastically. 'Amazing bash,' I added by way of changing the subject. And it was. Two hundred members of London's most fashiony party faithful were busily scoffing crustacean canapés and knocking back champagne. In the centre of the room was a revolving ice-sculpture, shaped like a giant leaping salmon. Two towering floral arrangements stood sentinel by the door.

'Yes, I think Jos is wonderful,' Lily enthused again. 'You just hang on to him Faith, otherwise some other woman will try and nab him, and we can't have that!'

'Oh no,' I agreed. 'We can't. And how's your love life?' I enquired as we dipped tiny meringues into a three-foot-high chocolate 'volcano' bubbling with molten menier.

'Oh, it's hell – as usual,' Lily sighed. 'I finished with Frank,' she informed me confidentially as she wiped sugary crumbs from her lips.

'Who?' I can never keep up.

'The conductor,' she explained. 'You know.'

'Sorry, I don't remember. Which orchestra's he with?'

'The number 11!' she guffawed. 'He was absolutely *gorgeous*,' she added ruefully, 'but he was hopeless between the – you know . . .'

'Ears?'

'No, darling, sheets. It was the way he'd shout "hold tight!" at the critical moment which began to get me down.'

'What about that pop singer, er, Ricky?'

'Oh, Ricky was tricky,' she replied. 'I adored him, Faith. But he was three-timing me, with his backing trio.'

'Oh dear. Well, maybe you ought to go out with someone more, you know, normal and down to earth; like a doctor,' I suggested, 'or a dot.com millionaire. Or what about that wine merchant?'

'He was a plonker.'

'How about that bloke from the BBC?'

'Too middle-waged.'

'And that nice stockbroker?' I enquired. 'The tall one with glasses?'

'Oh, *him*,' she said, rolling her eyes. She grabbed a cocktail sausage from a passing tray, then brandished it in front of my face. 'It was like *that*!' she announced contemptuously.

'Oh, Lord.'

'How's Jos in that department?' she went on knowingly, as we spotted him weaving his way back through the throng.

'Oh, he's . . . fine,' I said. I giggled self-consciously. 'In fact he's brilliant. It's nice to be, you know, active again,' I went on. 'Peter and I hadn't bonked for yonks.'

'Oh well,' she said indolently. 'No doubt he's *more* than making up for it now.' And when she said that I felt a stab of pain, like a knife to the heart; and I found myself wishing, as I often do, that Lily would sometimes think before she speaks. Because however much I'm moving on, and however happy I might be with Jos, the fact is I still *hate* the idea of Peter and Andie in bed. And now I found myself thinking about Peter, as I often do, and wondering how he was getting on. As I did so I suddenly looked across the room and saw Oiliver – my heart sank; worse, he was coming my way.

'Hello, Faith,' he said with impudent familiarity before I could escape.

'Hello Oliver,' I replied crisply. 'This is Lily Jago.' They gave each other a disinterested smile. I looked at his large, marsh-mallowy face which was beaded, as usual, with sweat. Clammy – that's what he was. Sticky. He seemed to leak and ooze.

'I'm so sorry to hear about your divorce,' he began. I said nothing. 'And of course,' he went on unctuously, 'we were all very sad to see Peter go.' I bet you were, you hypocritical wanker, I thought to myself.

'But Peter's doing *so* well at Bishopsgate,' I said.

'Really?' said Oliver with, it seemed to me, a slightly surprised smile.

'Yes. Really. He loves it there. And they love him.'

'Do they?'

'Yes.'

'I'm so glad to hear it,' he said oleaginously. Then he seeped away.

'He seemed a bit of a creep,' said Lily.

'You said it.'

'Oh look, here's Jos with our fizz.'

'Here you are, girls,' he said, handing us two glasses. 'Sorry

I took so long, but I kept bumping into people I know. In fact – ooh there's Melvyn Bragg – Faith darling, do you mind if I go and schmooze?'

'Of course not,' I replied.

'Sure?'

'Yes, sure,' I smiled. 'Go on.' Jos kissed my hand, then shot away and was soon deep in conversation with Lord Bragg. And I noticed that Lord Bragg was smiling and laughing, in fact he looked totally charmed. But then I've noticed that everyone – women and men – seem equally captivated by Jos. By now Lily and I were both feeling slightly tipsy as we circulated amongst the chic crowd.

'– didn't see you at Cannes.'

'– he manages Ali G.'

'– big friends with Zadie Smith.'

'– nah! It went to Faber.'

'– over there, look, with Graham Norton.'

'– we're calling it bonk.dot.com.'

I found the atmosphere oppressively trendy, but Lily was revelling in it all. I often think she must get bored of so many parties. But she doesn't. She's the Queen of the Night.

'Oh look, there's the novelist Amber Dane,' she said with a smirk. 'Her books are widely unread. And there's Zuleika Jones, the actress. Completely unspoiled by failure. Now, that tall bloke over there – see him?' I nodded. 'He's a brilliant politician.'

'Really?'

'Oh yes. Absolutely. One of the *best* that money can buy. Oh God,' she grimaced. 'There's that frightful fashion editor, whatshername, who writes that drivel in the you-know. I mean, how can someone who looks like a shopgirl possibly be an arbiter of beauty and style?' Sometimes I find Lily's constant need to be bitchy a complete and total bore, but now, gently anaesthetised by Laurent Perrier, I found myself laughing at her barbed *bons mots*.

'Ooh, isn't that the It Girl – Tarara Dipstick?' I asked as I spotted a long-haired blonde in a leopard-print sheath leaning against the bar.

'Past-It Girl,' Lily sniggered. 'She must be thirty-five at least. She thinks she's a siren,' she added dryly. 'But she only sounds like one. And you see that girl with her? That's Saskia Smith. Now, *she's* one for the money.'

By now I was vaguely looking round for Jos, but I couldn't see him. Melvyn Bragg had moved on and was talking to someone else. Where had Jos gone, I wondered, as Lily's caustic commentary rattled on.

'Oh God!' she exclaimed, digging me in the ribs. 'There's that cow Citronella Pratt – over there, that fat woman with the red hair. Isn't she gross! No wonder she's known as "*La Vag Qui Rit*"!' Where *was* Jos? I wished he'd come back and talk to me. Not least because I was really beginning to tire now of Lily's toxic observations. But suddenly her voice seemed to fade, as though someone had turned down the sound, because now, at last, I'd spotted Jos. *There* he was, standing by an illuminated green sign saying 'Exit'. And I was just about to go up to him when I saw someone else approach him, someone I vaguely knew. Who was it? Oh yes. That's right. It was Iqbal's boyfriend, Will. I've met Will once or twice, at our Christmas parties, although I can't say I liked him much. But that's partly because I know that he leads Iqqy a merry dance. He's not faithful – far from it – and I think it breaks Iqqy's heart. But Iqqy just won't give Will up because he thinks the world of him. Will's in opera, too; I think he's an assistant director. And there he was, heading straight for Jos. I instinctively wanted to rush up to Jos and drag him away, but it was awkward because I suddenly realised that they seemed to know each other quite well.

'Citronella writes this ghastly column in the Sunday whotsit,' said Lily. 'Quite dreadful! That bitch is always *vile* about other women, you know.'

'Really?' I murmured vaguely. But I wasn't listening to Lily any more. Because by now it seemed to me that something odd was going on. I'm no expert on body language, but something just didn't feel right. I looked at Will. He's thin, with short, blue-black hair and a sort of pinched, self-conscious expression. He's rather exotic-looking I suppose, with staring, ovoid eyes, thick eyebrows, and a curious, waxy sheen to his skin. He reminded me now of a camp version of that TV puppet, Captain Scarlett. That's what it was, I now realised – he looked somehow synthetic, and fake; unlike Iqbal, I reflected, who's so warm and real. I adore Iqqy, he's a lovely guy, but Will gives me the creeps. Standing next to him Jos looked so manly, with his dark blond hair just curling at the nape, and his broad shoulders, and his masculine physique, and his casually attractive clothes – a pale-green linen shirt above a pair of really nice jeans.

'But it was such a *scream*, Faith,' I heard Lily say. 'Citronella's husband ran off with a hairdresser. She was so awful she'd turned the man gay!'

It hadn't occurred to me that Jos and Will might know each other, but of course it made sense because they were in the same world. Looking at them together you'd have thought they were quite close friends. Yes . . . very close friends, actually. And now I felt my entrails twist and knot, because Will was standing much too near to Jos. Admittedly the room was crowded, but he didn't need to stand that close. He was right in his face. Invading his space. He was . . . yes, he was. He was hitting on Jos, I now saw with a shock as illuminating as sheet lightning. He was coming on to him. You could see it. It was obvious. How dare he, I thought. How *dare* he! And how awful for Jos. How embarrassing, too, I reflected, as my face now burned with vicarious shame. And I was just about to go over and rescue him when I suddenly stopped. Because I now realised that Jos wasn't backing away. If Will was standing too close to him, Jos didn't appear to mind. In fact he looked . . . yes, he looked as though he was almost *enjoying* it. He was staring straight back at Will and he was throwing back his head and laughing. He was . . . *no*. I looked again. Yes. He was. Jos was *flirting*. He was flirting with a *man*. My skin prickled, and rows of goosebumps raised themselves up on my arms. I didn't know what to do. I wanted to intervene. I wanted to go up to Will and tell him to back right off. But I couldn't because I felt like an intruder – no, *worse* – I felt like a *voyeur*. And now Will was putting both his hands on Jos's shoulders, then he reached up and kissed him on the cheek.

'Faith! Faith! You're not listening to a word I'm saying.'

'Wh-at?' I murmured. 'Oh, sorry.'

'Look, there's Jos, Faith, let's go and talk to him.' We made our way over to him through the heaving multitude, and I wanted to stop and tell Lily what I'd seen, but she was dragging me along in her wake, parting the crowd like Moses parting the Red Sea. And by the time we'd got to Jos, Will had disappeared.

'Darling,' said Jos. He flung his arms round me as though he hadn't seen me for weeks. 'I missed you,' he said as he drew me to him. 'Now,' he said with a wicked grin. 'Have you had enough?' I nodded mutely. 'Good. Because I think it's time we went home.' We left Lily still enjoying the party, then drove slowly back through west London in the enveloping midsummer dusk. Jos lowered the roof of his car, and I watched the sinking sun flare red and gold in the turquoise sky.

'Red sky at night,' said Jos. 'Shepherd's delight. Isn't that right?' he added with a laugh.

'Oh, er, yes,' I said.

I didn't feel like chatting, I felt too subdued and was trying to work out what I'd seen. I'd decided to say nothing about it, but now I felt that resolve crack.

'Jos, can I ask you something?' I said as we idled at a red light.

'Anything you like,' he replied. He grabbed my right hand and held it in his.

'Well, that chap you were talking to,' I began as the car nosed forward again. 'That chap, Will.'

'Yes,' said Jos. 'Do you know him?'

'I've met him. He lives with one of our make-up artists, Iqqy.'

'What about him?'

'Well, do you like him?' I asked.

'Do I *like* him?' Jos repeated as we turned left into Goldhawk

Road. He seemed surprised by the question. 'Do I like him? Er . . . no. Not much.'

'Then – why on earth did you kiss him?' My heart was banging and my palms felt damp.

'I didn't kiss him, Faith. Don't be silly.'

'Yes, you did. I saw.'

'No I didn't. He kissed me.'

'Well, all right, but why did you let him? You're not gay. I was . . .' I swallowed. 'To be honest, I was a bit shocked.'

'Oh Faith, darling,' he replied with an indulgent smile. 'That's only because you're so shockable – and so naïve. You always take things at face value, don't you? But they're never quite what they seem.'

'What am I supposed to think when I see my boyfriend kissing a man?'

'Well,' he said as he changed gear, 'you're supposed to think that these days it's perfectly acceptable for a straight man to let a gay man kiss him.'

'Oh,' I said unhappily. 'I see.'

'Just on the cheek, that's all. I mean, really, Faith,' he added with a smile, 'French men kiss each other the whole time. Do you think that they're all gay?'

'No, of course not. But it's not the same, because their culture's different from ours.'

'Oh, Faith!' Jos exclaimed with a huge smile as we passed a red No Entry sign. 'Did it make you think that I'm gay?!'

'Well, no, I mean, not really, I was just . . . wondering,' I added feebly. And at this Jos burst out laughing. But it wasn't his usual, good-natured chuckle. It was a rather mocking, high-pitched kind of laugh, a laugh I'd never heard before.

'My girlfriend thinks I'm gay,' he exclaimed. He seemed almost tickled by the idea. He thumped the steering wheel with the heel of his hand. 'Oh that *really* takes the biscuit!' Now he was shaking his head and laughing – it seemed to crack him up. And all of a sudden I found myself laughing, too. I guess I was laughing with relief.

'Of course I'm not gay,' Jos said as his giggles subsided. He

215

wiped the tears from his eyes. 'Not at all. Really. No way. But the point *is*,' he added, 'that I have to play the game.'

'Oh,' I said. 'What game?'

'Well, in my world, Faith, the fact is that a lot of the guys *are* gay.'

'Yes, but why do you have to flirt with them? That's what I don't understand. And you *were* flirting with Will, Jos. I could see.'

'Darling, I flirt with everybody,' he said as we drove under a sign saying 'All Directions'. I like to flirt. Haven't you noticed? That's how I get on.'

'That's how you get on?' I repeated. I felt a twinge of something like revulsion mingled with a kind of contempt.

'That's how I sometimes get work,' he explained as we turned towards Stamford Brook.

'I thought you got work because you're brilliant at what you do.'

'Well, yes, up to a point. But there are a lot of good designers, Faith,' he added. 'So I have to keep my end up.'

'You what?'

'I mean,' he stumbled, with a giggle, as we turned into Chiswick High Road, 'I mean,' he reiterated awkwardly, 'that I have to oil the wheels. Now,' he went on, 'I'll happily admit that I know Will fancies me. So I make sure I flirt with him because I don't want to alienate the guy.'

'Why ever not?' I asked. 'He's not important.'

'Oh yes he is,' he replied. 'He's doing *The Rake's Progress* at the New York Met next year, and I want to design the set. And if I have to flirt with that creep to get the gig, then, quite frankly, Faith, I will.' Now I found myself freshly confused – for which, I wondered, was worse? Flirting with a gay man when you're straight? Or flirting with a man whom you don't even *like*?

'Flirting's essential for business,' I heard Jos say. 'I do it all the time. You see you have to make yourself attractive to other people. That's all I'm doing. Do you understand?'

'Mmmm. I suppose so,' I said.

'If you make good eye-contact, use the right body language, then you make the other person feel good which means you can get them on your side.'

'Oh,' I said, faintly. 'I see. So it's just . . . strategic, is it?'

'Yes,' he said. 'It is. And it's quite harmless. Because the fact is, Faith, that although I flirt with lots of people, I choose to date only you.' We drove on in silence and then drew into Elliot Road. I looked at the house, the window panes flashing crimson in the setting sun. The wisteria which had looked so lovely two weeks ago looked sad and faded now. I made a mental note to dead-head it. And now there was Graham, doing guard duty in the window. Jos saw him, too, and groaned.

'I won't come in if that's OK. I've got a *Madame Butterfly* meeting at nine o'clock and I've got some sketches to rework. In any case,' he added ruefully, 'I'm not sure I could cope with Graham.'

'Don't worry,' I said. I smiled at him. 'Really, I quite understand.' In fact I was relieved. For although Jos's explanation had reassured me, a part of me still felt disturbed. I wanted to digest what Jos had told me, so I took Graham out for a quick walk, then called Lily on her mobile phone.

'Yes, darling?' she said. She was on her way home in a cab. I told her what I'd seen.

'Oh, I wouldn't worry about it,' she said airily. 'It's probably exactly as he says.'

'Yes, but Peter never flirted with men,' I pointed out.

'No,' said Lily. 'That's true. He flirted with women, didn't he? With rather unfortunate results. Look, Faith,' she went on emphatically, 'if Jos says he's not gay, then he isn't. Why on earth would he need to lie?'

'Well, maybe he's got a gay past?' I said. 'It's quite possible, you know. And if he did, then I'm not at all sure how I'd feel about that.'

'Mmm,' said Lily, thoughtfully now. 'Well, yes, I see what you mean. And we don't want him running off with a bloke like Citronella Pratt's husband did.'

'And the reason why I don't feel completely reassured is because when we were discussing it in the car, he said this funny thing. He said he flirted with men because he "had to keep his end up".'

'Oh!' she said darkly. 'What an unfortunate choice of phrase.'

'Yes. *Exactly*,' I agreed. 'And then he corrected himself rather quickly, which made me think it might have been a Freudian slip. And he was so emphatic in denying that he was gay. He said, "No I'm not. Really. Absolutely not. No way," so I felt he was slightly over-doing the denial. Protesting too much and all that. Lily, maybe Jos *is* gay, but has decided to date women for a while.'

'Mmm. Well, does he ever mention any ex-girlfriends?'

'Not really. I've never really wanted to ask.'

'And is he close to his mother?'

'Very.'

'Mmm. That doesn't necessarily mean he's gay. Does he cut recipes out of newspapers?'

'No.'

'Does he know lots of musicals?'

'Yes.'

'But can he sing all the words?'

'No.'

'Has he got lots of house plants?'

'Yes. Oh Lily, I'm feeling very disturbed – I just don't know what to think.'

'Poor Faith,' said Lily with a hollow laugh. 'I mean, three months ago you were obsessing about whether your husband was being unfaithful, and now here you are obsessing about whether or not your new man is gay. We could do something on it in *Moi!*' she giggled. 'Is Your Boyfriend Gay – Our Top Ten Tell-Tale Signs!'

'Please be serious about this, Lily, I'm worried.'

'OK. Sorry. Look, is there anyone you could ask?'

'Sophie at work might know.'

'Then talk to her,' Lily advised me. 'Get her to spill the beans.

Because I agree, you've *got* to get to the bottom of this. Oops! Sorry Faith – Freudian slip!'

The next morning I wrote my script in record time, then dashed downstairs to Make-Up just after six, as that's the time Sophie goes in. As usual AM-UK! was in chaos.

'– where's Terry's script?'

'– the psychic granny wants to know when she's on.'

'– has Sophie gone to Make-Up?'

'– if she's psychic she should know!'

'– who's got the hedgehog-racing VT?'

'– oh no! The singing parrot's gone sick.'

I opened the door of the make-up room. There was no sign of Sophie, but there was Iqbal, looking depressed.

'You're down early, Faith,' he said as I sat down.

'Yes, I got my script done quite quickly today. How are you, Iqqy?' I added.

'Oh, don't ask,' he groaned. 'Marian's ill which means I'm frantic, and to be honest I'm not feeling that great.'

'I'm sorry,' I said as he draped the nylon gown round my shoulders. 'Have you got a headache?' I enquired disingenuously.

'It's not physical . . .' he began as he pinned my fringe back from my face. 'I wish it was. I could deal with that. It's . . . emotional,' he sighed.

'Oh, dear. Look, tell me to mind my own business, but is there anything I can do?' He shook his head wearily.

'Thanks, but no-one can help. It's the usual problem, I'm afraid.' I looked at Iqqy's face in the mirror as he sponged foundation onto my skin. His jaw was grained with stubble and there were bags beneath his eyes.

'It's Will,' he murmured bleakly. 'We had a really bad row last night. He crucifies me,' he went on as he blended the make-up over my jaw. 'I mean, I know he's naughty,' he added. 'I've always known that. But what I can't bear is the way he . . . taunts me. He likes to make me feel bad.'

'Oh, Iqqy,' I said, 'you don't deserve that.'

'No,' he said. 'I don't think I do. Oh, hi, Sophie,' he added as the door opened. 'I'll be with you in a tick.' Sophie shut the door quietly behind her and gave me a friendly smile.

'Buggeration!' Iqqy suddenly expostulated as he rummaged through the cosmetics on the counter. 'No more powder – that's all I need! There's some more downstairs,' he added as he sped to the door. 'Hang on a tick, you two.' Sophie and I smiled at each other as she sat down, and then she looked at her script. Here was the chance I'd been seeking to ask her about Jos, but the words almost died on my lips.

'Sophie,' I began nervously. 'Can I ask you something?' She nodded. 'Well, you remember you said you know my, er . . . friend, Jos?'

'Yes,' she replied carefully. 'Or rather, I know one or two people who know him. Why do you ask?' she enquired.

'Because, well, this is going to sound idiotic really,' I said with an awkward little laugh. My pulse was racing and my mouth felt dry. 'But, um, someone I know, er, this, er, friend of mine, she suggested – quite absurdly, of course – that um, Jos might be, or perhaps had, at some stage been . . . gay.' Sophie was looking at me in a peculiar way, and her face had suddenly flushed red. Oh God, oh God, it was true. He *was* gay, that's what she'd been hinting at in the Ladies' that day.

'Gay?' she repeated.

'Yes. Er, have you, er, you know, ever, um, heard anything to that . . . effect?'

'No!' Sophie exclaimed. 'Gay?' she repeated again wonderingly. She emitted a hollow laugh. 'Good heavens, no – that's a new one on me!'

'Oh, so it's not true, then,' I said. Now I began laughing, and felt my heart flood with relief. 'I didn't for a minute think it *was* true,' I stuttered, 'but you know how it is, you hear such silly rumours, I mean, I'm sure there are some people who think *I'm* gay,' I added gaily.

'Oh no,' said Sophie emphatically. 'I'd never, ever think that. But no, Faith, to answer your question, I do not think Jos Cartwright is gay.'

'Oh good,' I said. 'Great. I mean, really, what an absurd idea!' I laughed loudly. Then there was a few seconds' silence, in which I could hear the pounding of my heart. 'So he doesn't have a gay past, then?'

'No,' she said, shaking her head. 'I've never heard anything like that.'

'And how long have your friends known him?'

'Oh, about five years.' So that was that. Now I knew. It had been absolutely horrible asking, but at least she'd said what I wanted to hear. Jos wasn't gay. Thank God. He *wasn't*. Of *course* he wasn't. And now, filled with relief, I smiled at Sophie, but she wasn't smiling back.

'Faith,' she said seriously as we looked at each other in the mirror. 'We're friends, aren't we?'

'Of course we are,' I replied.

'Then in that case I hope you won't mind me sounding just a word of caution. About Jos.' Oh. I felt my revived spirits flag and then droop again. 'I mean, I hope it's all going to work out for you,' she went on. 'And I'm sure you find him very charming, as most people do. And although I really don't want to interfere, I would advise you to be just a little bit . . . careful.'

'Careful?' I said. I looked at her as her words sank in. Careful? What on earth did she mean? A part of me felt annoyed that she didn't just say it, that she didn't just tell me, outright. And I was mustering the courage to ask her, when the door opened and Iqqy ran in.

'OK Sophie,' he said slightly breathlessly as he put down the powder. 'In the hot seat, please.' So now I couldn't ask Sophie to explain what she'd meant about Jos. The moment had passed, and I was annoyed. But then I was glad, yes, I admit it, I was glad, because I didn't really want to know. Still, all that morning I kept turning over the possibilities in my mind.

'I just can't imagine what Sophie's getting at,' I said to Lily when I phoned her after lunch to report.

'I think it makes him more mysterious,' she replied. 'Maybe

221

he's into drugs,' she speculated. 'You know, nasal refreshment. Does he have a runny nose?'

'No.'

'Maybe he's got a drink problem?'

'I'd have seen it by now.'

'Maybe he's got a criminal record,' she suggested. 'Or dodgy connections. Does he talk about his "associates" a lot?'

'Nope.'

'Maybe he's got perverted sexual tastes? Spotted any chains or whips?'

'No.'

'Maybe he likes frocks,' she went on.

'I don't think so!' I laughed.

'Maybe he's already married,' she suggested.

'No.'

'Mad wife in the attic?'

'I haven't heard any screaming.'

'Well then, Faith, relax. I really wouldn't worry,' she added expansively. 'So far the only thing he's done wrong, in your view, is to flirt with a man. But now we know he's definitely not gay I wouldn't get too worked up about that. I mean, the world of opera is very lovey-dovey. You've got to take that into account. I suspect Jos is just a social chameleon,' she went on, 'he adapts to his environment – that's no crime.'

'But why would Sophie warn me about him?' I said. 'That's what I don't understand.'

'Well, maybe she's after him herself.'

'I'm sure she's not,' I said. 'Not only do I get the feeling she doesn't really like him, she's got a chap called Alex.'

'Maybe he's a cannibal,' mused Lily facetiously. 'Or a Tory-voter.'

'Or maybe he's an alien,' I said. 'Oh Lily, you're right. I'm just being neurotic, because he's perfect in every other way.'

'Yes,' she agreed, 'he is. So why go looking for trouble? I've said it before and I'll say it again. Jos is attractive, he's talented, he's sexy and he's fun. He's also considerate, solvent, and he's very nice to your kids.'

Lily's right. He is. In fact he's wonderful to them. It's really touching. He can't do enough for them. On Saturday, for example, it was Katie's fifteenth birthday, and Jos arrived with this enormous cake. And he gave her Anthony Clare's new book, which was not just signed but also inscribed to her by the author. When she read the flyleaf, 'To Katie, from one psychiatrist to another', I thought her eyes would pop out of her head.

'Wow! Thanks, Jos, that's *really* nice.'

'You're welcome,' he said. 'Now, have you had many cards?'

Suddenly we heard the bang of the letterbox and Graham flew, barking, to the mat. On it were five birthday cards for Katie, a few letters for Matt and a single brown envelope for me. I looked at it, shuddered, and put it straight on top of the boiler along with all the other unopened brown ones. Peter could take care of those ones the next time he came round. Then the phone rang – it was my mum. She was calling from Budapest on her mobile phone. Katie talked to her for a couple of minutes and then she shouted to Matt to come.

'Granny wants to talk to you – as usual. But you'll have to yell, the line's bad.' Once again I thought how nice it is, the way my mother's bonding with Matt. In fact she talks to him more than anyone else these days. They seem to chat for hours. And as Katie, Jos and I sat in the garden in the sunshine, snippets of their conversation floated out. 'Bolivia . . . government . . . Amazon . . .' I heard him say. Of course, he was very interested in Latin America. 'Bears . . . predator . . . poached . . .' And now he sounded slightly agitated. He and Granny were obviously having some engrossing discussion about bear conservation in Hungary. And you know, I'm so pleased to think that at long last Matt's really coming out of his shell. That's why he got rid of all his computer games, because he realised he'd outgrown them and was ready to interact with the grown-up world.

'New technology . . . no,' I heard him say. Maybe he's going to be a journalist, I thought happily, given his new passion for current affairs. Then he came and joined us in the garden as we had coffee and cake in the warm summer sun. Katie and Jos were discussing Wagner while Graham was sitting by the flowerbed, snapping at bees.

'Graham!' I said. 'If you get stung, don't come running to me.'

'At least he'll stop doing it then,' said Katie. 'It'll be a kind of Aversion Therapy. He'll learn to associate the sting with the bees and stop.'

'Are you sure he's that rational?' said Jos.

While this conversation was going on Matt had whipped out his brand new laptop and was now tapping away, with a slightly anxious expression on his face.

'I wish we could do a little Aversion Therapy on you, Matt,' I joked, 'to stop you using your computer so much. Look, as it's Katie's birthday do you think you could give it a little rest?'

'OK, Mum,' he agreed. As he reluctantly closed the lid, I suddenly realised that I'd never seen the computer before.

'Matt,' I said carefully, 'that laptop. Is it new?' He nodded. 'Where did you get it?' I enquired.

'Er, nowhere,' he replied.

'What do you mean, nowhere?'

'Honestly, Mum. Nowhere.' But his face had flushed bright red.

'Matt,' I said as I shaded my eyes against the sun, 'please would you tell me where you got that laptop?'

'Erm, I, er, can't remember.'

'Darling,' I said, 'I happen to know that laptops are very expensive and your pocket money is only ten pounds a week. So I'd like you to tell me how you got it.' By now Matt was stuttering and fidgeting, and I almost felt sorry for him. But I felt disappointed too, because I've always taught my kids to tell the truth.

'Matt . . .' I tried again, keeping my voice low and calm because I didn't want to embarrass him in front of Jos. 'Matt, please just tell me how you come to own such an expensive machine. Dad didn't buy it for you, did he?' He shook his head and blushed again. And then I got it. Of course. It was from Andie. How slow of me. And how *outrageous* of her. She'd been bribing the children again. Anything to get them on her side. But Matt was too embarrassed to tell me, because he knew that I'd feel hurt.

'It's from Andie, isn't it?' I said. He was silent. But I wasn't going to let it go. 'Is it from Andie?' I repeated. Matt shook his head. 'Please tell me who it *is* from, then.'

'No,' he said. 'I can't.'

'Why ever not?' I enquired.

'Because it's private,' he explained. 'I'm sorry, Mum,' he said as he fiddled with his cuffs, 'but I really can't say.'

'Well, I'm your mother, Matt, and I don't want you to have a big secret like this from me.' He looked at me, then stared at the ground, and I could see that the tops of his ears were bright red. I was beginning to feel quite cross by now, but then I was struck by a terrible thought.

'Matt,' I said. 'I hope you came by it honestly.'

'What do you mean?'

'I hope you didn't . . . no, you wouldn't do that, would you? You'd never steal anything.'

'No, of *course* not!' he exclaimed, looking shocked. 'Oh Mum, I wish you wouldn't ask.'

'Matt,' I tried again. 'You are only twelve years old, yet here you are with a very expensive new computer and you refuse to say who it's from. But I really would like to know. Now, I think Andie gave it to you, and if she did, you must return it, because I will not have her bribing you like this.'

'Honestly, Mum. She *didn't* give it to me. I wish you'd just *believe* me.'

'Well then, who on earth *did*?'

'I can't say, Mum,' Matt whined. 'I really can't.' Oh God, he looked close to tears.

'Darling,' I said patiently. 'If Andie didn't, and Dad didn't, and I didn't, then who did?' He didn't reply.

'Matt,' I said. 'I think I'm about to get cross. Please tell me.' There was an ominous silence.

And then Jos said: 'Actually, it was me.' I looked at Matt. He looked as shocked as I felt.

'I was . . . updating my computer system,' Jos explained, 'and I realised that the laptop I had wasn't . . . quite what I needed any more. So, I offered it to Matt.'

'Oh,' I said, dumbfounded. 'But that's a very expensive thing.'

'Well, their second-hand value . . . isn't much,' he explained with a shrug. 'And I thought he might . . . find it useful.'

'Is this true, Matt?' I said. He looked at me blankly and said nothing. It obviously was.

'Why didn't you tell me then, Jos?' I said. 'I don't really understand.'

'Well, because I thought you'd disapprove,' he explained. 'Because if you don't want Andie giving the children expensive things, then that rule would also apply to me. I didn't want you to think I was trying to bribe your kids. So Matt and I agreed that we wouldn't say. I'm sorry if it's caused an argument,' he added. 'That's the last thing on earth I wanted.'

'Matt,' I said, swallowing hard. 'I owe you an apology. I'm sorry for doubting your word. And you're a very, *very* lucky boy.' Matt nodded mutely. 'And, Jos,' I went on, 'thank you. It was incredibly kind of you to give him that.' And now I found myself wondering how I could ever have doubted him. He was such a wonderfully generous and thoughtful man. I reached for his hand and squeezed it gratefully, aware that my eyes had filled with tears.

July

Highs and lows. That's what it's about. The weather, I mean. And at the moment we're on a high. The temperature's rising and the skies are deep blue, without even a wisp of cloud. At night the sky glows crimson; the barometer is fixed on fair. The little woman has emerged from my weather house, and the seaweed on my desk is bone dry. In short, it's hot. All the signs, technical and natural, point to that one simple fact. It's hot. It's very hot. And it's getting hotter by the day.

'Phew,' said Jos. He was standing in my bath, in a T-shirt and shorts, making pencil marks on the walls. He paused, then drew his hand across his brow. 'It's a bit on the warm side, what?'

'Mmm,' I said dreamily, 'it is.' Jos's right arm swung back and forth like a metronome as he sketched the curving fronds of a palm. A few deft strokes and a shoreline appeared, and then, in the foreground, a shell.

'Where is it?' I asked.

'Mystery location,' he replied, tapping the side of his nose.

'Go on, please tell me,' I said.

'All right, it's Parrot Cay on the Turks and Caicos. It's my favourite place in the world. And when this mural's finished, Faith, I'm going to go there with you.'

'When will that be?' I smiled.

'Around Christmas time, I'd say. Christ, it's hot,' he sighed as he sketched a solitary bird into the sky. 'I guess this is what's known as a warm front.'

'Nope. It's an anti-cyclone.'

'A what?'

'An area of high pressure, that's all. Anti-cyclones create calm, dry weather, unlike depressions which bring wind and rain. And anti-cyclones are stable,' I explained. 'They can sit in the same place for days.'

'Which presumably means this is going to last.'

'Yes,' I said, 'it is. In fact it's shaping up to be a serious heatwave, which makes for boring weather reports. "Good morning everyone," I say. "And it's going to be another very hot and sunny day, so put a hat on the baby, keep the dog inside, and slap on that factor fifteen!" I find fine weather dull,' I added ruefully, 'because there's not really much I can say.'

'Well, fine weather's fine by me,' said Jos as he clambered out of the bath. 'The hotter the better, I say. Look at that sky!' he added, glancing out of the window. 'It's like a Hockney or an Yves Klein. Why don't we go down to the coast?' he suggested as he leaned back and squinted at his work. 'We could take the kids,' he said.

'And Graham.'

'Yes,' he sighed as he wiped the back of his neck. 'But only if he's nice to me.'

'Do you hear that, darling?' I said to Graham, who was lying doggo by the door. 'If you're nice to Jos and promise not to bite him, he'll take you to the seaside for the day.' Graham raised a cynical eyebrow, then closed his eyes with a disgruntled sigh.

'Why don't we go next weekend?' said Jos. 'We could go down to Hastings or Rye.'

'The fifteenth?' I said. 'That's school speech day. I've got to go down to Kent.'

'Would you like me to come with you?' he suggested. 'To give you moral support?'

'I . . . well,' I was slightly taken aback. 'That's very sweet of you, Jos,' I said carefully, 'but I'd better discuss it with Peter first.'

So that evening I called him. I realised, as I dialled his number, that I'd never phoned Peter at his flat. Now, as I heard the ringing tone, I tried to imagine what it was like. The children had tactfully refrained from telling me, and I hadn't wanted to ask. Was the interior spartan, I wondered, or had it been tastefully done? Were there lots of mod cons in the kitchen? And what were his neighbours like?

'Hel-lo?' Suddenly I heard Andie's slow, transatlantic tones and felt a vicious stab of pain. 'Hel-lo?' she repeated. 'Who is this?' I felt my face begin to burn.

'It's Peter's wife,' I said with cross crispness. 'May I speak to my husband, please?' Then I was instantly furious with myself for having accidentally asked her permission.

'Hu-un,' I heard her call in her cigarettey drawl, 'it's for yo-ou.' By now my heart was banging so loudly I thought Peter would hear it down the line. Knowing he was involved with Andie was one thing. Hearing her voice was quite another. How *stupid* of me to have rung him at home when there was a high chance that she'd be there.

'Faith!' Peter exclaimed warmly. His friendly tone took me by surprise. 'How are you?'

'I'm . . . OK,' I replied.

'You sound a bit pissed off.'

'No. Not at all,' I said.

'Just phoning for a nice little chat, are you?'

'No,' I said briskly. 'I'm not. I'm phoning to ask if you're coming to school speech day. It's on the fifteenth.'

'Yes of course I'm coming,' he replied. 'Why do you need to ask?'

'Because arrangements will have to be made. And also,' I added carefully, 'because I was wondering about bringing . . . Jos.'

'Jos?' he repeated. 'Your lover?'

'My partner,' I corrected him with frosty hauteur.

'Your partner? Oh, how modern. So you're thinking of bringing him along? Hmmm,' he went on judiciously. 'I'm not sure how I'd feel about that. I can't say I'm gagging to play gooseberry all day. I know!' he exclaimed happily, as if struck by some novel thought. 'You bring Jos and I'll bring

Andie. What do you say to that? We can have a civilised little foursome,' he enthused. 'Wouldn't that be fun?'

'It's quite all right, Peter,' I said firmly. 'I find I've suddenly changed my mind.' However happy I am with Jos at the moment, I still couldn't face seeing *her*.

'Oh well,' he sighed theatrically. 'We'll just have to go down together then and present a united front. You can get the train and meet me there, or I'll give you a lift – you choose.'

So on Saturday morning I went to meet Peter at his flat in Ponsonby Place. The house was a white, flat-fronted terrace in a rather stark, treeless street near the Tate. It looked 'smart', and rather sterile after the warm cosiness of Elliot Road. I pressed the bell, heard rapid steps, then suddenly the door opened and there he was. I was terrified that I'd see Andie standing proprietorially behind him, but mercifully there was no sign. There was an awkward moment when Peter and I greeted each other and didn't quite know what to do. What does protocol require when you're in the middle of a divorce? A kiss on the cheek? A handshake? A diplomatic smile? We opted for the air-kissing, which felt unnatural and contrived. It was as though we were actors in a play we'd insufficiently rehearsed and were suddenly unsure of our lines. Peter was wearing a pale linen suit which I'd never seen, and another expensive silk tie. His sartorial style had changed since our split; he had never dressed like this when we were married.

'You look a bit smart,' he remarked as he eyed up my Miu Miu linen shift. 'You never dressed like this before.'

'Thanks,' I said uncertainly, unsure of whether or not that was a compliment. We smiled awkwardly at each other again as I stood there on the step.

'Do you want to come up?' he said.

'Sorry?'

'Don't you want to see my flat?' Oh.

'Yes,' I said suddenly. 'Why not?' And then I immediately regretted it, because I knew there'd be evidence of *her*. It would be horrible opening the bathroom door and seeing Andie's face creams ranged on the shelf, or peeping into his bedroom and seeing her sexy nightwear spread out on the bed.

'It's . . . all right, actually,' I stuttered. 'I, er . . . some other time perhaps.'

'Oh,' he looked slightly disappointed. 'Whatever you say. Well then!' He clapped his hands together with artificial brightness. 'In that case, let's get going. It's that blue Rover parked over there.'

'Does this go with the job?' I enquired as he beeped open the door.

'Yes,' he said. 'I could have had a Merc or a Beemer,' he went on, 'but I felt I should do my patriotic duty.' It was only ten thirty, but the sun was beating down and the sky was yet again a hot, searing blue. As we crossed the river we could see a miasma of smog already enveloping the city like a shroud.

'Isn't this fun, Faith?' he said as we drove along with the windows down. 'And I'd just like to say that I have absolutely no intention of asking you to share petrol.'

'Thank you,' I said wryly.

'This one's on me. It's complimentary. It's gratis. F.o.C.'

'Very kind,' I said as I pulled down the visor against the glare.

'Isn't this a laugh?' he said. I gave him a sideways glance. I realised that this was the first time I'd been alone with Peter for any length of time since he'd moved out. He appeared to be in an odd, flippant kind of mood which I found slightly unnerving. He seemed happy. Unnaturally so. No doubt, I reflected suspiciously, because he was having such a good time with Andie.

'Isn't this fun!' he exclaimed again as he drummed his fingertips against the steering wheel. 'It's just like old times, eh?'

'Not really,' I said warily as I put on my shades. 'The old times are over now.'

'Yes,' he conceded with a wistful sigh. 'Yes. I suppose they are. Now, where are we up to on the divorce?' he went on pleasantly as we followed signs for Blackheath. 'Are you fighting me for the house, or am I trying to get custody of the kids? Who's going to get the record collection, and is there going to be a tug-of-love with Graham?'

'I don't know what's happening on that front,' I said, refusing to respond to his facetiousness. 'I haven't heard from Rory Cheetham-Stabb for weeks.'

'Well I've done my bit, Faith,' he said as we drove through Catford. 'I've sent back that Acknowledgement of Service form, so any delays are not due to me.'

'You seem very cheerful about it all,' I sniffed.

'It's gallows humour. I'm just resigned. I mean, if you want to go to Splitsville I can't stop you, but as you know, it's not my choice.'

'Well it wasn't my choice that you should run off with your headhunter,' I retorted as we went round a roundabout.

'I didn't run off with her, that's not fair. Damn! Where's the sign?'

'No, but you did get involved.'

'True,' he conceded as we went round again. 'But only after you'd kicked me out.'

'Yes. But I wouldn't have kicked you out, as you so inelegantly put it, if you hadn't had an affair – QED.'

'Oh, Faith,' said Peter as the road circled round again. 'It's so lovely and logical and simple for you, isn't it? One plus one equals two.'

'I know that one plus one plus one equals *three*,' I shot back, 'and in a marriage that's fifty per cent too many!'

'You know, your arithmetic's stunning,' he said. 'It should be you getting the maths prize today, not Matt. In any case,' he went on quietly, 'you seem to have got yourself fixed up with impressive speed.' I didn't say anything. I knew it was true. 'Now,' he said as we followed signs to Sidcup, 'the kids tell me that your new bloke, whatshisname, Mr Glyndebourne, has industrial quantities of charm.'

'They're quite right,' I replied. 'Jos does. He's also considerate, generous and kind. Do you know, he gave Matt his old laptop. Wasn't that sweet? And today he's volunteered to look after the dog.'

232

'Well that *is* nice of him,' Peter agreed.

'It's *very* nice of him,' I reiterated, 'especially as he doesn't even *like* Graham.' There was a moment's silence as Peter took this in.

'What do you mean, he doesn't like Graham?' he asked quietly as he changed gear.

'Look, Peter,' I said. 'Just because we're crazy about our dog doesn't mean that everyone else has to be.'

'But Graham isn't just any dog, Faith. He's a very special dog.'

'Yes,' I said, 'I *know*. But Jos doesn't feel the same way. And that's not really surprising because Graham's not exactly mad about him.'

'Isn't he? Oh, that's interesting. And why not, may I ask?'

'I don't know,' I replied. 'He's being a bit . . . tricky at the moment. Katie thinks it may be because of the divorce.'

'Or maybe it's because he knows something you don't,' Peter suggested as we pulled up at a red light. 'I always said that dog was a genius, Faith, from the day he first followed you home. So Graham doesn't like your boyfriend,' he chuckled. 'Oh dear. What does he do?'

'Well, it's very embarrassing really,' I began slightly stiffly as we followed signs for the motorway. 'If Jos tries to, you know . . .'

'What?'

'Well, without being too personal – to kiss me, then Graham tries to bite him.'

'I'm not surprised. I'd probably do the same myself.'

'Also,' I said, ignoring him, 'Graham is conducting a psychological campaign against him. He conspicuously refuses to be friendly, and is often cold and withdrawn. But today Jos has magnanimously set his personal feelings aside in order to help me out.'

'Well, that's very good of him,' said Peter.

'Yes,' I said, 'it is.'

'Or,' Peter added judiciously, 'he's trying to demonstrate what a great bloke he is.'

'There's no need to be quite so cynical,' I said. 'Maybe he *is* just a great bloke.'

'No need to be touchy, Faith,' said Peter as we turned onto the motorway. 'I'm simply suggesting that to voluntarily spend several hours confined with a dog which is quite likely to savage you is somewhat beyond the call of duty. So I have to say I find myself wondering what Jos is trying to prove.'

'He's not trying to prove anything,' I said hotly. 'And in any case he doesn't need to, because he knows I think he's *great*.'

'Oh, really,' said Peter in a bored sort of way. 'Lucky old Jos.'

'Look, Peter,' I said crossly as we picked up speed. 'I'm not in the mood to quarrel, and in any case it's much too hot. So can we please have an agreement that we leave each other's partners alone? I promise not to bitch about – *her*,' I spat, 'if you don't criticise Jos.'

'OK,' he said. 'It's a deal. Pax?' he added with a smile.

'Yes. Pax,' I agreed. And I was just about to steer the conversation onto the safer territory of Peter's new job when he suddenly put on his indicator and the car swung left into a garage.

'I need some petrol,' he said. 'Hang on, won't be a tick.' While he filled up the car on the forecourt I went into the shop. I wanted some water, some Polos and a paper. *The Times* had sold out so I bought a *Mail*.

'And how's Bishopsgate?' I enquired pleasantly as we set off again.

'It's going *very* well,' he replied. He looked into his mirror as he overtook the car in front. 'It's much more commercial, of course,' he explained as I handed him a reconciliatory mint. 'It's all self-help guides and coffee-table books and no fiction, which I miss. But on the other hand I have far more responsibility, no Oiliver, and a lot more dosh.'

'Well, Rory Cheetham-Stabb will be relieving you of some of that,' I said.

'No doubt,' he groaned. 'And the house. For richer, for poorer,' he added wryly. 'But it was in marriage I promised that, not divorce.' At that a wave of sadness engulfed me, and I felt my throat constrict. I looked ahead at the long perpendicular ribbon of black motorway stretching far, far ahead, and I thought, Peter and I are on a road like this, which is taking us inexorably towards divorce. We're on it now, and we're stuck, and there are few opportunities to get off. And a U-turn is out of the question because there's this huge barrier in the way. Or rather, a central reservation, I realised bitterly. A reservation about Peter's fidelity, which I knew I could never overcome. And here we were driving down together to see the kids as though nothing were amiss, when the reality was that we had embarked on a process which would split us up in less than six months. It was surreal. *Un*real. And as we drove along, the heat threw up spectral mirages which shimmered in the distance, like ghosts. I heaved a painful sigh, aware of the relentless swish of the tyres.

'OK, we're passing Maidstone,' I heard Peter say a while later. 'Will you look out for Nettlebury Green? I always miss the turning. Faith, will you help me look out for the signs, please? Faith? Are you listening?' I wasn't. I was reading the paper and had just turned to the gossip page. Occupying the top part of it was a photo of Rory Cheetham-Stabb, on a tropical beach, with a louche smile on his face, and a glamorous blonde on his arm. So that's why I hadn't heard from him recently – he was on holiday at his house in Mustique. Then I lowered my gaze and now, to my astonishment, I found myself staring at another, much smaller photo. It was of Peter and me. It was captioned: *Weather girl Faith Smith in happier times*.

'Here's the sign,' I heard Peter say as the car began to slow down. 'You've gone very quiet, Faith. Faith?' I didn't respond as, with growing indignation, I read the diary piece. *AM-UK!'s Faith Smith is divorcing her husband Peter*, it proclaimed. *The attractive weather girl has confessed to friends that she's 'had enough' of his womanising ways. The only question now is what Smith's new bosses will make of his domestic troubles. And what of his place on the government's Family Ethics Committee? Can he in all honesty remain? Some say that Smith should do the decent thing and resign.*

'Faith, what's up?' said Peter as we turned left through the wrought iron school gates. 'What is it?' he repeated as he followed the drive, then nosed into a parking space.

'Look at this,' I said bleakly as he pulled up the handbrake. I handed him the paper, his eyes scanned the page, and his relaxed expression changed.

'Who the *hell* is doing this?' he said. 'I'll bloody well sue. Womaniser?' he expostulated. 'I am not a womaniser – I was faithful to you for fifteen years! Who the *hell* is behind this?' he repeated angrily as we opened the doors of the car.

'I don't know,' I said as I retrieved my jacket and bag from the back. 'But I've got a good idea.'

'Oh yes? Who?'

'Well, *I* think it's Andie,' I said carefully as I leaned against the car.

'Andie?' said Peter. 'No way!'

'I think it is her,' I repeated quietly. 'It certainly makes sense.'

'Faith,' said Peter firmly, 'I know you don't like her, but it makes no sense at all.'

'Yes it does,' I insisted, 'though I agree the logic is a bit odd. But she . . .' I swallowed. I hated saying this. 'She wants to marry you, doesn't she? I mean, I assume that's her aim.' I looked at Peter and he looked away into the middle distance.

'And how,' he now asked, pursing his lips, 'would this kind of behaviour help her to achieve that?'

'Rory Cheetham-Stabb thinks that's her subtle way of putting pressure on you. He thinks – and I agree – that *she* fed that story to *Hello!*'

'But why would she? I still don't understand.'

'Because if your divorce makes life a bit awkward for you with Bishopsgate, because you're getting some negative press, then Andie can quietly assure them, as her client, that your personal life will soon be "normal" again – with her.'

'Faith,' said Peter, 'Rory Cheetham-Stabb is talking out of his expensively besuited backside. He knows nothing about the terms of my contract. Of course they're not going to kick me out just because I'm getting divorced. If that were a condition of employment, then half the staff would have to resign. These gossip pieces are just spiteful speculation. They have no basis in fact. In any case,' he went on, 'if I was sacked before my first year is up then Andie would have to refund most of her fee. Cheetham-Stabb is quite wrong, Faith. The only purpose this drip-feed of poison serves is to damage and discredit me. But the question is, who's doing it, and why?'

'I don't know,' I replied.

'I mean, who would have such a big grudge against me that they'd be this vindictive and low?' Who would, I thought. Who? And then I knew.

'Oiliver,' I said. Of course.

'*Oiliver*?' Peter repeated. 'No! Although he's certainly vicious enough, and he definitely bore me a grudge.'

'I think he still does,' I said. And I told him about Oliver's nasty remarks at the book launch in June.

'Mmm,' said Peter. 'That's rather interesting. So he's still got it in for me, then.'

'Though it's hard to understand why, now that he's got what he's always wanted, namely your absence and your job.' Peter didn't reply. He was staring into the middle distance again. That's what he does when he's thinking. 'So why would Oliver want to damage you,' I went on, 'when you're no threat to him any more?'

'I wonder,' he said quietly. 'I *wonder*. But you may have hit on something there. Yes,' he added thoughtfully, 'as it happens, I really think you may. But I tell you what, whoever it is, I'm going to damn well find out. Mmm. Oiliver,' he mused as he locked the car. 'In fact that's quite an interesting thought. Anyway,' he added wearily, 'let's go and find Katie and Matt.'

We set off across the car parking field, the parched grass crisp beneath our feet, and as we passed under the school gateway with the other parents I read the Seaworth motto carved above. *Garde Ta Foy*, it declared. Well I did keep Faith,

I thought. I kept Faith for fifteen years. And this, I knew, would be the last time that Peter and I would come here as man and wife. By this time next year we'd be divorced, and despite the heat a shiver convulsed my frame at the thought that my life could have changed so fast. But then I made myself stop thinking about it, because I'd spotted the kids. Matt looked very grown up, I realised, though he had a slightly anxious expression on his face. Probably because he felt nervous at the thought of going up to collect his prize. Katie looked smart in a green linen dress we'd bought for her in Hobbs. They ushered us into a huge marquee on the main lawn for the buffet lunch. As we circulated amongst the throng I spotted a few familiar faces. We'd met the Dobbses a couple of times, and the Blacks – their children were in the same house. I'd also met the Thompsons, at the school play last year. They had a son in the same year as Matt, Johnny, and another boy of sixteen. I smiled at the Dobbses and their son James; to my great surprise, they didn't smile back.

'Peter,' I whispered as we stood in the queue. 'Am I imagining it or do the Dobbs seem a bit hostile?'

'Funny you should say that,' Peter replied. 'David Black has just been a bit off with me.'

'It can't be because of that gossip piece in the *Mail*, can it?' I asked. He shrugged.

'I don't see why. I mean, loads of people here are divorced.' I looked around. It was true. There was the rock singer, Rod McShagg, he'd been married three times. On the side of the marquee was that actress Sheryl Love – that was her fourth husband she was with. And that chap over there – he was a successful record producer – I'd read about his colourful private life in *Hello!* So why on earth should anyone be sniffy about Peter and me?

'Hello, Mrs Thompson,' I said to a woman in a frumpy lilac suit. 'How nice to see you again.'

She gave me a strange little smile, then said, 'Well, I suppose Matt must be pleased with himself.'

'Matt?' I repeated. I was totally taken aback.

'Yes. Matt,' she said.

'Oh, er, you mean because he's getting the Junior Maths Prize?' She emitted a hollow laugh.

'I don't know *why* he's getting it,' she said as she patted her rigid-looking perm.

'Well,' I said, dumbfounded, feeling my mouth open and close like a fish. 'Well, I believe he's getting it because he happens to be good at maths.' Mrs Thompson gave me a withering smile, then walked away. I was so shocked by her rudeness that I was shaking. What an awful thing to say! And why on earth had she said it? Then I realised. Of *course*. She was jealous, because her son, Johnny, isn't up for a prize. For God's sake, I thought, how petty can you get? It's not Matt's fault he's so bright. It's not Matt's fault that he's brilliant and her son Johnny is moronic and mediocre. I mean, why do other parents have to be so competitive, I reflected crossly.

Now the Ellis-Joneses were giving us odd looks as we nibbled our bits of cold quiche. I was beginning to feel quite annoyed, and far too hot in my jacket and dress. But I was determined, despite the aggravation, to act as though nothing were amiss.

'Hello, Mrs Ellis-Jones,' I said breezily. 'Hello Jack,' I said to her spotty sixteen-year-old. 'How are you?'

'I'm . . . OK,' he said. 'Considering.' Considering? What on earth did that mean?

'And have you got exciting holiday plans?' I enquired breezily.

'No,' he replied flatly. 'I haven't. I *did*,' he added darkly. 'I'd saved up to go inter-railing with Tom North. But I can't afford it now.'

'Oh dear,' I said. 'What a shame.' And I had not the slightest idea why he was telling me this, but I didn't press him to explain.

'Katie,' I whispered. 'I can't help feeling that we're not exactly popular today.'

'Mmm,' she said. 'We're getting bad vibes. There's some group hostility. I thought that this might happen.'

'What do you mean?' I said.

'Well, Mum,' she went on thoughtfully as she popped a strawberry into her mouth. 'I think there's something you ought to know.'

'What ought I to know? What are you talking about?' But I didn't have time to find out. For at that moment a bell was rung; and we were summoned inside for the speeches. All the children went down to the front of the hall, while the parents sat at the back.

'Peter,' I whispered as we took our seats. 'I find the atmosphere rather strained.'

'Mmm,' he assented. 'You're right. There's something decidedly odd going on, or maybe it's just the heat.' I began to fan myself with the service sheet, which listed the names of all the prize-winners. I experienced a stab of maternal pride as I read Matt's name at the end. Now the headmaster stepped onto the podium, to make his annual address.

'Over the past year . . . progress . . . community spirit . . . cricket results . . . excellent . . . unfortunately . . . expulsions . . . perspective . . . illicit substances . . . violence . . . new science wing . . . expensive . . . shortfall . . . much appreciated . . . bucket. And now,' he added warmly, 'the annual prize-giving, for which we are profoundly grateful to all our benefactors whose generosity has made it possible for us to present these valuable awards. We are particularly grateful to Mr Bill Gates for endowing the new junior maths prize with a splendid ten-pound book voucher!' We all applauded dutifully. And then the headmaster cleared his throat and announced the winners.

'The Ali G prize for grammar goes to Caroline Day.' A lanky girl with black hair went up to collect her book voucher, then returned to her seat in a shower of applause. 'The Emin prize for painting is awarded to Laetitia Banks.' We all clapped enthusiastically as the pint-sized Laetitia shook the head's hand. 'The Mark Thatcher prize for orienteering goes to Rajiv Patel.' We all applauded as the boy swaggered, hands in pockets, across the stage. 'And the Archer prize for acting goes to Britney Scott.' We all showed our appreciation

240

in the conventional way as Britney Scott collected her prize. 'The al Fayed prize for politics – this one's a cash award – is awarded to Mary Ross.' By now my hands were beginning to sting. 'The Barbara Windsor prize for elocution goes to Jennifer Johns. And the Ken Livingstone debating prize goes to Barbara Jones. Finally,' he said as we all applauded again, 'the Bill Gates junior maths prize, which is awarded to Matthew Smith.' Peter and I clapped enthusiastically as Matt got up from his seat. But as he stepped up onto the stage, we suddenly realised that we were alone. The hall was virtually silent, our applause pinging off the walls. How rude! I'd clapped all the other parents' kids, I thought indignantly, so why couldn't they clap mine? I felt my face burn with barely repressed fury, but now, at last, they did. Thank God. They were all clapping. They'd been a bit slow to react, that was all. Then I realised that it wasn't polite, appreciative applause. Far from it – it was a slow hand clap. I saw Matt's pale face flush bright red. Clap, clap, clap, they went. Clap. Clap. Clap. It was getting louder and louder and more rhythmic, and then, to my horror, someone booed. And as Matt shook the head's hand, there were shouts of, 'Rubbish!' and, 'Get him off!' And the headmaster, seeing things getting out of hand, called the hall to attention.

'We must applaud our prize-winners in a spirit of generosity,' he said. 'Matt is a very gifted young mathematician. Very gifted indeed. Although,' he went on judiciously, 'he doesn't always get it *quite* right.'

'Too right he doesn't!' someone called out from the third row.

'And some of Matt's recent calculations have been a *little* wide of the mark.'

'You're telling me!'

'But we're confident,' the headmaster went on benignly, 'that his recent run of bad luck is just a . . . blip.'

'Bloody well hope so!' piped up another boy. It was Johnny Thompson. 'He lost me three hundred quid.' *What*?

'He lost me five hundred,' said a thin girl sitting behind.

'He lost me six hundred and fifty,' said Jack Ellis-Jones. 'I was going to go round Europe with that.'

'Well, I do think he needs to do a little more work on his percentages,' said the head carefully. 'But I'm sure that's something he'll conquer next term. And we're confident that he'll be able to assist the bursar in the fund-raising effort for the new science wing.'

'What the hell is going on?' hissed Peter.

'I wish I knew,' I said.

'Well, that brings us to the end of the prize-giving,' said the headmaster, 'and so congratulations to all concerned.' Matt trooped disconsolately off stage, and Peter and I made our way through the crowd to the front. He was sitting, head bowed, in the front row, dejection personified.

'Matt, what's this all about?' I said. 'What's been going on?'

'It's not my fault,' he mumbled as he fiddled with his book voucher. 'I told them there was a risk.'

'What do you mean?' He was silent. 'Katie,' I said, 'will you please tell us? Has Matt done something bad?'

'No,' she replied carefully. 'Not really. He was . . . speculating, that's all.'

'On the horses!' I gasped.

'No, of course not,' she said. 'On the stock exchange. He made loads of money to start with,' she explained. 'He had a really good run. He was working it all out on his computer.'

'You were investing on the stock market?' I said. 'How, may I ask? And with what? Matt, where did you get the money? We only gave you eighty pounds a term.' He shuffled his feet, sighed and then he spoke.

'I sold my computer games,' he said quietly. 'That's how. I set up a website and advertised them. I made nearly two thousand pounds.'

'Two thousand pounds!' Peter said.

'I thought you'd given them all to charity,' I pointed out.

'No,' he said, 'I didn't. I sold them all, for twenty pounds each – that's cheap, you know. People would e-mail me their orders and then send me the cash.' Ah. That's why he'd had so much post.

'And you invested that money in stocks and shares?' I said wonderingly.

'Yes,' he said quietly. 'I did.'

'But you're too young to do that,' said Peter. 'You can't trade until you're sixteen. In fact,' he continued, 'you're too young even to have a bank account. So how did you do it?' Matt stared at the floor. 'How did you do it?' Peter pressed him gently. 'And where did you put the cash? Please just tell us, Matt. We promise we won't be cross.'

'Well . . .' Matt looked at us beseechingly. I could see he was close to tears. 'I can't tell you,' he said, 'it's a secret. A big one.' A fat tear coursed down his cheek.

'We don't want you to keep big secrets from us,' I said. 'We'd like you to tell us the truth.'

'Look Mum, I really can't. I just . . . *can't*.'

'Why not?'

'Because I promised Granny I wouldn't.'

'Granny?' we said. Matt looked stricken as he realised his gaffe, and then his head sank into his hands.

'Yes. Granny,' he croaked. 'The money went into her account. She put in two thousand as well, so we had four thousand for me to invest. I gave her all the tips, she did the trading, and we split the profits down the middle.'

'Are you saying that Granny has been encouraging you to gamble on the stock market?'

'Well, no, not really. We were doing it together.' Right. Now I understood why she was always so keen to speak to him.

'She even bought him that laptop,' said Katie. 'To make it easier to keep in touch.'

'Granny bought you that?' I gasped. 'I thought Jos gave it to you. I thought it was an old one.'

'Oh no,' said Katie, shaking her head. 'It's a brand new powerbook, state of the art.' And now I found myself wondering what Jos was doing lying to me. Why the hell did he say that *he'd* given it to Matt?

'How much money did you make?' I asked quietly.

'To begin with, a lot,' he sniffed. 'I made a profit of five hundred per cent.'

'How much is that?'

'Twenty thousand pounds.'

'Good God!'

'Some of the older kids heard about it,' said Katie. 'And so they asked him to give them tips.'

'I didn't want to,' Matt said. 'But Ellis-Jones and Thompson, they're prefects, and they made me tell them which shares to buy. And at first they made lots of money too,' he wept. 'But then the dot.com stocks all crashed.'

'Dot.coms?!' Peter exclaimed. 'You might as well have bought lottery tickets.'

'I know,' said Matt. 'I told them that. I said we should get out of that sector. I went into Bolivian silver mines for a bit, but that wasn't much good, either. Then we tried trading in soya harvests. But they said they wanted to buy dot.coms and hold them, and they were furious when they crashed. Up until then we'd been doing well.'

'I see,' I sighed. And I did. I saw it all, as clear as day. I saw how my mother had afforded all her fabulous holidays, and why the other parents had been hostile. I understood why Matt kept going out to the letterbox, and why he'd been receiving so much post. I also saw that his intense new interest in current affairs wasn't quite what it seemed. And I saw red, that my mother had been encouraging Matt to gamble instead of study.

'Ellis-Jones and Thompson were really angry,' said Matt. 'They said it was all my fault.'

'How much was their stake?'

'A hundred. And it went up to over six hundred, then it dropped right back down to almost what it had been at the start. But I warned them that that could happen. It wasn't as though they didn't know.'

'Oh dear,' said Peter quietly. 'So you've been dicing with debt. Oh well. All is explained.'

'Not quite,' said Katie. 'The headmaster was having a flutter as well. For the new science wing. They're trying to raise three million, but they've lost a lot too.'

In the circumstances we decided not to stay for tea. The children collected their cases and we went home. I dreaded to think how much school work Matt had missed out on as we drove silently back in the car. Of course, it would all have to stop. We'd have to write to the parents and apologise and, oh God, we'd have to reimburse them. And I'd have to have strong words with Mum. And I wanted to know why Jos had lied to me about the computer. That didn't make sense at all. I wondered whether he'd still be there when we got back, and was rather relieved that he wasn't. The lie about the laptop had unnerved me, and I wasn't ready to introduce him to Peter yet. In any case the stress of the day had left me seriously wrung out.

Graham leaped up like a rocket when I turned the key in the door, and he was so overjoyed to see Peter that he practically knocked him to the ground. He was crying, almost singing, with happiness as Peter got down on his hands and knees.

'Hello Graham darling, have you missed me?' Graham licked his ears and whimpered with joy. 'Do you like having all your family in one place? Is that it, then? All your little flock?'

'Yes,' said Katie firmly. 'That's it.'

'Now,' said Peter. 'Where's Jos? Oh, Graham,' he said, looking shocked. 'You haven't . . . have you? Oh, that *is* naughty. I'm afraid Mummy's going to be very cross. Faith,' he called out to me as I went into the kitchen. 'I'm afraid that Graham's eaten Jos.'

'No he has-n't,' I replied airily as I read Jos's note on the table.

'Honestly, Faith, I think he has. He's got that guilty look.'

'Jos is alive and well,' I said, 'he left half an hour ago.' He'd left Graham lots of water, and a few biscuits which he hadn't touched. But now, thrilled at our return, he came in search of his bowl. Peter followed him into the kitchen and stood there, framed in the doorway like a handsome portrait.

'Would you like to have supper with us, Peter?' I asked.

'Yes, I would,' he replied.

'Great.'

'But I'm afraid I can't.' Oh.

'What a pity,' I said breezily. 'Why not?' I added fatefully, although of course I knew.

'Well, because Andie's expecting me,' he said. I nodded. 'I told her I'd be home by eight.'

'You are at home, Dad,' said Katie matter-of-factly.

'Well, yes,' he said ruefully. 'I suppose I am.' He looked at me and smiled. It was a smile of painful resignation. We were standing a few inches away from each other, but we were just so far apart.

'Right,' I said brightly. 'I guess we'd better not keep you, then. Thanks for taking me, I mean, taking me down, there. I mean, giving me a lift. That's what I mean.' I glanced at Katie, who was giving me one of her old-fashioned looks – I don't know *what* that girl's problem is! Peter kissed the children goodbye and ruffled Graham's ears. Then, to my astonishment, he put his arms round me, gave me an awkward hug, then pressed his cheek, for a moment, to mine.

'So long,' he murmured.

'Yes,' I said. 'So long.'

'So long,' he said again. 'Fifteen years.' Then he turned and walked out of the house. As I listened to his retreating footsteps I felt a great wave of regret. And I know that Graham did too. Because after Peter left, he sat at the window, looking out, and stayed like that for a long, long time.

July Continued

This morning I left Jos fast asleep in my bed and slipped off to eight a.m. Mass. I was in the mood to reflect quietly on recent events and on the concept of guilt – and penance.

'To prepare ourselves to celebrate Mass,' said the priest, 'let us call to mind our sins.' I didn't call to mind my own sins, however – I called to mind my mother's. We'd had a bruising encounter over the phone.

'It was just a bit of fun,' she'd said.

'Fun!' I exclaimed.

'Well, Matt loves working things out, and it was our little secret.'

'I bet it was,' I said. 'There's no way Dad would have approved if he'd known about it, and you know *my* views on stocks and shares. I mean, you might as well go down the casino.'

'Darling, the stock market is absolutely fine,' said Mum calmly, 'as long as you know what you're doing.'

'Matt obviously didn't,' I said. 'But then why should he – he's only twelve. I can't believe you exploited your own grandson for financial gain.'

'I didn't do it for financial gain, Faith,' she pointed out earnestly. 'I had no *idea* we'd make so much. I just thought it would be good for him.'

'Oh yeah?'

'That it might broaden his education. I mean, to do it successfully you have to follow current affairs. He knows all about Bolivian politics now,' she added enthusiastically. 'And US soya harvests, too.'

'Yes, but he knows nothing *useful*,' I replied. 'He's way behind with his Latin, and his Ancient Greek is dire. As for his French and history,' I added, 'he got D minus for those. I'm furious, Mum.'

'Well, I'm sorry, Faith,' she replied. 'I really am. But I've thought of a way of putting things right.' So last week she and Dad took the kids to France for a month. They've hired a small *gîte* near Bordeaux so that Matt can improve his French, and Mum's going to help him catch up on his schoolwork, too. That's her penance. It was quite a good one really, I reflected as we bowed our heads in prayer, and a lot more fun than reciting strings of Hail Marys and Glory Bes. The children were thrilled at the prospect, and I was pleased, too – not least because it gives me the chance to spend a little more time with Jos. You see, when he told me about the laptop, I was really quite upset. I didn't like the fact that he'd lied to me; no, I didn't like that at all. But when I finally understood *why* he'd lied, I felt overwhelmed with grateful affection.

'You see, Faith,' he confessed the day after speech day, 'I've become very fond of Matt. He's such a great kid – they both are – and I couldn't bear to see him distressed. Obviously I didn't know where the laptop *had* come from,' he'd added, 'but seeing that Matt was in a tight corner, I pretended it had come from me.'

'And Matt clearly wasn't going to contradict you,' I went on, 'because you'd just got him off the hook.' He nodded.

'Oh darling!' I exclaimed, throwing my arms around him. 'You covered up for my son. That was so *wonderfully* kind and selfless of you.' He just looked at me and smiled. So, yes, Jos lied to me, that's the truth, but he lied for a very good reason.

Now, I'm afraid to say that Katie has a slightly more sceptical take on this. She claims Jos covered up for Matt to make me feel emotionally indebted. I told her that's a ridiculous theory, because he couldn't know that I'd find out the truth.

'Look, Mum,' she said wearily. 'Jos knew he was in a no-lose situation. Either he's the generous donor of the laptop; or he's the devoted boyfriend, nobly covering up the "sins" of his girlfriend's son. He must feel awfully inadequate,' she added matter-of-factly, 'to go to such lengths to make himself liked.'

'That's very mean of you,' I said crossly. 'Especially when he gave you that *extremely* expensive book for your birthday – *and* that *enormous* cake. He didn't have to do that, did he?'

'QED Mum,' she said.

I must say I find Katie's cynicism very depressing, especially in one so young. But now, as I sat in church, I felt the strain of the last few days flood away. As the sun poured through the stained-glass windows, it scattered refracted beams in red, gold and blue, like the fragments of a shattered rainbow.

'God be with you,' said the priest, his hands upturned.

'And also with you.'

'The Mass is ended. Go in peace.'

And I did go in peace. I felt very peaceful indeed, because for once everything was well with the world. Peter was being reasonable to me; we seemed to have established a more civilised rapport. Perhaps we could become 'apartners', I thought optimistically, like Mick Jagger and Jerry Hall. At the same time my mother was trying to atone for her bad behaviour by taking the children on a lovely trip; and I was dating, quite seriously now, a man who was talented, devoted and kind. I looked at my watch as I turned right into Elliot Road. It was only ten to nine. Jos would still be in bed, I reflected. Just time for us to have breakfast, and then we were driving down to Windsor for the polo. Lily had invited us to the Cartier – I'd never been before. Oh yes, all is well with my world, I realised happily as I clicked open the gate. To my surprise, I suddenly heard raised voices – or rather one raised voice. I slipped the key in the lock and went upstairs. In my bedroom, still in his pyjama bottoms, standing with his back to me, was Jos.

'Just what is your *problem*, Graham?' he yelled as I stood there, paralysed with amazement. 'Just what is your *effing problem*? Eh?' Graham was staring at him with an expression of aloof disdain. 'Why don't you *like* me? *Why*?' Jos shouted, putting his hands on his hips. 'Everyone *else* likes me. But *you* don't. You have to be *different*. And I don't know *why* you don't like me, you stupid *mutt*, because I've been very *nice* to you!' Graham continued to fix him with his cool, contemptuous gaze. But this only seemed to enrage Jos more. 'Boy, have you got problems,' he added vehemently, shaking his head. 'You really need *help*, dog. You know that, don't you? Do you *hear* me, Graham?' he said, wagging an admonitory finger at him. 'You're *sad*! Yes! That's what you are. *Sad*! And let's face it, you need *help*. You. Really. Need. *Help*. Because you have got *serious*. PSYCHOLOGICAL. *PROBLEMS*!!!'

'Jos,' I said quietly. He spun round and looked at me, his face a mask of shock. 'Jos,' I repeated as Graham bounded up to greet me. 'I'd rather you didn't shout at the dog.'

'Well, I'd rather the dog didn't bloody well *bite* me!' Jos shot back. I'd never seen him angry before. His face was puce; the veins in his temple stood out, he was trembling and seemed close to tears. Now he pointed down at his left ankle while looking accusingly at Graham.

'Er, I can't see anything,' I said.

'Then you're not looking properly,' he replied. I crouched down and inspected his foot, and indeed, just below the ankle bone I could see that the skin had been slightly broken.

'Oh dear,' I murmured. 'Not again. I'm really sorry.'

'So am I, Faith. I'm *very* sorry. And I am also very, *very* upset that despite the fact that this dog has known me for two whole months, he continues to treat me like Bill the fucking *Burglar*! All I was doing was trying to get out of bed,' he went on furiously. 'He just went for me.'

'Perhaps he thought you were going to kick him,' I suggested.

'I bloody well will next time.'

'OK I'm sorry,' I said again, impotently. 'But it really doesn't look too bad. Would you like me to put a plaster on it?' I added. Jos nodded his head, lips pursed.

'That dog is dangerous!' he called out as I rummaged in the medicine cabinet. 'He could bite someone he doesn't know.'

'Well, he's never done that,' I replied. And I was about to point out that Jos was, in fact, the *only* person Graham's *ever* been tricky with, but just managed to stop myself in time.

'He could bite someone in the street,' Jos went on indignantly as I returned with the pack of Elastoplast. 'He could bite a child!' he added vehemently as I peeled off the backing strips. 'There's only one thing for it,' he added furiously as I applied the plaster to his bloodless 'wound'. 'I think you should have him done.'

'What?' I said, looking up at him.

'I think you should have him done.'

'Done?' I echoed non-comprehendingly.

'Snipped,' he snapped as I stood up again. 'It would be the kindest cut of all.'

'You mean, a – vasectomy?' I ventured. I felt sick.

'No,' he said. 'I mean castrated. As in having his bollocks chopped off.'

'No!' I exclaimed, horrified. 'I'm not letting anyone mutilate my dog.'

'You may be forced to, Faith,' said Jos, 'and it would be the right thing to do. If you really loved him,' he added, 'then you *would* do it, to get rid of his vicious streak.' But he hasn't *got* a vicious streak, I thought. 'Now, I'm not thinking of myself,' Jos added, lowering his voice, 'my only concern is for you. Because if Graham bites someone else, and they complain, which in this climate of victimhood they would, then he might have to be destroyed. And that would get reported in the papers.' My hands sprang up to my mouth.

'Yes, Faith,' Jos said, clicking his tongue, 'that could get you some very negative publicity.' *Publicity*?

'I don't care about any effing *publicity*!' I yelled. 'I just don't want Graham being killed.'

'But that's what they do, Faith,' Jos added, shaking his head. 'If a dog is dangerous, then I'm afraid it's destroyed.'

I had visions of Graham tied to an execution post, with a blindfold over his eyes. I had visions of him in a cell, on death row, awaiting the electric chair. I had visions of some unknown hand hovering over him with a syringe. And then I didn't have visions any more because my eyes were blinded by tears.

'I don't want him to be put down,' I wept. 'He's *my* dog, he's mine, and I love him. I love you, Graham,' I sobbed as he jumped up and licked my face. 'I don't want you to die – *ever*!'

'Look, darling,' said Jos. 'I didn't mean to upset you, and I'm sorry to have to spell it out. But the hard fact is that however sweet *you* find him, Graham is what is euphemistically known as a dog of "uncertain temperament". He's savage,' he added simply. 'You have to protect people from him, and you have to protect him from himself.' I lifted up a corner of the duvet and pressed it to my eyes. 'And you know, Faith, don't you, that the Dangerous Dogs Act is still in force.' Oh God, oh God, that was true. Maybe Jos was right. I didn't know. All I knew was that the peaceful start to my day had been utterly ruined.

'Honestly, Faith,' Jos said gently as he came and sat next to me on the bed. He put his arm round me and drew me to him. 'I really *do* think it's best. And it makes them much nicer dogs, too,' he went on soothingly. 'It stops them running after bitches.'

'Yes, but he's never really done that before,' I said. 'He's not that interested in girls.'

'Maybe he's gay,' said Jos contemptuously.

'No he's not,' I shot back.

'Anyway, we can talk about it another time,' he added wearily as he went into the bathroom. 'But we'd better get ready to go.'

I changed for the polo match, feeling bleak and depressed, while Jos had his shower. The doorbell rang; Graham ran, barking, to the door, and there was Sarah, who was puppysitting for the day.

'I'm so grateful,' I said to her as she came into the house.

'Well, it's the least I can do,' she replied. 'To make up for Peter's appalling behaviour! Poor darling Faith,' she said as she put her arms round Graham and gave him a big kiss.

'It's nice of you to take my side,' I said as I made her some coffee. 'Not all mother-in-laws would.' But I knew why she was being so sympathetic, of course, because of what her husband, John, had done. Twenty years previously, when, *she* was thirty-five, John had left Sarah for an American girl. History has repeated itself in our family, as Katie often likes to point out.

'Like father, like son,' Sarah sighed, yet again. 'Maybelline!' she spat. 'What a ridiculous name! And what sort of life is it for him?' she went on crossly. 'Living in Florida, playing golf all day!' She sighed, then shook her head. 'I'm refusing to meet her, you know.'

'Who, Maybelline?'

'No, Andie of course.'

'Oh. Well, maybe you ought to,' I said. 'She'd probably give you a huge present.'

'I'm ashamed to think of the pain Peter's caused,' Sarah carried on with a bitter sigh.

'Yes, it was painful, as you know, but we're dealing with it now,' I explained. 'I'm not quite as angry as I was – especially since I've met Jos.' Now I looked at Sarah and thought it sad that she'd never met anyone else. Lily was right, life *was* tough for divorcées. But I'd met Jos, and I knew on which side my bread was buttered, and I was going to hang on to him and give thanks. Because despite our little areas of, as it were, well, tension, I still think that he's a good thing. Now, suddenly, there he was, standing in the kitchen in his blazer and chinos, looking an absolute dream. He'd calmed down completely and was urbane and self-possessed once more.

'Hello Mrs Smith,' he said warmly, holding out his hand. 'How lovely to meet you. I've heard so much about you.' Sarah smiled at him delightedly. He'd scored yet another diplomatic triumph. 'I'd love to come and see your book shop one day,' he added. 'It sounds wonderful.'

'Well,' she said, slightly flustered by his attention, 'I'd love to see you there.'

'Thanks so much for looking after Graham,' Jos went on.

'He's such an adorable dog, we wouldn't like him to be moping while we were out enjoying ourselves.'

'Be sure that you *do* enjoy yourselves,' said Sarah warmly as she ushered us out. 'I'm going to sit in the garden and read.'

'Be careful of the sun,' Jos warned her gallantly. 'It's going to be another scorching day.'

'It's my job to say that!' I laughed. 'Now, how's your ankle?' I asked him as we got into the MG and sped south.

'It's fine,' he said, slightly grudgingly above the noise of the car. 'I'm sorry we quarrelled, Faith. Let's just forget about it, shall we, and have a lovely day.' That wasn't going to be hard, I thought as we drove through Windsor Great Park half an hour later in the hot sun. Despite the heat, a cool scene met our eyes. Glossy looking women strolled along in floaty little dresses and feminine shoes. The men were all in white chinos and dark blazers – some wore Panama hats. Every car was a gleaming convertible. Designer shades adorned every face. This event was evidently an opportunity for those who had it, to flaunt it. Jos and I attached our blue entry tags to our lapels, then went in search of Lily's hospitality tent, which had been laid on by Madison's, the publishers of *Moi!* We passed stalls selling saddles, and riding hats and Hermès scarves; we saw horses, their fetlocks neatly bandaged, their tails in elegant braids. Then we came to the white *Moi!* marquee, its pennant hanging lifeless in the heat.

'Faith, darling! Jos!' Lily exclaimed, embracing us in a shared hug. She was wearing Egoïste – she must have drenched herself in the stuff. 'How lovely to see you,' she squealed. 'You look terribly pukka, may I say.'

'And you look gorgeous,' I responded. It was true. She was wearing a strappy, coffee-coloured shift which emphasised the cinnamon tones of her skin. Two shining bronze amulets adorned her elegant arms. On her feet were flat gold sandals, from which protruded ten perfectly manicured toes. She was so beautiful. I was filled with pride to think that this amazing woman was my best friend.

'What a great marquee,' I exclaimed. It had a yellow striped lining and parquet flooring, and even windows with a kind of double glazing.

'It's what's known in the trade as a Viagra,' she snorted. 'A semi-permanent erection! Now go and grab some alcoholic refreshment,' she said, 'while I flooze and schmooze.'

Lily's guests were as well-groomed as the horses we'd spotted outside. The women had legs like thoroughbreds and glossy, shining manes. The men had equine faces, were well shod and radiated good breeding. There were lots of blue genes here, I reflected wryly as Jos and I walked round.

'– yah, we went to Cowdray.'

'– visited Jemima in Lahore.'

'– little bolt-hole in the Highlands.'

'– *great* chums with Prince William.'

'– the smart money's on Bishopsgate.'

'– just three thousand acres or so.'

On the flower-bedecked tables were copies of *Moi!* fanned out like playing cards. As Jos went to get us drinks, I idly looked at the cover. 'Star Wards! – Private Healthcare Uncovered'; 'House Work-out – Get Lean While You Clean'; 'Going for a Thong – See our Beachwear Special'; 'Hit and Myth – the Truth about Female Violence' and 'Bristols Fashion – Our Top Ten Bras'.

'Lots of divot dollies,' said Jos approvingly as he returned with two glasses of Pimm's.

'What?'

'Polo chicks. Girls who follow the game.'

'I see,' I said with a suspicious smile.

'But you're my divot dolly,' he said as he put his arm around me. Suddenly there was a soft, marshmallowy 'pop' and a burst of fluorescent light. A photographer had lifted his camera and snapped us; and now he did it again.

'You don't mind, do you?' he asked as he clicked away. 'Lily asked me to photograph you both for the society section, "I Spy".'

'No, it's fine,' I replied with a smile. Lily had said she'd get me a bit of coverage, and in any case, I thought, why shouldn't I be photographed with Jos? He was my boyfriend after all.

And it was certainly no secret that I was getting divorced – it had been in *Hello!* and the *Daily Mail*. And now, from outside we could hear the Tannoyed commentary as the polo got under way.

'Let's go and watch,' said Lily. 'May I introduce the managing director of Madison's, and *Moi!*'s publisher, Ronnie Keats.' We smiled and shook hands with the pleasant-looking fiftyish man, then went and stood by the low white, perimeter fence. From a distance the huge, seated crowd looked as festive and colourful as a shower of confetti. The smell of horse dung mingled with scent and cigars hung on the stifling air. As I'd never been to polo, Jos and Lily quickly explained the rules.

'They're not mallets, Faith, they're sticks; the players aren't wearing jodhpurs, they're wearing trousers; they're not riding horses, but ponies, and the pitch isn't a pitch, it's a lawn. There are four players on each side, and the game is divided into six seven-minute sections, called chukkas. And at half-time the ponies are changed. Got that? Now, this is the third chukka, OK, and it's England against Australia in the semi-final for the Coronation Cup.'

And now the eight ponies thundered up and down the lawn, in a drumroll of hooves, sending the divots flying. The players stood, almost upright, in the saddle, holding their sticks aloft like lances. Indeed, with their helmets and face-grilles they looked like latter-day knights.

'And away we go again,' said the commentator as a stick described a huge arc through the air, sending the ball flying towards the far goal. 'Great shot ... at least eighty feet ... good control from Gilmore there ... and a lovely sharp turn from White. *Very* nice backhand now ... and Hardy picks it up ... picks it up ... back the other way and come on, come on, come on and ... oh, yes, yes, yes ... GOAL!' There was the blast of a hooter and we all clapped as the players cantered back into the centre of the lawn. I looked at the snorting ponies, their ears pricked up, their necks and flanks gleaming; who was sweating more, I wondered, them or us? It was just *so* hot. My cheeks were burning and my brow was damp; a bead of sweat was working its way into the hollow of my back. My dark glasses could barely keep out the intense, stinging glare of the sun. And now, as play resumed, I glanced into the middle distance at a screen of magnificent oaks, two of which had been struck by lightning. Their nude, jagged branches pointed towards the sky like accusing, skeletal fingers. I glanced upwards and, for the first time in a month, I could see long wispy strips of cirrus. Ah. That meant there was a little moisture in the air. That meant the weather was on the turn.

'And a fine ball there by Gilmore,' said the commentator as we heard the sharp, bright click of stick on ball. 'Australia's in the lead, nine goals to seven and with thirty seconds on the clock . . . twenty . . . and . . .' The hooter sounded again and then, over the Tannoy we heard: 'That brings us to the end of the first half. Ladies and gentlemen, would you care to tread in!'

Suddenly everyone surged forward and invaded the pitch like triumphant football fans. We all began to stamp down the upturned divots, like tribal dancers, laughing and giggling as we did. Jos was talking to Lily, so I began chatting to Ronnie Keats. It transpired that he knew Peter.

'I know your husband professionally,' he explained as we trod in the bits of broken turf. 'We distribute books for Fenton & Friend in South Africa, you see. Peter's a really nice guy,' he went on. 'He's very smart, too. They say he's doing *great* things at Bishopsgate,' he added warmly.

'Oh yes, yes, he is,' I said.

'He's got very good judgement, has Peter,' he went on.

'Yes, that's right,' I replied. Though not when it comes to fidelity, I reflected ruefully. Oh no – not when it comes to that.

'He's really respected in the industry, you know.'

'Yes,' I said. 'I do.' And I suddenly found it upsetting to be discussing Peter so favourably with a total stranger so I steered the conversation towards Lily instead.

'You must be really pleased with what she's doing at *Moi!*' I said.

'Oh yes,' he said. 'We're over the moon. The circulation's gone up by twenty per cent in the ten months since she took over. We took a big risk when we appointed her,' he confided. 'But she's doing great.' And I thought this was an odd, and very indiscreet thing to say. In any case, what did he mean? Perhaps he meant they'd taken a risk because of her colour, since no black woman had held the post before. But if that were true, then he should never have said it, especially to her closest friend. Maybe he'd had too much champagne, I reflected as we made our way back to the stand. And now, though the polo looked lovely, I found my attention wandering, so I began to flick through my copy of *Moi!* There was the *Chienne* section, with a photo byline of Jennifer Aniston in blue satin bow, dispensing tips on 'Dealing with the Puparazzi – How to Get Them Off Your Tail'; 'Obedience Classes for Naughty Owners' and 'Labradorable – New Directions in Canine Couture.' She was also giving her views on a range of grooming products. It's just a gimmick, I thought dismissively. Of course a dog can't give advice. Especially a *dim* dog like Jennifer. Although I did decide to try the herbal flea dip she was recommending – I've noticed Graham's been scratching of late. Then I read the rest of the magazine, occasionally glancing up at the match. And I was just about to put it down when I came to a questionnaire entitled, 'Are You And Your Partner Compatible?' Now, I love doing questionnaires. It's like competitions, I can never resist. So I got my pen out of my bag and began to read it through. There were three options: 'Yes', 'No', and 'Not Sure'. *Do you fancy your partner?* was the first question. I looked at Jos, as he stood there watching the match, his dark blond hair bleached white by the sun, and put a firm tick in the box marked 'Yes'. *Does your partner show you affection?* I ticked the 'Yes' box again. *Does your partner listen to your point of view?* I chose 'Yes', again. *If you have rows are they resolved fairly quickly?* 'Yes', I ticked once more. *Does your partner have any annoying little habits?* I thought about it for a second, then ticked 'No'. *Do you and your partner laugh a lot?* Yes, we do, I thought. *Does your partner always tell the truth?* Ah, that one was a little bit tricky. Although Jos only ever lies for a good reason, so, basically, a 'Yes' there as well. *Do your friends and family like your partner*? Affirmative – they do. *Does he broaden your horizons*? Oh, 'Yes'. '*Does your partner make an effort to please you*? All the time, I thought. By now I was semi-euphoric – this was going so well. *Are you proud of your partner's achievements*? it enquired. 'Yes', I am, thanks very much. And finally, *Do you ever have 'uneasy feelings' about some of the things your partner says or does?* I stared, with increasing irritation, at this question as my hand hovered over the page.

'Come on . . . come on . . .' I heard the commentator shout. 'Not long on the clock . . . come *on*!' Uneasy feelings? I mused again. I looked at Jos as he followed the game. I thought of him flirting with that gay guy, and of how he'd justified that to me. I thought of the girl who'd approached him at Glyndebourne, and of the way that had nettled him. I thought of what Sophie had hinted at, though I still didn't know what she'd meant. And I thought of the way Jos always listens to his answerphone with the volume turned right down. I also thought about his 'homemade' curry, and about Matt's laptop, too. And now I thought about what had happened this morning, and the way he'd shouted at Graham. And Jos must have sensed that I was staring at him because he suddenly turned, looked at me and gave me this heartbreaking smile. *Do you ever have uneasy feelings*? the questionnaire asked. I smiled back at Jos, then put a small, firm tick in the box marked 'No'. And now I added them all up. If you could answer yes to more than seven questions, you were a very compatible pair. If you had ten yes's – then yours was a match made in heaven. And that's what Jos and I had got – an amazing ten out of ten!

'That's an *incredible* score!' I heard over the Tannoy. Yes, I thought, it is. 'England, fifteen, Australia, fourteen – what a close finish, but it's England who go through!'

As we walked back to the marquee for tea, I felt happy again. Jos and I were a perfect match. Sure, we had little areas of tension, but that was only to be expected, wasn't it? When Peter and I married, we were so young that we didn't really have any sharp edges. We were as green and flexible as saplings. We grew up together, side by side, bending to each other's shape. But now, at thirty-five, any new partner was bound to have acquired a few emotional lumps and bumps. This meant being accommodating – we couldn't just expect them to fit in. That's what mature people do, I mused. They try to be flexible, and that's all I was doing with Jos. As we walked back across the grass, Lily was talking about nuisance telephone calls.

'It's a pain,' she said. 'Sometimes they're random nutters, or people I've sacked, but quite often they're just back issues.'

'What?' said Jos.

'Oh, ex-boyfriends,' she explained dismissively. 'But they're easy to deal with, you know.'

'Really?' said Jos. 'How?'

'Well, you can bar their calls.'

'*Can* you?' he said.

'Yes. It's called Choose to Refuse. You just dial 14258, then star, star, then tap their number in. Then the next time they call you an automated voice tells them to bugger off. I use it all the time,' she said happily. 'It's jolly good.'

'It certainly sounds it,' he agreed.

'Do you have trouble like that, then?' she enquired.

'Well,' he said. 'I . . . not really, but I keep getting calls from this . . . guy who's trying to sell me . . . insurance. It's a real drag. You know what they're like. He er, just won't take no for an answer.'

'Right, well, next time he calls, just punch in that code,' said Lily, 'and after that he won't get through.'

'Faith,' said Jos after a few minutes, 'the heat's getting to me, do you mind if we go home?' I shook my head. I'd had enough too. As we found our way to the car park, I looked up at the sky. The cirrus had lengthened and begun to curve, like boomerangs. This meant the anti-cyclone had hit a warm front, which signalled the onset of a new low. And as we drove back to London, the sky was already turning from cobalt to gun-metal grey. When I got in, I looked at the barometer and sure enough, it had switched to 'Change'. Then Sarah left, and Jos went home too, and as he kissed me goodbye Graham growled.

Jos looked at him contemptuously and said, 'You're for the chop, old boy.' I found myself wishing he hadn't said that. It was a sour note on which to end the day. As he walked down the path, I saw that the sky had turned pewter-grey. And there were churning cumulonimbus now, and the rumble of distant thunder. Uneasy feelings, I thought. Uneasy feelings. I'd never had them before. I mean, Peter could annoy me, of course. He might leave the loo seat up, or forget to put the top on the toothpaste tube. He might snore half the night or tell me jokes I'd heard fifty times before. But I'd never had the vague sense of disquiet I sometimes have now, with Jos. No, with Peter there were no uneasy feelings – at least not until the start of this year. That's when everything had changed, I reflected bitterly as I heard a loud thunder clap. That's when it began to go wrong. And now, overwhelmed by the urge to speak to him, I picked up the phone and dialled.

'Peter,' I said quickly. He was still my husband after all. 'Peter, I –'

'Oh, Faith,' he replied. 'It's so lovely to hear your voice. I –'

'Yes?'

'I,' he tried again, and laughed. I laughed too.

'You first,' I said.

'Well, I was just going to phone *you* actually,' he said.

'Really?' I said happily. I glanced outside where a fork of lightning had fissured the coal-black sky.

'Yes. Look, Faith,' he went on, slightly shyly I thought. 'I wanted to talk to you.'

'Yes?' I said, my heart quickening. Now there were raindrops the size of bullets beating down onto the path. As I stood there with the phone in my hand, I saw them scatter the dust.

'Faith, I just wanted to say . . .'

'Yes?' I could hardly hear him now above the rack-a-tack-tack of the rain.

'Well, to let you know really, that I'll be away for a few days.'

'Oh! Have you got a work trip?' I asked as a huge 'BOOM!' rent the air.

'Well, no,' he said, with what now struck me as a slightly awkward, apologetic air. 'It's a . . . holiday, actually.'

'A holiday! How *lovely*!' I exclaimed as a bolt of misery pierced my heart. 'So where are you going?'

'Norfolk –'

'Oh, that'll be nice,' I interrupted as the garden began to blur. 'All those long, sunny beaches and big skies . . .'

'No, it's Norfolk, Virginia, Faith. You see,' he added as a tear splashed my hand, 'I'm going to meet Andie's parents.'

August

I have different dreams these days from the ones I used to have. I know, because I write them down. At the beginning of the year, for example, I was dreaming about mobile phones. I guess that's because Peter and I weren't communicating very well. I was also having dreams about cucumbers which, I suppose, signified a suppressed desire for summer. When I first began to suspect Peter, I dreamed I was stuck halfway up a mountain. But the funny thing was that I didn't know whether I was trying to go up or down. When Peter confessed to his fling, I had recurring dreams in which I was falling off tall buildings. I felt terrified as I plummeted, face down, towards the ground. All I could see beneath me was concrete and tarmac – no grass. But as I'd braced myself for the impact I'd suddenly realised I had wings; and then I wasn't falling any more – I was flying. That was strange. Over the past few days I've been having dreams in which Peter's lying in bed. He just lies there, in this big four-poster, looking at me. And I guess that means he's made his bed now, and must lie in it, because of the affair. Bridges have also been featuring prominently. I think they symbolise the fact that I'm trying to cross the bridge to reach Jos. And I'd be crazy not to do that, because he seems keener than ever.

'I love you, Faith,' he murmured on Saturday morning as we lay in bed. He's said that a few times of late. He's also taken to sending me romantic little e-mails at work. 'Do you love me, darling?' he asked. I nodded. 'It's just that since the polo match you've seemed a little . . . remote. A little distant, as though there's – Faith, are you listening?'

'What? Oh, sorry.'

'As though there's something on your mind.'

'Oh no, no no no, not at all.' Then, not that I was trying to change the subject or anything, I began telling him about my dream.

'Was I standing on the other side of that bridge?' he asked me as he stroked my hair. 'Was it me, waiting for you on the opposite bank?'

'Yes,' I replied. 'It was. I could see your face quite clearly.' Now, this wasn't true. Jos wasn't in my dream, but I didn't want to hurt his feelings so I told him that he was. But I don't feel bad about it because, like Jos, I'd only lie for a very good reason.

'I expect you've got a fascinating *id*,' he murmured as he kissed me. 'And that's why you have vivid dreams. I had a funny one,' he added as he placed his hands behind his head. 'It was a kind of nightmare, in a way. I dreamed that I was standing in the foyer of the Opera House, and for some reason I began to get undressed.'

'Really?' I said with a laugh.

'Yes. And there I was, taking off my clothes, when people started to come in.'

'How embarrassing.'

'It would have been, but luckily they didn't seem to notice me. But I was terrified that they would. I was really scared that they'd see me without my clothes on.'

'And did they?'

'I couldn't tell. I suspected that they had spotted me, but were politely averting their eyes. By the end of the dream I was standing there, stark naked, and praying that no-one would see.'

'How weird,' I said with a giggle. 'I wonder what that means. I know!' I said. 'It means you're very honest, because you're prepared to strip off in public. I'll ask Katie when she's back,' I added. 'She's good on this kind of thing.' Oh yes, Katie's keen on dreams. She says she agrees with Freud that dreams 'are the royal road to the subconscious'. She believes that they contain important messages from ourselves to ourselves.

264

'I wonder what Graham dreams about?' I said as I looked at him dozing by the door.

'He's probably dreaming about knives and scissors,' Jos said with a grim little laugh. 'I'm serious, Faith,' he added. 'You ought to talk to the vet.'

'Do I really have to?' I sighed. He kissed me.

'Yes,' he said softly. 'You do. If Graham and I are to cohabit happily I'm afraid there's no other way. And how's the divorce going?' he added as he sat up in bed and stretched.

'It seems to have stalled,' I said. 'In fact it's pulled over on the hard shoulder. I haven't heard from Rory Cheetham-Stabb for weeks.'

'But I imagine Peter will want to get on with it,' Jos said as he stood up. 'It's clearly serious with Andie.' Oh yes, I thought, bitterly, it's serious. It's serious all right. And now, as he went into the bathroom, I mentally replayed my last conversation with Peter.

I have to go to the States, he'd said. *I've got to meet Andie's parents*. So their relationship's obviously going very well if it's Meet the Family time. I'd felt heartbroken when he told me that, even though we're splitting up, because it was as though the swing door of our separation had been replaced with a barred gate marked 'Keep Out!'. But in the week since Peter and I last spoke I've been rationalising things, as I do. And, as Lily is constantly telling me, the fact is I *have* to move on. I have to leave my old existence behind because – yes, of course, *that's* what my dream was telling me! – I have to cross the bridge, to my new life. A life in which Peter will no longer be at the centre, but at the edge. Andie went after his head, and she got it, I reflected; then she went back for the rest.

'When am I going to meet your parents?' Jos enquired as I followed him into the bathroom.

'Well, er, when they're all back from France, next week. Do you really want to meet them?' I asked as I put in my lenses.

'Yes,' he said. 'I do. After all, we've been together for three months now, so it's serious, isn't it?' *Serious*. That word again.

'Yes,' I said quietly. 'It is.'

265

Jos reached down his toothbrush from the family toothbrush holder. To be honest, I hadn't wanted him to put it there but I didn't like to say. Now he was squeezing the toothpaste, and I noticed that he always squeezes it very neatly, from the end, whereas Peter squeezes it from the middle.

'And it's time you met my mum,' Jos went on as he carefully replaced the cap. 'Wouldn't you like to, Faith?'

'Mmm, of course,' I said. He brushed his teeth, spat neatly into the sink, then gave me a minty kiss.

'I love you, Faith,' he said again with a smile. 'I've got designs on you.' At this I looked at the half-finished mural. The sea is a luminescent turquoise, the sky is vaulting and blue. The palm trees look so real I can hear their leaves rustling in the breeze. Jos has changed my perspective, I realised. I have vistas I never had before. And yet . . .

'I wish you'd say you love me,' he added plaintively as he inspected his face in the mirror.

'But I do.'

'Then just say the words, "I love you".'

'Yes. Yes. I do.' Jos looked at me, out of slightly narrowed eyes, then squished shaving foam into his hands.

'Jos – why do you love me?' I suddenly asked as I sat on the side of the bath.

'Why do I love you?' he echoed. He was smoothing the foam over his throat and jaw – it covered his lower face like a mask. 'Why do I love you?' he repeated. 'Well, because you're very loveable. That's why.' At that he looked into the mirror again, and his reflection smiled at mine. 'Why do you ask?' he said.

'Because I'm only *quite* attractive,' I said. 'And I'm not rich, or famous. I've got two teenage children, and a dog who you can't stand, plus there are millions of women out there. So what drew you to me?' I went on boldly. 'Out of all the women you could have had?'

'I'll tell you what,' he said as he lifted the razor to his left cheek. 'It was your cross little face, that's what. Women are usually smiling at me. They're flirting and they're trying too hard. But you were doing the opposite,' he went on as he scraped the blade across his skin. 'You were scowling at me, Faith. You were telling me to fuck off. You were giving me two fingers.'

'Yes, I was,' I agreed with a laugh.

'And the more hostile you were, the more I thought, I'm going to make that woman love me . . .'

I glanced out of the window; the sky was opalescent with the threat of summer rain. The sun was a blurred white disc as it tried to burn its way through a veil of cloud.

'Say it,' Jos said again as he wrapped his arms around me. I looked down at my toes, and noticed that the nail varnish was badly chipped. 'Go on, Faith. Say it. Tell me you love me.'

'Yes,' I muttered. 'I do.'

Jos gave me an odd little smile, ruffled my hair, then got dressed and went to work. There are often weekend rehearsals at Covent Garden, and today the cast of *Butterfly* were rehearsing on set for the first time. Jos needed to be there to make sure that it was all working well.

'I'll be home at seven!' I heard him call from the open front door. 'Did you hear me, Faith?' *Home*? 'Faith? Did you hear me? I'll be back here at seven!'

'Right-e-o,' I replied brightly, aware that this was not a word I ever used.

A few minutes later Graham barked as the post arrived. There was a card from the kids – *On s'amuse!* they wrote – and another hateful brown envelope. I put it on top of the growing pile in the boiler cupboard, then switched on Radio 4. It was *Home Truths* with John Peel and there was a feature on photograph albums. In the background they were playing that old song, 'Memories are Made of This'. I got down some of our photo albums and flicked through them as I sipped my tea. *Take one fresh and tender kiss* . . . I heard Dean Martin croon. *Add one stolen night of bliss*. There were Peter and I at university, our college scarves wrapped round each other's necks. *One girl. One boy*. It was hard to see where his ended and mine began. *Some grief, some joy*. He had his arm round me, and we were laughing wildly. I remember that photo – it was March '85 – we'd only been going out for a month. *Mem-ories are made of this*. I'd fancied him since the Freshers' Ball but had been too shy to make the first move. But one day he'd sat next to me at a lecture and, well, that was that. *Your lips, on mine. Two sips, of wine*. I looked at the photo again. *Mem-ories are made of this*. It was slightly discoloured, through age. We looked so in love, and so young; but then we were – we were only nineteen. He was my first boyfriend, and I was his third girlfriend. *Then add the wedding bells*. In the next album there were casual snaps from our wedding the following year. Peter looked happy, but slightly startled, in the way that young bridegrooms do. *One house where lovers dwell*. And I had a velvet cape to keep out the wind as we posed outside in the cold. There was Sarah, talking to Mum – she wasn't much older than I am now. And Lily, of course, looking elegant, but slightly, well, disappointed, I could now see. And there was Mimi – her hair was long then – chatting to my Dad. *Three little kids, for the fla-vour*. The next album contained some of Katie's earliest snaps, looking so serious, even then. *Stir carefully through the days*. There was Peter, on graduation day, in his academic gown, holding her up in his arms. *See how the flavour stays*. He's put his mortarboard on her head, and I'm standing next to him, in a Laura Ashley dress, hugely pregnant with Matt. *These are the dreams that you'll sav-our*. The next album was of a holiday we had in Wales – that must have been in '89. *Mem-ories are made of this*. Peter was assistant editor then at Fenton & Friend and we were very hard up. But we had a lovely week in Tenby, and Matt took his first steps on the beach. And every time he fell down, and I rushed to help him, he'd cry because he wanted to do it on his own. *Mem-ories are made of this*. And now, as John Peel's familiar tones droned soothingly away, I opened the next album which was labelled 'Chiswick, '93'. We'd just bought this house. It was a huge squeeze financially, but Peter had been promoted again and I was temping at AM-UK! And here we all were in the kitchen on our first night in Elliot Road. The children were so thrilled to have a garden, after having been in a flat, and I'd cooked a huge spag bol. *Serve it generously with love*. And we were all laughing as it dribbled down our chins, and Peter's got his arms round us all. *One man, one wife*. And I'm tucking a bib into Matt's bespattered little shirt. *One love, one life*. I must have put the camera on automatic timer for that one. *Mem-ories are made of this . . .*

'And now,' I heard John Peel say as the music faded out, 'a romantic tale of a woman who's found new love – with her ex-husband.' I listened as she recounted the grim tale of their divorce.

'Never saw it coming . . . someone he knew at work . . . it's like your heart's been put through a shredder . . . as though my life had stopped . . . no kids, so I moved down to Devon . . . left him to *her*,' she spat. At that I smiled a tight little smile of recognition. 'Slowly began to recover . . . one or two love affairs . . . new friends . . . but then . . .'

'Yes,' said John Peel. 'But then . . . ?'

'But then I just kept wanting my old life back. For five years I tried to suppress the memories,' she went on, 'but they just kept flooding in. All the years of shared experiences and shared history. The images in the photo album. The story of us – of who we'd been. I wanted it back, and it became overwhelming, this longing for the past. I'd found I couldn't just shed my old life like a lizard shedding its skin.'

'So what did you do?'

'Well, one day I just picked up the phone and called him at work. I hadn't spoken to him for six years. I had no idea what his situation was. I'd heard that the affair hadn't lasted, but didn't know if he was with anyone else. I hadn't a clue what I wanted to say. It was just one of those moments when you decide to act, and you know that if you don't act, right then, in that split second, you never will. I was so nervous as the receptionist put me through. My heart was in my mouth as the number rang. Then it picked up, and I heard his voice. And I just said, "Mark. It's Gill." That's all I said. There was a moment's silence and I thought, I have made a stupid, *stupid* mistake, and I'm going to regret this for the rest of my life. Then I suddenly heard him say, "Gill, just tell me where you are and stay there – I'm driving down." We haven't had a day apart since.'

'And what's it like now?' John Peel asked. There was a slight pause during which I heard the click of Graham's claws on the lino, then felt the gentle weight of his head on my lap.

'Well, I'd be lying if I said it's better than before,' she replied. 'Obviously it would have been better if the affair had never happened. But it's different. Yes, our marriage is "mended",' she went on as I absently stroked Graham's ears. 'Of course we can see the joins, but those joins are also part of our history, of who we are, and we know they have their place in the picture too.'

And now I was flicking through photos of the dog lying blissfully across Peter's lap, or catching tennis balls on the common, leaping six feet into the air with a corkscrew twist, the children screaming and clapping with delight. Then I turned the page and found myself staring at a photo of me. It wasn't a very interesting one, I was just ironing Peter's shirts. I've got no idea why he took it – he must have picked up the camera on a whim. I'm looking into the lens and laughing – that must have been in the autumn of '99. Before Peter began to have problems at work. When things were still going well. As I looked at it, I suddenly saw Andie there, in my place, ironing Peter's shirts and laughing. I couldn't stand the thought of her doing something as mundane for him as that. Or putting his clothes in the washing machine. Or scrubbing his back in the bath. I couldn't stand the thought of her knowing all the little things about him that I do. That he's missing the little toe on his left foot, for example, or that he likes Gladys Knight and the Pips. And I couldn't stand the thought of her sharing the infinite moments of domestic intimacy with Peter when it had always, *always* been me. And I knew that our cosy togetherness would only exist in fading photos like these. As the programme ended, and they played the Dean Martin again, I felt the familiar ache in my throat and the dragging sensation in my chest. Now I was looking at a snap of Peter and me, in the back garden, taken last May. We're sitting on the bench and I'm leaning right into him, encircled by his arms. *One man, one wife*. The image wobbled and blurred, then great, fat tears of self-pity began to course down my face. *One love. One life*. I heard a whimper – Graham hates it when I cry and he'd put his paws on my lap and was reaching up to lick my face. *Mem-ories are made of this*. They certainly are, I thought bitterly. In all these photos we were united. United. But soon we would be untied. A huge racking sob escaped me. Then another.

'Oh, Peter,' I said.

When you're going through a divorce, you feel unhinged. Your emotions are seesawing like a, well, seesaw, and your perspective is completely skewed. You simply daren't trust your own judgement.

'You've got to keep a tight rein on your feelings,' said Lily a week later as we sat in the Nail Bar in Maddox Street. She was having her weekly manicure while Jennifer Aniston sat, grunting, on my lap.

'The only reason you feel down,' she said as we perched on Barbie-pink stools at the zig-zag shaped bar, 'is not because you want Peter back, but because you don't like the idea of him being with someone else.' I hadn't thought of it like that, but now she said it it kind of rang true. 'It's a common psychological syndrome,' she went on as the manicurist, or rather, 'nail technician', swiftly removed her old Rouge Noir. It had been so long since her nail-beds had seen the light of day that they'd turned a virulent shade of yellow. 'I mean, you don't want Peter,' Lily added above the muzak.

'Don't I?' I replied.

'No,' she said. 'You don't. But you don't want Andie to have him.'

'That's certainly true.'

'And *that's* why you've been upset all week – because he's gone to the States with her.' At this I imagined Peter and Andie in Virginia, sailing perhaps, off Chesapeake Bay, or hiking in the Blue Ridge mountains. On the trail of the lonesome pine.

'I'm sorry to be so blunt, darling,' Lily continued between sips of elderflower juice which she delicately imbibed through a straw. 'You know that such plain-speaking is normally not

271

my style. But it's only by analysing things in this brutal way that I can demonstrate to you that it's true. You want Jos,' she said as a layer of undercoat was applied to her perfectly shaped talons.

'Do I?' I said as I inhaled the aroma of acetone.

'Yes,' she said. 'You do. But unfortunately you're allowing yourself to sentimentalise Peter.'

'But I *do* feel sentimental,' I said as she placed her elegant hands under the fast-drying machine. I stared at my ragged cuticles. 'I mean, I was married to him for fifteen years.'

'Yes darling, that's all very well, but don't get carried away. Though I think it's very nice of you to show such feeling for him when he's let you down.'

'I'm not showing feeling,' I said carefully. 'I'm *feeling* feeling.'

'Well, that's silly of you,' she said as a layer of Hard As Nails Vermilion was applied in short, rapid strokes. 'It's a bit self-indulgent, too. And you'd better not do it too much otherwise you'll end up driving Jos away.' She looked at me out of the corner of her beautiful, slanting eyes. 'And you don't want to do that, do you?' I was silent. 'Do you, Faith?' I was thinking. I was trying to imagine what life would be like without Jos.

'Do you want to be single, Faith?' I heard her say.

'No,' I said bleakly. 'I don't.'

'Do you want to have to go to social functions all on your own? Believe me, Faith, it's no fun.'

'You make it look like fun.'

'Well, I've always been single, so it's different. But for you it would be hell. You'd be consumed with shyness and fear and you'd feel vulnerable and alone. Combined with the fact that every time you met some man you liked there'd be five hundred other women after him too. The grass really isn't greener elsewhere, Faith.'

'Yes,' I said. 'I know. It's just that I feel a little . . . unsure.'

'Why? What's wrong with him?' she asked.

'I don't know,' I said. 'It's nothing that he does, as such. He

272

always behaves perfectly towards me. He's extremely attentive, and sensitive, and he's got lovely manners. Although he did shout at Graham the other day, which I didn't like at all.'

'Well, he and Graham obviously don't get on,' she observed. 'But you and Jos do. I thought you looked terribly compatible at the polo.'

'Compatible?' I murmured, remembering the questionnaire. 'Yes, I suppose we are. And he's so talented and so good-looking and I know I'm very lucky, but there's *something* . . .' I stared at her painted nails. 'I just can't quite put my finger on.'

'I think you've done very well for yourself,' said Lily. 'Lots of women would kill to have someone like him.'

'You make Jos sound like a raffle prize, Lily. It's not a competition, you know.'

'Of course it is!' she exclaimed. 'Don't be so naïve. In fact our beauty editor, Arabella, was looking at the pics of you and Jos at the polo. And she said, "My God, that man is gorgeous!"'

'Did she?' I said, slightly indignantly.

'Yes,' said Lily vehemently. 'She did. She fancied the pants off him. And so do quite a few other young things at *Moi!*'

'Oh,' I said, not knowing whether to feel proud or annoyed.

'So you *are* competing with other women,' said Lily softly, 'but so far you're in the lead. Still, he won't stick around if he thinks you're still hankering after Peter, so I'd make a big fuss of him if I were you.'

'Yes,' I sighed, 'you're probably right.'

'I know I am,' she said. She inspected her gleaming, blood-red claws. 'Right. All done,' she announced with a smile. Then she grabbed Jennifer Aniston from me, sat her on her lap and put her front paws up on the bar.

'Here's your next customer,' she said to the manicurist. 'And she'd like Perfectly Pink by Chanel.'

The following Friday, my parents dropped the children off. They didn't have time to come in because they were flying to Tierra del Fuego the next day. Matt and Katie were so brown, and they'd grown a little bit too. Graham went berserk when he saw them, barking and ululating with joy.

'Did you have a great time?' I asked as I hugged them.

'*Formidable!*' said Matt.

'Oh, that's rather good,' I said. 'So, Granny did her stuff?'

'Oh yes,' said Katie. 'We spoke French all the time.'

'*Tout le temps*,' said Matt with a grin.

'Well, that's . . . just . . . *très bien*,' I said. 'There's some post for you,' I added as they took their stuff upstairs. I looked at the blue airmail letter which Peter had jointly sent them. It had arrived the previous day.

'Is Daddy having a nice time?' I asked with as much casual interest as I could muster as Katie read it in the kitchen.

'Is he having a nice time?' she reiterated. 'Well,' she said, handing it to me, 'I'll let you judge for yourself.'

Such an interesting part of the US, I read. *The site of the first permanent European settlement in North America (1607) . . . state named in honour of Elizabeth I, the Virgin Queen . . . also known as the Old Dominion State . . . one of the original thirteen states of the USA. A leading producer of tobacco, peanuts, apples, tomatoes . . . timber . . . coal mining very important too. Many historic towns such as Williamsburg, Jamestown and Fredericksburg . . . population six and a half million . . . its chief landmarks are the Blue Ridge mountains . . . the Shenandoah River . . . Chesapeake Bay . . . Andie's parents seem quite nice.*

'He's obviously having a fascinating trip,' I said as I handed the letter to Matt.

'Yes, he seems very taken with the history of the state,' said Katie.

'Well, it sounds interesting.'

'And the flora and fauna,' she added.

'Indeed.'

'And the political background.'

'Mmmm.'

'Conclusion?' said Katie.

'He's hating it,' said Matt. My heart leaped like a salmon leaping upstream to spawn.

'It's the Freudian telling omission,' said Katie. 'He doesn't mention Andie at all. And as for this: "Andie's parents seem quite nice." He obviously doesn't like them one bit.'

'Is that what you think?' I said.

'It's what I know,' she replied. 'Poor Dad,' she went on, pulling a face. 'But she's got her hooks into him and she's not going to let him go. How's Jos?' she said suddenly.

'Oh. Jos is . . . fine,' I said. 'Just fine. He's coming to supper tomorrow, actually. Won't that be nice?'

'*Je m'en fou*,' she replied with a Gallic shrug.

'*Cela m'est egal*,' said Matt.

'You don't seem very enthusiastic,' I said.

'We're not really,' said Matt.

'I think that's a little bit mean of you,' I said, 'because he's always so kind to you. Anyway, what's wrong with him?'

'Oh, nothing really,' said Katie grudgingly. 'He just tries too hard.'

'Well, that's no crime.'

In the event it wasn't too bad. Jos had painted a 'Welcome Home!' banner for them and hung it over the banister – to be honest I wished he hadn't – and he'd bought them little presents, too. He asked them all about their trip and, as usual, made a huge effort. In return, they were a little cool and noncommittal, but that's teenagers for you, isn't it?

'And what did you do in the evenings?' I asked as we ate our boeuf bourgignon.

'Oh, er, we played cards,' said Katie as she pushed a piece of beef round her plate.

'Cards? What fun. And what did you play? Rummy?'

'Oh, er, yes, that's right,' said Matt as he fiddled with the pepper pot.

'Or did Granny teach you how to play Bridge?'

'Mmmm, she did,' they both said as I stood up to clear the plates.

'That was delicious, Mum,' said Katie.

'It certainly was,' said Jos. 'In fact,' he went on expansively, 'it was the dog's bollocks!' I looked at him, slightly startled. Matt and Katie laughed. 'And on that subject, Faith, I do think we ought to tell the kids about Graham's little . . . operation.'

'What operation?' They both looked shocked. 'Graham's not ill is he, Mum?' said Matt, rushing over to Graham who was lying in his bed.

'No,' I said. 'He's not. He's a healthy little dog.'

'Then what are you talking about?' said Katie.

'Well,' Jos began, 'although of course Graham's a *lovely* dog, he does have this unfortunate habit of snapping at people.'

'No,' said Katie. 'It's not a habit. He only snaps at you.'

'Katie!' I said, giving her a warning glance.

'But it's true, Mum,' she said. 'It's only Jos he does it with.'

'Well, we won't argue about that,' Jos carried on smoothly, still managing to maintain his pleasant smile. 'But the fact is that the best thing for a dog with aggressive tendencies is to have it . . .'

'Jos!' I interrupted him, looking anxiously at Graham. '*Pas devant le chien s'il vous plait*!'

'What do you mean?' he said.

'It means "not in front of the dog, please",' said Matt.

'I know *that*,' said Jos. 'But why ever not?'

'Because he understands everything we say,' I replied brusquely.

'Don't be silly, Faith,' said Jos wearily. 'You just like to think that he does.'

'Oh but he does,' said Katie. 'He understands loads of things. He's got a fantastically high IQ and we think he's got a vocabulary of at least five hundred words.'

'I very much doubt that "castration" is one of them,' said Jos. He was still smiling. I wished he wouldn't.

'Castration?' Katie repeated.

'What's that?' said Matt.

'It's where they cut off the, um, you know, um, thingys,' I said. Matt's face registered incredulity combined with naked fear. 'It's supposed to make them nicer dogs,' I explained.

'But he is a nice dog!' said Matt.

'But he has behavioural problems,' said Jos. 'Now, it's a

276

simple, routine operation, it doesn't hurt, and he won't miss them, believe you me.'

'How on earth do you know?' demanded Katie. 'You'd miss them, wouldn't you?'

'Katie!' I said. 'That's rude!'

'You know, Katie,' said Jos calmly, unfazed by her frank remark, 'lots of people have this little . . . procedure . . . done to their dogs. And it's a good thing, not least because it stops them chasing girls.'

'Why shouldn't he chase girls?' said Katie indignantly. 'You do.'

'Katie!' I said crossly. 'You are *not* being very nice!'

'Anyway, he doesn't even like girls,' said Matt. 'He only chases *cats*!' At this Graham leaped out of his basket and rushed, barking and whining, to the back door.

'You shouldn't have said that,' I groaned. 'Graham, there is *no* cat out there, so will you please go and lie down.' Graham looked at me, nonplussed, then trotted back to his bed.

'Anyway,' said Jos, resolutely refusing to be crushed, 'Faith and I think it would be better if we had Graham done.'

'I bet Mum doesn't think that,' said Katie matter-of-factly.

'Katie, I can speak for myself, thank you very much, and my opinion on this subject is that we should . . . that we should . . . wait until Daddy gets back.' I saw Jos roll his eyes.

'OK,' said Katie. 'We'll wait till Dad gets back. And I can tell you he won't have anything to do with it. Apart from anything else,' she went on, 'it would mean Graham couldn't have any children.'

'Yes, but that wouldn't matter,' said Jos, 'because he's not exactly a Pedigree Chum.'

'Jos,' said Katie with suddenly assumed hauteur, 'Graham may not, as you are kind enough to point out, have a pedigree. But he has true breeding. He is one of nature's gentlemen.'

'OK, OK,' said Jos, throwing up his hands. 'I wish I'd never mentioned it.'

'So do we,' said Matt. He'd given Graham his plate to lick.

'Don't do that, Matt!' I said. 'It's disgusting!'

'Well, so is cutting off his balls! It's to make him feel better,' Matt added as I snatched it away. 'In case his feelings are hurt.'

'No-one cares about *my* feelings,' said Jos. 'No one cares that I keep getting bitten.'

'Has he ever drawn blood?' Katie demanded.

'Well, no.'

'Then that's not a proper bite.'

'Yes, but one of these days he will bite me, good and proper.'

'Good and proper,' muttered Matt.

'Look, please can we just forget this conversation and change the subject,' I said as we all returned to the table. I removed the chocolate mousse from the fridge and began spooning it out. By now Graham had closed his eyes.

'Oh, good,' I said, 'he's asleep. Which reminds me, Katie, do you think dogs dream?'

'Oh yes,' she said. 'They have rapid eye movement just like we do, when their eyelids twitch. That's the time when humans dream, so I guess it's the same with dogs. And Graham sometimes whimpers in his sleep, as though he's having nightmares, or his legs "run" as though he's chasing rabbits.'

'Dreams are strange things, aren't they?' I said as we ate our pudding.

'They're usually wish-fulfilment,' said Katie, 'in which the *id*, the childish, pleasure-loving part of the subconscious, is indulging all its deepest desires.' I thought about that for a while as we ate on in silence.

'I had a funny dream last night,' I said. 'I dreamed that I was ironing some shirts. But I know exactly why I dreamed that,' I added, though I didn't explain.

'Dreams of ironing mean you would love to smooth over current troubles,' said Katie with a candour I found hard to take.

'Well, I had a *very* strange dream the other day,' said Jos, determined to melt the ice that had accumulated around him in the last half-hour. So now he described his dream in which he'd got undressed at the Royal Opera House. As he spoke, Katie

278

sat there, scrutinising him in a thoughtful way. She obviously wasn't sure what it meant.

'I think it means that Jos is a very honest person,' I said, 'that he's prepared to strip off in public. Why don't you get your book of dreams down, Katie, and look up what it might mean?'

'Oh, it's OK, Mum,' she said. 'I don't need to. I know exactly what it signifies.'

'Oh yes?' said Jos. 'And what's that, then? I'd love to know.'

'It's about exposure,' she went on calmly. 'Dreams of undressing are a sign that you fear that someone will discover something about you that you would rather remained a secret.'

Jos met Katie's unflinching gaze for a moment, then looked down at his bowl. 'This mousse is absolutely *delicious*, you know. I'd love some more,' he said.

Dear Alfie, I wrote on Monday, after my last bulletin. *A flash of lightning is a spark of static electricity zigzagging between a thundercloud and the ground, or between two clouds. If the lightning jumps out of the cloud, it's called fork lightning. If it jumps inside the cloud, it's sheet lightning. I hope this helps with your holiday project.*

Dear Vicki, I began. *The reason why thunder is so loud is because during a storm, flashes of lightning heat up the air to incredible temperatures – five times as hot as the surface of the sun. This heat makes the air suddenly expand, at supersonic speed, which produces the deafening crash we call thunder. It's the same effect as when Concorde flies overhead. I do hope this helps with your holiday work.*

Dear Anil, frost is just frozen dew. The reason why it's white is because the ice crystals are full of air. If the weather is very, very cold, then the ice crystals form in the shape of sharp needles. We call this hoar frost. Thanks for writing, and good luck with your project!

I looked up from my computer as I printed off the letters, saw Sophie and smiled.

'More fan mail?' she asked as she saw the pile of post on my desk.

'Not exactly. Just letters from school kids rushing to do their holiday projects before term starts again next week.'

'I don't get any letters,' she said ruefully.

'You must get some.'

'No. Practically nothing.'

'I'm astonished. Apart from anything else I'd have thought you'd get marriage proposals by the sackful.'

'Marriage?' said Terry, who was just walking past. He stopped and gave her an arch smile. 'Oh, Sophie's not interested in that. Are you Sophie?' he said.

'No,' she said calmly. 'Certainly not. At twenty-four I'm much too *young*.' I saw Terry flinch as she jabbed his Achilles heel. 'I intend to build my presenting career first,' she added.

'Don't bank on it,' said Terry with a hollow laugh. 'You might find you have a commercial break. So I wouldn't get too comfortable here, Sophie,' he added with a knowing smirk.

'Oh, I'm not,' she replied ambiguously. Then she turned her back on him and carried on talking to me.

'Nice one,' I whispered as he walked away. 'More power to your larynx.'

'Thanks.' But although Sophie seemed calm and self-possessed, I could see her hands shake. 'And how's everything going with you?' she asked as she perched on the side of my desk.

'Oh, fine, thanks. Fine, fine, fine. Jos is really busy,' I added. 'He's doing *Madame Butterfly* at the moment.'

'*Madame Butterfly*?' she repeated.

'It's a new production at the opera house. It opens in three weeks' time. He's taking my kids in to watch rehearsals this morning. He's so kind to them, you know.'

'*Is* he?' she said wonderingly. She was fiddling with my weather house.

'Oh yes, he's *fabulous* with them,' I went on. 'He simply can't do enough. To be honest they're a little, well, ungrateful at times, but you know how teenagers can be.'

'So he's good with kids, is he?' she echoed.

'Oh, yes,' I said. 'He's great.'

Matt and Katie had received Jos's offer of a backstage tour of the opera house with polite enthusiasm. They were still feeling a little chilly towards him about the dog but they knew a good offer when they saw one. And I secretly hoped that the trip to Covent Garden would help them all bond a little more. Perhaps watching Jos in his professional context, and seeing how respected he was would leave them with a better impression. I didn't know. All I knew was that today I was shattered. On Mondays I'm always exhausted, but by Wednesday I've adjusted again to the early start so it doesn't hit me quite so hard. But today I was aching for my bed. To my surprise Graham didn't come rushing to greet me when I opened the front door. I looked in the garden, and he wasn't there. They'd obviously taken him with them, I thought as I hauled myself up the stairs. But then he and the children are inseparable, I reflected as I undressed and fell into bed. He thinks he's their little brother and wants to do all the things they do. I was just so, so tired, and the second my head hit the pillow I was out. Once again I had strange dreams. I was in a shopping mall somewhere, and I was on the escalator, going up. I was standing there, with my bags of shopping, happily taking in the view. But then just as I was approaching the top the escalator stopped and went into reverse. So now I was going down instead, which struck me as very strange. But I remember thinking that when it got to the bottom it would probably ascend again. And I looked up, and standing at the top of the escalator were all these people and they were shouting at me. They were yelling at the tops of their voices. The strange thing was, I couldn't hear a word they were saying because I suddenly realised I'd gone deaf. I could see from their expressions, and the way they were gesticulating, that they were trying to warn me about something, but I didn't know what. And now I turned and looked down, and to my horror the shopping mall had gone, and in its place was this yawning chasm. And the escalator was carrying me inexorably towards the edge, and I was almost at the last step. So I began desperately running upwards, but my legs wouldn't go fast enough. And I was so out of breath, and I had a stitch, and as I looked up I could see Peter and the kids. They were at the front of the crowd and they were shouting at me, urging me on. And now at last, at last, I could hear. I could hear Matt and he was saying, 'Mummy! Mummy! Come *on*!'

'It's OK, I can hear you now!'

'Mummy!' he shouted again. And I could feel his hands on my shoulders. 'Mummy, wake *up*! We can't find Graham!'

'Wh-at?' As I opened my eyes, the dream receded and there was Matt, by the bed, looking distraught. I heard Katie's footsteps running up the stairs, and then she burst in too.

'I've been all down the street,' she said breathlessly. 'He isn't there.'

'What?'

'Graham's missing, Mum,' said Matt. He was crying. 'We can't find him.'

'But I thought he was with you!'

'No! We left him here. We've just come home, we came back on the tube.'

'He's missing?'

'Yes! He's gone.'

'Now, don't worry,' I said as I felt my pulse begin to race. 'We're going to find him, we're going to find him, we're going to find him, but we'll have to stay calm. What time is it? Half past four? Oh my God, he's been missing all day!' I put in my contact lenses, threw on some clothes and ran downstairs.

'Graham!' I called as I flew into the garden. I clapped my hands. 'Graham! Come on! Here boy! Graham!'

'We've been doing that,' said Matt, 'he's not here.'

'How did he get out?'

'Through the kitchen window.'

'But it was only open six inches.'

'I know, but he squeezed through. Look, here's a bit of his fur.'

'Oh my God! What shall we do?'

'Let's phone Dad!' said Katie. Of *course*! I rapidly dialled Peter's mobile phone and after five rings it picked up.

'Hello?' said Peter.

'Peter, it's me. Listen, we can't find Graham. He's got out. He's been missing all day. We're distraught.'

'He's got out? Christ! Now don't worry, I'll come and help you find him, I'll come and look with you and – oh no, I can't, I'm in America. Have you rung the police? You've got to ring the police, you've got to ring the police, you've got to ring the police and Battersea dogs and you've got to get in the car and drive round and look. I'll phone you back in two hours. Bye.'

I dialled Chiswick police station, got put through to the lost dogs department, and gave the station officer a rapid description.

'Collie cross . . . feathery red-gold coat . . . slightly foxy looking . . . white blaze on throat and chest . . . whippety back . . . long swishy tail . . . yes, of course he's got a collar and tag . . . no, no, no, not microchipped . . . very, very clever . . . but it's true – he really *is* . . . Graham. Yes, that's right . . . Yes, yes, I know it's odd . . . yes, of course I'll wait.' There was an agonising silence while the policeman checked the lost dogs logbook.

'I've got two Alsatians, a West Highland terrier a Jack Russell and three mongrels, none of which match your dog's description. But we'll phone you if we have him handed in. In the meantime you should phone Battersea Dogs' Home.'

'Yes of course.'

'And the animal warden – here's the number . . .'

'Thanks.'

'And your local vets.'

'The vets?' I repeated. 'Why?'

'In case he's been run over.' It was as though a knife had been plunged into my heart.

'You know why this has happened, don't you?' said Katie as I dialled the dogs' home. 'It's because he doesn't want to have that operation. He'd developed Castration Anxiety. We told Jos,' she added vehemently. 'We told him Graham understands everything we say, but he simply wouldn't believe us.'

'Hello, this is Battersea Dogs' Home,' I heard a voice say. I gave a rapid description of Graham, trying to fight the tears which were rising in my throat.

283

'He's never run away from us before.' My voice was trembling now. 'But he's got a collar and an identity tag, so if you've got him there, you'd know.'

'Lost dogs often arrive without their collars,' the woman explained. 'So can you tell me if he has any distinctive markings, because we get a lot of collie crosses coming in.'

'Distinctive markings?' I looked at the kids for inspiration. Matt was pointing to his ear. 'Oh yes, one of his ears is slightly shorter than the other,' I said. 'And he's got a very waggy tail.'

'I see,' said the woman politely. 'Well, I'm looking through our database right now and no matches are coming up. But we'll call you if we think we have him, and we're open until eight tonight.' Then I phoned the five vets' surgeries with a pounding heart. None of them had got him, and nor did the Chiswick dog warden.

'Katie,' I said, 'you stay by the phone while Matt and I go out again and look.' We went down to the common and called his name – he'd have come in a flash if he'd been there. Then we went up onto Chiswick High Road – the traffic was so heavy, and the thought of him trying to get across it filled me with utter dread. Matt went left, and I went right. I passed Waterstone's, and Marks and Sparks, and The Link, the Church, and Café Rouge, then headed up towards Kew Green. I must have looked a sight as I ran down the street with a desperate expression on my face, calling out his name. But I was beside myself with anxiety and didn't give a fig what anyone thought. By the time I got back to the house again it was half past five.

'Any calls?' I said to Katie. I was panting and bathed in sweat.

'Dad rang for an update, and you've just missed Jos,' she said. 'I told him about Graham and he's going to come and help us look.'

'Oh, that's so nice of him,' I said as I sank onto the stairs.

'Yes,' said Katie guiltily. 'It is.' Then Matt appeared from upstairs with some 'Missing' posters which he'd designed on his Apple Mac.

'I'm going to stick them on lamp-posts,' he said. 'Here are

twenty for you.' As he went off, Katie and I tried to work out where Graham might have gone.

'Where does he like going?' I said.

'Chiswick House,' she said. 'He loves it there. And the river – oh look, here's Jos.'

Jos hooted his horn, I ran outside with Matt's posters and some sticky tape and jumped into his car.

'Thank you,' I said. I squeezed his hand.

'Love me, love my dog,' he replied with a shrug. 'I just hope we're lucky.' We crossed over the high road and went down Duke's Avenue, driving along slowly while we scanned the gardens and side roads for a flash of ginger fur. At the end of Duke's Avenue was the Great West Road. I looked in horror at the thundering juggernauts and speeding cars, and imagined Graham trying to cross.

'He'd never survive,' I said faintly. 'It's like crossing a motorway.'

'I think he'd be too clever, and too frightened, to try.' We negotiated our way over it, then turned left to get to Chiswick House. Jos pulled up, parked the car and we went through the side gate.

'Graham!' I called. 'Graham! Here boy! Come on!' There were hundreds of dogs out with their owners. There were setters and pointers, Dalmatians and Alsatians; we walked for twenty minutes past the Ionic Temple, and the Conservatory and the Camellia house. By now the light was fading with our hopes. So I put a few posters up on trees, praying as I did so that someone might know where he was. And now, as dusk descended, we drove down to the Thames. We parked by the tennis courts and walked for a mile, just shouting his name. But all we could hear was the lapping of the water, and the wind swishing through the trees.

'We ought to get back,' said Jos. I nodded. And as we drove slowly along I imagined Graham lying injured somewhere, or wandering around distressed and disorientated, unable to find his way home. As I clicked open the front gate I felt oppressed and sick at heart. I lifted my hand to put the key in the lock, but Katie had got there first. She was crying. Oh God. Oh God.

'Tell me,' I said. And now I was weeping, too.

'He's at Battersea,' she croaked, wiping her eyes. 'They've just phoned. He's OK. We can go and get him tomorrow.'

So at ten thirty this morning we were first in line on the pavement outside the dogs' home.

'Come on!' said Matt impatiently. 'Open up!' At last the metal grille was raised and we went in. On the floor were trails of coloured pawprints. The receptionist told us to follow the yellow ones to the Lost Dogs department. As we did so we could hear a cacophany of indignant barking, baying and whining. I filled in the form, provided proof of our identity, and then the kennel maid processed our claim. While we waited we looked at the noticeboard which was plastered with 'missing' posters like ours, offering rewards of a thousand pounds and more. Some dogs had got lost or run away, but many had been stolen. There was a photo of an Alsatian called Toby which had been taken from outside Sainsbury's in Kenton, and of Bumble, a greyhound puppy, 'last seen being dragged away by four males who then bundled him into a van'.

'How horrible,' said Matt. Now, at last, the kennel maid took us through to the pens in which strays are held. The air was sharp with the tang of disinfectant mingled with dog.

'He's at the end,' she said as we passed along the row. Staffordshire bull terriers and elderly labradors gazed mournfully out at us. A sprightly looking springer spaniel offered us his toy. A Jack Russell leaped up, yapping, at our approach. We passed two Alsatians, a three-legged chow, a sleeping Maltese terrier, then finally we stopped and gazed into the end pen.

'Is this him?' said the kennel maid. Same colour. Same size. Similar type. But to us it might as well have been a great Dane. We drove back to Chiswick in silence, then sat disconsolately in the kitchen. Matt filled Graham's water bowl and put some biscuits on his plate.

'He'll be hungry when he gets back.'

'Yes, darling,' I said, 'he will.'

'We'll have to give him a bath. He'll be dirty.'

'Mmm. Probably,' I said.

'I've got him this,' he added, holding up a video of *The Naked Chef.*

'That's very sweet of you, Matt, I don't think he's seen that one.' To make the waiting less agonising, we played cards and Scrabble. And the kids told me about their trip to the opera house, and about Jos's brilliant designs. Then at lunchtime Peter phoned again, and we said there was still no news. A little later Jos rang from work on his mobile. Then at five the phone went again.

'Is that Mrs Smith?' said an unfamiliar male voice.

'Yes, it is,' I replied.

'I'm calling from Westminster City Council. I'm the animal warden. I thought you'd like to know that we've got your dog.'

'Thank God!' I murmured, sinking onto the hall chair. I clapped my left hand to my breast. 'Thank God,' I repeated wearily. 'But is it definitely ours?'

'Oh, no doubt about it,' he replied. 'He's got his collar and tag on. Tell me to mind my own business, but I think Graham's a funny sort of name for a dog.'

'I know,' I said, laughing now as tears of relief pricked my eyes. 'It's a very funny name,' I wept. 'In fact, it's a ridiculous name for a dog. Thank you so much,' I sniffed. 'We've been distraught. But where on earth did you find him?' I added as I scribbled down the address.

'Very near the Tate.'

'The Tate?' I repeated wonderingly.

'Yes, he was sitting outside a house in Ponsonby Place.'

'Ponsonby Place?'

'That's right. Number seventy-eight.'

'Number seventy-eight?' I echoed.

'Do you know anyone who lives there?'

'Yes. My husband,' I said.

September

DOG BONES

Ingredients:
3 cups wholewheat flour
1 1/2 cups cornmeal
1 cup rice flour
1cup chicken stock
2 ozs melted butter
1/2 cup milk
1 whole egg
1 egg yolk.

Method:
Mix together the flour, cornmeal and rice flour. Blend the stock, melted butter and milk, then stir into dry ingredients. Add whole egg, then egg yolk. Knead the dough until it is very stiff, roll out half an inch thick and cut into bone shapes. Place on baking parchment in an oven preheated to 325 degrees for 45 minutes. Cool, then store in an airtight container. Makes 24–30 biscuits.

I read Lily's accompanying note again, which she'd stapled to the recipe: *Darling F, The chef at the Four Seasons in LA gave me this. Such a treat, and I think it will cheer Graham up after his ordeal. I always make some for Jennifer whenever she's had some horrid shock. Woof woof! Lxx.*

I reflected that the only shock Jennifer was likely to receive was being forced to wear her Burberry collar instead of the

Gucci, but I knew that Lily meant well. As for Graham, he seemed none the worse for wear, though still indignant at being prised off the pavement outside Peter's flat. According to a neighbour he'd been sitting there for twenty-four hours.

'Don't you *ever* pull that trick on me again,' I said to him as I kneaded the biscuit dough. 'In any case,' I added, 'you won't be able to because I've had that window fixed. Daddy was *very* upset,' I added. 'You could have been killed, you know.'

'Yes,' said Matt, wagging an admonitory finger at him. 'You put us through absolute hell.'

'It was extremely irresponsible of you,' added Katie seriously. Graham heaved a regretful sigh. He'd had the ecstatic welcome home, the hugs, kisses and tears, and now he was getting a bit of grief.

'Don't *ever* do that again,' I said crisply. 'You can dig holes in the lawn, you can moult all over the house, you can even throw up in the car – but you are *not* allowed to go missing.' By now he looked decidedly hangdog.

'You put us to a lot of trouble,' said Matt.

'And you seriously increased our stress levels,' added Katie. 'We were all running around trying to find you – even Jos.'

'Yes,' I said. 'Even Jos. Which was nice of him when you think about it.' Graham seemed magnificently unimpressed. 'But how did he know the way to Peter's flat?' I wondered aloud, yet again.

'He'd been there once before, on Easter Day,' said Matt. 'He'd obviously remembered the route.'

'It was his sense of smell,' Katie opined. 'Dogs have a sense of smell two hundred and fifty thousand times more powerful than ours. Apparently they can detect a drop of vinegar in forty thousand gallons of water.'

'Not all dogs,' said Matt judiciously. 'I mean, Jennifer Aniston wouldn't be able to detect the vinegar in a fish and chip shop. But Graham's so clever,' he added, stroking his ears. 'Though he's a bit naughty, aren't you?'

'Well, I think we've all said enough now,' I pointed out

fair-mindedly as I put the biscuits in the oven. 'All's well that ends well, as they say.'

At that precise moment the phone rang.

'It's your solicitor!' Katie yelled.

'Hello, Mrs Smith,' said a pleasant female voice. 'It's Mr Cheetham-Stabb's secretary here. He asked me to chase you up about the papers he sent you in June.'

'Oh. What papers are those?'

'The Affidavit by petitioner in support of the petition, which you have to sign in front of another lawyer, then return. On that form you are also required to swear that the signature on your husband's Acknowledgement of Service form is his.'

'Why do I have to do that?'

'That's to stop women from forging their husbands' signatures in order to obtain a divorce.'

'Do they do that?'

'They certainly try. We sent you the document three months ago,' the woman went on. 'Now that Mr Cheetham-Stabb's back from his vacation, he wants to get things going.'

'Yes,' I sighed. 'Of course.'

'I'm very surprised you haven't received it,' she added. 'It was in an A5-sized brown envelope.'

'Ah. Well, I never open brown envelopes,' I explained. 'It's a sort of phobia I suppose. I always leave those ones to my husband, but he's in the States until next week.'

'In that case I'll send you a duplicate. In a white envelope.'

'Yes,' I said. 'That would be . . . great. But no hurry, you know. Whenever. I'm sure you've got lots of other things to do.'

The white envelope landed on my mat at eight a.m. the next day. I opened it but was too busy getting the children ready for school, and didn't get round to reading the contents for several days. But on Sunday I finally sat down in the kitchen and looked through the cream-coloured form. It was set out in a simple, question-and-answer way. *QUESTION: State briefly your reason for saying that the respondent has committed the adultery alleged. ANSWER:* 'He confessed.' *QUESTION: On what date did it first become known to you that the respondent had committed the adultery alleged? ANSWER:* 'Valentine's Day.' *QUESTION: Do you find it intolerable to live with the respondent? ANSWER:* 'Well, yes, I suppose I do.'

Oh God, this was awful. Awful. I put the form away. I didn't feel like filling it in now – I was much too depressed. The children had just gone back to school and I hadn't seen Jos for almost a week.

'Darling, I'm sorry. I'm neglecting you,' he said when he phoned me later that night. 'I'm afraid it's going to be like this until *Butterfly* opens,' he explained.

'It's OK,' I said. 'I understand. I know you're working all hours.'

'Why don't you come in to work tomorrow?' he suggested. 'You can watch a bit of the technical run, then we can sneak off for a cup of tea.'

So the following afternoon I got the tube to Covent Garden and walked to the Stage Door in Floral Street. The Tannoy was on in reception, and as I sat there, waiting for Jos, I could hear banging and hammering on-stage.

'The technical rehearsal will continue in twenty minutes,' I heard a stage manager announce. 'Would all technical staff please return to the stage in twenty minutes' time.'

While I waited for Jos to appear I looked at the programme he'd given me, and as I read his name and biography my heart expanded with pride. Then I studied the synopsis again. It explained that Butterfly, a fifteen-year-old geisha, enters into a 'marriage' with the handsome American, Lieutenant Pinkerton. For him it's just a casual affair, but she is infatuated with Pinkerton, even converting to Christianity for him. When Pinkerton's ship sails for America, Butterfly is confident that he'll return. Three years later, he does, and she joyfully prepares to greet him, not knowing that he has since married an American woman called Kate. Pinkerton sends the consul, Sharpless, to prepare Butterfly for this fact. But Sharpless discovers not only that she still worships Pinkerton, but also that she has had his child, a son. He cannot bring himself to tell Butterfly the awful truth. The following morning Pinkerton goes to the house, where she is asleep, having been watching for him all night. When he sees the child, who resembles him, he is shocked and filled with remorse. But Pinkerton is too cowardly to speak to Butterfly himself, so he leaves Kate and Sharpless to explain. When Butterfly wakes, and sees Kate standing in the garden, she intuits the awful truth. Kate explains that she and Pinkerton wish to adopt the little boy. Butterfly agrees on condition that Pinkerton comes in person to collect him. Now, left alone, she kisses her child goodbye, then kills herself, having nothing left to live for.

'Terrible,' I murmured. My skin had gone bumpy with goosepimples and my eyes were stinging with tears. 'Terrible,' I whispered again.

'Faith!' Suddenly the glass doors slid back and there was Jos, smiling at me. 'Hey!' he said as he kissed me. 'What's the matter?'

'Oh, nothing,' I said.

'You look a bit serious. Cheer up!'

'Oh, I am cheered up,' I said. And I was. Puccini's tragic story had suddenly receded, and it was as though the sun had come out. Here was Jos, all smiles, and I felt glad. His curly hair was tousled and tangled, his chequered shirt was hanging out; his jaw was stubbled with growth from the long hours he'd been putting in. Even in this unkempt state, he was such a handsome man. And I'd fallen in love with him all over again after the sweet way he'd looked for the dog. 'I'm lucky,' I'd told myself after that. 'It's not perfect, and yes, sometimes I'm not quite sure . . . but Lily's right. I'm incredibly lucky to have someone like Jos in my life.' Now he was signing me in and proudly introducing me to the receptionist as 'my lovely girlfriend, Faith'. Then he whisked me inside along smartly painted grey corridors and up two flights of stairs.

'I've just got to get some notes I left in the Model Room,' he said. 'Then we'll go down to the auditorium for the start of Act Two. The Model Room,' he added, 'is called the Model Room because we're all so damn good-looking.'

292

'I know you are,' I smiled. In reality the Model Room resembled an architect's practice. Designers sat hunched over drawing boards, marking lines on sheets of tracing paper or cutting card with Stanley knives. To one side were several tiny replicas of opera and ballet sets. There was one marked *Coppelia*, another marked *Rosenkavalier* and now I peered at the model for *Madame Butterfly*. It was like looking into a doll's house.

'We make them to one twenty-fifth of the actual size,' Jos explained as he rummaged in his desk. 'It's accurate in every detail, down to the garlands of flowers Butterfly decorates her house with when Pinkerton returns. Luckily *Madame Butterfly* is a simple work,' he explained. 'So the set is usually simple too.' I peered at the model. There was Butterfly's house, a small square structure with a white blind made of gauze. Inside was a futon, and in the corner, an American flag and a vase of flowers. There was even a tiny mirror on the wall. Around the house was a verandah, the planks no wider than lollipop sticks: in front was a small garden, with a lily pond and a bridge. And there was the figure of Butterfly herself, by the cherry tree, looking out for her beloved Pinkerton. And, in the background, instead of the boat-filled harbour of Nagasaki, was that ugly tenement building.

'Do you like it?' said Jos.

'Oh, yes,' I said. 'Although the tenement building looks a bit stark.'

'That's deliberate,' Jos replied. 'It's meant to emphasise that Butterfly is blind to the harsh realities of life. The director wasn't sure about it,' he added, 'but I talked him round in the end. When Butterfly meets Pinkerton,' he went on, 'she thinks life's a bowl of cherry blossom. But she's forced to recognise that she was deluded in believing that.'

'Poor Butterfly,' I murmured. 'She really suffers.'

'Oh, she's a little idiot,' said Jos. I looked up, startled.

'Isn't that a bit harsh?'

'No, because it's true. She brings it *all* on herself,' he went on with a grim little smile. 'Everyone warns her that her devotion to Pinkerton is foolish, but she refuses to listen. I mean, she *knew* the rules,' he went on irritably, his left hand cutting through the air. 'She *knew* it was just a temporary arrangement so she has only herself to blame.'

'Yes, but knowing is different from feeling,' I said. 'Then of course she's very young.'

'She's a fool,' he said, ignoring me. 'Doubly so because a Japanese prince offers to marry her but she won't have him, stupid girl.'

'Well, she won't compromise,' I said. 'She can't. She's even prepared to die for love.'

'Her suicide is just a selfish act,' he said contemptuously, 'designed to punish Pinkerton.'

'But Pinkerton's a shit. He *should* be punished.'

'I don't agree,' he said. At this he looked quite angry and I suddenly thought: this is *mad*. We're having a heated argument about a woman who doesn't even *exist*.

'Well, I think her suicide is tragic,' I went on quietly. 'She renounces everything. It's noble and it's wonderful, too.'

'I'm sorry, Faith,' said Jos briskly as he picked up his file. 'I just can't sentimentalise some crazy, pathetic bitch who's bent on victimhood. But fortunately for us opera folk, an awful lot of people do.'

I was taken aback by Jos's heartless comments, but resolved to put them to the back of my mind. There are times, yes, there *are* times when he says things I really don't like. Things that make me tense up inside. So I find the best thing is just to ignore them, and think about his good points instead. In any case, I reasoned as we went downstairs, we can't always view the world in the same way. How could we, when our experiences of life have been very different. So if he wants to get all steamed up about *Madame Butterfly*, well – let him, I said to myself. I mean, he's worked with the opera for months so he's bound to have a more sophisticated view than mine. By now we were in the back stage area, where sound engineers and lighting technicians were standing around in small groups. I stood in the wings as Jos walked about on the gently raked set. He was conferring with the lighting designer, and the director, and the production manager, and there were a number of people wearing headsets, staring up into the flies. A carpenter was adjusting the blind on Butterfly's house while three set painters – they looked very young – put the finishing touches to the backdrop.

'This is another world,' I reflected as I went and sat in the auditorium. I sank into the plush, red velvet seat as Jos strode about like a creative king. Everyone was looking at him. Everyone wanted to speak to him. Everyone wanted to know his opinion. He seemed to command such respect.

'This is what people will remember,' I realised as I gazed at the stage. 'They'll remember the singers, and the orchestra for a while, but for most of the audience their abiding memory will be of what it all looked like, and what they wore.'

I'm lucky, I thought again as the house-lights dimmed and the run-through began. Oh yes, I'm lucky. I repeated it, like a mantra. 'I'm very, very lucky indeed.'

'You're *very* lucky,' said Peter a few days later. 'You know that, don't you?' He was down on his knees in the kitchen, eye to eye with Graham, who was nervously wagging his tail. 'You are one helluva lucky dog. So don't push it, puppy.' Graham licked his nose. 'And next time you want to come over to my place, just phone me first, OK? Right. Lecture over. Gimme five.' Graham held up his right paw. 'I hated not being able to help you look for him,' Peter said as he straightened up.

'Well, you couldn't,' I said. 'But we all went out, and Jos helped too.'

'That was nice of him,' said Peter. 'That was very nice, when you consider that they don't really get on.' I poured some coffee into his mug. 'I'll look at these in a minute,' he said, indicating the pile of brown envelopes. 'You really ought to try and conquer your fear of manilla, you know.'

'Yes,' I agreed. 'But I can't.'

'You might have to,' he said. 'Because once the divorce comes through –' he drew an imaginary knife across his throat – 'I won't be doing it for you.' I nodded. I knew it was true. 'So how's it going with you and Jos, then?' he suddenly enquired. And I was slightly taken aback by that question, and by the bright, friendly way in which it was asked. I'd assumed Peter wouldn't really want to know about Jos any more than I wanted to know about Andie. 'Going well, is it?' he added casually.

'Oh, yes, it's fine,' I said. 'It's fine. You know. Fine.' I felt uncomfortable discussing my boyfriend with the man I was still married to. 'It's just, absolutely . . . fine,' I reiterated with a sigh.

'Good,' he nodded. 'Good. That's good.' We sipped our Arabica in silence. 'So it's progressing nicely then,' he added pleasantly.

'Well, yes,' I said, fiddling with my spoon. 'It is. Really, although . . .'

'What?'

'Although, he's very busy at the opera house.'

'Of course. That's a *really* interesting job he's got there.'

'Mmm.' I nodded. 'It is.'

'So it's going really well, is it?'

'Um, yes. It is. Absolutely. Usually.'

'*Usually*?' he echoed with a quizzical air.

'Yes. Usually,' I repeated. 'I mean, it's great, it really is. It's great. But it's not *perfect*, you know.'

'*Isn't* it?' he said. He was fiddling with the sugar bowl.

'No. Not perfect as such.'

'In what way?'

'Oh. Nothing really. Just small things.'

'Like what? Graham?'

'Oh no, not that. That's getting a bit better. Just other, trifling things.'

'Things?'

'I mean, areas of conflict.'

'Conflict? Oh dear.'

'Well, you know – differences of opinion. That's all I mean. Differences of attitude. But they're pretty piffling, really. And I guess that's normal, isn't it?'

'Is it?' he repeated.

'Oh, yes. I mean, I'm sure we had our differences too. At the beginning.'

'Did we?'

'I think so.' There was silence. 'Yes,' I said. 'I'm pretty sure.'

'Like what?'

'Well . . .' I looked at him blankly. I couldn't remember anything. 'I'd have to think about it. It was a long time ago.'

'That's true,' he said. 'It was. It was a very long time ago. I remember one thing!' he suddenly announced triumphantly. 'You didn't care for my taste in popular music.'

'Didn't I?'

'No. You used to tease me.'

'Really?'

'Mmm. Because I liked Gladys Knight and the Pips.'

'Oh yes,' I said. 'I remember.' We looked at each other and smiled.

'You're the best thing that's ever happened to me,' said Peter softly.

'Sorry?' I said. My face felt hot and my pulse had begun to race.

'You're the best thing that ever happened to me,' he repeated.

'Really?'

'Yes. I think that's their best number.'

'Oh. Mmm. I suppose it is. I wasn't mad about them myself.'

'No. You preferred Tom Jones.' I nodded.

'It's Not Unusual,' I said.

'I always thought it was, as he was a bit before your time.'

'No, "It's Not Unusual" is my favourite song,' I explained. 'And actually he's been continually popular. His appeal spans the generations.'

'Yes, I suppose it does. So it's going well with you and Jos?' he repeated brightly. I nodded. 'Good. Nothing big worrying you, then?'

'Heavens, no.'

'No major concerns?'

'Nope.'

'Or areas of incompatibility?' I shook my head.

'Why do you ask?' I said.

'Well, because the kids phoned me from France, and Katie hinted that there might be, you know, one or two, little things.'

'Did she? Well I'm afraid she's quite wrong. In any case, you know how she loves to over-analyse.' He nodded.

'She certainly does. So you're really happy with Jos, then?' he added.

'Yes. And since we're being so personal, what about you. Do you have any?'

'Any what?'

'Major concerns?' I asked.

'What? With Andie?' I nodded. 'Oh. No,' he said, shaking his head. 'Like you, there are just a few, you know . . .' I heard the air being drawn through his teeth. '. . . Small things.'

'What things?' I asked. Not that I was curious, of course. Now he exhaled, quite audibly, blowing air through his lips.

'Oh,' he said, 'just piffling, insignificant, and not very important tiny, well, baby little things really.'

'Like what?'

'Oh, well . . .'

'Yes?'

'It would be disloyal of me to say.'

'Of course it would. Ditto here.'

'And in any case they're only tiny things.'

'Well, that's . . . great.'

'Yes.'

'Because tiny things don't matter.'

'No.'

'So did you have a good holiday?' I enquired.

'Oh. It was . . . great,' he said, stirring his coffee again. 'It was . . . great. It's an interesting part of the States, you know.'

'Yes,' I replied. 'So I hear.'

'Virginia was the site of the first permanent European settlement.'

'1607,' I said.

'It was named Virginia in honour of Elizabeth the First. The Virgin Queen.'

'Of course.'

'It's also known as the Old Dominion State.'

'Mmm. I also hear it's a leading producer of tobacco.'

'Oh yes,' he said. 'Peanuts, too. And apples, and tomatoes.'

'Tom*ay*toes!'

'Of course,' he laughed. 'And timber.'

'I understand that coal mining is an important sector too.'

'Oh yes. Yes. It is. And there are so many historic towns. Like Norfolk, of course, and Richmond, and Jamestown. Now that's a *very* interesting place.'

'Well, it certainly sounds like you had a wonderful time.'

'How's your mother?' Peter said.

'Oh. Well, Mum is contrite,' I replied carefully. 'She has redeemed herself by working really hard with Matt, who seems to have caught up quite a bit. His French vocabulary is pretty good now. She taught them to play Bridge as well.'

'Oh, that's a good game. I'd like to take them out this weekend,' he went on. 'As I haven't seen them for almost two months. I thought we could go to the Tate Modern.'

'Good idea.'

'Or the Royal Academy.'

'Great.' We smiled awkwardly at each other. 'Right. Well, I'd better go through these,' he added as he picked up the pile of brown envelopes. 'Gas bill,' he announced. 'Seventy three pounds, sixty. Here you are. And this is from your accountant. This one's a reminder from the Inland Revenue and this,' he said, ripping open the envelope, 'is from . . . ooh . . . the manufacturers of Impulse body freshener. Congratulations, Faith! You have won *another* competition. A weekend for two in Rome.'

'Have I?' I grabbed the letter. 'Wow!'

'You'd better phone them up to accept. So, tell me, what was your slogan?'

'Oh, what was it? I can't remember. Oh yes. It was: "Men Can't Help Acting On Impulse because . . . they ignore common scents." That's s.c.e.n.t.s.,' I explained.

'I know,' he said. 'I got it in one. Well, that's brilliant. What a great prize. Not quite as good as a divorce though, is it?' he added briskly. 'On which note, this envelope here contains some nasty looking documents from Rory Cheetham-Stabb.' He peered at the pale yellow form. 'Affidavit by petitioner in support of the petition.'

'Oh yes,' I said. 'I know about that. They sent me a duplicate.'

'And have you filled it in?' he enquired casually.

'Yes,' I said quietly. 'I have.'

'When?' He looked out of the window. It was raining.

'Yesterday. I got Karen to witness it this morning. The decree nisi will come through in late November.'

'Precipitating,' he said.

'What?'

'The weather. There's precipitation. Isn't that what you fore-casters say?'

'Oh, we don't really talk about precipitation these days,' I explained. 'We talk about percentages instead. As in, "There's a sixty per cent chance of rain this morning." Or, "There's a ten per cent chance that it will snow."'

'And there's a one hundred and ten per cent chance that I'll be in trouble if I'm late for Andie,' he said, suddenly standing up. 'So I guess I'd better go. Bye, darling,' he said as he turned. 'I do love you, you know.'

'Bye darling,' I replied. I was slightly taken aback by his declaration of affection, but suddenly realised he'd been talking to the dog.

'Bye poppet,' he said, putting his arms round Graham. 'No more freelance walkies, OK? I'll see you again very soon.' And I thought there was a chance that Peter might kiss me too. But he didn't. He gave me a slightly joyless little smile, then walked out of the house.

'So long, Faith!' I heard him call from the door.

'So long!' I replied. I waited to hear the click of the latch, but it didn't come. How *very* odd. He'd left the door ajar.

* * *

'Ten, nine, eight . . .'

'So the picture's rather unsettled,' I concluded in my nine thirty bulletin on Monday morning.

'Seven, six . . .'

'Rather than the clear, fine weather we'd expect at this time of the year.'

'Five . . .'

'There's a good deal of rain and murk.'

'Four . . .'

'This is because of these spiky lines here on the isobars, which indicate an occluded front.'

'A *what*?' I heard in my ear.

'An occluded front arises when a warm front meets a cold front and that generally leads to a very cloudy, unclear period, which is what we're going to get for the next few days.'

'Three, two . . .'

'With a fifty per cent chance of rain.'

'One . . .'

'Which on the other hand means there's a fifty per cent chance of sun.'

'And zero . . .'

'See you all tomorrow.'

'Thanks, Faith.'

'And thank you all for watching,' said Terry. 'In the programme tomorrow we'll be interviewing the woman who set up Two Awful – a dating agency for incredibly ugly people – and we'll be meeting some of her clients.'

'Also,' said Sophie, 'we'll have more Decorating Disasters. And we'll be talking to the authors of *The Great Pantyhose Crafts Book* – a complete guide to making useful things out of old tights. But just before we finish,' she added, 'I'd like to thank everyone who's sent me fan-mail. I'm sorry not to have written back to you all, but there seems to have been a little local problem with the post which has now been sorted out.'

With that she gave the camera a dazzling smile, let the credits roll, then strode off set with a purposeful air. I removed my make-up with Simple moisturiser, checked the satellite charts once more, then went into the boardroom for the weekly planning meeting. There was Terry indolently picking his teeth, Tatiana whispering into her mobile phone, and there were the producers and researchers with their clipboards and folders and notes. And Darryl, of course, at the end. There was a hiatus while we waited for everyone to arrive, so I looked through the pile of magazines. At the bottom was the new, October edition of *Moi!* I flicked through it to the back, to the diary section, 'I Spy'. And sure enough, there it was, at the top of the page. The photo of Jos and me at the polo. It was simply, but correctly captioned, *Jos Cartwright and Mrs Peter Smith*. Jos had his arm round me, and we were both smiling. It was a flattering picture, though I noticed that despite my happy expression my smile didn't quite reach my eyes. But of course that was the morning that Jos had shouted at Graham. Things had been tense that day. But now, well, they were pretty good. All in all. I mean, nothing's ideal, is it? There's no such thing as the perfect man. With relationships, especially new ones, you have to take the wider view. My thoughts were suddenly interrupted by the sharp tapping of a pen on the table. It was Darryl, and he didn't look pleased.

'Where's Sophie?' he said irritably. 'I want to start.'

'Just coming!' she called. She came into the boardroom, smiling but slightly breathless, clutching a huge cardboard box.

'So sorry I'm late,' she said.

'What's that?' said Darryl.

'I'll show you,' she replied. She smiled at Terry and Tatiana, then suddenly tipped it up, disgorging a sea of letters. Out they spewed, in a papery slick as thick and slow as lava. There were white envelopes, and pink ones, and yellow ones and brown. There were parchment-blue aerogrammes with pretty foreign stamps. There were postcards, plain and pictorial, there was Conqueror and Basildon Bond. There was green ink, and blue crayon, and smudged pencil and mauve felt-tip. Many were typed, some were scrawled, while others were in smart copperplate. A number had stars and hearts stuck to them, and some were emblazoned S.W.A.L.K. There must have been more than five hundred, and they were all addressed to Sophie.

'My missing fan-mail,' she announced pleasantly. 'I found it this morning. Isn't that funny? I just thought you'd all like to know.'

'Good God!' said Darryl. 'Where was it?'

'It really is the strangest thing,' she said innocently, giving Terry and Tatiana a beady stare. 'Before we went on air I was looking for a highlighter pen, and so I went to the stationery cupboard. And right at the bottom of the cupboard there was this box, and, well, *imagine* my surprise when I looked inside! This is six months' worth.'

'Terry?' said Darryl. 'Can you enlighten us?'

'Don't look at me,' Terry replied.

'Well, do you have any idea who might have done this?' Darryl asked.

'Er, the post boy,' Tatiana suggested. 'He had ambitions to be a presenter, you know.'

'*Did* he?' said Sophie, her eyes like saucers. 'Well, why don't we ask him?' she said.

'We can't,' Darryl replied. 'He left last week.'

'Where's he gone?' she asked.

'To work at the Savoy, I think.'

'Well that's not going to advance his TV career much,' Sophie pointed out. 'Is it, Tatty?' Tatiana shrugged.

'It's a complete mystery,' said Terry smoothly. 'But as I don't think we'll ever get to the bottom of it, I suggest we get on with the meeting.' But Darryl wasn't listening, he was reading the letters as Sophie passed them to him.

'Of course I haven't opened them all,' she explained. 'There are so many – I haven't had time. But let me just give you a taste. I'm sure Terry would love to hear what the viewers think of me.

'"Dear Sophie,"' she read, '"I think you are the best thing on breakfast TV. Dear Sophie, without your sunny smile and witty words I wouldn't be able to face the day. Dear Sophie, I get up early just to watch you. Dear Sophie, you are so much more intelligent than that fourth-rate old git on the sofa next to you." Oh sorry, Terry,' she said with theatrical exaggeration. 'I didn't mean to be tactless. "Dear Sophie,"' she read, picking up another one, '"why aren't YOU the main presenter?"' She ripped open a small brown envelope. '"Dear Sophie, why are you doing crappy breakfast TV? You should be presenting Newsnight!"' By now Terry's mouth was as thin and hard as a hairgrip.

'Well, it's good to know you're so popular,' said Darryl. 'But do you want to pursue this matter – it's theft?' She shook her head.

'I have no wish to make trouble,' she said, staring at Terry. 'But I just wanted everyone to know.'

'Good,' said Terry. He folded his arms and leaned back in his chair. On his face was an insolent smile. 'It's right that everyone should know. It's absolutely right that everyone should know,' he repeated vehemently, 'about *you*.' The temperature in the room suddenly dropped from boiling point to minus twelve. 'There are some things about you, Sophie, that everyone should know,' Terry added with a sly smile. At that a look passed between them of utter, visceral, hate. The cut and thrusts of the last ten months had been mere skirmishes. This was a declaration of war. 'Are there many letters from men here?' asked Terry innocently, picking one up. He tossed it back on the mountainous pile. 'Or do you find you're more popular with the ladies?'

'It seems I'm popular with everyone,' she snapped. But her throat was blotched and red.

'Hmm,' said Terry with a sceptical smile. 'Are you? I'm not sure about that.'

'Er, OK,' said Darryl. He swallowed nervously, his Adam's apple dipping by at least three inches. 'Anyway, thanks for drawing this to our attention, Sophie, and er, let's start the meeting. OK, everyone. Ideas please. And don't forget – it's a family show.'

*   *   *

On Friday evening the children came home; I collected them from Charing Cross. The following morning they got the tube over to Peter and didn't return until eight.

'Did you have a nice day with Dad?' I asked as I washed some salad.

'Oh, yes,' said Matt. 'It was great. We went to the Tate Modern in the morning.'

'And what did you do in the afternoon?' I asked. They were silent. 'What did you do?'

'Well, nothing really,' said Matt.

'You must have done something,' I said. 'You've been out all day.'

'Well, we just went out for tea, that's all. Nothing special, you know.'

'So where was that then?' I said. 'Come on. Spill the beans.'

'Nowhere worth mentioning,' said Matt.

'Oh, let's stop this charade, Matt,' said Katie. 'We went to Andie's, Mum.'

'Oh,' I said crestfallen. 'I see.'

'Well, if Jos can come here so much, then I don't see why Dad can't go to her place.'

'I suppose so,' I said. But it hurt. I knew he went there. Of course he did. But I still loathed the thought of my kids going there too.

'You've got to accept it, Mum,' said Katie briskly. 'It's six months since you and Dad split.' I looked at her and sighed. She was quite right. I couldn't have it all ways.

'So what's her place like?' I said, swallowing hard.

'Luxurious!' Matt exclaimed.

'That figures. Where is it?'

'Notting Hill.'

'That figures too.'

'There are *five* bedrooms,' he said, round-eyed.

'Surprise me.'

'And she's got a *huge* double bed!' I felt sick. 'And do you know what she's got on her bed, Mum?' he went on.

'No, and I don't want to –'

'Cuddly toys!' he exclaimed.

'What?'

'Lots of cuddly toys,' Matt repeated. 'Dozens. And they've all got names.'

'That's a bit weird,' I said. 'For a thirty-six-year old.'

'Oh no, Mum,' said Katie.

'I think it is.'

'No, she's more than thirty-six.'

'Is she? How do you know?'

'Because I saw her passport. She'd left it on the kitchen table so I just sneaked a teeny little look.'

'Katie! That's really naughty. So tell me – how old *is* she?'

'She's forty-one.'

'Gosh. Does Daddy know?'

'I don't know. I didn't ask.'

'But she's really funny,' said Matt.

'Funny? I can't imagine that,' I said, remembering the humourless blonde I'd seen on TV.

'I mean funny *peculiar*. You see, she's started calling Dad all these names. Baby names,' he added with a laugh.

'Baby names? Like what?'

'Well,' he began. He was giggling. 'She calls him her "little Petie-Sweetie".'

'No!'

'And her Pumpkin-Pie!'

'Yeeeuch!'

'And her honey-bunny.'

'How ghastly.'

'And her Baby-Waby.'

'Eeeeuuugh.' Graham put his paws on my lap. 'I never did that. Did I, my little puppy wuppy? And how does Daddy react?'

'He just sort of smiles,' said Matt.

'And what does he call her?'

'Andie. But she calls herself . . .'

'No, don't tell me!'

'Yes,' said Katie. 'Andie *Pandy*!' By now my eyes were on stalks. 'Dad doesn't like it much. I think he finds it demeaning and silly. I don't think he understands why she does it,' she added. 'But I do. It's a form of self-infantilisation,' she explained matter-of-factly, 'because Andie's clearly sensitive about her age. She's also trying to project a child-like vulnerability to cover the fact that she's rapacious and hard. The cuddly toys tie in with that too, and of course, at a deeper psychological level it all connects, together with the five bedrooms, with her obvious desire for –'

'But *hang* on,' I interrupted. 'This woman's a hard-nosed headhunter. She doesn't want to be seen as a little girl.'

'She does at home,' said Katie. 'She wants to be Dad's ickle baby, so that he'll look after her, because she knows that men like powerlessness, which is, of course, why Lily's still single. The other thing about it,' she went on knowledgeably, 'is that it's also a form of manipulation. She calls Dad all these toddler names so that she can push him around. It's a way of emasculating him,' Katie concluded. 'So that she can get what she wants.'

'Oh,' I said. 'Poor Dad.'

'It's also a way of displaying ownership,' she said. 'All her endearments are prefaced with the tell-tale word "my". That's the real give-away – it's an obvious sign of desperation.'

'My God,' I said. 'How weird. Are you sure you're not over-analysing all this, Katie? I mean, Dad seems happy enough. He told me he didn't have any major worries, and he always tells the truth.' At this the children were silent. 'He is happy, isn't he?' Matt shrugged.

'Dunno.'

'We haven't asked him outright,' said Katie carefully. 'We can only go on what we see. But I'd say that Dad's about as happy with Andie as you are with Jos.'

'I'm *quite* happy with Jos, thank you,' I said stiffly. 'And it's, you know, serious.'

'Yes,' said Katie archly. 'We know.' At this she just looked at me and smiled this peculiar little smile – an annoying habit she gets from her father. She's like Peter in so many ways.

That night her irritating remarks revolved around my head,

making it hard to sleep. I must have drifted off at some stage, because I remember having an odd dream about an iceberg. But it can't have been a deep, peaceful sleep, because I was woken by the clatter of the letterbox when the paper arrived. Graham and I went blearily downstairs. I made him a cup of tea – milk, no sugar, not too strong – then I looked at the *Sunday Times*, holding it about an inch from my face as I didn't have my lenses in. I went straight to the *Culture* section, imagining that there might be some small preview piece about the opera. Instead, to my astonishment, there was a double-page spread about Jos. It was headed, 'Butterfly's Designer in Full Flight' and there he was, smiling out at me, hair tousled, looking as divine as ever. There's something about his large, grey eyes which just draw you right in. It was a flattering piece – the journalist had clearly been charmed. In fact it was very like the piece in the *Independent* six months before. *I guess I've been very lucky* . . . Jos was quoted as saying . . . *Passionate about what I do* . . . *Stefanos Lazaridis' work is wonderful* . . . *Director's wishes always come first*.

That last remark suddenly struck me as odd, and now I remembered what Jos had said when he was showing me the set. He'd said, 'The director wasn't sure about it, but I talked him round in the end.' That was strange. But then it went right out of my mind because now, to my amazement, I was suddenly reading my name. *Cartwright has recently been linked with AM-UK!'s weather girl, Faith Smith*, the journalist had written. *I don't know what I'd do without Faith*, Jos had said. *Six months ago I fell under the warm spell of her sunshine and now I'm quite bewitched.* I think I read that sentence ninety-five times. Then I read it again. Now he was talking about *Madame Butterfly. Puccini's most powerful opera* . . . *I wanted to show Butterfly's vulnerability* . . . *Her pretty house is dwarfed by ugly tenements against which she looks fragile and alone* . . . *Yes, I think she's Puccini's greatest heroine*, he went on. *Her wings are made of steel. She renounces everything for the man she loves* . . . *Her nobility and courage are unforgettable*, he concluded. *Her heartbreaking sacrifice fills me with awe.* I felt my eyes widen and my jaw go slightly slack. I went upstairs and put my lenses in, then read it again, to make sure. Then I gazed out of the kitchen window where I could see the weather vane on the house next door swinging in the morning breeze. Now I returned my gaze to the newspaper, and looked at the photo of Jos. How could he say that, I wondered, as I felt my insides twist and coil. How was it possible to speak so contemptuously of Butterfly in private, then heap such lavish praise on her here? I stared, sightlessly, into the middle distance, trying to work it out. Suddenly I started as the phone rang out. Who the hell was ringing me at seven thirty on a Sunday morning?

'FAITH!' shouted Lily. 'GET UP RIGHT NOW AND GO AND GET THE *SUNDAY TIMES*!'

'It's OK,' I said. 'I am up. I've got it.'

'And have you seen the piece about Jos?'

'Mmm,' I murmured. 'I have.'

'But, darling, isn't it just *unbelievable*?'

'Yes,' I said quietly. 'It is.'

The first night of *Madame Butterfly* was to be a celebrity-filled gala opening – a major social event. I should be feeling thrilled, I reflected; instead I felt depressed. I felt as low and flat as a stratus, I mused as I looked up at the sky. I'd have felt better if Lily was coming along, but she had to go to some charity ball. I hadn't even decided what to wear, so odd was my mood, so now I went through my things. Here was my old Principles 'best' dress; it was a safe choice, black velvet and quite smart, but I hadn't worn it for a very long time. On the neighbouring hanger was a pretty frock from Next – an impulse buy which had never looked right. There was also – don't laugh – a satin dress from What She Wants, which, though cheap, looked rather nice. But I knew it wouldn't do for this. I didn't really have anything suitable, I realised, so I asked Lily if she'd mind lending me the pink Armani again.

'That dress you wore to Glyndebourne?' she said.

'Yes, that one.'

'Don't be ridiculous. Of course you can't.'

'Oh. Sorry I asked.'

'It's out of the question darling, because someone might spot it!' she said. 'How can you possibly go to a gala night at Covent Garden wearing a dress that everyone's seen?'

'But it's lovely, and anyway, they won't all be there.'

'Faith,' she said firmly. 'You simply cannot run the risk. You're going to be on show tomorrow night, darling. You're going to be spotted and snapped. Not just because of your own, admittedly minor celebrity, but because you'll be there with Jos. Now, I've got a gorgeous Clements Ribeiro sample. I'll lend you that instead.'

She sent the dress round by company car on Tuesday afternoon, five hours before curtain up. It was made of a dark grey silk jersey fabric, cut on the bias, with pretty, diamante straps. It looked lovely: sparkly without being overdone, glamorous but very discreet.

'Lily knows what she's talking about,' I said to Graham as I gazed at myself in the glass. I phoned Jos and told him I'd get the tube up to town, but he hit the roof.

'Darling, you are *not* getting the tube,' he said.

'Why not? I can meet you there.'

'Because, Faith, we are arriving together, by limo. You've obviously forgotten. I told you this last week.' So at six fifteen a large Mercedes, as black and shiny as a raven, pulled up outside the house. I stepped into its darkened interior, then we drove to Burnaby Street. Jos emerged from his house in a white tuxedo, looking like something out of a *GQ* shoot.

'You look lovely,' he said as he got into the car. I squeezed his hand.

'So do you.'

'This is the most important event of my life,' he said. 'Did you see the *Sunday Times* piece?'

'Yes,' I whispered. 'Oh yes, it was great.' He looked anxiously at his watch a couple of times as we idled in rush-hour traffic. By the time we were driving down Haymarket it was already ten past seven. But now we were moving slowly along the Strand, then turning left up Wellington Street. And here was Bow Street, and the Corinthian portico of the opera house, and the massive arched window of Floral Hall. Lily was right

– the paparazzi were out in force. Who was it they were photographing? I craned forward a little to see. It was Anna Ford and her new man. There was Emma Thompson with Greg Wise, and wasn't that Stephen Fry?

'The stars will be twinkling tonight,' said Jos. 'OK. Breathe deeply. It's us.' The driver stopped, ran round and opened the door, and I stepped out first.

'Faith! This way! Faith! Over here!' We paused on the bottom step, turned and smiled. I felt Jos's hand on the small of my back.

'One more,' he whispered. 'Very good. And in we go.' The foyer spangled with the refracted beams from diamonds, crystals and gold. The air was voluptuous with *un*common scents, and the tang of expensive cologne. We went up the wide, red-carpeted stairway and took our seats in the Grand Tier. I looked at the great swagged, red velvet curtains with their golden embroidery and royal crest. Just below us were the stalls, and rising vertiginously above, the tiered balconies, like the decks of an ocean liner. I glanced discreetly to left and right. We get celebrities coming into AM-UK! but this was something else. At the end of our row was Cate Blanchett with her husband, and just in front were William and Ffion Hague. On the left side of the stalls I spotted the Michael Portillos and, well to their right, the Blairs. In one of the boxes I spied Joanna Lumley, and in another, Michael Buerk. There were so many famous people I was suddenly possessed by the urge to start a Mexican wave.

'How's your Italian?' said Jos with a smile.

'Not too *caldo*, I'm afraid. I'll be reading the surtitles,' I said. And now the house-lights momentarily flared, then dimmed, and a reverential hush came down. Then the conductor came on in a burst of applause. He walked through the pit, stepped onto the podium, bowed once, then turned and raised his baton. There was a moment's silence. Just a beat. Then, against a sudden flurry of violins, the huge red curtain lifted and there was Pinkerton, on his 'wedding day'. Already the lyrical, lush beauty of the music was in stark contrast to his cynical words:

'I will marry according to Japanese custom . . .' he sang, 'And I can get divorced any time . . .' Now he was drinking a toast to, 'The day when I marry a true American bride.' Then, from off-stage came Butterfly's voice, sweet and high, as she approached the house with her maidens.

'I am the happiest girl in Japan,' she sang. 'This is a very great honour.' And now there she was in her ceremonial kimono, with flowers in her hair, stepping forward to greet Pinkerton.

'Butterfly can flee no longer,' he sang as they were 'married'. 'I caught you, and now you are mine.'

'Yes. For life!' she replied ecstatically. I felt my head shake with pity for her terrible fate. And I must have sighed, because I suddenly felt Jos's arm pressing on mine; out of the corner of my eye I saw him lift his right index finger to his lips. But I couldn't help it. I couldn't. I felt for her. And as the curtain fell on Act One half an hour later my throat was aching with a long-suppressed sob.

'Darling, I hope you're not going to blub all the way through,' said Jos as we made our way to the bar.

'Probably,' I said with a thin smile.

'Well, please try not to. It's annoying.'

'OK. But it's just *so* sad. They ought to staple a couple of tissues into the programme,' I joked. Jos didn't laugh, but then he had other things on his mind. After all, this was a very big night for him, and I'd been forgetting that fact.

'The set looks wonderful,' I said again as he came back with our champagne. 'You're just so, so brilliant, Jos. I'm so proud of you.' And now, at last, he smiled. The bar in Floral Hall was a crush of *haute couture* and black serge.

'– fabulous voice he's got.'

'– prefer Laurent Perrier.'

'– oh, I've never heard him. Is he any good?'

'– *super* little place down there.'

'– not mad about this libretto.'

'– our two youngest are at Stowe.'

Now the bell was ringing, then it rang again and we made our way back to our seats. But the champagne had made me feel dizzy, and as we sat there, waiting for the lights to go down, I could feel my head starting to swim. I *mustn't* cry in the second half, I thought, because Jos won't like it one bit. So in order to distract myself, I glanced around the auditorium again. I scrutinised the boxes, then dropped my gaze to the stalls. All of a sudden my heart began to beat so fast I thought it would burst from my chest. For halfway down, on the righthand side, was Peter – with Andie. It was as though I'd been pushed out of a plane.

'Anything the matter, Faith?' asked Jos as my heart hurtled to the ground.

'Oh, no,' I murmured. 'I'm fine.' My face was burning and my mouth felt dry; the hairs had risen on the back of my neck. My stomach was churning like a cement mixer and someone was trying to push a blunt knife into my chest. Oh God. Oh *God*. I'd never seen them together before. But now here they were, side by side, my husband of fifteen years – and *her*. I stared, miserably, at them. It was masochistic, but I couldn't *not* look, even though I didn't want to see. Peter was in a dinner jacket, she was in a red silk dress, and she was chatting to him and picking lint off his collar, and suddenly she leaned her head on his shoulder. And I wanted to stand up and shout, 'TAKE YOUR FUCKING HANDS *OFF* MY HUSBAND, YOU PREDATORY BITCH!' But I just managed to remember where I was. This was purgatorial. Why the *hell* did they have to come *tonight*? And why didn't Peter tell me? He could have guessed I'd be here. Now Andie was taking hold of his hand as the house-lights began to go down. What was that she was whispering to him, I wondered blackly. 'Ooh, it's getting dark, Petie-Sweetie, so will you please look after your ickle Andie-Pandy because she's a teensy bit afwaid.' I felt sick, and faint, and the champagne didn't help, and now the orchestra were playing, and the curtain was rising. A bitter sigh passed my lips.

'Sssshhh!' whispered Jos. The music seemed to match my mood. It was plangent, funereal even, with the relentless slow beat of a drum. There was Butterfly, three years later, alone in her house, and poor. She'd abandoned her kimono and was wearing Western dress, and had unfurled the American flag. Her maid, Suzuki, was telling her she didn't think that Pinkerton would ever come back.

'He will return,' said Butterfly defiantly. 'Say it! He *will* return.' Then she sang 'One Fine Day', in which she imagined Pinkerton's ship sailing into the harbour, and him walking up the hill to her house.

'He will call me, "my little wife", you "fragrance of verbena", the names he used to call me when he first came here.' She was still so in love, and so deluded – you'd have to have a heart of stone not to care. Now Sharpless had come, with a letter from Pinkerton, and it's so obvious what it means. But Butterfly wilfully insists that Pinkerton is still in love with her. Sharpless tactfully tries to spell it out, but she just won't hear. He's about to give up, and the music is building, in this ominous crescendo, when she suddenly darts into the house. And now she was emerging with the child in her arms. This tiny boy. She was standing there, holding him defiantly, as the music swelled to an unbearable pitch. There was a blast of trombones, and bassoons and French horns, then the deafening crash of a vast gong.

'What about *him*?' she sang, as she stepped forward with her child, her voice soaring into the gods. 'Could he also forget *him*?' Sharpless looked shocked.

'Is the child his?' he asked faintly.

'Whoever saw a Japanese child with blue eyes?' she sang. 'Look at his mouth, and his golden hair.' I felt Jos stiffen beside me. I glanced at him, but he wasn't crying. Not one tear. I guessed he was concentrating on the set and costumes rather than the music and plot. Then I glanced blindly down into the stalls, to see if I could make out Peter in the gloom. I wondered if he was crying – he probably was – he's sentimental, like me. He wouldn't have abandoned Butterfly, I thought feelingly. Oh no. He'd have done the right thing. Now, still determined that Pinkerton was hers, Butterfly was strewing her house with flowers and putting on her wedding kimono. Then she was waiting, and falling asleep. I could feel the audience stiffen into immobility as the drama intensified. For now at last, here was Pinkerton, with his wife, and Sharpless. Sharpless reminds him that he had always known that Butterfly would become profoundly attached.

'Yes,' sang Pinkerton. 'I can see my mistake. And I fear that I will never be free of this torment. Never! I am a coward!' he sang. Yes, I thought. You *are*. 'I am a coward!' Then, as he saw Butterfly stir, he ran away. And I thought, how could any man – let alone a brave naval officer – run away from a woman and a small child? By now I could hear stifled weeping as Butterfly realises the terrible truth.

'Everything is dead to me!' she wept. 'Everything is finished! Ah!' Then came the awful moment when she says goodbye to her son.

'Is it you, my little darling?' she sang sweetly. 'I hope you never find out that Butterfly died for you . . . Farewell, my love. Go and play.'

All around me, I could hear suppressed weeping. I tried to swallow my own tears as I felt my eyes brim, then overflow. I couldn't look as she took out her father's ceremonial sword, then plunged it into her side. There were suppressed sobs and sniffs as the music swelled once more, then gradually faded and died.

The ensuing silence, as the curtain dropped in front of Butterfly's lifeless body, must have lasted thirty seconds or more. Then the clapping started, building gradually, rolling like thunder, until it rang to the roof. Now people were cheering and shouting *Bravo*! And I wanted to do that, too, but I couldn't – I felt too drained. I wiped my wet cheeks with my stole. The heavy curtain was parting, and, one by one the cast reappeared.

Bravo! *Bravo*! *Encore*! Suddenly Jos stood up.

'I'm expected on stage too,' he whispered. 'I'll see you in the foyer afterwards.' Now Butterfly was taking her bow, spreading wide her arms to acknowledge the rapturous appreciation and the roses that rained down around her feet. People were standing and clapping and cheering, but still my eyes were full. On and on it went. Then the conductor came on stage, with the director and Jos, and the applause erupted again. They took their bow, smiled, then clapped the orchestra, still seated below them in the pit.

As the lead violin stood up, I looked into the stalls and saw Peter wiping his eyes. But now the applause had finally subsided and the house-lights were shining again. As reality returned, I felt myself engulfed by a wave of panic. What should I do? Stay in my seat until it was all clear? I couldn't *face* seeing Peter with her. I resolved to stay put, but then found I couldn't because the rest of the row wanted to leave. So now I was being swept towards the exit in a human tide. I glanced at the faces around me – they all looked shattered and drained. Many had been crying, but then it was so big, so terrible; it had been like watching someone being crucified. Now we were going down the stairs – there was the foyer – and still there were tears in my eyes. As I got to the bottom, I nervously looked behind me to see if Andie and Peter were there. I turned my head for a split second, no more, when suddenly, my contact lens flipped out. Oh God! It had gone. My vision had blurred and I felt it drop, its edge lightly brushing my cheek. Oh Christ! This was all I needed. There were people all around me and I was terrified it would get stepped on, so I dropped to my hands and knees. So there I was, groping about on the carpet, and it was impossible to see. I was aware that a space was being cleared around me as I probed the floor with my fingertips.

'Lost a lens, have you?' said a man. I nodded. 'Let's see if we can find it.'

'Oh, thanks.'

'Hard or soft?' I heard a woman ask.

'It's a hard one,' I replied. And even with my blurred, trombone vision I could see about six people starting to look.

'Thank God it's not a soft one,' said another voice. 'They're a complete nightmare to find.'

'Really?'

'Yes. They dry out and disintegrate, and they're much harder to spot.'

316

'– but on the other hand they're easier to wear.'

'– oh I don't find that at all.'

'– no, you can wear them for a lot longer.'

'– prefer hard ones myself.'

'– got it! Oh no, it's a sequin.'

'– sequin and you shall find!'

'– mine are tinted, actually.'

'– give me specs any day.'

'Have you been wearing them long?' someone else asked me.

'Oh, years,' I replied. 'I don't often lose them. But it just, you know, popped out.' And although it was nice of everyone to help me, I felt an utter fool. Jos, I knew, would be livid. He'd come downstairs after his triumph to find his girlfriend grovelling on the floor.

'I hope you've got some spares,' said a woman.

'No,' I said ruefully, 'I don't.'

'Well, then we've *got* to find it – otherwise you'll be in the soup.'

'What we need is a torch,' said a man in a dinner jacket. 'Anyone got one?'

''Fraid not.'

I sighed; we'd never find it. I'd have to go into work tomorrow half blind. Oh God, oh God. What a *terrible* night. And what a farcical way for it to end.

'I give up,' I said. 'It's very kind of everyone, but I don't think I'm going to have any luck.'

Suddenly, a hand stretched out beneath me, and resting in the palm was my tiny lens.

'Thank God,' I breathed. I picked it up, spat on it, then quickly put it in. 'Thank you *so* much,' I said as I blinkingly looked up. 'I –'

'That's OK,' Peter said.

'Found it, has she?' I heard someone say. 'Has she got it or not?'

'Oh yes, yes, I have, thanks very much. Thank you, Peter,' I said. We both got shakily to our feet as the crowd now flowed around us and out. He was smiling at me, but I noticed that the whites of his eyes were veined and red.

'Did you enjoy the opera?' he asked.

'Yes. No. Not really. Too sad.'

'Ditto,' he said. 'Terrible.'

'Terrible.' We gave each other a watery smile. 'I didn't know you'd be here,' I added quietly.

'Nor did I. It was a surprise.'

'Well, how lovely!' I said brightly while inside I felt as bleak as a Yorkshire moor. My nerves were jangling painfully as I waited for Andie to appear. Peter smiled again. A sad smile. Then he suddenly grabbed my hand. 'Oh, Faith,' he said. Then he swallowed hard. He'd enclosed my hand in both of his. 'Faith, this is *mad*,' he added. 'I can't bear it. This crazy . . . thing we're doing. Faith,' he said imploringly, 'I don't want to get divorced.'

'No,' I said, faintly, 'I know. Where is she?' I added quickly.

'In the Ladies. She'll be down in a second. And where's he? Where's Jos?'

'He's on his way too.'

'We don't have long, Faith,' Peter said. He was holding my hand so hard I thought my fingers would break. 'We've got to talk,' he added. 'We've got to talk properly, Faith. We don't have much time, you see. We've got to –' Suddenly he dropped my hand as though it were white-hot.

'Peter, darling!' It was Andie. She was sweeping down the stairs like a Harpy come to snatch the feast away. 'Come on, pumpkin,' she said in that gravelly voice. 'I want you to take me home.' Suddenly she registered me, standing next to him, and stopped dead in her tracks. Then she gave me a brittle smile, turned on her heel and led Peter away.

October

This Butterfly has Wings! trumpeted the *Telegraph*. *A Soaring Butterfly!* announced *The Times*. *Perfect Puccini!* proclaimed the *Guardian*. *A Butterfly Ablaze!* said the *Mail*. The critics were united and unanimous – the production was a huge triumph. I read and reread the reviews with Jos as we had breakfast on Saturday. *Absolutely heart-searing ... Covent Garden awash with tears ... Li Yuen's Butterfly more than a victim ... proud and dignified ... Mark Bell's Pinkerton callous, but revealing a bewildered agony too ... Jos Cartwright's thrilling design puts him firmly in the front rank.*

'You've done it,' I said. 'You're a star.'

'Well, it worked pretty well,' he said judiciously. 'And today I feel . . . satisfied.'

'So you should,' I said warmly. 'The whole world's after you now.' For already Jos is being deluged with offers of work. He's been approached to do *The Turn of the Screw* at Glyndebourne, *The Rake's Progress* at The Met, *Don Giovanni* in San Francisco, and *Rigoletto* in Rome. He's being commissioned now to do operas that won't be staged for three or four years.

'I'm going to choose very carefully,' he said. 'I don't want to travel as much as before. And the reason for that,' – he lifted my fingers to his lips – 'is because I don't want to be too far from you. That's why none of my relationships have worked out,' he added, 'because I was always away. But I feel different now, Faith. I'm thirty-seven. What I'd *really* like to do,' he added with a knowing smile, 'is *The Ring Cycle*.'

'*The Ring Cycle*?' I repeated. 'Oh.'

'Why not?' he murmured as he stroked my left hand. 'After all, it's serious now. And what about the divorce,' he went on smoothly, 'is that still on track?'

'Mmm. As far as I know.'

'And I want to book that trip to Parrot Cay,' he went on as he stood up to go and play squash. 'Can you get away in early December?' I nodded. 'Good, we'll try and go then. Right, I'd better be off,' he said as he picked up his sports bag. 'The court's booked for half past ten.' He went to the kitchen dresser to get his car keys, then something caught his eye and he stopped.

'That's pretty,' he said, picking up the greetings card I'd bought the previous day. 'Who's it for?'

'Oh, it's for an old school friend,' I replied. 'It's her . . . wedding anniversary soon.'

'You send your friends anniversary cards?' I nodded. 'Oh Faith, that's so typically sweet. Anyway,' he added as he kissed me, 'I'll see you in a couple of hours.'

I found myself feeling slightly shocked at the smooth way in which I'd just lied. The card wasn't for a school friend at all – it was for Peter's birthday the following week. I looked at it again as I heard Jos's MG rev up, then drive away. As I did so I thought once more of what Peter had said that night: 'This is mad . . . This thing we're doing. We don't have long. We've got to talk . . .' He'd looked at me with such a blazing intensity, but I hadn't heard from him since. Perhaps he'd been carried away by the emotion of the opera. Perhaps he'd had too much champagne. Perhaps he was getting on better with Andie. Perhaps he'd been working too hard. But he was still my husband and I wanted him to know that on his birthday he'd be in my thoughts. I took the card out of its Cellophane sleeve and a slip of paper fell out: *This card has been left blank for your own message*. But what should my message say? Happy birthday, obviously. I wrote that down. But how should I sign off? 'Love from Faith', I suppose. Or, perhaps, 'With love from Faith'. 'Much love, Faith', maybe? 'Lots of love from Faith'? 'Love and kisses, Faith'? Oh, no. Too forward. Perhaps I should just sign it 'F'. Maybe I should add an x. Or two. Or possibly even three. I tried that out on a piece of scrap paper but still I wasn't quite sure. Perhaps I should stick on a little PS – 'It was so nice to see you the other day'. Though the fact was, it had been one of the most stressful events of this year. I sighed at the memory then quickly wrote, 'With love from Faith, and Graham'. I added a small cross by my name, and two paw prints, then scribbled, 'I hope you're OK'. Pleased with this affectionate, yet casual salutation, I looked at the card again. On the front was a drawing of two outstretched hands – they were almost touching. There was no particular reason for buying that one, it was just the one I liked best, that's all. Anyway, I addressed the envelope to Peter's office, then dropped it straight in the mail. Not that I was in a hurry to post it, or anything, but it was time for Graham's walk. Nor was I hoping he'd get in touch – I mean, it was only a birthday card. As Graham and I walked on Chiswick common, I wondered how Peter would spend the day. Perhaps Andie would throw a drinks party for him. Perhaps they'd have dinner *à deux*. Perhaps she'd take him to the theatre. And what would her present be? Gold cufflinks, quite possibly. Or rather, gold manacles. Or perhaps an extending lead. She'd sunk her piranha teeth into him, and she wasn't about to let go.

As the days went by and I didn't hear anything from him, I tried to push Peter to the back of my mind. In any case Jos was being so attentive – we're seeing a lot more of each other now – and things were pretty busy at work, though Terry and Sophie were still being cool. But if it was uncomfortably chilly in the studio, at least the temperature had lifted outside. The occluded front had moved away, and a belt of high pressure was drifting in.

'So the temperature's lifting nicely,' I said on Thursday morning at five to eight.

'Counting out please, Faith.'

'And as you can see from the isobars,' – I pressed the clicker – 'the pressure is starting to rise.'

'Eight, seven . . .'

'So some really glorious sunshine should be on its way.'

'Thank Christ.'

'After a disappointing September.'

'You're telling me. Six, five . . .'

'And with any luck we may even have . . .'

'Three, two, one . . .'

'A real Indian summer.'

'Zero.'

As the news headlines rolled I went upstairs to check my charts. I looked at my weather house – the little man was inside now, and his wife was coming out – and I was just reading the latest faxed briefing from the met office, when my extension rang.

'Faith, this is reception,' said a female voice. 'Could you come down? Your husband's here.' Shocked, I half walked, half ran down the corridor. What on earth was Peter doing here at this time, I wondered as I hit the button on the lift? Alarm bells were clanging and jangling – something bad must have occurred.

'What is it?' I said breathlessly when I saw him in reception. 'Just tell me – why are you here?'

'Well . . .' he began. He looked tense, and emotional.

'Yes?' I was hyperventilating. 'What?'

'You see . . .' he tried again. This was *agony*.

'Just tell me, Peter. What's going on?' He blushed.

'It's . . . my birthday,' he announced rather sheepishly. *What?*

'Yes,' I said wonderingly. 'I know.'

'And . . . I just wanted to thank you for your card.'

'Oh,' I said faintly. 'I see.'

'It arrived yesterday, and I thought it was . . . lovely. And I wanted to say so in person. But I knew I wouldn't be able to see you tonight,' he went on, 'because I've got to go out with Andie; and I can't come round during the day because I'm at Bishopsgate. So I thought I'd just, you know, drop in to see you on my way to work.'

'Ah,' I breathed. 'I see. But – it's in the opposite direction, Peter,' I pointed out. 'It's a detour of at least eight miles.'

'Well, yes, I . . . suppose it is. But the point is,' he went on, reddening again, 'that I've always seen you on my birthday, and I wanted to see you this year, too.' By now I was smiling, and heard myself sigh with relief.

'Well, many happy returns, Peter,' I said. He was just staring at me, so I stepped forward and kissed him on the cheek. 'Many happy returns,' I repeated, now trying to stifle the urge to laugh. 'So, is that it, then?' I smiled. He nodded. 'Well, thanks for coming by.'

'No. Don't go.' He'd put his hand on my arm. 'I just had to *see* you,' he said quietly. 'But you see it's awkward because –' Suddenly For He's A Jolly Good Fellow, spilled forth from his sports jacket with a tinny whine. He flinched, then took out his mobile phone and flipped up the lid.

'Yes. Hi. Yes,' he said. 'Mmm. Look, I'm in a breakfast meeting. Let's speak later. Yes, of course I'll call you. Bye.' He put the phone away and looked at me guiltily. 'She likes to know where I am.'

'Peter,' I said. 'I'm so glad to see you – I really am. But I've got to go – I'm on air in ten minutes' time.'

'Of course. OK.' I smiled my goodbye.

'Faith!' he said suddenly.

'Yes?' I turned back. Perspiration was beading his brow.

'Faith there *was* something else, actually.'

'There was?'

'Yes. Something I wanted to say.'

'Really?'

'Something I wanted to ask you, in fact.'

'Yes?'

'Look . . . Would you have dinner with me next week?'

On Monday I got ready to meet Peter, a bubble of apprehension building in my breast. A date with my husband, I mused sardonically. But what on earth should I wear? The bedroom floor was already strewn with discarded garments as I selected outfits, then changed my mind. I put on my sleeveless pink Principles dress – not because Peter likes it, though he does

– but because it was gloriously warm. I hadn't told Jos I was seeing Peter; there was no need for him to know. In any case, I reasoned, why look for trouble? Better to keep it quiet. However, there was a slightly tricky moment when Jos phoned to suggest a film.

'I'm sorry, darling,' I said, 'but I'm afraid I can't tonight.'

'Oh, why not?' he said.

'It's just a . . . work thing. You know . . .'

'A work thing? What?' Now, I hadn't expected him to ask me that. As I groped for a plausible alibi, I felt my pulse begin to race.

'It's a . . . seminar,' I explained.

'Really? What's it about?'

'Er, global warming,' I said.

So at six fifteen I checked my appearance in the hall mirror once more, then got the tube to Chalk Farm. Peter had asked me to meet him in Regent's Park Road, at Odette's. A waiter showed me to his table, downstairs, in a discreet little alcove at the back. When Peter saw me he stood up, kissed me on the cheek, then suddenly gave me an enveloping hug.

'Oh, Faith,' he said. 'It's so nice to see you.'

'Well . . . ditto,' I replied.

'I like your dress,' he said with a smile as we sat down.

'What? This old thing? I've had it for years.'

'I know,' he replied. 'I remember it. You always look so nice in pink.' The waiter came to our table and I ordered a glass of white wine. Now we sat there looking at each other over the tops of our menus, feeling slightly shy. Our fellow diners could never have guessed that we'd been married for fifteen years.

'It's lovely to see you again,' he said wonderingly. 'I'm sorry to drag you up here,' he added, 'but you see, it's safe – from her.'

'Oh. That doesn't sound good.'

'It *isn't* good.'

'So where does she think you are now?'

'At a book launch in the City. I told her I'd be back by ten.

324

But I needed to talk to you Faith, because . . .' He sighed. 'Well, I just *did*.' He stared mournfully into his gin and tonic. 'Faith,' he croaked, 'it's absolute hell.'

'I see,' I murmured as I fiddled with my fork. Perhaps he just wanted advice.

'That's what I was trying to tell you at *Madame Butterfly*,' he explained with a bitter sigh. 'I wanted to ring you the next day, but I was worried I wouldn't sound sane.' He had another big gulp of his drink while I slowly sipped my white wine.

'I've had enough,' he groaned as he gripped his napkin. And suddenly, out it all came. That Andie was suffocatingly possessive; that she was manipulative, and low; that he found her baby-talk embarrassing; that the holiday had been dire; that she didn't possess a single book; that she'd lied about her age.

'She told me she was thirty-six,' he added bitterly. 'She's not. She's forty-one.'

'Well, I never thought I'd find myself defending Andie,' I said with a reasonableness which astounded me, 'but loads of women deduct a few years – that's not a crime.'

'Yes, but the point is Andie lied about it for six months. It was only when Katie saw her passport that I found out the truth. So now I keep wondering what else she'd lie about. The relation-ship's just plain wrong, Faith, so I'm cashing in my chips.'

'You are?' He nodded.

'I'm getting out. As soon as I decently can. I could just leave a note on the kitchen table,' he added, 'but that's the coward's way out. However I do it, she isn't going to like it – there'll be an awful scene.' Peter looked at me across the table, then suddenly reached for my hand.

'Faith,' he said. 'Faith, I'm really sorry about all this . . . mess.'

'It's OK,' I whispered. 'It's . . . OK.'

'It's my fault – I know that. I was an idiot to tell you about my fling.'

'No, Peter,' I said firmly. 'That's not the point. You were an idiot to *have* a fling.'

'Well . . . yes. But she flattered me. She was attractive. It was exciting, and I got carried away. I never stopped loving you, Faith, but we hadn't been getting on well.'

'We hadn't been getting on badly,' I pointed out.

'No, but we'd been together so long. So *long*,' he repeated wonderingly, as though he couldn't quite believe it himself. 'Fifteen years, Faith,' he said. '*Fifteen years*. I mean, didn't *you* ever get bored?'

'No, not really,' I said sniffily. 'So I'm sorry to hear that you did.'

'Then Andie came along and the excitement of her interest made me feel more . . . *alive*. Didn't you ever want that, Faith? Didn't you ever want something to . . . *happen*? Something to hit you, just – out of the blue?'

'No,' I said, fiddling with the pepper pot. 'I was perfectly happy as things were.'

'You never wanted even a *little* change?'

'I think we've had enough change, thanks.' I looked at him. 'Peter, you were playing with fire.'

'Yes,' he said, 'I was. And I *loved* it. I loved the way it shook me up. And you were going on and on at me about being unfaithful to you, and I thought dammit, I'll have a fling. And that's all it was. Just a fling. I didn't intend it to damage *us*, but before I knew it our marriage was lying in broken shards. But it's not too late, Faith,' he added desperately. 'Can't we stick it together again?' Ah. I stared down at my plate of dressed crab, conflicting thoughts shouting in my head:

He's just in a panic at the thought of being single!
Stick with Jos, he treats you well!
There's too much blood under the bridge now!
He did it once, he could do it again!

'Say something, Faith,' said Peter urgently. 'Tell me we can work it out.'

'Peter,' I began carefully. 'It's not that easy.'

'Isn't it? Why not?'

'Because the fact is, I'm . . . involved.'

'But you're not happy, are you?'

'That's very presumptuous of you, Peter, and actually – yes. I am.'

'I don't think so.'

'I'm very happy,' I said as I snapped a breadstick in half.

'I don't believe you, Faith. That birthday card you sent me, for instance, hinted at a desire to be reconciled.'

'No it didn't,' I said indignantly. 'I just happened to like the design.'

'And it was significant that you didn't say, "Happy birthday" to me, Faith. You said, "Many Happy *Returns*."'

'You're reading far too much into all this,' I said. 'The fact is, I'm happy with Jos.'

'Faith,' said Peter, 'you can't lie to me. I know you off by heart. Freud said the truth leaks out of us from every pore. And I've seen the truth about you.'

'I *am* happy with him,' I insisted as my salad arrived.

'Really?'

'Mmm. Of course. Admittedly we had our teething problems,' I added as I picked up my fork, 'and he can be a little . . . complex. And sometimes there are things I'm not quite sure about.' I found myself staring into the middle distance now. 'But apart from that we're very compatible,' I concluded, 'and, well, we're . . . together now.'

'But *why* are you together? I mean, what do you like about him?'

'For God's sake, Peter!' I said suddenly. 'It's bad enough getting this from Katie. I'm not climbing onto the psychiatrist's couch for you.'

'But I'm simply curious to know what draws you to Jos. If you were really keen on him, you'd say.' Ah. Right.

'Well,' I began matter-of-factly, 'he thinks a lot of me, and I was feeling very lonely and insecure after you and I split up. Jos came along at that time, and made a beeline for me. I find him very attractive, and he's also very talented, and he's good to the kids and um, oh, I don't know, Peter, I've sort of got used to him now.'

'Used to him? You make him sound like a piece of furniture

you don't really like. So is that it, Faith? Are those the reasons?'

'Yes,' I said. 'They are.'

'It's not enough.'

'*Isn't* it? People stay together for *much* less.'

'But there's one thing you didn't say, Faith,' he added as he picked up his knife. 'There was one vital telling omission.'

'What do you mean?'

'You didn't say that you love him. Did you?'

'Well . . .'

'That's the *one* thing you didn't say.'

'I didn't *need* to say it,' I shot back, 'because . . . obviously I do.'

'It isn't obvious at all.'

'You're beginning to annoy me, Peter!'

'And you're kidding yourself,' he replied.

'Look,' I said crisply. 'I'm sorry your affair has turned out to be so disappointing, but if you think that gives you the right to pick holes in my current relationship, then I'm afraid you're quite, quite wrong.' Peter smiled one of his irritating little smiles – then leaned back in his chair.

'*Current* relationship?' he said quizzically. 'Are you sure you intend it to last?'

'Of course I'm sure,' I snapped. 'Jos and I are going to get spliced.'

'Spliced? What does that mean – split?'

'No. You know, spliced. As in getting married.'

'Really? Oh. So it's serious, then?'

'Yes. It's very serious indeed.'

'So where does he think you are now?'

'Sorry?'

'Where does Jos think you are tonight?'

'Er . . .' I swallowed.

'I mean, does he know you're with me?'

'Well, no,' I said as I sipped my white wine. 'He doesn't, actually.'

'Ah *ha*!'

'He thinks . . .'

'Yes?'

'That I'm at a seminar.'

'So you lied to him, then.'

'No.'

'Yes!'

'Oh, not *really*,' I repeated as I fiddled with the stem of my glass.

'You did,' he said triumphantly. 'You lied to him because you didn't want him to know you were seeing me.'

'Well . . .'

'But if the relationship was as good as you say it is, you'd have told him the truth.' I drummed my fingernails on the table cloth. 'You didn't want him to know.'

'Look,' I said crossly, my face beginning to burn. 'The fact is I'm with Jos. *He's* never *hurt* me,' I added pointedly. 'And yes – I like him a lot.'

'But do you *love* him?'

'That's not the point.'

'It *is*. And why don't you look me in the eye?'

'Let me repeat: I can't simply ditch Jos, Peter, just because you've decided to dump her.'

'Yes you *can*!' he said intensely. 'Of course you can! What's six months compared to fifteen years? Come back, Faith,' he added. 'You don't love Jos. Come back, and let's start again.'

'I can't, Peter,' I said. 'It's dishonourable, and Jos and I are enmeshed. I mean, we see a lot of each other these days, and we've got a holiday planned.'

'Oh Christ,' Peter exclaimed, looking at his watch. 'It's nine thirty. I've got to go.' He paid the bill, then we both stood on the pavement waiting for a cab.

'You'd better take this one,' I said as an amber light came into view. He gave the driver Andie's address, then turned to me once again.

'I don't want to lose you, Faith,' he said quietly. 'So please think about it, before it's too late.' I looked at him.

'I can't.'

'You're tempted, Faith,' he added. 'I know you are. You're tempt*ing* Faith,' he added with a smile.

'Look, Peter,' I sighed. 'I really don't want to hurt your feelings, and I am glad we met tonight, and I'm very sorry you're not happy, and I appreciate that it was hard for you to admit you'd made a big mistake, but if you think I'm going to get myself into another serious emotional mess just because you've now decided, having caused a *huge* crisis in our marriage, that we should conveniently get back together like characters in some romantic novel, then I –' Suddenly Peter had grabbed me, wrapped his arms round me, and planted his lips on mine. A wave of adrenaline shot through me like forked lightning. He hadn't kissed me like that for years.

'I'm sorry,' he muttered as he pulled away. 'But I love you, Faith. I always have – and I think you still love me.' He opened the cab door and climbed in, then pulled down the window. 'Don't you?' he said.

'No,' I replied faintly. 'I don't.'

'Oh yes you do. You're still angry, so you're making it hard. But you do love me, I know you do.'

'Didn't you hear me?' I said crossly. 'I *don't*!'

'That's a *lie*!' he shouted cheerfully as the cab pulled away.

'I AM not LYING!' I shot back.

'You DO still love me, Faith,' I heard as the cab rounded the bend. 'That's why you're still standing there!'

'I don't bloody well STILL LOVE YOU!' I shouted back. 'And I AM not still standing HERE!'

'Oh, it was *really* interesting,' I told Jos the next day when he phoned to ask how the seminar had gone.

'And where was it?' he enquired.

'At the Royal Geographical Society,' I replied with a plausibility which filled me with a strange kind of pride. 'Global warming is a very serious issue,' I said, warming, as it were, to my theme.

'Any new developments?' he asked.

'Er . . . yes,' I said. 'A few.'

330

'Like what?'

'Well, meteorologists are . . . re-evaluating the situation.'

'In what way?'

'Well, we're convinced that the atmosphere *is* getting warmer, but what we don't yet know is – whether or not it's temporary. It's a fascinating phenomenon,' I added. 'In fact, there's a series of twice-weekly lectures coming up on the subject and I'm rather tempted to go. You see, the point about greenhouse gases is that –' Suddenly Graham emitted a volley of rapid barks. 'Sorry, Jos, there's someone at the door, I'll call you back.'

'Mrs Smith?' said the delivery man. He was clutching a huge bouquet.

'Yes?'

'Floribunda. Could you sign here?' I took the proffered bouquet of fat pink roses and, smiling wonderingly, shut the door. Then I ripped open the envelope and read the message. *I'd like to keep Faith*, it said.

'Thank you, Peter,' I said, thirty seconds later, my fingers trembling on the phone. 'Thank you,' I repeated. 'They're lovely.'

'Well, I know you like pink.'

'Oh, I do.' Then there was a silence in which neither of us seemed sure what to say.

'It was lovely to see you last night,' he added.

'Mmm.'

'I don't want to lose you.'

'I know.'

'Have you given it all some more thought?'

'Yes.'

'And?'

'I'm afraid the answer's still no.'

'Then we'd better have dinner again, don't you think, mm?' I fiddled for a moment with the telephone cord.

'Well . . . yes. I suppose we had.'

I decided not to tell Lily about my little meetings with Peter. Normally I tell her everything, but in this case I felt she'd disapprove. She'd say I was mad to do anything to risk my relationship with Jos. But it was quite innocent. After all, I reasoned, I wasn't being unfaithful. So no-one was going to get hurt. In any case, I mused, why *shouldn't* I be friends with my soon-to-be-ex-husband? After all I didn't answer to Lily, or, for that matter, to Jos. I was careful, however, to conceal the card Peter had sent with the flowers. When Jos asked me who had sent them, I said they were from a fan.

'Who is he?' he said as he stared at the thirty long-stemmed roses in their vase.

'I don't know,' I replied. 'Some bloke.'

'Well, he's obviously very keen on you.'

'Mmm,' I said vaguely. 'I suppose he is.'

'Do you know anything about him?'

'Well, you know, just a bit.'

'Perhaps you should build up a psychological profile.'

'Yes. You may be right.'

'Be *very* careful of stalkers,' said Jos, seriously. 'If he develops an obsession, then let me know. Will you do that, Faith? Will you tell me?'

'Don't worry,' I said. 'I will.'

The following Thursday I met Peter again, this time in Docklands, at the Pont de La Tour. It was lovely sitting outside in the gloriously warm air as the Thames glinted like beaten silver in the sun.

'It's magnificent, isn't it?' said Peter as we gazed up at Tower Bridge. I nodded. 'I dream about bridges,' he went on. My glass stalled in mid-air.

'That's funny,' I said. 'So do I. I dream about icebergs, too,' I went on as a river cruiser chugged by. 'And I have recurring dreams about spiders' webs.'

'How's Lily?' he suddenly asked.

'She's fine. Same as ever. Very busy working on *Moi!* and she's been away quite a bit for the new collections. I haven't told her that I'm seeing you, by the way. I didn't think it was wise.'

'Seeing me?' he echoed with a smile. 'You *are* seeing me,

aren't you?' I leaned forward and picked a piece of fluff off his collar.

'Whatever makes you think that?'

'And where does Jos think you are tonight?' he added quietly as he stroked my hand.

'At another seminar on climate change.'

'So is the atmosphere getting a little warmer, then?' he smiled.

'Well, yes. I think it probably is.'

'You see,' I explained later to Jos, 'the climate has always had natural variations, but the main problem with what's going on now is that no-one knows precisely by how much the temperature's going to rise. It could get warmer, or it might just stay the same. But that's what we need to know.'

'How's it caused?' he asked.

'Well, by greenhouse gases,' I explained, 'notably carbon dioxide which comes from car pollution. Burning coal, oil and wood also produces CO_2, and methane from rice fields and cattle farming is a major contributor as well. Then there are the CFCs of course – otherwise known as chlorofluorocarbons – from aerosols and fridges.'

'You do seem to be getting a lot out of these seminars,' he said.

'Do you know, Jos, I think I am.'

Over the next few days Peter rang me more often, and his calls became the highlight of my day. When he told me he was going to the Frankfurt book fair I felt a huge pang of regret. But despite the fact that he was so busy there, he still phoned me a lot.

'How's it going?' I asked him, aware of the babble of publishers in the background.

'Well, you'd find it very interesting Faith, because there's an awful lot of hot air. In fact there are enough inflated egos here to launch the *Hindenburg* – and speaking of big egos, guess who I just saw?'

'Not Charmaine and Oiliver?'

'The very same! He was carrying her bag!'

'What a creep. Did they talk to you?'

'Oh, no!' he snorted. 'It's no speakies. They think I've got too big for my books.'

'Well, you've had the last laugh there, Peter,' I giggled.

'Mmmm . . . Not quite,' he replied.

'What do you mean?' I asked.

'Oh, nothing,' he said.

'Now – when are you back?' I enquired.

'On Saturday. I'd love to see you again. Do you think you'll be going to any more of those seminars, Faith?'

'Well . . . yes. I think I probably will.'

I found it surprisingly easy to deceive Jos about what was going on. If he suspected anything, he didn't show it. In fact he was more attentive than ever.

'You seem very happy these days,' he remarked as we drove back to Chiswick on Saturday night. We'd been to see *All's Well That Ends Well* at the Globe.

'Oh, I am happy, Jos.' He squeezed my hand. 'I think I'm getting happier all the time.'

'That's what love does, doesn't it?' he said as he parked his car.

'I couldn't agree more,' I replied as he pulled up the hand brake. As I opened the front door I noticed the green light of the answerphone wink and flash. I waited until Jos went upstairs, then lowered the volume and pressed 'play'.

'Hello darling, it's Mum. Just to say we're off to the Maldives.' BING-BONG! 'Would all passengers on Icarus Air Flight 666 please make their way to Gate thirteen. Gerald! GERALD! Where are the passports? Back in ten days' time . . .'

'Mum, it's Katie. Just to let you know that Matt and I won't be coming home for the next few weekends. We've got rehearsals for the school play . . .'

'Darling! It's Peter!' I slammed the volume down to level one and pressed my ear to the machine. 'Back from Frankfurt . . . longing to see you . . . love you to bits, Faith. Bye!'

'Faith!' It was Jos. He was standing on the bottom step,

staring at me. I hadn't heard him come down. I straightened up so fast I almost ricked my back. 'What on earth are you doing?' he asked.

'I'm just checking my messages, that's all.'

'Well, why so furtive, then?'

'Furtive?' I said indignantly. 'Honestly, Jos, I'm *not* being furtive,' I said. 'I'm *never* furtive. Have you ever seen me be furtive? Furtive, darling, is *not* a word I know.'

'No, but it's just the way you were listening to the answerphone as though you didn't want me to hear.' But that's what *you* used to do, I thought to myself, though I didn't dare say it out loud.

'The reason I was doing that,' I explained, 'was because . . . I'd had a . . .' I sighed. 'A funny message.'

'Funny?'

'A bit dodgy,' I said.

'My God! Can I hear it?'

'No. I've – wiped it off.'

'Was it your stalker?' He looked horrified.

'Well, yes, it was actually,' I replied. 'I wasn't going to tell you because I didn't want to worry you.'

'How did he get your number?' I shrugged. 'You *must* get this thing which enables you to bar calls from people you don't like.'

'I'll look into that,' I said.

'Yes. I think you should. Have you got a busy week coming up, Faith?' he asked me a little later as we got into bed.

'Just the usual,' I replied. 'I've got another seminar on Monday,' I told him.

'Well, as long as you enjoy them,' he said.

'I feel a complete heel,' I said to Peter on Monday as we sat in Frederick's in Islington. 'I've never done this before.'

'I'm glad to hear it,' Peter said with a smile.

'I mean, secret meetings in unfamiliar restaurants in distant parts of town. Listening to my answerphone with the volume turned right down. Being evasive with Jos, where I was always truthful. Thinking about you, and not him.'

'Do you think about me?'

'Yes,' I murmured, 'I do. I think about you all the time.' We smiled at each other through the flickering candle. 'What about Andie?' I said. 'Has she noticed anything yet?' He shook his head. 'And when are you going to tell her the truth?'

'At the end of this month. She's got a very busy patch at work, so I'm going to wait until that's over and then I'll tell her about us. She'll be furious,' he added. 'But she'll be OK. There are plenty more heads out there.'

'I used to hate her,' I said. 'But now I pity her, in the same way that she must have pitied me.'

'Don't bank on it,' he said. 'Compassion isn't in her emotional repertoire.'

'I feel so . . . deceitful,' I said. 'These . . . assignations I'm having. Perhaps I should go and confess.'

'But you haven't done anything wrong, Faith.'

'No I haven't. That's true.'

'I mean, it's just platonic at the moment, isn't it?'

'Oh, yes. It is. You're right. It's quite innocent,' I added airily as I felt Peter's foot pressing on mine.

'I mean, we haven't – you know – have we?' he said as he caressed my right instep with his toes.

'No,' I murmured, 'we haven't. Peter,' I added. 'Did I tell you Jos is going to New York next weekend?'

'Oh, really? That's interesting.'

'Mmm. I thought you'd say that. He's got to see some people at the Met. He wants me to go too,' I added, 'but obviously I can't, because of Graham.'

'Of course you can't go,' said Peter. 'It's out of the question. Because you're going to come away with me.' He suddenly covered my hand with his. 'Will you do that, Faith?'

'Peter,' I said. My face was aflame. 'You're not suggesting, are you, that I should actually be unfaithful to Jos?'

'That's *exactly* what I'm suggesting,' he said, smiling shyly. 'Come away with me, Faith.'

'Well, maybe. I – I don't know.'

'Why are you hesitating, darling?' He stroked my cheek.

'Because this flirtatious banter is all very well, but I've never two-timed anyone before.'

'Well then, I'll make it easy for you,' he said. 'We'll go to a country house hotel,' he added. I sighed. It sounded bliss. 'I'll choose a really luxurious one,' he went on temptingly. 'In the Cotswolds. One that takes dogs.'

'A country house hotel?' I said wonderingly.

'Yes. With a jacuzzi, and champagne on ice.'

'And luxury toiletries in the bathroom?'

'Of course.'

'And beribboned bowls of fruit?'

'Mmm.'

'And a fully stocked minibar.'

'Naturally. With Toblerone.'

'And fluffy towels as well?'

'Oh yes.'

'Will they be *very* fluffy towels, Peter?'

'Extremely fluffy.'

'In that case, the answer's yes.'

'Darling,' said Jos the next morning, 'I'm a bit worried about you.'

'Why?' I said dreamily. 'I'm *fine*.'

'Well, because twice last night I heard you say Peter's name in your sleep.'

'*Really*?' I said, sitting bolt upright in bed. 'I must have dreamed about him, I suppose. It was probably a nightmare,' I added with a short, sardonic laugh. 'I was probably dreaming that he was having another affair. Yes! That's what it was!' I muttered bitterly. 'Oh, I don't know – that man!'

'Now don't upset yourself,' said Jos, kissing me. 'It's over now. And you're with me. Are you quite sure you can't come to New York next weekend?'

'I'd love to, darling, but I can't leave Graham.'

'Can't your parents look after him?'

'They'll still be in the Maldives,' I lied.

'What about Peter?'

'Er, he's got something on.'

'Well, this is one weekend when I wish he *didn't* have anything on.'

'I know what you mean,' I said.

'But what will you do about Graham when we go to Parrot Cay?'

'That's still six weeks off,' I said. 'I think I'll have worked it all out by then.'

'And next month I want us to visit my mum,' he added. 'You do want to, don't you?'

'Of course.'

I felt hollow and cheap that day as I plied Jos with my smooth lies. I'd never been unfaithful to him, but that's what I was contemplating now. I thought of my new La Perla, still in its tissue paper, at the back of my knicker drawer.

'We're going to have a little holiday with Daddy,' I whispered to Graham in the kitchen later. He licked my nose, then swept the floor with his tail. 'But Jos mustn't know. It's a big secret, OK? Shake on it?' He offered me his left paw.

'I'll miss you in New York,' I heard Jos say. 'But I'll call you every day.' I renamed myself Judith Iscariot as I sat there and smiled. The fact was Jos trusted me, and by Friday I'd have broken that trust. But I had to spend time with Peter alone. I had to. And then I'd know . . .

'So a glorious weekend coming up,' I said enthusiastically just before nine thirty on Friday morning.

'Six, five . . .'

'A real *scorcher*. Very high temperatures. Summer's last hurrah.'

'Four, three . . .'

'So let's all make the most of this golden period.'

'Two, one.'

'I, for one, certainly intend to.'

'And zero.'

'So have a really great time, everyone.'

'Thanks, Faith.'

'See you again next week.'

I practically ran out of AM-UK! and went home to sleep, and then pack. I'd packed Graham's lead, and his bowl, and his beanbag, and some food and some Scooby Snacks.

'We're going to a luxury hotel,' I explained as I brushed his fur, 'so you've got to look your best.'

I'd arranged with Peter that he'd pick us up just round the corner, so that the neighbours wouldn't see. After all, they'd got used to seeing me getting into Jos's MG. 'So where are we going?' I said with a smile as Graham and I clambered in at half past five.

'Mystery destination,' he replied.

'Chipping Camden?'

'No. A bit further south.' Graham was standing up on the back seat, as he always does, with his head resting on Peter's left shoulder.

'He likes your new car,' I remarked as I pulled down my visor against the glare.

'Of course he does. He likes Rovers. Does he still snap at Jos, by the way?'

'Now you come to mention it – no. He seems to have called a truce. Perhaps he's got bored of it,' I added.

'Nah, he just feels sorry for him. Don't you, Graham? I bet he sits there thinking, "Poor sod, if only he knew."'

'So what have you told Andie?'

'That I'm in Scotland, with an author, doing some intensive editing on a new book.'

'Did she buy it?'

'As far as I could tell.'

'Won't she be calling on your mobile phone?'

'I'll make sure I call her every couple of hours just to keep her off the scent.'

We headed north-west, up the M4, past Bracknell and Reading, eating up the miles. Graham was curled up, asleep, lulled into oblivion by the soothing rhythm of the car. Then we left the motorway and headed for Cirencester, along wooded, country roads. To our left plunging hillsides, bisected by dry-stone walls, were aflame with the colours of the fall. Then we drove through Bisley where honey-coloured houses glowed like old gold in the evening sun. Finally, we drove into Painswick and pulled up outside a Georgian manor house.

'Welcome to the Painswick Hotel,' said Peter.

'What bliss,' I breathed as he parked. The house was wide and deep, Palladian in style, with a profuse pink rose rambling up the front. To the left an Italianate balcony, threaded with an ancient wisteria, overlooked a smooth croquet lawn. The panes of the floor-to-ceiling sash windows winked in the setting sun.

'What name is it, please?' asked the receptionist.

'Mr and Mrs Smith,' said Peter. The woman gave us an indulgent smirk. She was used to this kind of thing.

'And this is . . .' She looked at the dog.

'Graham Smith,' I said as he stood up on his back legs and offered her a kiss.

'Your room is number one, on the first floor. I'll get someone to take up your bags.'

Whenever Peter and I were really hard up, which was most of the time, I used to fantasise about a country house hotel, and in my dreams it looked like this. In our room was a four-poster bed, with sumptuous drapes and Colefax and Fowler paper on the walls. There were gleaming antiques and a dressing table with a selection of silver-backed brushes and combs. A great bay window with a soft, padded seat gave out onto rolling, sheep-dotted hills. In the bathroom was a jacuzzi big enough to do breaststroke in and – oh bliss! – a bale of fluffy white towels. Suddenly, I was struck by an awful thought.

'Peter,' I said. 'How do you know about this place? I mean, I . . . Did you come here with *her*?'

'No,' he replied. 'Of course not. I just looked it up on the Web.'

Suddenly there was a knock on the door. It was room service.

'Your champagne, sir.'

Five minutes later, Graham was installed in front of the TV

watching Delia Smith while Peter and I were up to our necks in bubbles in the whirlpool bath.

And now I'm going to show you how to make poppyseed rolls . . . said Delia.

'This book you're supposed to be editing,' I said wryly as I sipped my champagne. 'What's it about?' He slid his foot up my leg.

'Body language.'

'Body language? I see.'

And the delicious thing about them . . .

'Yes. Body language.'

Is that they don't take long to rise.

Peter put down his glass, then pulled me towards him as our limbs entwined.

So pour the liquid yeast into a well in the centre . . .

'This, for example,' he said, kissing me, 'is positive body language.'

'Really?' I murmured. 'What about this?' I whispered as I placed my hand on his thigh.

And mix to a good, stiff dough . . .

'Yes. That's very positive too.'

It should feel springy and elastic by now.

'It does.'

'And this,' he said, sliding his hands over my breasts, 'is a sign of more than casual interest.'

'You don't say?'

Then leave it in a warm place to rise . . .

'And this,' he said as he slid his hand between my thighs, 'is a sign that we're getting on terribly well.' We stood up, still kissing, and collapsed onto the bathroom floor.

Then place them side by side . . .

'Oh, Faith,' said Peter as his face hovered over mine.

Add a really good sprinkling of seeds . . .

'Oh, Peter,' I said.

'I love you, Faith.'

'And I love *you*.'

Then pop the buns in the oven.

* * *

341

When I woke the next morning, I lay on my back, enjoying the whisper of pure linen on my skin. I listened to Peter's low, regular breathing as raptly as if it were music. And as the sun poured through a chink in the curtains I felt as though some miracle had taken place. I also felt wanton – like Madame Bovary. '*J'ai un amant,*' I said. For this was no longer innocent. It was an affair. I had been unfaithful, I realised with a shock. I had broken the seventh commandment. I had committed adultery, in a way. And it was unadulterated *bliss*. As I thought of Jos I experienced a pang of regret, but not exactly guilt. In my mind our relationship was already over: it had ended last night. And on my return I would tell him, as kindly as possible, that we couldn't go on. I wondered how he'd react, then realised that I didn't particularly care. Peter was right. I didn't love him. I'd found him attractive, and intriguing, and so attentive, and of course I'd got used to having him around. But now I banished Jos from my mind and turned to Peter, encircling his sleeping form in my arms. This is the man of my life, I thought as I laid my cheek against his bare shoulder. I will never want anyone else. We were lying so close together that my eyelashes tickled his skin. He stirred, opened his eyes, then smiled.

'I love you, Faith,' he said sleepily.

'I love *you* Peter,' I replied.

'How long is it since we've slept together?' he murmured.

'I don't know. Over a year.'

'We must make up for that, mustn't we?' I nodded. He kissed me, then stroked my face. 'This is our new beginning, Faith,' he said seriously.

'Yes,' I said. 'I know.'

'This is our new chapter,' he added. I smiled. 'I mean, you took a little *Persuasion*,' he went on, teasingly now. 'You were full of *Pride and Prejudice*.'

'No. It was just *Sense and Sensibility*, I pointed out. 'Because of your . . . *Liaison Dangereuse*.'

'You had *That Uncertain Feeling*, didn't you?'

'Yes. So I gave you a . . . *Dusty Answer*.'

'But now, here we are, *Far From the Madding Crowd*.'

342

'In *A Room With A View* . . .'

I knew I would always look back on that weekend as one of the most magical of my life. There was not a cloud in the sky. The air was so clear it seemed to shine. The woods were clothed in antique gold and bronze and red. I will remember this all my life, I thought as we walked with Graham over the Cotswold hills.

'What is an Indian summer, exactly?' said Peter as we strolled through an avenue of copper beech.

'I looked it up the other day,' I said, as the leaves rustled beneath our feet. 'An Indian summer is "a period of mild weather, occurring in the autumn or early winter; or an unexpectedly pleasant, tranquil, or flourishing period."'

'This is *our* Indian summer,' he said, drawing me to him and kissing me. 'It's the end of this awful period of being apart. Isn't it, Faith?'

'Yes,' I said. 'It is. It's the end. Or rather it's the beginning of the end.'

'We'll stop the divorce,' he said.

'I'll phone Rory Cheetham-Stabb and call it off.'

'It's usually engagements that get called off, not divorces,' Peter remarked wryly as we walked on. At that moment Peter's mobile phone rang with Andie's signature tune. He'd thought it would arouse her suspicions if he left it switched off, so now he flipped up the lid and spoke.

'Hi, Andie. Yes, I'm fine. Oh, sorry, but I'm very busy. Well, I told you I would be. Yes. It's going very well. Are you OK? Good. We're right in the middle of things here. Birdsong? Oh, no, we've just got the windows open, that's all. Yes I'll call you later, OK? Of course I'll call you. Bye.'

'I'm sorry,' he said as he put the phone away. 'I don't like lying to her in front of you. I don't like lying to her full stop. I have to for now, but not for much longer because I'm going to end it next week.'

The rest of the weekend passed in a haze of food and champagne and walks and talks and shared jacuzzis and shared papers, and love. We played croquet, and backgammon, and walked through the Slad Valley, and visited Laurie Lee's grave. Then on our last evening we strolled in Painswick churchyard amongst the topiarised yews, watching as their lengthening shadows stretched across the lawn. Then we got into the car and drove back to London, sated with contentment and love. Peter dropped me off round the corner, with Graham. We didn't want to be spotted kissing each other goodbye, so we just squeezed hands.

'I'll see you on Tuesday at Snows, Faith,' he said. 'We'll decide on everything then.'

'Trick or Treat?' said a couple of small boys in black cloaks and vampire masks as I walked to Snows on Tuesday. 'Trick or treat?' they repeated defiantly. I'd forgotten it was Halloween.

'Er, treat,' I replied, opening my purse. In an access of love-induced generosity, I gave them a five-pound note. I pushed open the door – Peter hadn't arrived – and was shown to the very table in the window where we'd sat for our anniversary party ten months before. That had marked the beginning of our split, I mused. This summit meeting marked the end. In January the cold spell had set in, but now our frigidity had melted like the dew. As I glanced out of the window, I saw Peter approaching. He looked so happy and relaxed.

'Hello, darling!' he said. He kissed me. 'Let's have some champagne.'

'Champagne?' I said doubtfully.

'Yes. We've got something to celebrate, after all.'

'Darling, I'm not sure we should. After all,' I added guiltily, lowering my voice, 'we're about to hurt two people.'

'This is true,' he said, chewing on his lower lip. 'We're about to behave rather badly. Out of respect for our soon-to-be former partners, then, we'll have the Italian sparkling instead.' So the waiter brought it, and we sipped it like a couple of lovestruck teenagers at their first disco.

'Have you told Lily?'

'Er, no, I haven't, not yet.'

'You're scared she'll disapprove, aren't you?'

'Oh don't be silly, darling,' I said.

'And did you ring Rory Cheetham-Stabb?' Peter asked as he perused the menu.

'He was busy all day, but I left two messages for him to call.'

'He's going to be pissed off, isn't he? Losing his client?'

'Oh, he's got loads of other wives to sort out.'

'Oh, Faith,' said Peter, 'I'm so happy.'

'So am *I*. But aren't we naughty?' I said with a grin.

'We're terrible,' he replied. By now I was feeling slightly light-headed with love and the sparkling wine. 'But we'll let them down nicely,' Peter added seriously.

'Absolutely,' I agreed.

'We'll be decent about it.'

'Oh, yes.'

'We'll dump them very, *very* sensitively,' he said.

'Very sensitively,' I agreed. 'In fact, we'll dump them *so* nicely that they'll actually enjoy being dumped.'

'Yes,' he agreed. 'They will. For example,' he added expansively, 'I'll buy Andie a lovely present. To make it up to her.'

'Well, I'm going to send Jos on a holiday,' I said, determined to go one better.

'Oh, you're so thoughtful,' Peter said.

'I'll send him on a round-the-world cruise on the *QE2*.'

'Oh Faith, you're so sweet,' he said. 'He'll *really* appreciate that.'

'I'll give him the big E *really* kindly,' I said tipsily. 'And what I shall say to him *is*,' – at this I leaned across the table and gazed into Peter's eyes – 'I'm sorry, Jos, but there's something I have to tell you. I'm afraid it's over. We can't stay together. Why? Because that's what Fate has decreed. So I'm *terribly* sorry to let you down, but I will always think of you with huge affection and respect. I will always think of you with love . . .'

'Steady on!' said Peter.

'Oh, all right. Er . . . I shall always think of you as my friend.

And I'm sorry it couldn't work out between us . . .' I could almost feel a lump coming to my throat. 'And I know I've hurt you,' I added, swallowing now, 'but I will always be so grateful for the time I've spent with you. And I will always be proud to have been your girlfriend, for a while.'

'That's *brilliant*, Faith!' Peter was clapping.

'I must say I thought it was rather good. What about you?'

'I won't get the chance to make a nice speech like that,' he replied. 'She'll be throwing things before I've even got to "Andie, there's something I've got to tell you." But she'll cope,' he added matter-of-factly. 'She won't be single for long.' He stood up. 'Excuse me, darling, I must just pop to the loo.'

I watched Peter walk to the back of the restaurant, and as he did so I suddenly spotted a man who looked vaguely familiar, but I couldn't for the life of me think why. He was seated alone, reading the paper. I knew I knew him but couldn't remember how, and the effect of sparkling wine didn't help. Who *was* he? I mused. He was somehow both memorable and yet non-descript.

'I've got it!' I said to myself suddenly. 'I know exactly who it is.' It was the private detective, Ian Sharp. I looked at him again and tried to catch his eye, and almost waved, but then restrained myself. After all, I reasoned, he might be on a job.

'Darling, do you know that man?' said Peter as he returned to the table.

'What? Do I know what man?'

'That man sitting over there. You were staring at him just now.'

'Oh, oh no, I've no idea who he is,' I lied. For how could I admit to Peter that I did? Peter gave me this slightly odd, disbelieving look, but then the waiter arrived with our main courses and the awkward moment passed. I had chump of lamb again, like last time, and Peter had lemon sole. And as we chatted away I could hear that song, 'I Can See Clearly Now'.

I can see clearly now, the rain has gone, crooned Johnny Nash.

'I love this,' I said to Peter. 'It could have been written for us, today.'

I can see all obstacles in my way . . .

'Now. Plans,' said Peter. 'Why don't we move house? We can afford it, after all.'

Gone are the dark clouds that had me blind . . .

'And it would give us a fresh start.'

It's gonna be a bright, bright, sunshiney day.

'We could get something down by the river.'

I think I can make it now the pain has gone . . .

'With four bedrooms, instead of three.'

All of the bad feelings have disappeared . . .

'After all,' said Peter, smiling, 'we might want to expand the family.'

'Mmm.'

'I'd love another baby, Faith, wouldn't you?'

Here's that rainbow I've been praying for . . .

It's gonna be a bright, bright, sunshiney day . . .

Out of the corner of my eye I saw Ian Sharp shift in his chair. Then he seemed to mutter something to himself. Then suddenly I was aware of two things simultaneously: that the door had been flung open behind me, and that there was an expression of horror in Peter's eyes.

'Oh God,' he murmured.

It's gonna be a bright, bright, sunshiney day . . .

'Peter!' It was Andie. She was standing by our table. 'Mind if I join you, darling?' she said with a tight little smile. 'Having a cosy little dinner *tête à tête*, are we?' she added as she grabbed a neighbouring chair and sat down.

'Look, Andie,' said Peter, shaking his head. 'I really think you should leave.'

'But I don't want to leave,' she replied. 'I want to talk to you.'

'How did you know I was here?' said Peter flatly.

'Oh, a friend of mine tipped me off.' I looked at Ian Sharp's table. He'd gone. Of *course*. I felt strangely betrayed.

'Listen, honey,' said Andie to me, grabbing a bread roll. 'I hate to poop the party, but you are onto a loser here.'

'I don't think so,' I said.

347

'Having a sordid little affair with my boyfriend. Well, that's not on, is it?' I stared at her in silence. 'And did you enjoy your stay in the Cotswolds? I had you followed all the way.'

'Andie,' Peter whispered irritably, 'we'll have this conversation elsewhere.'

'The Painswick Hotel sounds delightful, Peter. You must take *me* there some time.'

'Andie,' he persisted, 'there's something I want to tell you. I was going to tell you tomorrow, but I'll tell you now.'

'Oh, and what's that, darling?'

'That I'm going back to Faith. If she'll have me,' he added.

'Of *course* I'll have you,' I said.

'I'm leaving you, Andie,' said Peter more boldly. 'I'm very sorry to hurt you, but it's true.'

'Oh no you're not,' she whispered back. She looked both menacing and slightly smug.

'I'm sorry, Andie. But it's true.'

'I really don't think you *are* leaving me, darling,' she said calmly. 'Because the fact is,' – she smiled – 'I'm pregnant.'

November

'Well, that's the end of the Indian summer!' I said with uncustomary sharpness on Thursday.

'Eight, seven, Faith's in a strop . . .'

'I did say to enjoy it while you could.'

'Six, five . . .'

'Because now, look, out of the blue . . .'

'Four, three . . .'

'We have this *vicious* Atlantic front . . .'

'Two, one . . .'

'Which is going to cause a *major* depression.'

'Who rattled her cage?'

'Giving us nothing but November murk.'

'Zero.'

'Thank you, Faith,' said Sophie. She gave me a slightly surprised-looking smile, then turned back to camera Two. 'And if you've just joined us, you're watching AM-UK! Coming up after the commercial break – the beast of Bodmin, is it a genetically modified kitten? Ten new ways with dahlias, and remember, remember, the fifth of November.'

'Yes,' interjected Terry smoothly as he smirked into the autocue, 'it's Guy Fawkes night on Sunday, so we've some helpful hints on safety. Will you be having a bang, Sophie?' he asked innocently.

'I'm sorry?' she said; she shifted awkwardly on the sofa and covered her embarrassment with a thin smile.

'And which "Guy" forks out for you?' he enquired facetiously.

'Well, I . . .'

'Oh never mind, Sophie,' he said, his cheesy smile barely covering his air of quiet menace. 'I'm sure your fireworks night is going to be an absolute *cracker*!'

'It's eight thirty,' said Sophie, ignoring him. 'And now the news and traffic . . . wherever you are.'

I didn't know what Terry was talking about. He's always having a go at Sophie, and in any case I was absorbed in my own distress. I struggled to suppress my emotions as I went upstairs to my desk. I pretended to look engrossed in my satellite charts as I blinked back the angry tears. I mean, there I am – a professional forecaster. I make my living by looking ahead. But in my blind bliss at being with Peter again, I hadn't predicted this. It was *hideous*. It was dismal. I felt as though I'd been shot. The harpies had swooped down, out of the blue, and snatched my feast away. I stared mournfully at the swirling black clouds on the screen, then picked up the phone and dialled Lily.

'Something *terrible*'s happened,' I whispered, aware of a lemon-sized lump in my throat.

'What?'

'Something . . . unbearable.'

'Jos hasn't dumped you, has he?' she demanded. She sounded distraught, almost panic-struck.

'No, no, he hasn't,' I said as the desk began to blur. 'It's just that, well . . .' I looked up, aware that several pairs of eyes were swivelling discreetly in my direction. 'I can't tell you over the phone,' I whimpered. 'But I – uh-uh – need to talk to you.'

'Now, don't cry, Faith,' she said. 'Don't cry! Jennifer and I will take you to lunch, OK? We'll meet you at Langan's at one.'

'Do you have a reser*vation*, madam,' said the head waiter slightly sniffily three hours later.

'Yes,' said Lily, giving him an imperious stare, 'I'm not sure about the wallpaper. Come on, Faith,' she said, tossing her pashmina over her shoulder like a matador, 'we'll sit over there.' She parked Jennifer Aniston under the table, then listened while I tearfully told all.

'You were carrying on with *Peter*?' she gasped, her eyes the size of saucers. She seemed absolutely dumbfounded. 'My God, Faith, you were playing with *fire*!'

'I know,' I whispered, shielding my eyes with my right hand as I dissolved into tears again.

'Jos doesn't suspect, does he?' I shook my head. 'Thank *God*!' she breathed, clapping her left hand to her breast in a gesture of tremendous relief. 'You nearly blew it, Faith,' she added crossly, and this struck me as an odd thing to say.

'What do you mean, "I nearly blew it"?' I repeated. She shifted on her chair, then gave me an awkward little smile, her tobacco-brown eyes darting from the table to my tear-stained face.

'Well, all I meant,' she began, sipping her mineral water, 'is that if Jos had found out, he'd have chucked you, and then you'd be right up shit creek.' I looked at her and nodded. I'm ashamed to admit that that thought had already crossed my mind.

'So it could be a lot worse,' she concluded.

'That's hard to imagine,' I croaked. 'It's just so, so *awful*, Lily. God I hate that *bitch*! She's having Peter's *baby*,' I wailed softly as my shoulders started to shake.

'Darling,' said Lily firmly, as a hot tear snaked down my cheek. 'There's no point in being angry with Andie, when *you* were the one having the affair. Let's face it, you were carrying on with her boyfriend, and to be honest, that wasn't very nice. No, that really wasn't very nice of you, Faith,' she went on irritably. 'But I'm your best friend and I don't want to judge.'

'Well, *you've* carried on,' I pointed out hotly. 'You've had affairs with married men. At least I was only having an affair with a married man who was married to *me*!'

'Yes, but you were betraying Jos, darling,' she said querulously. 'I must say, I'm a bit surprised.'

'Oh, don't be so disapproving,' I groaned as I felt my lenses

351

slip and slide. 'I wouldn't have told you if I'd known you'd be like this. You're my friend – I want *sympathy*!'

'Faith,' she said carefully as she handed me a tissue, 'it's only because I *am* your friend that I'm being a bit hard on you now. I'd hate to see you wreck your chances with Jos, and let's face it – you nearly did.'

'So what if I did?' I shot back as my eyes brimmed again. 'It's Peter I want, Lily – Peter – and I don't know why you've got a problem with that!'

Suddenly Lily grabbed my hand and we gazed at each other across the table. 'Faith,' I heard her say gently. 'You're my one real friend in the world. I have only your *best* interests at heart.' And for all Lily's funny, obsessive ways I knew that she spoke the truth. 'I'm very sorry you're unhappy,' she went on earnestly, 'but I think you can put the situation right.'

'*How*?' I wept, pressing the mascara-stained tissue to my eyes.

'By forgetting your little – indiscretion,' she said simply. 'And Jos will never know. In any case, Peter wasn't the answer to your problems,' she said. 'Peter *was* the problem.'

'That's not true.'

'It is true,' she insisted. 'I mean, first of all he has an affair with Andie, and hurts you; and now he's had an affair with you and hurts Andie. I really don't think that's on.'

'You make it sound so much worse than it was, Lily,' I said as the waiter brought our salads. 'Yes, he had an affair. But he regretted it, and so he tried to come back to me. Isn't that understandable? And that's what I wanted too. Because Peter's my *husband*!' I said passionately as my eyes overflowed again. 'He's ineradicable,' – I pinched my forearm – 'he's *here*, he's right under my skin. And you don't understand that, Lily, because you've never been with anyone for more than a *week*!' Lily stared at me, dumbstruck. I'd never spoken to her like that before. But out of the depths of my despair – and my exhaustion – I seemed to have found a new voice.

'I love Peter,' I groaned. 'I always have – I know that now – and I want him back.'

'But you can't have him,' said Lily simply.

'No,' I croaked. 'Not now.'

Peter had wanted us to stay together. He'd come round the next day – we were both distraught – and he'd said we could work it out.

'We can, Faith,' he said quietly. 'We can work it out.' I stared at him, red-eyed. 'I've been thinking about it,' he added. 'And it's not going to break us up.'

'Isn't it?' I said bleakly.

'Well, why should it?' he said.

'Because a baby is such a huge thing – that's why. I can get over a fling, Peter – I know that now – but I don't think I can get over a *child*.'

'But I want to be with *you*, Faith. I want my old life back.'

'But this is too big, Peter,' I wept. 'A *baby*. A baby which will *always* be there. And the thought of your child growing inside Andie makes me feel physically *sick*. Now I know why I've been dreaming about icebergs,' I wept, 'because we were about to crash into one!'

'Stay with me, Faith,' he said quietly.

'I just don't think I can. Because now Andie and her child will always remind us of this miserable part of our lives. We could pretend to be happy,' I went on. 'Oh yes, we could put on a good show. But inside we'd both feel so *bad*. I don't think I can deal with this, Peter. It's the kind of thing that splits couples up. I mean, Jerry Hall had put up with loads of Mick Jagger's affairs, but it was that baby that broke them up.'

'I have to do the right thing by Andie,' he said.

'Yes, of course,' I said. 'I *know*. I, of all people, know that you will always do the right thing. But it would make life so hard for me, Peter, and it would give Andie a hold over you. She'd be there for ever. We could never forget. I just don't think it would work.'

'Is that really how you feel?' he said. I nodded.

'And I've thought about it so hard. I've looked at the situation from every possible angle, but I think my answer has to be no. I imagine myself being stepmother to Andie's child, and I simply don't think that I can. Perhaps some women could cope with it, but I know I can't. I feel that everything's ruined now, Peter, so I guess we have to move on.'

Oh yes, everything was *ruined*, I'd realised bitterly. Andie had had a Lucky Strike and it had all turned to ashes in our hands.

'You were chasing an illusion, Faith,' I heard Lily whisper. 'You were living in a fool's paradise. Because, quite apart from Andie's pregnancy,' she explained, 'the fact remains that Peter let you down.'

'Yes,' I said faintly as I picked at a lettuce leaf. 'He did let me down. That's true. But I was able to forgive and forget. I thought I'd never get over his infidelity, but in the end I knew that I could.'

'Then you're an idiot!' said Lily contemptuously. I stared at her across the table. Her eyes were shining with scorn and her mouth was set in a hard, cruel line. Now, emboldened by despair, I asked her something I'd wanted to ask for a very long time.

'Lily,' I said quietly. 'Why are you always so hard on Peter?' She didn't reply but just stared back at me, as though irritated, then blinked and looked away. 'Why are you so set against him?' I repeated. 'I just don't understand. I mean, I know you've never really liked him,' I went on.

'No,' she agreed. 'I haven't.'

'But before you've always tolerated him.'

'Yes,' she agreed as she sipped her mineral water again. 'I've tolerated him. For your sake.'

'But recently,' I persevered, 'over the last year or so, you really seem to have had it in for him. As though you really *hate* him. You just won't give him a break.'

'Why *should* I give him a break?' she said with sudden vehemence. 'He's never given *me* one.'

'Lily,' I said wonderingly, 'I don't think that's true. You behave as though he has some animus against you. But I can only tell you that he doesn't.'

354

'Oh, really?' she said with a quizzical little smile.

'Yes. Really,' I replied. 'But you seem so hostile to him these days. As though you bear him some sort of grudge.'

'OK,' she said, pushing her rocket around her plate. 'I admit it. I have had a bit of a downer on Peter recently. But the *only* reason for that,' she explained vehemently, 'is because of what he did to you. And although you may have been ready to forgive him, I'm afraid, the truth is, I wasn't.'

'But it isn't for *you* to forgive him, Lily,' I pointed out. 'It's for *me*. And if I'd decided to have Peter back, then why the hell should you mind?'

'I'm sorry, Faith,' she said with a disdainful shrug, 'but I just can't help how I feel. The simple fact is that if Peter hurts you, then he hurts me as well. Oh *yes*,' she added as she stabbed at her plate, 'Peter hurt me too.'

I looked down at the table and shook my head. For, however she tried to explain it, Lily's reaction seemed so extreme. But now I remembered what Katie had sometimes said – that at some deep level, Lily had always been jealous of Peter, because she thought of me, somehow, as 'hers'. As I gazed at her across the table I was transported back twenty years. I remembered her talking so animatedly, when we were sixteen, of all the fun we'd have when we left school. She spoke of the trips we'd make together, and of the parties we'd throw in the flats we'd share. But in the event I'd married at twenty. I'll never forget the shock and disapproval on Lily's face when I told her that I was engaged.

'You never wanted me to marry Peter, did you?' I asked as she lit a cheroot. There was silence. Then she blew the smoke away.

'Not really,' she admitted with a shrug.

'Why not? Why did you mind?'

'It seemed to me – a waste.'

'Of what, exactly?'

'Well, of your degree for a start.'

'But you didn't finish *your* degree,' I pointed out. 'You left Cambridge in your second year.'

'Yes, but I only did that,' she explained, 'because I'd had

this wonderful opportunity to get cracking on what I'd always wanted – to work in magazines.'

'And I'd got *my* opportunity to get cracking on what I'd always wanted – to be a wife and a mother.' She rolled her eyes. 'You can despise it as much as you like, Lily,' I said, 'but that was my aim. I was never going to have a fantastic career like yours,' I went on. 'I wasn't brilliant and ambitious, like you. I met Peter at nineteen and that was that – Cupid's arrow struck home the very first time. You could do a feature on it for *Moi!* – 'When Your First Love is Your Last Love' – and that's what Peter was to me. You've always, somehow, resented him, Lily; but it's not your life – it's *mine*. I'm desperate to be with Peter again,' I finished quietly. 'And it kills me to know that I can't.' She looked down at the table as she shuffled the pepper pot around, and for the first time I thought I saw a flicker of something like guilt pass across her lovely face.

'Well . . . Is it definitely his baby?' she enquired awkwardly.

'Yes, there's no doubt about that.'

'And how does he know she's pregnant?'

'Because she did the test.'

'And how far gone is she?'

'Two and a half months.'

'So it must have happened when they were in the States.'

'I don't know when it happened,' I murmured bleakly. 'I only know that we're both distraught.'

'Have you told the children?'

'Not yet. There's no need. Peter's going to tell them at the end of term.'

'Well, I'm – sorry,' said Lily as we stood up to leave. 'I'm sorry you're unhappy. I truly am. But I also think you're genuinely lucky that you've still got Jos.' I gazed out of the window, my eye momentarily drawn to a red No Entry sign.

'Yes,' I said, flatly. 'I suppose I am lucky that he's still around.'

'And you're sure he doesn't know?' she added as she scooped Jennifer up.

'Do you know, it's very odd,' I said. 'But he hasn't suspected a thing.'

As I got the tube back to Chiswick I thought about this some more. I thought it very strange that Jos hadn't seemed to notice when, for the past month, I'd hardly been myself. My excitement at seeing Peter again must have shown – quite apart from the fibs I'd told. That's why I'd been dreaming about spiders' webs, I mused – because I'd become so expert at spinning lies. But not only had Jos seemed oblivious to my furtive behaviour, he'd been even more affectionate than before.

I *was* lucky, I realised with a bitter sigh, and Lily, though brutal, was right. My *rapprochement* with Peter had been an illusion. A *del*usion. No more than a shimmering mirage. What would I do now, I wondered bleakly as I rattled westwards on the train? The thought of being single filled me with dread – I couldn't face being on my own. And the idea of having to start all over again with someone new made me feel sick and faint. So I decided to count my blessings and to stick with Jos. I wasn't proud of this decision. In fact it filled me with self-disgust. But what would you have done in my place? For Jos was still there, and he still wanted me, and I didn't want to be on my own. And though I despised myself for it, I guess people make these emotional calculations all the time.

When I got back to the house, there was a friendly message from Jos on the machine: 'I'll pop round on Sunday evening, darling,' he said. 'We could go and watch the fireworks display.' And when I heard that I felt a surge of relief, that we could carry on as before. There was a second message, from Rory Cheetham-Stabb. I hadn't heard from him for weeks.

'So sorry to have been a bit out of touch, Mrs Smith,' he said suavely when I called him back.

'That's all right,' I replied.

'I've had a lot of clients to see to.'

'I'm sure you have,' I said.

'I imagine you're champing at the bit now, aren't you?'

'Well, not really. I mean – yes.'

'Thanks for returning all those papers.'

'That's OK.'

'But now I think it's time to press on. So let's get this divorce on the *road*. I mean, there's no reason why not, is there, Mrs Smith?'

'Not any more,' I replied.

'Your decree nisi will come through at the end of this month, and it will become absolute, or final, in another six weeks and one day. This means you'll be divorced by January.' January? Our wedding month. 'Now, do you want to authorise me to apply for the decree absolute for you? It makes it so much simpler, and means you don't have to sign any more of those nasty forms. Shall I do that for you, Mrs Smith?'

'Yes,' I said bleakly. 'Please do.'

'Right. Now, are you quite sure you're happy with that?'

'Oh, I'm ecstatic,' I said.

'Penny for the Guy?' said two small boys as I walked to the newsagent on Sunday morning.

'What?' I said, looking up.

'Penny for the Guy, miss?' they repeated. I surveyed their battered little scarecrow effigy and reluctantly opened my purse.

'Here you are,' I said with an irritated sigh, handing one of them a twenty pence coin.

'Is that *all*?' he said indignantly.

'Yes,' I said crossly. 'It is.'

'Most people give us at least a pound,' piped up his friend resentfully.

'Well, I'm not going to,' I said.

'Oh, go on, miss, give us a bit more.'

'No, you ungrateful little beasts!' Graham's eyebrows shot up in surprise. As I say, he's very sensitive to my moods. In any case, I thought splenetically, it was begging – that's what it was. It shouldn't be allowed, I reflected angrily. I had never let Matt do anything like that. And now, horror of horrors, a pregnant woman walked past, and the sight of her huge stomach – like

358

a wind-filled spinnaker – made me feel physically sick. Then a young mother pushed by me with her baby buggy, and I was nearly felled by a wave of distress. I had prenatal depression, I realised bitterly. I had mourning sickness, that's what. For the thought of Peter's baby growing inside Andie filled me with venom and bile. Misanthropic. That's how I felt. I was Miss Anne Thropic, I mused with a grim little smile. Then I went into the newsagent and what do I see? *Parenting Magazine* – that's what. Oh God! And *Mother and Child*. But then my anger evaporated like steam as I stared, in stupefaction, at the tabloids.

SEX SCANDAL AT AM-UK! screamed the *Sunday Express*.

SHAME OF BREAKFAST TV STAR! shouted the *Mail*.

MY STEAMY ROMPS ON THE SOFA WITH SOPHIE! yelled the *Sunday Mirror*.

TV SOPHIE'S SHAMEFUL SECRET! howled the *News of the World. Exclusive Report! See pages, 2, 3, 4, 5, 6, 7, 9 and 23!*

I felt my jaw go slack, my eyes widen and my heart begin to pound. I rushed back home with an armful of papers and spread them out on the kitchen table. I was so stunned by the story my contact lenses nearly fell out.

AM-UK!'s Sophie Walsh may appear to be cool, calm and collected in front of the cameras every morning, said the *Mail. But the twenty-four-year-old Oxford bluestocking has been hiding a sordid secret which now threatens to ruin her career. A former lover is seeking the return of valuables and jewellery given to her during a two-year relationship,* it went on. *Lavinia Davenport, forty-five, chairwoman of Digiform, the broadcast equipment company, has applied to have items worth ten thousand pounds returned. Her relationship with Walsh ended acrimoniously eight months ago, after Walsh started an affair with glamorous fashion PR Alexandra Jones, twenty-three. Following these revelations, Walsh's future at AM-UK! is now in jeopardy.*

Ah, I thought to myself. Alexandra. So 'Alex' was a girl. Then I thought, *why* is Sophie's future in jeopardy? So what if she's gay? What a bunch of idiotic prigs these tabloid editors are. Then I read on, and felt my heart sink into the soles of my shoes.

Lavinia Davenport has given an interview to a Sunday newspaper in which she relates how the two women met while Walsh was working as a lesbian stripper in a Soho nightclub – the Candy Bar. Davenport admits putting a twenty-pound note in Sophie's bra …

I turned to the *News of the World*, and there, on pages two and three, were two huge photos of Sophie, looking slightly younger and wearing nothing but a strategically placed feather boa and a pair of white evening gloves. Oh God, I thought. Poor girl. This was dreadful. Darryl wouldn't like it at all. And in that instant I remembered something that Sophie had once said: *The tabloids would have a field day with me.*

Now I turned to pages four and five. There was a photo of Lavinia Davenport looking lachrymose, spilling her guts about her 'disappointment' in Sophie.

I was distraught at Sophie's infidelity … I'd bankrolled her for two years … I kitted that girl out … Chanel, Ferragamo … now I feel used and betrayed … I believe the mothers who watch her every morning should know the shabby truth about her past.

How *vile*, I thought dismally. How vile. This woman was chair of a successful company – she didn't need to do this. There was only one reason why she'd done it – revenge. She was out to destroy Sophie's career. And now I recalled Terry's vicious remarks to Sophie on Friday about her having a 'cracker' of a fireworks night. This was certainly explosive, I realised, as I threw the papers away. Terry and Tatiana. Of course. Who else? Then I recalled Terry's vicious comments at that planning meeting. Oh yes, those two had been digging away.

All that day, random fireworks had been going off like sniper fire, making Graham and me start. At seven, Jos came round and I cooked him supper, and everything seemed fine. We decided not to go to the big display in Ravenscourt Park. Instead, we stood in the garden and watched as the sky lit up in a *blitzkrieg* of orange and red.

BOOOOOOM! BANG! we heard, like World War One cannons; then 'KER-ACK-A-TACK-A-RACK-A-TACKKKK! Like machine-gun fire. The roman candles flew up like distress flares, blazing a fiery trail through the dark. Then – WHEEEEE-EEEEEEEEEEEEEEEE!!!!!!!! WHEEEEEEEEEEEEEEEEEEEEE!!!!!! – we heard, like the sinister whistle of falling bombs. And now dozens of huge silvery tadpoles were wriggling across the sky; they reminded me, depressingly, of sperm.

'OOOOOOOH!' we breathed, and then, 'AAAAHHHHH!' as the last rockets shot away like ground-to-air missiles; they flared for an instant as they strafed the dark, then dimmed, dissolved and died.

We could hear desultory detonations from neighbouring houses long after we'd gone to bed. I lay there, staring at the ceiling, hearing them 'pop' and 'crack'.

'Are you all right, Faith?' I heard Jos whisper. 'It's half past one.'

'Sorry?'

'You don't seem to be able to sleep.'

'Don't I?'

'Is there anything worrying you?'

'Oh, no, no, no,' I lied. 'It's just the fireworks, that's all.'

But I must have finally drifted off, because at three-thirty came the sharp shock of the alarm, puncturing my semi-consciousness like jabbing needles. I wrenched myself out of bed.

When I got into work at four fifteen, I had two double espressos then looked at the papers. Sophie was still on every front page.

SUSPENSION FOR SOPHIE! screamed the *Mirror*.

LESBIAN LAID OFF! shrieked the *Sun*.

SOPHIE'S COMMERCIAL BREAK! yelled the *Mail*. There were photos of her leaving her Hampstead flat looking pale and distraught. In the *Daily Express* there was a nauseating interview with Terry in which he said how 'sad' he felt. *Such a pity . . . her career was going so well . . . she should have been more open from the start . . . no, no, none of us guessed . . . well this* is *a family show . . . no, no, of course I'm not pleased about it . . . in fact I'm* terribly *upset.*

'I bet you are,' I said to myself furiously as I watched him strutting around like a prize cock.

'Poor kid,' said Iqbal when I went down to Make-Up. 'And she was doing so well.'

'She's a brilliant broadcaster,' Marian pointed out. 'She doesn't deserve all this crap. Anyway, Tatty's got what she wanted,' she added. 'Look!' On the monitor, in the corner, we watched as Tatiana took her coveted place on the sofa next to Terry.

'Do you think Sophie will come back?' I asked as Iqbal dabbed foundation over my cheeks.

'I very much doubt it,' he replied.

'But this has nothing to do with her career.'

'Yes, but you know what Darryl's like. Apparently he's been saying she's brought the programme into disrepute.'

'Disrepute!' I exclaimed. 'How can a programme which dishes up a daily diet of psychic grannies and roller-blading cockatiels be brought into disrepute?'

I struggled through the morning, my distress about Peter compounded by the fact that I missed Sophie's friendly presence. I wouldn't say we were close friends, but we'd become allies over the past few months. I'd never forgotten how nice she'd been to me, and I wished I could help her now. But what on earth could I do? I had her home number and resolved to ring her when I got back from work.

'I'll call her this afternoon,' I said to myself when I got home at ten fifteen.

I took Graham onto Chiswick common, where spent fireworks speckled the grass. Then I went back and sank into bed. But though I was shattered, my mind was in such ferment that sleep eluded me. In desperation I flung out my hand and turned on my tranny, which was tuned to Radio 4.

'And you can hear *Woman's Hour* again tomorrow at the same time,' said an announcer. 'The programme was presented by Jenni Murray and produced by Mimi Clark.' Mimi, I reflected exhaustedly. I hadn't heard from her for months. But then she'd been busy with the baby, and I'd been avoiding mutual friends during the divorce. I remembered her saying that she wanted to invite Lily onto *Woman's Hour*. That was a good programme, I mused. *Woman's Hour* . . . Of *course*! I threw off the duvet, ran downstairs and telephoned Broadcasting House.

'Faith!' Mimi exclaimed warmly five minutes later. 'What a lovely surprise! I've been thinking about you,' she added. 'What with all the ructions at AM-UK!'

'That's why I'm ringing, actually,' I explained slightly breathlessly, 'because Sophie Walsh is a friend of mine. She's been badly stitched up, Mimi, and she needs some instant PR. Would you have her on the show?'

'Well, we could,' she replied judiciously. 'But I'm not quite sure in what context. Look, let me talk to my editor, but I promise I'll do what I can. Any idea who her agent is?' she added.

'Swann Barton – they're in the book.'

'And are you OK, Faith?' Mimi added gently. 'I'm sorry not to have been in touch.'

'Oh, I'm OK,' I sighed. 'I'm . . . fine.'

'I heard a lovely rumour that you might be getting back with Peter.' It was as though a knife had pierced my heart.

'That's not true,' I said bleakly. 'We're getting divorced.'

'I'm sorry, Faith,' she murmured. 'You always seemed so happy.'

'We were happy,' I replied. 'For fifteen years, Mimi. We were as happy as clams at high tide.'

As I put down the phone I realised that Peter and I hadn't spoken now for over five days. It was probably just as well – after all, what on earth would we say? Wounded animals run for cover, and that's what we had done. And because the kids weren't coming home at weekends, there was no need for him to call; and though I missed him desperately, I was very relieved about that. For talking to him would hurt so much more, when there was no chance of our being together. As for seeing him – it would be torture, I'd have to view him in a different way. I must look *ahead*, I told myself firmly. I must get on with my life. I must try and get some – what do they call it? – 'closure' on this, because my marriage would soon come to an end. So, now, after the disorienting effects of my affair, the needle of my emotional compass began to swing slowly back towards Jos. As we had supper that night I told him about Andie's baby. He seemed genuinely shocked.

'Did he know she wanted to get pregnant?' he asked.

'Not really. She just went ahead.'

'I don't think women should do that,' he said. At that, a tiny shudder convulsed his frame, but I knew the reason why.

'It's OK,' I said gently. 'You don't have to worry. I'd never do that to you.' He reached across the table and squeezed my hand.

'I know you wouldn't,' he said.

'But Andie did,' I went on. 'And she calculated, quite correctly, that Peter would stick around. You see, Peter's very decent,' I added. 'He always does the right thing.' Jos put our plates on the worktop, then enfolded me in his arms.

'So is her pregnancy the reason why you've been a little distant lately, Faith?' I nodded, relieved to be handed an excuse. 'I guess it was a bit of a shock,' he added.

'You *bet* it was,' I said.

'What?'

'I mean, yes . . . it was a shock, because – well, we're not even divorced.'

'But it's not as though it makes any real difference to you,' Jos went on smoothly. And I thought – *if only you knew*. 'I mean, Peter's obviously moving on,' he added reasonably, 'and so are you. Now, let's talk about something nice. I want to book the holiday in the Turks and Caicos. Can we discuss dates?'

I felt cheered by the prospect of a holiday. I hadn't been away for more than a year. The total change of scene, and the warm sunshine would probably improve my mood. The chance to spend some time with Jos, just on our own, would help us bond again. So the next day I asked for leave, then Jos booked our flights to the Caribbean; we would be leaving on December the fifth. As I brushed my teeth that night I looked into the mirror and stared at the reflection of the mural behind. I looked at the trompe l'oeil palm trees and azure sea and thought, that view will be real, quite soon.

In the meantime, lips were zipped at AM-UK! about Sophie's departure from the show. She'd been airbrushed out of the station like a Soviet dissident being excised from a history book. By Monday afternoon her name had gone from her dressing room door. Sophie was finished. She didn't exist. I phoned her three times but kept getting her answerphone, so guessed she didn't want to talk. So it came as something of a surprise to turn on Radio 4 on Wednesday evening and to hear *The Moral Maze*.

'Our witness this week, on the subject of press freedom, is Sophie Walsh,' announced Michael Buerk.

'It's Sophie!' I exclaimed to Graham. He wagged his tail.

'Sophie Walsh,' began Michael Buerk, 'your private life has been splashed across every tabloid and most of the broadsheets this week. Presumably you're in favour of a privacy law?' I bet she is, I thought. I heard Sophie inhale to steady her nerves, and then she spoke.

'It was the French historian Alexis de Toqueville who suggested that in order to enjoy the inestimable benefits that the liberty of the press ensures, it is necessary to accept the inevitable evils it creates,' she began quietly. 'I am emphatically against prior restraint when it comes to press freedom, and wholly in favour of what we already have – self-regulation.' This drew a gasp from the other panellists.

'Are you saying you don't mind what you've had to put up with this week?' said David Starkey almost indignantly.

'No, I'm not saying that at all,' she replied calmly. 'Of course I mind. You'd mind having eight photographers outside your house, snapping you every time you stepped outside. You'd mind having someone going through your rubbish, or trying to steal your mail. You'd mind having some tabloid hack phoning up anyone you ever knew. But I can only say that my passion for the rights of a free press are greater than any annoyance I may personally feel at having my privacy infringed.'

'But your privacy hasn't just been infringed, it's been grossly invaded,' said Janet Daley hotly.

'Yes,' agreed Sophie. 'It has.'

'And the government, through the European Declaration of Human Rights, may now make it impossible for newspapers to justify running stories such as yours, which have no public interest whatsoever.'

'That's true,' Sophie replied. 'But I believe it to be wrong. For the end result will be that we will ultimately have parliament policing the press, and I can imagine nothing worse. After all,' she went on, 'for much of the world the reality for journalists is either that they are mouthpieces of the powerful, acting merely as propagandists, or they are independent watchdogs – and are therefore at great physical risk. Do we want to see that here? Of course not. A free press – free occasionally to be *bad* – remains a vital safeguard of democracy. How else would crooks such as Maxwell, or Jonathan Aitken, have been exposed if the papers could easily be gagged? If a cabinet minister is cheating on his wife while promising a less sleazy government to the electorate, then surely it is right that the electorate should know?'

'Yes, but your story had no public interest factor, did it?' pointed out Michael Buerk.

'No,' she replied. 'It didn't. It was mere titillation, that's all. But the fact is, it was true,' she added, 'so how can I complain? No-one has defamed me. Though I emphatically reject Ms Davenport's claims for the return of certain items she willingly gifted to me, and though I dispute the value she assigns them, I can fight that corner myself. But basically,' she concluded, 'to answer your question, I'd say that I was pretty fair game.'

'How can you sit there and say that?' said Janet Daley incredulously. 'Are you a masochist?'

'No, I'm a realist,' Sophie replied. 'I knew that this episode was in my past and that it might one day come to light. But I had willingly taken a job which put me in front of five million people every day. And if you do that, then to some extent you forfeit your right to total privacy. I minded losing my job,' Sophie concluded. 'Not only because it wasn't necessary, but also because I know I was doing it well. But that's an entirely separate issue from the one we're discussing here and my lawyers will be taking that up.'

'Sophie Walsh, thank you,' said Michael Buerk. I picked up the phone and dialled Mimi.

'Mimi, I've just heard Sophie. She was *fantastic*!' I said. 'You must have done that – thanks.'

'Well, I heard *The Moral Maze* were planning something on press freedom,' she explained, 'so I gave the editor a call. They were all raving to me afterwards about how incredibly impressive she was.'

I dropped Sophie a line, via her agent, telling her how brilliant I thought she'd been, and expressing the hope that she'd get in touch some time. In the meantime, Tatiana was made a permanent fixture as Terry's co-presenter, and life went on as before. Jos was due to start work for Opera North in January and I began to look forward to Parrot Cay.

'Of course we'll look after Graham,' said Mum when I called. 'Turks and Caicos – how super. It's only a short hop to Cuba from there, darling, old Havana's *fascinating* you know, and then of course Haiti's not far, and you could have a quick whizz to the Dominican Republic.'

'Mum,' I interjected. 'I don't *want* to do all that. I just want to stay in one place. I've been through a lot this year,' I added wearily. 'I just need a . . . holiday.'

'Of course you do, darling. So it must be going well with Jos, then,' she added, 'if you're going away. Have you met his parents yet?'

'I'm meeting his mother next week. She lives somewhere near Coventry.'

'And what about his dad?'

'He doesn't see his father,' I explained. 'And he never talks about him, so I don't ask.'

'Well, we look forward to meeting Jos some time soon, Faith. How's Peter?' she added.

'All right, I guess. Well, to be honest, I don't really know.' I couldn't bring myself to tell Mum about Andie's pregnancy. I could hardly bear to think about it, let alone discuss it with someone else. I was trying to vanquish thoughts of Andie's swelling stomach as I mended bridges with Jos.

'I know my mother will love you,' he said as we drove up the M1 towards Coventry the following week. 'She already feels she knows you,' he added happily, 'because she's seen you so often on TV.'

'Well, I'm sure I'll like her,' I said. Then I took a deep breath and added, 'Jos, I hope you don't mind my asking you this. But what about your father? Don't you ever see him?'

'No,' he said sharply. 'I don't.'

'I'm sorry,' I said, looking at his darkening face. 'I didn't mean to probe.'

'It's all right,' he said apologetically. 'You're entitled to ask, but there's not very much to say. Basically, my father wasn't much good to us,' he explained. 'He let my mother down. I was three when he left, so I can hardly remember him.'

'Why did he leave?' I asked.

'He claimed that Mum had lost all interest in him and had become obsessed with me. Before long he'd taken up with another woman and they went to live in France. That was in 1967, Faith, and I haven't seen him since.'

'Do you want to?' I said gently.

'No. No, I don't. He does,' he added. 'He writes to me from time to time, but I'm afraid it's just too late.'

I looked out of the window as we sped along, absorbing what Jos had just said. How sad, I thought. How incredibly sad, to feel rejected by your own father. That would explain certain things about Jos, I realised, not least his transparent need for approval and love. Poor Jos, I reflected. He'd probably been compensating for that loss all his life. By now a blanket of pale grey stratus had descended and a clammy rain was starting to fall. I peered through the metronomic swing of the windscreen wipers onto the black ribbon of road ahead. The silver birch trees along the verges looked derelict, having already been stripped of their leaves. We passed Northampton, then signs for Coventry, then turned onto the M6. Soon we were pulling up outside a semi-detached house somewhere to the north of the city. As Jos parked the MG, he honked twice, the door flew open, and there was his mum. They looked so alike, Jos's strong features a masculine rendition of her own. But the planes of her face, though softer, were similar to his, and she had the same large grey eyes and curly hair.

'Hello, Mrs Cartwright,' I said, extending my hand. My slight nervousness evaporated like the dew as I found myself clasped in a warm embrace.

'Faith!' she exclaimed, beaming delightedly. 'How lovely to meet you. Jos talks about you *all* the time. And please don't call me Mrs Cartwright,' she added, 'my name's Yvonne.' Disarmed by the warmth of her welcome, I smiled and followed her inside. I was relieved to find her so friendly as I'd had no idea what she'd be like. I took off my coat and handed it to her, then looked up and blinked. For every available bit of wall was covered with Jos's work. Sketches from his opera and theatre designs were crammed alongside his Olivier awards. And there were framed posters of his productions going all the way up the stairs. There was *Carmen* at the Coliseum; *The Pearl Fishers* in Rome; *Othello* at the National Theatre, and *Hedda Gabler* at the RSC. Every square of the house seemed to bear some tribute to Jos's success. But what struck me most was all the photos; there must have been at least eight of him hung on the side of the staircase, and a further six ranged on a table in the hall. In the small sitting room his face gazed out from at least ten or twelve silver frames. There he was on his first day at school; and there, aged about twelve, on his bike; and there he was at art school, going up to receive a prize. Now here he was in his paint-spattered overalls, working on some set; there he was again, on holiday somewhere, his dark-blond hair bleached white by the sun. There were photos of him with Bernard Haitink, with Sam Mendes and Trevor Nunn. Here he was again, snapped with Darcey Bussell, and there were several of him with Yvonne.

'Wow!' I said politely. 'You're obviously very proud of Jos.'

'Oh yes,' she said. 'I *am*.'

'Sorry about all the photos,' Jos said with a grin. 'It's very embarrassing for me, but Mum likes to put them on show.'

'I certainly do!' she exclaimed with a peal of laughter. 'I'm his number one fan.'

As Jos helped his mother in the kitchen, I thought about the photos I have at home. There are just one of each of the children on my desk in the sitting room, and the wedding photo, long since consigned to a drawer. We sat and had tea and she enquired about my work and the kids. I enjoyed talking to her, though she missed no opportunity to lavish praise on her son.

'He's such a good boy, really . . . done ever so well . . . never forgets me, do you darling? . . . I go to most of his shows . . . couldn't get down to *Madame Butterfly* . . . wasn't feeling too well . . . yes, much better now, thanks . . . oh yes, London's such a long way.'

Jos is her whole life, I realised as she chatted away. She has no husband and no other kids. Jos is the fulcrum of her existence, and all her thoughts seemed to revolve around him. He went into the kitchen to make more tea, and so we were left alone. To avoid any awkward gaps in the conversation I decided to tell her about Parrot Cay. But before I could open my mouth she'd started to speak, and what she said took me by surprise.

'I want to thank you, Faith,' she announced in a conspiratorial whisper.

'Thank me?' I said wonderingly. 'For what?'

'For making Jos so happy.' I blushed. 'I've never seen him so contented before.'

'Really?' I said, and smiled. I thought it best to change the subject, but she clearly had more to say.

'He's had a few girlfriends, you know,' she said as she brushed a stray crumb from her skirt.

'Has he?' I said. 'He's never talked much about his past.'

'Oh my goodness, *yes*,' she confided with a breezy little laugh. 'But then he's a very attractive man.'

'Yes, he is,' I agreed.

'And an exceptionally attractive and talented man like that is always bound to attract women.'

'Well, that's true.'

'Some of them were mad keen to marry him.'

'Were they?' I said politely. This was more than I wanted to know.

'And I'm afraid one or two of them have been very persistent.'

'Really?'

'Oh yes. *Very* persistent.' What on earth did *that* mean? 'Sometimes he'd bring them here,' she went on, 'and they'd get very upset. And they'd say to me, "Yvonne, he just won't *commit*." Of course I felt sorry for them,' she went on benignly, 'but what on earth could I do? You see he wasn't ready to make a commitment – at least not until he met you. He adores your children,' she added.

'Well, he's very nice to them,' I said.

'And I'm sure he'd be a *marvellous* father.'

'Yes, I'm sure he would.'

On the way back to London, I turned to Jos in the car.

'Your mother was telling me about your exciting past,' I confided with a smile.

'What?' he said, slightly irritably.

'She was divulging all your dark secrets,' I joked.

'Oh. And what did she say?'

'Ooh, all kinds of things,' I added teasingly. 'About all your girlfriends. Quite a harem.'

'No, but what did she . . . *say*?' he repeated. By now his mouth was set in a hard, thin line.

'I'm only joking, darling,' I said reassuringly. 'She didn't say anything bad. Of course she didn't – she thinks the world of you. All she said was that you'd be a very good father. But I already know that.' At this he turned on the radio. It was the repeat of *Start the Week*. To my amazement I heard Sophie's voice again. That's why she hadn't called back; she'd been busy. She was talking about the EU.

'Two-speed Europe a dangerous concept . . . France and Germany a hair's breadth apart . . . fully fledged political union . . . extension of majority voting . . .'

'That's my friend Sophie!' I declared happily. 'You know, the girl from work.' Suddenly Jos's hand went down to the dial. 'Oh darling, please don't change channels, I'd like to listen.'

'Europe should remain a community of equal states . . . The EU's institutions belong to all its members . . . And of course our power of veto must remain.'

'She's so brainy,' I said warmly. 'She's brilliant at politics – she was wasted at AM-UK!'

'Did you . . . get to know her well?' he asked carefully.

'Not very well,' I replied. 'But I liked her enormously. She was always very friendly and nice.' Then I suddenly remembered – I'd somehow put it out of my mind – what Sophie had said about Jos. She'd told me she'd never actually met him, so what could she have meant? Perhaps she was concerned because she knew he'd had quite a few girlfriends – a fact which his mother had just confirmed. That must be it, I thought. But I didn't really care because Jos seemed so devoted to me. The next day, as I was busy packing for the Caribbean, I decided to call her again.

'Sophie,' I said. 'It's Faith here. Just ringing to say that I keep hearing you on Radio 4 – you sound fantastic. I'd love to see you, so do call. I'll be away for a fortnight from next Tuesday, but back by the fifteenth. So I hope we can get together, maybe before Christmas? Here's my number again . . .'

I carried on packing, feeling my spirits lift as I put my new bikini into the case with my sarong and the three dresses I'd got from Episode, plus my flip-flops and two books. I was just reaching down my old sun-hat, when I heard the phone ring. Maybe that's Sophie, I thought.

'Is that Faith?' said an unfamiliar female voice.

'Er, yes,' I said. 'It is.'

'You don't know me,' she said hesitantly. 'My name's Becky.'

'Oh. Er, how can I help?'

'Well,' she began. 'Well . . .' Suddenly her voice cracked, then trailed away. 'Oh God, this is very difficult.'

'What is it?' I said wonderingly. 'Would you tell me what this is about?'

'I really don't like to do this,' she said. By now she was in tears. 'But I don't know what else to do. I've been plucking up the courage for days. I don't want to hurt you,' she added miserably, 'but, you see – I just can't go on.' My grip tightened on the handset and goosebumps raised themselves up on my arms. 'I've seen you,' she went on tearfully. 'I've seen you on TV . . .' My God – a deranged fan! 'And I know all about you . . .' she wept. Oh God! 'From Sophie.' *Sophie?* 'And then I saw the photo of you both at the polo . . .'

'The photo?' I said faintly.

'In *Moi!* magazine. I happened to see it. The one of you and Jos. You see, I'm just *so* desperate,' she gasped. 'But he won't talk to me. In fact he's blocked my calls. But I thought you looked nice,' she went on. 'And Sophie told me that you were very nice, so I thought you might understand.'

'Understand what?' I said. By now I felt sick and confused. '*What* am I supposed to understand?' I repeated.

There was silence. Then I heard her say, 'Hasn't he told you, then?'

'Told me what?'

'About me?' Oh God, I thought. A disappointed ex. One of the 'persistent' women that Jos's mother had mentioned the other day.

'I'm sorry,' I said, 'but, no, Jos hasn't mentioned you. And to be honest I'm not sure what it is you want or how you possibly think I can help.'

'But hasn't he told you about . . . *her?*' she went on.

'Her?' I repeated. My God – *another* woman? 'Look,' I said, feeling irritable by now, 'I really don't know what you mean.'

'But hasn't he told you about Josie?' she sobbed.

'About who?'

'Josie.'

373

'Who's she?' There was a momentary silence.

'She's our baby,' I heard her say.

The hall carpet rushed up to greet me as I sank onto the stairs.

'I haven't had an unbroken night in months,' she wept. 'But Jos just doesn't want to know.' My head was spinning and I put my left hand out and steadied myself against the wall. And now I could hear the girl's breath coming in ragged little gasps as she became increasingly distraught.

'Please, *please* would you ask him to call me,' she sobbed. 'Please tell him we need his *help*! I just can't carry on, and I'm – uh-uh – so *tired*. I haven't worked since January. Well, it's impossible when she's so small. And I can't get any benefits unless I give them his name. I don't want to do that behind his back, but he's refusing to talk to me. And now every time I – uh-uh – ring him,' she wept, 'this annoying woman says, "the person you are calling is not" – uh-uh – "accepting your calls."' By now Becky was in full flow. I didn't know what she looked like, but I could imagine her red eyes, wet cheeks and puckered chin.

'You've had Jos's baby?' I said faintly. 'My God. I didn't know. *When*?'

'In February. She's nine months old.' Suddenly, in the background, I heard a lusty cry go up. 'Shhhh! Darling, sshhh! I'm sorry,' she said. 'I'm really sorry. You obviously had no idea.'

'No,' I murmured. 'I didn't. I've known him for seven months and we've become very close, but he's never said a thing. I'm just . . . stunned,' I added miserably.

'I knew about you,' she said, swallowing her tears, 'from Sophie. But I didn't think it would last. It never lasted with any of the others. He'd always come back to me. But then when I told him about the baby . . . He was livid. He told me to – but I refused. I thought he'd come round in the end. But he hasn't and now I just don't know what to do.'

'Hasn't he given you any money?' I said incredulously.

'Not a penny,' she wept. 'He refuses to accept that she's his. But she *is* his,' she added passionately. 'You only have to see her to know. He says that he won't accept paternity without a DNA test, and they cost six hundred pounds. But if he just came and looked at her face then he'd see that she could only be his.'

'How did you get my number?' I asked. I felt sick and faint.

'I was at Sophie's the other day, when you called. She was in the bathroom and the answerphone was on. When I realised it was you I wrote down your number and decided to phone. Sophie said I shouldn't. She assumed you knew but didn't want to get involved.'

'So, are you a friend of Sophie's, then?' I asked hesitantly.

'No. I'm her sister,' she said.

December

'Why didn't you tell me?' I said to Sophie the next day as we sat in the Kensington Café Rouge.

'How could I?' she replied. 'I didn't know you very well, and in any case, what would I say? Don't touch Jos with a bargepole, Faith – he abandoned my pregnant sister.'

'Well, if she was *my* sister I think I would.' Sophie sighed, then sipped her cappuccino.

'When I first realised you were going out with him I *was* very tempted to tell you the truth. But I stopped myself because I could see how happy you were, and I knew how miserable you'd been before. I didn't want to spoil things for you, Faith, and it was up to him to tell you, not me.'

'I wish you had told me,' I said as I stared into my café latte. 'As it was such a big thing.'

'But the other reason for keeping mum was because Becky had sworn me to secrecy. She adores him,' she explained simply. 'She's always adored him, and hoped – and believed – he'd come round. So the last thing she wanted was me going round slagging him off.'

'But you dropped . . . hints about him. I remember now.' Sophie tucked her short blonde hair behind one ear.

'Yes,' she said, 'I did. But I couldn't push it too far. In any case,' she added, 'I thought you'd find out – I mean, my God, you can't hide a *child*!'

I looked again at the photo of the baby that Sophie had brought with her. She beamed out from her buggy, chubby arms and legs waving exuberantly, her face Jos's in perfect miniature.

'And he's never *seen* her?' I said wonderingly.

'Never. Not once,' she replied.

'Does his mother know?'

'Oh, yes,' said Sophie vehemently. 'Becky sent Yvonne a photo,' she explained, 'hoping she'd put pressure on Jos. But the woman's so deluded about her darling boy that she refuses to accept what's happened. She thinks the sun shines out of his arse.'

'I know. Her house is a shrine to his gifts.' I glanced out of the window onto Kensington Church Street where a bucolic, red-besuited Father Christmas was handing out flyers for some new store. And now I suddenly remembered something Yvonne had said. She'd said that Jos would make a 'marvellous father'. But he already *was* a father, I thought sardonically, though marvellous wasn't quite the word.

'Becky was stupid, of course,' Sophie went on quietly. 'She just couldn't leave him alone.'

'Did they ever have a proper relationship?'

'Not really,' she replied. 'She met him in '97 when she was an art student at the Slade. Jos did a series of lectures on set design and they had a brief fling. A month later he told her it was over, but by then Becky had become obsessed. It became a fatal attraction. She even left college and got a scene-painting job at the Coliseum so that she could work with him. He was thirteen years older,' Sophie went on, 'so he had all the power. He told her he'd never marry her,' she added dismissively, 'but at the same time he went on seeing her whenever there was no-one "better" around. But of course *she* kidded herself that it was a real relationship. She believed that, because he always came back, ultimately he'd "see the light". That's what she'd say to me: "He'll see the light, Sophie. He will – he'll see the light." But when she told him she was pregnant . . .' Sophie drew her right index finger across her throat. 'He was vicious about it,' she went on simply. 'He was screaming at her to get rid of it and refused to accept it was his. As though Becky could ever have *looked* at another man!'

'What did she do?'

'She decided not to contact him again until after the baby was born. She was terrified she'd miscarry if they had another big row. So she lay low for seven months; then in February, when she had Josie, she finally phoned him to say. He didn't even ask her what sex the baby was – and he hasn't seen Josie to this day.'

Now, as I listened to Sophie's soft voice, I thought of how I'd met Jos. In March he'd been driving along in his open-topped sports car, without an apparent care in the world, gaily throwing his business card into the laps of strange women like me. Yet all the time he knew that Becky had just given birth to his child. I felt sick to think of it. And sick, too, to recall the efforts he'd made for my children when he'd completely neglected his own.

'He ignored all Becky's calls,' Sophie went on. 'She threatened to come round to his house with the baby, but in the end she didn't – she was too upset. So she sent him a photo, which he ignored. He changed his mobile phone so she couldn't ring him, and he'd leave the answerphone on at home.' I remembered the furtive way in which he'd listened to his messages whenever I was there, crouched over the machine secretively with the volume turned right down.

'Then in July,' Sophie continued, 'Becky found that she couldn't get through – he'd blocked her calls.'

'Ah. Choose to Refuse,' I said.

'What?'

'Choose to Refuse. It's a British Telecom service. My friend Lily told him about that because he said he was getting "nuisance" calls.'

'He did regard Becky as a nuisance,' said Sophie flatly. 'But because she no longer had any way of contacting him she told me she was going to ask you to intercede. She warned Jos by letter that if he didn't get in touch with her that's exactly what she'd do. I told her not to phone you. You must have had a bit of a shock.'

'That's an understatement,' I said. 'I just couldn't believe that

I'd known him for seven months and that he'd never mentioned his child.'

'It's such a *mess*,' Sophie sighed. 'There she is, twenty-four years old, with no job, no man, and a kid. I've been paying her rent all year, and her friend Debbie has been a huge help.'

'Debbie?' I said. 'That sounds familiar.'

'She's Becky's best friend from the Slade. Becky asked her to be Josie's godmother; she's a young set designer, making her way.' Debbie . . . She was the girl at Glyndebourne. The girl who'd made that odd remark. What was it? Oh yes – *I hear you've been involved in some* very *exciting productions*. And now I knew what she'd meant. Then I recalled the lie Jos had told me about Debbie being angry with him for not giving her a job on *Madame Butterfly*. *Madame Butterfly*, I thought with a hollow laugh. No wonder he'd got so worked up about the plot – it obviously touched a deep chord.

'He's a shit,' I said to Sophie. This realisation didn't upset me. On the contrary, I felt curiously calm. 'He's just a shit,' I said again.

'Yes,' she shrugged. 'He is. He could easily afford to support Josie – in the end he'll be forced to – but so far he hasn't paid a thing.'

'But what about your parents?' I asked.

'They're both dead,' she replied. 'They died in a car crash six years ago. That affected us enormously, of course,' she went on. 'Becky, perhaps, more than me. It made her very clingy, and of course Jos is a needy man, too. But her excuse is that she's very young. He just exploited her.'

'But didn't she *mind* that he was seeing other women?'

'Of course – it tore her apart. Worse, he'd tell her about his other girlfriends knowing that she'd always forgive him. I'm ashamed to say it about my own sister, but I'm afraid Becky has no pride. There's nothing she wouldn't do for Jos,' she added. 'He can commit no crime in her eyes.'

'Even *now*?' I said wonderingly.

'Yes,' she said. 'Even now. He's the love of her life,' she went on. 'She'd have him back like a shot. She believes that, ultimately, when he sees the baby he'll come round – but I know he won't. I mean, just look at his background,' she went on vehemently. 'To Jos, a father is someone who runs away, because that's what *his* father did. I've never actually met him,' she explained. 'I don't want to. But I know all about him from Becky. He craves love and approbation,' she added, 'but once he's got it, he feels contempt. All he wants to hear is that women love him, but the second they say it, he moves on. He was perfectly happy to keep seeing Becky casually. He thought it was no strings attached – he was wrong.'

'I've never told him I love him,' I said thoughtfully as I stared out of the window again.

'Clever you,' Sophie replied. 'That's why it's lasted so long. But if you had said it, you wouldn't have seen him for dust.'

'It wasn't deliberate,' I explained. 'I just couldn't bring myself to say it because I knew it wasn't true. I don't love Jos,' I said calmly. 'I never have. I love my husband, but we're getting divorced.'

'I'm sorry,' said Sophie sympathetically. 'So you couldn't . . . forgive him then?'

'Yes,' I replied, swallowing hard. 'That's the funny thing – I could. But then . . . well,' – I didn't want to tell her – 'it just all went wrong again. So I took this desperate, and rather despicable decision to stick with Jos.'

'Have you confronted him yet about the baby?' she added as I called for the bill.

'Not yet,' I replied. 'I needed to talk to you first. He thinks I've gone shopping in Chiswick, he's got no idea I'm meeting you.'

'And what will you do?' she asked as we stood up to leave. I looked at the photo of Josie.

'I'll see him once more,' I said.

As I walked to High Street Kensington tube through the throng of Christmas shoppers my thoughts now turned towards Lily. I hadn't confided in her about Jos yet because I didn't feel like being in touch. I was cross with her – no, not cross, *angry* – for pushing him at me. That's what she'd done, I realised. She'd been doing it all along. Of course she didn't know about the baby – if she had done, she'd have told me, for sure. But ever since I'd met him she'd promoted him relentlessly, and now I seriously wondered *why*. I remembered too how she'd almost panicked the other day when she thought I could have been dumped by Jos. Now, as I rattled westwards on the train, I recalled all the things she'd said.

He's handsome and he's talented.

He'd never let you down.

It's a nightmare being single, you know.

Peter's done it once, he'll do it again!

You're so lucky to have met Jos, Faith.

Jennifer and I are just thrilled!

I thought too of the things Lily had *done*. Of the way she'd lent me Armani frocks and other smart clothes, and offered to babysit. I thought of the way she'd had us photographed together for *Moi!* And now I recalled her scarcely concealed fury when I finally confessed to my 'affair'.

I thought about Jos and about how, though I'd suppressed it, I'd been uneasy from the start. I remembered the lie about the 'homemade' curry, and Matt's computer, and the way he'd flirted with a man to get work. I recalled his hysteria over *Madame Butterfly* and his subsequent lies in the *Sunday Times*. I remembered the way he'd shouted at Graham – it was both horrible and absurd. Now I recollected his dream about being naked at the opera house. I'd naïvely interpreted this as a sign of honesty, but it was Katie who'd intuited the truth: *dreams of undressing are a sign that you fear someone will discover something about you that you would rather remained a secret.* And that's clearly how he felt about his child. The fact that he had a baby didn't bother me – why should it? – it was his failure to do the right thing. But, above all, it was his lies – his bare-faced, blatant lies. Peter never lied to me, I reflected. Peter always told me the truth. What else would Jos lie about, I wondered, if he could lie to me about this?

I opened the front door and Graham bounded up to greet me with a volley of joyful barks.

I crouched down and put my arms round him and looked into his soft brown eyes. 'I owe you an apology, darling,' I said. 'Because you were right all along.'

'Krug!' Jos exclaimed happily the following night. 'I say, that's a bit of a treat.'

'I know it is,' I said. 'But then why not? I'm afraid it's only non-vintage, though.'

'Never mind,' he said with a grin. 'I think I'll be able to cope.'

'Apparently Krug is very popular for christenings.'

'Really?' he said vaguely. 'I wouldn't know.'

'So you haven't been to any christenings lately?' I said.

'Oh, no – not for years. I say, how adorable!' he exclaimed, peering at the advent calendar I'd hung on the wall. 'I love advent calendars, but you haven't opened today's window. I'll do it, and it's – ooh – a trunk. Which reminds me, Faith, have you packed yet?'

'Not quite,' I replied.

'Do you travel light?' he asked as he slipped his arm round my waist.

'Not usually, but I will this time.'

'And are you looking forward to the break?'

'Oh, yes.'

'Mmmm – duck!' he exclaimed appreciatively half an hour later as we sat down to eat.

'Actually it's duck*ling*,' I pointed out as I put the vegetables on the table. There were tiny new potatoes, and mange-tout, and baby sweetcorn, and miniature carrots, and little zucchini.

'It's a vegetable kindergarten!' he quipped.

'Well, I just love baby vegetables, Jos, don't you?' He smiled and shrugged. 'I just love sweet, dinky little baby carrots and peas and sweetcorn. Do you like baby things, Jos?' He nodded, then sipped his champagne. '*Do* you?' I repeated. 'I'm really not sure that you do. Oh no, Jos,' I sighed, shaking my head, 'I'm not sure about that at all. You see, I get the impression you really *don't* like babies much – especially your own.'

He slowly lowered his knife and fork, then he gazed at me with a blowtorch intensity as though he was trying to read my mind. But I'd decided I'd played with him for long enough. I'm not the sadistic type.

'Jos,' I said quietly. 'I *know*.' There was a silence during which I was aware of the slow tick of the kitchen clock.

'What?' he said, irritably. 'What do you know?'

'About the baby,' I said. Jos rested his knife and fork on the side of his plate.

'I suppose Becky told you?' he said.

'Yes. She did. But why on earth didn't *you*?'

'Because it's none of your business,' he replied calmly as he picked up his fork again.

'Are you sure about that, Jos? I mean, what makes you think you can have a serious relationship with me for eight months and not tell me about your child?'

'Look,' he was beginning to bluster. 'It's been a very . . . difficult time for me. I've had awful problems with her.'

'So I hear,' I replied quietly. 'And I hear that she's had awful problems with you. You lied to me,' I went on pleasantly. 'Just like you've lied to me about so many things. But this is a very big lie, Jos, because you told me you didn't have kids. When we first met, don't you remember? I asked you, and you said no.'

'I didn't think it *was* mine,' he said defensively, 'and I still don't believe it now.'

'Oh, I do,' I said calmly. 'And by the way it's not "it", it's "she".' I stood up, went to the dresser and took out the photo which Sophie had lent me.

'Are you sure she's not yours?' I said as I placed it in front of him. He flinched, then looked away. 'She looks awfully like you, you know, Jos. Same big grey eyes, same mouth, same fair curls. She's even got the same name.' I put the photo back in the drawer, then sat down again.

'It's my problem,' he insisted. 'This has nothing to do with you.'

'Well, to be honest Jos, I think it does. Because in theory she could be my stepchild, so of course I'd like to know. But the main thing is that I'm wondering what else you'd lie to me about, if you were prepared to lie about this?'

'It's been a nightmare,' he groaned, running his left hand through his blond hair. 'I didn't want to bother you with it, Faith, because it just wasn't fair.'

'Oh, come on, Jos,' I said wearily. 'You just didn't want to be bothered your*self*. Sophie says you've never given Becky a penny. Not a thing. Is that true?'

'It's none of your business what I have or haven't given her!' he retorted. 'And you shouldn't have listened to that, that, fucking . . . *lesbian*!' His aggression didn't surprise me. After all, I told myself, this is a man who screams at dogs.

'You're right, Jos,' I said calmly. 'It *isn't* any of my business. Not now. Because you and I are going to part.' He looked down at the table.

'I don't see why this should make any difference to us,' he groaned.

'The fact that you can't see that only proves how incompatible we are.'

'So you're trying to dump me, are you?' he said angrily, his lips pursed in a now familiar hard, thin line. 'Are you trying to get rid of me? Is that it?'

'Well, yes, I suppose I am.'

'I will not have you doing that!' he said.

'I'm sorry, Jos, you don't have much choice. I know you usually do the dumping, but in this case it's going to be me. Not because of the baby, but because I don't trust you. You're a liar,' I said. 'I've always known that and, to be honest, I wasn't in love with you.' At this he stared at me, shock shining in his eyes. 'There was something about you that never felt right,' I went on. 'And now I know what it was. You don't feel quite real. You're all surface. You're like one of your lovely trompe l'oeil paintings. You're just a charming illusion, that's all.'

'I've treated you very well,' he spat.

'Yes,' I said. 'You have. But only because you wanted me to fall for you. "I'm going to make that woman love me" – isn't that what you said? And recently you've been exceptionally nice to me, and now I've worked out why – because you knew that Becky might spill the beans, so you were trying to soften me up. But to be honest, Jos, your niceness means nothing when you've been such a four-letter-word to your child.'

'How would you feel if you were me?' he said vehemently. 'How would you feel if you categorically told a woman it was casual and then she goes and does *that*! You ought to feel sympathetic to my situation given that it's just happened to Peter.'

'But the difference between you and Peter is that Peter will do the right thing. Becky needs money,' I said. 'And you can easily afford to pay.'

'Oh, she'll get her money in the end,' he said petulantly. 'I'm just not going to make it easy for her when it's all her fucking fault.'

'Why is it all her fault? After all, you had sex with her, knowing she was obsessed.'

'Yes, I did. But I was honest. I *told* her there was nothing in it for her. I kept telling her,' he said, his voice rising now to a kind of tenor bleat. 'I kept telling her she ought to get herself a proper boyfriend.'

'How chivalrous of you,' I said.

'I never thought she'd *do* that,' he whined, the planes of his handsome face twisted with discontent.

'Jos, *why* did you think she wouldn't?'

'Because it would be emotional suicide, that's why. I didn't pretend to love her. So why would she want to have my kid?'

'Because *she* loved *you*. You knew that. So you should have taken care.'

'I did take care. I gave her money.'

'You gave her *money*?' I said weakly. 'For what?'

'For the morning after pill.'

385

'Is that your idea of contraception?' I said with a hollow laugh. 'My God, you must have had a deathwish to carry on like that! Poor Becky,' I said. 'The more you say, the more despicable you sound. You were like Pinkerton,' I remarked calmly. 'You were no better than that.'

'But she *knew* the rules!' he hissed. He had stood up now and was glaring at me. 'She *knew* the rules,' he repeated as his left hand sliced through the air. 'She knew it was just a temporary arrangement, so she has only herself to blame!' And I thought, I've heard that before. That's exactly what he said about *Madame Butterfly* when we were in the Model Room. 'She's just a crazy, pathetic bitch,' he added contemptuously, 'bent on victimhood. I told her not to have it!' he hissed as he poured more Krug into his glass. 'I told her I'd pay for the abortion, but the silly little cow refused. I hoped she'd have a miscarriage,' he went on, hysteria creeping in now. 'I prayed she'd have one,' he yelled. 'I got down on my knees and I *prayed*. Oh, *yes*!' he shouted as he waved the bottle of champagne about. 'If Becky had had a miscarriage, it would have been vintage Krug ALL *ROUND*!' His words hit me like a punch to the solar plexus. I looked at him, feeling derelict now of every emotion except contempt.

'I'd like you to go now,' I said quietly as I felt my insides twist and coil. 'And please phone the travel agent tomorrow and tell them you'll be going to the Caribbean alone.'

After he'd left I sat in the sitting room, with Graham, just staring into space. Knowing I was unhappy, he'd laid his head on my lap.

'You're so clever, Graham,' I said as I stroked his ears. 'You got it in one. I thought Jos was my Faith healer, but he was just a brilliant deceit.' I idly picked up the copy of *Moi!* magazine I'd got at the Cartier. I reread the compatibility questionnaire with dark laughter rising in my throat and a burning sense of shame.

Does your partner have any annoying little habits? it asked. Yes, I'm afraid he does. *Does your partner always tell the truth?* Unfortunately not – in fact, he lies. *Do your friends and family like your partner?* Not really – especially the dog. And finally, *do you ever have uneasy feelings about some of the things your partner says or does?* With a grim smile I rubbed out the 'no' I'd pencilled in in July, then picked up my pen and ticked, 'yes'.

Three days later I arrived back from work at half past ten to find a pile of letters on the mat and the answerphone winking away.

'Darling!' I heard Lily shout as I picked up the mail. 'Happy birthday!'

'Thanks,' I said miserably.

'Long time no hear! I've been thinking of you because Jennifer Aniston got out last night.'

'How tragic,' I said.

'Yes – she'd gone all the way down the King's Road, naughty thing.'

'I'm surprised she could find it,' I said.

'I expect Jos is taking you somewhere fabulous tonight, and I guess you're off to the Caribbean any day.'

'No, I'm *not*,' I said crisply as I opened the first letter – a birthday card from the kids. 'If I don't speak to you before you go, have a wonderful time. But I'm ringing you because the January *Moi!* has just come back from the printers and I wanted to read you your stars. Your horoscope's absolutely brilliant, darling. Everything's going to be great.'

'Oh, really?' I said.

'Now, just listen to this.' I heard her clear her throat theatrically. 'Sagittarius, planet of big dreams, romance is very much on your mind this month.' I emitted a mirthless laugh. 'And by the time of the full moon on the sixth of January you'll have worked out why one particular person seems to hold for you an undying appeal. Isn't that fabulous, darling?'

'No it isn't,' I hissed.

'Just thought I'd share that with you. Byeeeee!'

There was another message from Mum, wishing me a happy birthday and asking me when I was bringing Graham down. Christ! I'd forgotten to tell her. I rang her back straight away.

'I don't need you to puppysit after all,' I said. 'I meant to tell you – it's off.'

'Oh, darling. What a pity. Why?'

'I've just . . . changed my mind,' I explained.

'But the Turks and Caicos are divine.'

'I'm sure they are, Mum, but I don't want to go.'

'So what about Jos, then? What's happened to him?'

'I did Choose to Refuse.'

'You did what?' she said.

'Choose to Refuse. I don't want to see him any more.'

'Oh dear,' she said. 'Why not? I mean, weren't you compatible?'

'No, we weren't,' I replied. I thought of my three new summer dresses. 'It was just an Episode.'

'So what are you doing tonight then, darling? It's your birthday, after all.'

'Oh God, Mum, I really don't know, and to be honest I don't much care.'

Now I opened the rest of my mail. There was a lovely card from Peter – no message – but simply signed with a 'P' and a cross. Sarah had sent me a card too, and there was one from Mimi and Mike. And now I opened the letter from Rory Cheetham-Stabb and found myself staring at my decree nisi. Here it was. *This came through ten days ago*, said an accompanying note, *but I thought you'd like a copy to keep*. Not really, I thought. I studied it with an air of defeat and a dragging sensation in my chest. For this was it. The palpable proof that my marriage had failed. I felt I was clutching a time-bomb, primed to explode in just a few weeks. The children would soon be home from school, so I hid it in my desk. I wanted to protect them from the details of our split, though they'd soon have to know about Andie.

Then I trudged upstairs, aware of the irritatingly merry jingle of an ice-cream van, and sank into bed. But it was one of those days when, despite my exhaustion, I just couldn't sleep. Not least because the phone just wouldn't stop ringing. Usually I let the answerphone take it, but today I kept getting up. First it was

Sophie to find out how my meeting with Jos had gone, and to tell me she'd got more work with the BBC. Then it was Sarah, fulminating against Andie who she'd seen the previous day.

'The fuss she's making about this pregnancy!' she exclaimed. 'It's ridiculous! She wouldn't eat this, and she wouldn't eat that, and she was quizzing me about what I'd cooked, and accusing me of giving her unpasteurised cheese. And I mean, she can't be that pregnant yet, Faith, but she was wearing this sort of marquee, and Peter just looked so dismal,' she went on breathlessly, 'I've never seen him like this. He spent most of the time working – on a Sunday – to avoid being with her, I should think! Like father like son,' she added bitterly. 'I'm afraid he's done *just* what my husband did. Maybelline!' she spat contemptuously. 'I mean – what a ridiculous name!'

I humoured her for another five minutes and then went into the kitchen, made some coffee, and opened the window on my advent calendar. As I did so a shower of glitter was loosened, and fell, like frost, to the ground. Well, things *have* lost their sparkle, I reflected. Inside the tiny window was a bowl of cherries. Mmm. Just like my life, I thought.

I spent the rest of the day feeling dismal; I felt like a small boat that's being swept out to sea. For my divorce was no longer hypothetical but all too real, and Peter would soon take the rest of his things. I walked round the house, followed by Graham, identifying everything that was his. Those two old jackets in the hall, and his gumboots, and some shoes, and now I went through his books. Peter has so many – hundreds of them – they line the sitting room walls. I inhaled their sweet, musty fragrance with profound feelings of regret. There were shiny new paperbacks, and hardbacks, and a few treasured first editions. There were orange Penguins, and classic black ones, and all his authors' novels, of course. And it's funny the things that you notice when you're in a certain kind of mood. For I found my eye inexorably drawn now to *The End of the Affair*; yes, I thought ruefully, our affair *did* come to an end. Then I spotted *Can You Forgive Her?* by Trollope. No, I thought bitterly, I can't. *Bleak House* caught my eye now, and I thought, yes, this house *is* bleak. *Hard Times* were coming, I realised, there'd been a *Decline and Fall*. And here was *The Rainbow* but where, yes, *where*, was *mine*? Then I pulled out *Things Fall Apart*. Things had indeed fallen apart, I mused, leaving only *A Handful of Dust*. My reconciliation with Peter had failed catastrophically and Jos had proved to be a false dawn. For the first time in my adult life, I was utterly alone.

I'm on my own now, I said to myself as I sat in the bathroom with Graham that night. I'm thirty-six, the children are growing up and I have no partner, no spouse. I surveyed Jos's Caribbean creation, with its swaying palm trees and turquoise sea. It was tantalisingly beautiful, but it just wasn't real. I went downstairs to the cellar, found a tin of white silk vinyl and a paintbrush, and carried them upstairs. Then I began to go over the mural with strong, deliberate strokes. Back and forth went the brush, with a gentle slap, obliterating the lapis sky and gleaming sands. A drip of paint ran over the conch shell as I covered the distant fishing boat. And now a small sob escaped me, and then another, and soon my cheeks were wet; and I think I would have cried for a long, long time, if the phone hadn't rung again.

'Happy birthday, Mum!' said Matt happily.

'Thank you, darling!' I croaked.

'Have you had a nice day?'

'Oh, it's been *lovely*,' I said.

'Have you got a cold?'

'No,' I said, swallowing my tears. 'I mean, yes. Yes, I have . . . just a sniffle.'

'Is Jos taking you out?' he asked.

'No,' I said quietly. 'He isn't. In fact I might as well tell you that Jos won't be taking me anywhere now.' There was a moment's silence, then I heard hand-noise as the phone was passed over and then Katie came on the line.

'Mum? It's me. What's happened?'

'Oh, nothing. It's just one of those things.'

'Aren't you going to the Caribbean then?'

'Er, no. I'm not. Not now.'

'Have you dumped Jos, then?'

'Um . . .'

'I hope you have.'

'Well then, since you ask – yes.'

'Oh, good. We thought he was a bit of a creep,' she remarked. 'Not nearly as nice as Dad. Do you want to talk about it?' she added cheerfully. 'I can work through it with you if you like.'

'No thanks, Katie!' I said crisply.

'I think you need a little cognitive behaviour therapy.'

'I assure you that I do not.'

'But you're bound to have some negative feelings coming up.'

'I do not have any negative feelings whatsoever,' I said as I pressed a sodden tissue to my eyes.

'So what are you doing tonight?' Katie asked.

'I'm staying in. I've got some . . . painting to do.'

'Oh, that'll be a coping mechanism.'

'It's no such thing, it's just a little chore that needs to be done. Now, let's change the subject – tell me, how's the play coming along?'

'Oh, it's fine,' she replied airily. 'We've got dress rehearsals this week. I've got quite a big part actually, and Matt's in charge of props. Are you going to come down and see it?'

Was I? I'd been too distracted to give it a thought.

'Go on, Mum,' she urged me. 'Come and watch.'

'All right,' I said suddenly. 'I will. Yes, of course I'll come,' I added. I wanted to support my kids, and after all my recent troubles it might cheer me up. 'But Katie, remind me what the play is again?'

'It's *When We Are Married*,' she said.

Getting divorced is like falling into a big, black hole, I realised the following week as I drove down to Seaworth on my own. No, it was even worse than that – it was like falling out of a plane. But now I knew I had reached terminal velocity and that surely I would soon hit the ground. It wouldn't kill me

– I felt confident of that – but my injuries would be severe. So I'd just have to splint up my shattered bones, get out there again, and *live*. It's going to be awful, I reflected quietly. It's going to involve years of pain. I would have to be brave, I told myself. I'd have to do things I'd never done before. And as I crawled along in the slow lane, I imagined myself doing evening classes, or attending dinner parties on my own. I saw myself going on dates with hideous men, who'd bore me to death about golf. I'd often wondered what it was like to be single, and now I was going to find out. There were so many situations I'd have to cope with, I realised. I'd never ever been down to the school without Peter, for example. But this is what it's going to be like now, I told myself grimly. From now on I'm on my own. Maybe I'll be on my own for ever, I thought miserably as the amber streetlights strobed the car. What was it Lily had said? Oh yes. *Just think of all the sad divorcées who never find anyone new*. I'll probably end up like that, I reflected – frustrated, and bitter and sad. I struggled to find the turning off the motorway and wished that it was Peter at the wheel, not me. The kids had told me that he wasn't coming down to see the play, and I was vastly relieved. They said he'd told them he was very busy at work, but I knew the real reason why. He didn't want to come because he knew it would distress us both too much. I remembered the last time we'd come down, on speech day. It was just so, so hot. And Peter was upset because of that nasty piece in the *Mail*, and then there'd been all that fuss about Matt. Well, I'd just have to cope alone this time, I realised as I parked the car.

When We Are Married, I thought grimly as I took my seat in the crowded hall. *When We Are Parted*, rather, or, *When We Are Divorced*. The play was billed as a 'serio-comic assessment of married life'. I glanced at the programme and read Katie's name with a stab of pride. She was playing one of three Yorkshire wives celebrating their silver wedding. Peter and I would never get to that milestone, I realised with a bitter sigh. We'd got to fifteen years – our crystal anniversary – and then we'd smashed it all up. But now, as the curtain rose I forgot my troubles and gradually got lost in the play. Katie was playing Clara Soppit, the bossiest of the three wives.

PARKER: 'Marriage is a serious business.'
CLARA: 'That's right, Albert. Where'd we be without it?'
SOPPIT: 'Single!'
CLARA: 'That'll do, Herbert.'
PARKER: 'So we're all gathered 'ere to celebrate the anniversary of our joint wedding day, friends, I give you – the toast of *marriage*!'

But then they discover that the vicar who jointly married them wasn't properly qualified, and that – shock horror for those days – they'd been living 'in sin' for twenty-five years.

PARKER: 'You might *feel* married to him – but strictly speaking – and in the eyes of the law – the fact is, you're *not* married to him. We're none of us married.'
CLARA: 'Some 'o t'neighbours ha' missed it. Couldn't you shout it louder?'
PARKER: 'All right, all right, all right. But we shan't get anywhere till we face facts. It's not our fault, but our misfortune.'
CLARA: 'Let me tell you, in the sight of Heaven, Herbert and me's been married for twenty-five years.'
PARKER: 'And there you're wrong again, in the sight of Heaven, nobody's married at all.'

The curtain fell for the interval in a burst of applause and we all trooped outside. This was the part I'd been dreading most as I'd never been to a school function alone. I clocked all the people we'd met on speech day and gave them a polite but disinterested smile. Then, in order to cover my embarrassment at being alone, I pretended to be absorbed in my programme.

'Mrs Smith?' I looked up. Oh God. It was that ghastly

woman, Mrs Thompson. She was the one who'd been so sniffy in July about Matt getting the Junior Maths Prize. The old bag was probably coming to beat me up again, I thought, as she bore down on me with a gleam in her eye. Without Peter here to protect me I felt my metaphorical fists go up. This is what it's going to be like now, I realised. I'd have to fight my corner alone. But as she approached me I noticed she was beaming, and that she looked – different, somehow.

'How lovely to see you!' she exclaimed. I was almost cata-tonic with shock. 'How are you, Mrs Smith?' she enquired solicitously.

'I'm fine, thanks,' I lied. 'You look well.'

'Oh, I *am* well,' she said with a smirk. And as she babbled away about the play, I took in the change in her appearance. She'd lost quite a bit of weight, she was nicely made up, and her rigid perm had been replaced by soft, subtly highlighted layers. She was wearing a very expensive-looking angora coat-dress, and she exuded a delicious scent. I've got quite a good nose, but I couldn't for the life of me recall which one it was.

'Isn't Katie fabulous!' she gushed as we sipped our coffee.

'Oh, yes, well . . . thanks,' I replied. And hearing her com-pliment my daughter like that, I suddenly regarded her as my New Best Friend. 'Johnny's *marvellous* too,' I added warmly. She gave me a rapturous smile.

'But he's not as good as Katie,' she said generously.

'No, honestly, he is,' I replied.

'Katie's such a natural.'

'But so is Johnny – and his diction's divine.'

'No really, Katie's the star turn today. Her comic timing is *great*.'

'But Johnny's just – *fantastic*!' I insisted, determined not to be outdone.

'Oh, that's *awfully* nice of you, Mrs Smith, but I think your children are great – I mean, they're so attractive, and incredibly bright.' By this stage I loved Mrs Thompson so much I wanted to kiss her on the lips. 'And the way Matt's paid everyone back,' she added. 'Well, we're all *so* impressed.'

'I'm sorry?' I said.

'Oh, didn't you know?' she went on as she stirred her coffee. 'He's reimbursed all his friends.'

'Er, has he? Good. I . . . didn't know.'

'Yes. He won some money.'

'He won some money? How?'

'By playing poker.'

'But he doesn't play poker,' I said.

'Oh yes he does. Apparently he's brilliant at it. He told Johnny his grandmother had taught him in the summer.'

'No, no, that's not true, Mrs Thompson, you see she just taught him . . . Rummy. Oh,' I said slowly. '*Oh.*' Was there no end to my mother's antics?

'Johnny said Matt was playing on the Internet, using his granny's credit card. Very enterprising of him, Mrs Smith – apparently he won five thousand pounds. *So* much better than gambling on those silly dot.coms, don't you think? But changing the subject,' she went on smoothly, 'I just wanted to say . . .'

'Er, yes?' I said faintly, resolving to have it out with Mum when I felt stronger.

'And I do hope you don't mind my mentioning this –'

'No . . .'

'That I'm so sorry about your divorce.'

'Oh,' I said with a pang, 'that's fine.' And I realised that everyone would know about it because the kids would have told their friends.

'Are you bearing up all right?' Mrs Thompson asked solicitously.

'Oh, absolutely,' I lied.

'You've got Rory Cheetham-Stabb, haven't you?'

'Um, yes, I have, that's right. Er, how do you know I've got him?' I added.

'Because I've got him too!' she declared.

'*Really*?' I said. 'I didn't know.'

'Oh yes,' she replied. 'My husband's gone off with his temp, Mrs Smith, but to be frank I couldn't care less. I'm enjoying myself too much,' she added happily. 'I'm having a *wonderful* time. I've been married for twenty years, I've brought up three kids, and now I'm going to have some *fun*.'

'Well . . . good!' I was laughing by now.

'But isn't he fantastic?' she said, her eyes misting over.

'Who? Johnny? Oh *yes*.'

'No, not Johnny,' she said with a girlish giggle. 'I mean Rory Cheetham-Stabb.'

'Oh, well . . .'

'I think he's just *marvellous*!' she gushed.

'Well, he's certainly efficient,' I pointed out. 'He's a bit ruthless,' I added.

'Oh, *yes*,' she said enthusiastically, 'he *is*. I'm so glad I've got him seeing to me, Mrs Smith,' she went on. 'I mean, he really does the business, don't you find?'

'Er . . .'

'He's just what I've needed really,' she went on with this odd little sparkle in her eye. 'Do you know what I mean, Mrs Smith?'

'Well, yes,' I lied. 'I do.'

We exchanged protestations of undying friendship, then went back in for the second half; and now the three couples were suddenly not sure they wanted to stick with their 'spouses' after all. Now that they knew they were technically free, the worms were turning all round. Clara's henpecked husband, Herbert, rebels, and the others glimpse the possibilities too. And I was just sitting there, reflecting on this, when suddenly the name of Mrs Thompson's scent came to me – it was called No Regrets.

The following week the kids came home. This would be the first time we weren't all together at Christmas, so I tried to make it fun. We went to a carol service, and made mince pies, and strung up the Christmas cards. Then, on the Sunday, the kids spent the day with Peter.

'How was he?' I asked Katie casually that night as we decorated the Christmas tree.

'Oh, he's all right,' she replied. He told us about Andie by the way, Mum. She's got him now.'

'Is he – living with her?'

'Oh no, he's still at the flat. Poor Dad,' she added as she untangled the fairy lights. 'Poor you, too.'

'I'll be OK,' I lied. For the truth was I felt as fragile and hollow as the glass bauble I was holding in my hand. Just one little knock and it would shatter into fragments – that's all it would take. 'You were quite right about Jos, by the way,' I offered. 'All he wanted was to be loved.'

'He must have been compensating for something in his childhood,' she said.

'Yes. I'm sure he was.' Then I told her what I'd found out about him – she was old enough to know.

'Oh! So it wasn't Graham who needed the snip,' she remarked indignantly, 'it was *him*! Lily liked him though, didn't she,' Katie added.

'Yes,' I said crisply. 'She did.'

'But then she's a bit like Jos in a way – still looking for her inner adult. Mum,' she continued, slightly hesitantly as she draped red tinsel over the lower boughs, 'I've never asked you this before, but why are you and Lily such close friends?'

'Well, to be honest, there are times when I wonder that myself,' I said as I hung up a gold star. 'I mean, Lily can drive me mad.'

'She always has to be the centre of attention,' Katie offered as she placed the fairy on top of the tree. 'And she always has to win.' I rolled my eyes. It was true. 'But you're totally different, Mum, so I've sometimes wondered why you two became close?'

'Because at school a lot of the girls were pretty nasty to her, and I hated that, so I decided I'd be her ally. Then, as she grew in confidence, I realised what fun she was. And because I was rather unadventurous and sensible, I found Lily liberating because she was wild.'

'So it was the attraction of opposites, then?'

'Yes, I suppose it was. To me, she was such a tonic. She was so daring. And she liked me because I never really threatened her in any way. I always imagined, especially once I'd got married, that we'd slowly drift apart. But we didn't, and, to my surprise, she's always kept in close touch.'

'Well, it's obvious that she needs you, Mum.'

'Yes. Perhaps.'

'I mean, you're her only real friend. And because she knew you when she was so young, you probably remind her of just how far she's come.'

'Perhaps that's true,' I sighed as I hung a tiny glitterball on the tree.

'And of course it's obvious that she adores you.' My hand suddenly stopped in mid-air.

'Is it obvious?' I said wonderingly.

'Oh yes. No doubt about it. You're very important to Lily. But then you've been close for twenty-five years. Perhaps you should have a silver anniversary party!' she added with a laugh.

'Mmm . . . perhaps we should. But the longer you're friends with someone, Katie, the more meaningful that friendship becomes.'

'She's obviously a bit jealous of Dad,' she remarked. 'As though she knows you better than him. Maybe that's why he doesn't really like her,' she suggested. 'Three's a crowd and all that.'

'Oh, I don't know,' I replied. 'I think he finds her a bit shallow and vain. He admires her intelligence tremendously,' I added, 'but he thinks she's wasted her gifts. He says she could have been a brain surgeon, or a scientist. He thinks she's sold out to fashion and glitz.'

'But it's up to her what she does with her life, not Dad.'

'Yes. Of course it is.'

'I do *like* Lily,' said Katie judiciously. 'She's funny. And she's intriguing.'

'Intriguing . . . ?' I murmured. 'Yes.'

'She's very complex,' Katie added. 'I mean, she's so obsessive, and so driven. Mind you, Dad works really hard too.'

'He always has,' I said.

'No, he's working incredibly hard on something at the moment, but he wouldn't tell Matt and me what it is.'

'He's probably negotiating to buy some expensive new author,' I suggested, 'or striking some big foreign deal. Now, will you both be all right tomorrow night?' I enquired as we appraised the tree. 'I won't be out for long.'

'We'll be fine,' she said airily. 'We're almost grown-up, you know.'

'Yes,' I said, sadly, 'I *do* know that. I know it all too well.' And as Katie switched on the lights, and they began to wink and flash, I thought, wistfully, of how she and Matt would soon be leaving home. Peter had wanted me to have another baby. But now Andie was having it instead.

'Will it be a good party?' Katie enquired as we put the boxes away.

'Not really,' I said. 'Office parties rarely are.'

In fact I always found the AM-UK! Christmas party a bit of a strain. Standing in the boardroom drinking cheap white wine wasn't my idea of fun. But they're my colleagues, I told myself as I got into work on Monday morning, and it would be unsporting of me not to go.

I had my usual espresso from the machine, then glanced at the papers before starting work. I looked at the *Mail*, then picked up the *Independent* and suddenly my plastic cup stalled in mid-air. 'BISHOPSGATE BOOKS FENTON & FRIEND.' I experienced a huge surge of adrenaline as I quickly scanned the piece: *Latest blockbuster merger . . . Fenton & Friend snapped up . . . Bishopsgate paid £35 million . . . rumours began six months ago . . . further gossip at Frankfurt . . . Smith showed real financial flair . . . MD Charmaine Duval's desk already cleared . . . Oliver Sprawle poised to go.* My hands shook with shock as I put the newspaper down. *That's* what he'd been working on, I realised. That's why he'd been slaving away. Good God! I thought. Last December Peter was about to be sacked by Charmaine; now, just a year on, he had sacked *her*. As I tried to concentrate on my weather charts, one thought wouldn't go away – that Peter must have been right in his presumption that Oliver was behind the drip-feed of poison to the press. I now knew he'd had a motive, if he knew of Peter's plans to take over the firm. I glanced at the article again. It said that Peter had been planning to buy up Fenton & Friend for more than six months. Oliver's brother was a banker, and could easily have told him what was afoot. Hence Oliver's continuing attempts to undermine Peter – now, at last, it began to make sense. I remembered Peter had hinted at things at the Frankfurt book fair. I'd told him he'd had the last laugh on Charmaine and Oliver, and he'd replied, 'Not quite.' But now he had, I realised, and they'd got what they deserved. I was so thrilled for Peter, and so proud of him I thought my heart would burst. Then I was knocked down by a wave of regret because I remembered we were getting divorced. Tonight Peter would be celebrating his success – but not with me.

'Are you OK?' said Darryl.

'What?'

'You look a bit down.'

'Oh, no,' I murmured. 'I'm . . . fine.'

'Coming to the Christmas party?' he added brightly.

'Oh, yes,' I said. 'I'll be there.'

So at half past seven that evening I found myself standing in the throng, clutching a glass of cheap Chardonnay.

'– bloody funny!'

'– a singing ferret?!'

'– the Princess Diana tragedy special.'

'– did you see Sophie on *Newsnight*?'

'– yeah, that girl from the *Big Breakfast*.'

'– Selina Scott was there!'

Terry was looking cock-a-hoop, then the music started and I could hear that annoying 'Merry Christmas' song. Well it wasn't a merry Christmas for lots of people, I reflected miserably, least of all for me.

So here it is, Merry Christmas, everybody's having fun . . .

I'm not, I thought. Far from it.

Look to the future now, it's only just be-guuuuuuun.

'Faith!' It was Iqqy. I kissed him. 'How are you, darling?'

'I'm OK,' I shrugged. And then, because he's so sympathetic, I added, 'Actually, I'm feeling dreadful – my divorce is about to come through.'

'Poor darling,' he said compassionately. 'And I've just finally dumped Will.'

'You have?' I said. 'Well, that's a good thing. He treated you very badly from what you said.'

'He certainly did,' he sighed. 'I decided I couldn't stand it any more, so I told him it's over this time. Bye bye.'

'Then that means you're going to be happier,' I said.

'Yes, I am, Faith. And so are you.' I smiled at him and thought that I'd never felt less happy in my life. By now I was beginning to feel slightly tipsy as the wine and music flowed. Iqqy went off to chat to someone else, and I had a quick word with Marian, and with Jane on the planning desk, but I avoided the whining Lisa who'd messed up Sophie's autocue. In any case she was deep in conversation with Tatiana. And now I found myself standing next to a girl called Jan, who'd started temping the week before. She'd clearly drunk quite a bit, and seemed in the mood to talk. I established that she'd temped for newspapers and magazines before she came to AM-UK!

'I like being a temp,' she said as she knocked back her glass of wine. 'It's fun,' she added as she grabbed a passing vol-au-vent, 'and it means you're not tied down. I'm not the faithful type, professionally,' she giggled. 'I like to play the field!'

'Did you enjoy working on newspapers?' I asked politely.

'Oh yeah – I did. Especially on the gossip columns, that was a laugh!' she exclaimed.

'Where did you do that?' I asked, aware that my interest was being suddenly aroused.

'Ooh, all over,' she replied. 'At the *Express*, and the *Daily Telegraph*; and I did a few weeks on *Hello!* I also worked on *TV Quick!* for a bit, and then I had a stint on the *Daily Mail.*'

'Did you?' I said. 'When was that?'

'Between March and July of this year.'

'Really?' I said. 'How interesting. Because I had some nasty gossip at around that time.'

'I know, I remember it,' she said with an inebriated laugh.

'Really?' I said again. 'Did you read it?'

'I typed it up,' she replied.

'And were you . . . sworn to secrecy?' I asked as she drained her glass.

'In theory, yes,' she said. 'But you know how it is with us temps, we come and go.'

'In that case,' I said meaningfully, 'could you reveal the source for those pieces?'

'Do you really want to know?'

'Yes. Actually, I do know who it was,' I added, 'I'd just like you to confirm it, that's all.'

'All right,' she agreed. 'I'll tell you if you're right. Hit me with a name!'

'Oliver Sprawle.' She looked blank. 'He used to work with my husband at Fenton & Friend,' I explained. 'We were both convinced it was him.'

'Oliver Sprawle?' she repeated, chewing on her lower lip. 'No, that name doesn't ring any bells.'

'There were two nasty little pieces,' I explained. 'One was in *Hello!* in April, and there was a piece in the *Mail* in July.'

'Well, I was working on those titles at those times,' she said. 'And I can tell you that it wasn't him.'

'Are you sure?' She nodded. I was confused. 'But, I was convinced it was,' I said. 'So who was it, if it wasn't him?'

'I'll tell you,' she said. 'As long as you promise not to beat them up – I could get into trouble for this.'

'I swear not to do them any acts of violence,' I added. 'But I just need to know.'

'OK, then. It was Lily Jago – that woman who edits *Moi!*'

I took the stairs two at a time as I went up a floor to my desk. I punched Lily's phone number into the pad, inflamed by a mixture of fury and drink.

'Lily!' I said. I was hyperventilating. 'I want to talk to you, I –'

'This is Lily Jago . . .' I heard her answerphone click on.

'Lily, I know you're there. Will you please pick up?'

'Thanks for calling me . . .'

'Pick up the phone, Lily! Do you hear me? I want to talk to you!'

'But I'm away now in St Kitts for Christmas . . .' Oh. Oh God. I'd forgotten. 'And I'm not back until the thirtieth – late.'

I hung up, then stared out through the plate-glass window, trying to work it out. Why would Lily do that to Peter? Because she didn't like him, of course. But on the other hand, she did like me. And she would know that if she hurt him in any way, then that would damage me, too. In any case, those nasty little pieces had no basis in truth. They were just spiteful speculation, designed to make him look bad. How *dare* she, I thought furiously. How dare she! But what the hell was it all *for*? And now, as I felt confusion furrow my brow, I heard laughter and music from below. Above the alcohol-fuelled babble, up floated the words of a familiar song.

There are more . . . questions than answers, I heard Johnny Nash croon. There certainly were, I thought. *And the more I find out, the less I know.* Quite, I thought miserably. *Yes, the more I find out . . . the less I know.*

'Peace be with you,' said the priest on Christmas Day. I'm going to *kill* her, I thought.

'Now, in this season of goodwill to all mankind . . .' I will, I'll kill her, the treacherous *bitch*. 'Let us call to mind our sins . . .' I'd rip out her heart and feed it to Graham if I didn't think it would poison him. As for Jennifer Aniston, I'll have her turned into a Shih Tzu-kebab. Then came the first reading, which was all about Mary being pregnant and giving birth in the manger, and the baby being wrapped in swaddling clothes and all that, and I thought I was going to be sick. I glanced at the infant Jesus lying in the crib and thought, I've really *had* it with babies this year. Then, oh

403

God, from the back of the church, this sweet treble voice piped up.

In the bleak mid-winter . . . Oh no. Please no. Not that. *Frosty wind made moan*. Tears sprang to my eyes. This was the bleakest mid-winter of all. *Earth stood hard as i-ron*. So bleak. *Water like a stone*. This year's been so hard, I reflected. *Snow was falling, snow on snow*. That's when it all began, I reflected, at Snows, in January. *Snow on snow. In the bleak mid-winter, lo-ong ago*. The priest's purple vestments blurred and I felt Katie squeeze my hand. I hadn't told the kids what I'd found out – they wouldn't understand it any more than me. In any case, I had to talk to Lily first, which I couldn't do for six days.

That no-man's land between Christmas and New Year's Eve passed in a painful blur. My parents came, and Sarah, and the kids went to see Peter, of course. I hardly ate, and everyone said I looked ill, but they put it down to the impending divorce. Some strange, residual loyalty to Lily prevented me from telling them the truth. But on the night of the thirtieth I sat up, alone, Katie's words ringing in my ears.

She adores you, Mum, you can see that.
You're my dearest friend in the world.
You're important to her. She loves you.
I have only your best interests at heart.

I lifted the silver kaleidoscope to my eye and gently twisted the end, watching the technicolour sequins slither and slide and regroup into ravishing shapes. They were mesmerisingly complex and beautiful, and impossible to pin down.

'So, things are *pretty* frosty!' I said brightly when I went back to work the next day.

'Seven, six . . . she doesn't look well, you know.'

'There's a massive cold front building up.'

'Five, four . . . They say it's the pressure of the divorce.'

'In fact it's been building up for quite a while.'

'See Sophie on *Question Time*?'

'And there's a lot of black ice about.'

'She was fantastic. Two, one . . .'

404

'Which can be *extremely* treacherous.'

'Zero.'

'So it's best to watch out.'

Lily had better watch out, I thought crossly as I made my way to Chelsea that night. I hadn't told her I was coming over, as I favoured a surprise attack. In any case, I knew that New Year's Eve is the one night she always stays in. I marched down the King's Road, the thin wind stinging my cheeks. The Christmas lights, like gaudy necklaces, swung back and forth in the bitter breeze. The shop windows were spangled with tinsel and plastered with red sale signs like bleeding wounds. *Massive Reductions*! they announced. I thought, there's going to be a massive reduction all right. I was going to cut Lily down to size.

'Happy New Year!' I heard someone call out. It damn well won't be, I thought. Oh no, thanks to Lily, I was going to have a miserable new year. As I passed Wellington Square, I tried to piece together the events of this year. On January the sixth, I told myself, I was a perfectly happily married woman. Now, thanks to Lily's interventions, I was miserable and alone. It's all her fault, I said to myself, and I'm going to make damn sure she knows.

'Faith, darling!' she exclaimed as she opened the garlanded front door. 'What a lovely surprise. Oh, what's the matter?' she added, peering at me. 'You look a little . . . *distrait*.'

'I *am distrait*,' I said crisply. 'I'm very *distrait* – thanks to you.'

'What on earth are you talking about?' she said wonderingly.

'Lily, you know perfectly well.'

'Faith,' said Lily calmly, 'Christmas is a notoriously stressful time – you obviously need a drink.'

'I don't need a drink,' I said as I followed her into the flat. 'What I need is the *truth*!' In the huge sitting room, Jennifer Aniston was sprawled on the white leather sofa watching *One Man And His Dog*, her face, like a furry chrysanthemum, fixed rapturously on the screen.

'Why aren't you looking more tanned, Faith?' asked Lily suddenly. 'You've just been to the Caribbean, after all.'

'I have not just been to the Caribbean,' I announced briskly. 'I decided not to go.'

'Why ever not?' she demanded.

'Because I didn't feel like it, that's why. And the reason for that is that Jos – marvellous, gorgeous, fabulous Jos – to quote you – turned out to be a prize shit!' I told her about Becky and the baby. I thought she'd choke on her canapé.

'My God!' she breathed. 'How utterly caddish. But . . . he seemed so perfect,' she said.

'Well, *you* clearly thought so,' I hissed.

'Oh, I see what this is about,' she went on, nodding slowly. 'Christmas has obviously been a bit of a turkey, so now you want to blame me.'

'I do blame you,' I said.

'Why? Because of Jos?'

'Yes,' I said. 'That's right. I mean, you really pushed him at me, Lily. Ever since I met him you've been promoting him, going on about how suitable he was, and how attractive.'

'Well, I thought he was!' she exclaimed.

'You couldn't just let me get on with it, you had to interfere.'

'But Peter had let you down, Faith, and I wanted your new relationship to go well.'

'Oh Lily, it was much more than that. You were almost stage-managing the whole thing. You were manipulating it from the sidelines, as though you had some agenda of your own.' I suddenly thought of the scheming maid, Despina, in *Cosi Fan Tutte*. She'd been up to no good, and so had Lily, I realised. Katie had said Lily was intriguing – she *had* been intriguing, I now knew.

'I mean, there you were,' I went on resentfully, 'kitting me out in designer gear and offering to babysit, and having me photographed with Jos in *Moi!* so that everyone would see we were together, and generally promoting him as enthusiastically as if he were the latest new bag from Chanel. But all along I knew there was something about him that felt hollow and wrong.'

'Well, if you knew that you shouldn't have gone out with him,' she said irritably. 'It's your life, after all. My God, you're still so naïve,' she said. 'Faith Value, Faith – that's you.'

'Yes, and you knew that. You've known me for twenty-five years. You've known I'll always listen to you, and, as usual, I did. But the point is, Lily, that you've been giving me persistently bad advice.'

'Then why did you take it?' she snapped.

'Well . . . because I was feeling so unhappy and so vulnerable, because of what Peter had done.'

'What Peter did was shocking,' she said crossly.

'Was it?' I replied. 'I'm not sure. In any case that's a bit rich coming from a woman who's dated truck-loads of married men. Yes, Peter had a fling, Lily. Lots of people do. You insisted I'd never get over it, but actually, I *did*. And then, when I told you I'd taken him back, you were horrified, almost angry, and I thought your reaction was *weird*. But now I understand that there was more to all this than met the eye. You've wanted me to get divorced,' I said simply. 'That's been your aim all along. You wanted Peter and I to split up. You see, over Christmas, I worked it out. It all started in Snows, didn't it, with that nasty little remark of yours. "I think you're marvellous to trust him" – that's what you said, out of the blue: you dropped it into the conversation like a sharp stone. That's when I first began to suspect Peter, Lily. That's when everything changed. And you fanned my suspicions like a fire,' I went on. 'You stoked my insecurity, because it kept you warm. You sent me that infidelity article of yours, and got me to look at the IsHeCheating.com website. My God, you even paid for the private detective,' I added, 'to make damn *sure* I got my proof. But you were so subtle about it. Pretending that you were certain that he wasn't up to anything, while making sure I found out that he *was*. Pushing me, against all my instincts, to ask him about the cigarettes and the gum. Then, the minute he confessed to his fling – you pounced. And every time I was tempted to go back to Peter, you'd persuade me to stick with Jos.'

'I thought Jos was a desirable property,' she said. 'It's not my fault he's no good.'

'No, but it *is* your fault that I got so involved. Because if I hadn't listened to you, I'd have forgiven Peter. But I did listen to you – to my eternal regret. You've destroyed my marriage!' I shouted at her. 'We were happily married, and now we're getting divorced. And it's all your effing fault!' Lily sipped her champagne with a look of benign contempt.

'You self-deceiving idiot,' she announced calmly. 'You weren't happily married at all.'

'Oh yes we *were*!' I shot back. 'We were as happy as sandboys, Lily. We were as happy as pigs in shit. We were as happy as Larry, whoever he is. So yes, Lily, to answer your question, I was very happily married, thanks, very.'

'And very, *very* bored. You were, Faith. It was written all over you. You were just desperate for change.'

'What the hell would you know about it? You've never been married.'

'I only know what I saw. You were catatonic with marital tedium, Faith – you both were – it stuck out a mile. So I reckoned I was giving you a helping hand. But I guess I'd be bored too after fifteen years with the same man. With your boring little trips to Ikea, and your boring little house, and your pathetic little sexual fantasies which you'd joke about, but as Freud so tellingly said, Faith – "There is no such thing as a joke."'

'I loved Peter,' I insisted. 'We were happy.'

'You could have fooled me,' she replied. 'You told me you hadn't slept with him for over a year. You preferred to sleep with the dog!'

'Why not? I like sleeping with my dog. You sleep with yours. And Peter was having difficulties at work,' I added, 'and as you well know, I work horrible hours.'

'Faith,' she said, 'you were utterly frustrated and so was he. Ennui oozed from every pore. Remember that weird little speech he made in which he accidentally described his anniversary as a "millstone"? So don't give me this, "we were so happy together" rubbish, because I know for a fact it isn't true.'

'It *is* true!'

'It isn't.'

'It is.'

'It *isn't*.'

'What do you know?'

'Because if you *had* been happy, you moron, you would *never* have listened to me!'

I stared at Lily, rendered speechless by the shocking logic of what she'd just said.

'If you'd been as happy as you say you were,' she added calmly, 'you'd have told me to piss off.'

'I wish I had.'

'But what you still don't realise, Faith, as you stand there and abuse me, is that I had only your best interests at heart.'

'You *keep* saying that, but it's a lie.'

'No. It's not. It's quite true.'

'It's a bare-faced lie, Lily. Because if you'd had my best interests at heart, you would not have gone round planting vicious pieces about my husband in the press!' Lily's champagne glass stopped in mid-air. 'It was you,' I added simply. She brushed imaginary crumbs off her skirt. 'It was you, wasn't it?' I said.

'Whatever are you talking about?' she said tetchily.

'It was you feeding that trash to the papers.'

'Faith, I –'

'Don't bother to deny it, because I have it from an impeccable source. And, worse, it wasn't even true. It was just spiteful speculation designed to discredit Peter as much as possible, and to give our divorce a helpful little push. It was you,' I said wonderingly. 'For a long time I thought it might be Andie, and then I figured it was Oliver from work. But for all your funny, obsessive ways, Lily, I never ever thought it could be you. Because we're best friends, don't you remember? We go back twenty-five years.'

'I –' Words clearly eluded her. In any case I didn't give her a chance.

'Why did you do it?' I went on. 'I'd really like to know. What did I ever do to you, to incur your famous wrath? How did I hurt you, that you could feel justified in doing this? All I know is that it goes back to that anniversary dinner. Something happened that night . . . I've got it!' I exclaimed suddenly. '*Othello*. Is that it? Because I accidentally mentioned the play. I tactlessly reminded you of the one instance when you didn't win. That was always a sore point with you, wasn't it, so perhaps you decided, then, that night that you were going to punish me.'

'Oh, don't be so *ridiculous*,' she said. 'As though, eighteen years on, I could care.'

'Then what motivated you, Lily? I need to know. All this crap about having my best interests at heart when you were trying to wreck my marriage and Peter's career. And why did you have it in for Peter so much? I mean, he's never hurt *you*.'

'That's where you're wrong!' she shot back. 'He *has* hurt me!'

'How?'

'There are things you don't know about Peter,' she explained, her voice rising to a reedy whine. 'You don't know what he tried to do to me. Oh yes, there are things you don't know,' she reiterated shrilly. 'Things I found out, last year.'

'*What* things?' I said wonderingly. 'What the hell are you talking about?'

'I'll tell you,' she said quietly. Then she sat down again.

'Just over a year ago,' she began nervously, 'in November, I had dinner with *Moi!*'s publisher, Ronnie Keats. That man you met at the polo match.'

'I know. But what's he got to do with all this?'

'Well,' she said, breathing deeply now, as though in physical pain. 'I'd only been in the job for a month when Ronnie – he shouldn't have done it, really – told me this *terrible* thing.' Lily was inhaling through her nose now, and there were tears standing in her eyes. 'He told me,' she began, her lower lip trembling, 'that when I was being considered for *Moi!* he sought references from four different people. One of them was Peter.'

'Yes. I know.'

'Well, Ronnie tends to blab, and he got a bit drunk and he told me . . .' She whipped a tissue out of a box. 'That one of these referees had given me the thumbs down.'

'Yes?'

'And that as a result there'd been *considerable* discussion as to whether or not I should get the job.'

'Yes?'

'And apparently it was really touch and go. So, knowing that Peter has never liked me, I knew it could *only* be *him*.'

'But you did get the job,' I pointed out.

'But I very nearly *didn't*!' she exclaimed.

'And you blame Peter for that?'

'Yes! I do!'

'Ah! I see. So you plotted your revenge.'

'Yes,' she snarled, standing up now. 'I did. I decided I'd pay him back. Because in this life, Faith, you're either a wimp or a terminator – and I'm a terminator!' I wanted to laugh.

'You're mad,' I said quietly as I stood up to face her. 'In fact you're mad, bad, and sad.'

'I am *not* mad!' she spat.

'Yes you are – you're crazy. You're certifiably insane.'

'But don't you *understand*, Faith? This was the pinnacle of my career. To edit *Moi!* meant everything to me – I'd striven for it all my life. I was going to make those snotty little cows at school eat their words. Don't you remember how they all laughed when I said I was going to edit a glossy magazine? They laughed at me, Faith – those little rich girls with their ponies and their mummies and daddies and their expensive frocks. And I thought to myself then, I'll show you. And I *had* shown them, Faith – I'd got the last laugh. Then I discovered that Peter had nearly stopped it.'

'That's where you're wrong.'

'He *did*,' she insisted. 'It was him.'

'It *wasn't* him,' I said.

'And I tell you it WAS!'

'Really? Well, where's your proof?'

'Oh come off it, Faith, I don't *need* proof. He's never liked me, so who else could it have been?'

'One of the other three. Because I know *exactly* what Peter said to Ronnie Keats about you. Shall I tell you, Lily? Do you want to know? Now, I can't remember it verbatim, but it was full of words like "huge talent, vision and drive". Oh, and he mentioned your "superb visual imagination" too, as well as your "brilliant editorial skills". He also praised your "enormous intellect", your "well-stocked mind", and said that you could write "like a dream". He swore me to secrecy as it was confidential, but that's exactly what he said.' By now Lily looked as transfixed, and confused, as though I was speaking in tongues. 'You've got it wrong, Lily,' I said quietly. 'Peter gave you a glowing report.' She stared at me, too shocked even to blink. Then her eyes opened wider still and she clapped her left hand to her mouth.

'Oh. *Shit*,' she said quietly.

'You've been barking up the wrong tree.'

'I –'

'You've got ego all over your face.'

'But I . . . don't understand,' she whimpered. 'I was convinced.'

'You were wrong.'

'But I know Peter doesn't like me, so why would he say such nice things?'

'Because he wouldn't let any personal feelings influence his high opinion of your work.'

'But I don't . . . understand,' she repeated faintly.

'Well, how very sad that you don't. You can't understand that Peter would never lie about your professional ability. I suppose some people would – perhaps *you* would, Lily – but Peter always tells the truth.'

'Oh,' she murmured. She sank onto a chair. 'Oh, *shit*,' she said again. By now she looked horrified, almost guilty, as she contemplated her appalling mistake. 'But I was *sure* it was him,' she croaked. 'I was certain, I was . . .'

'Obsessed, that's what you were. But it's all been based on a delusion, Lily. A misconception, you might say. And now, thanks to you, I'm almost divorced and Andie's having Peter's baby.'

'Faith, I –'

'Or rather it's *my* baby she's having. Peter and I were going to have another one, Lily, because we'd fallen in love again. I never realised how much I loved Peter until the past few weeks. And now, thanks to you, it's all lying in ashes and I'm getting my decree absolute in a *week*!' Jennifer Aniston started barking now, as I got more and more worked up. 'Andie's having my BABY,' I repeated, 'and I'm going to have to live with this for the rest of my LIFE! So I hope you're SATISFIED,' I yelled, my throat aching, 'because you couldn't have done me more harm if you'd TRIED!'

'No, but wait –'

'It's all RUINED . . .' I said, tears streaming down my face now. 'It's all completely fucked UP . . .'

'Faith, listen –'

'It's just so, so *terrible*!' I wept as the floodgates opened and my hands sprang up to my face.

'But there's something I want to say.'

'I don't want to HEAR IT!' I screamed. 'Don't ever tell me anything again! Because I've had it with you, Lily! I've heard ENOUGH!'

'But it's important!'

'Woof woof!'

'Oh shut up, Jennifer!' I said. 'You fat little . . . GAR-GOYLE!'

'Faith!' Lily shrieked. 'She's *not* fat!'

'She *is* fat!' I flung back. 'She's FAT! Because all she does is sit on her furry arse all day, stuffing her ugly little muzzle with canapés and fantasising about *Graham*!'

'My God, Faith, that's very rude!'

'I don't care! I put my faith in you, Lily – what a mistake!

413

I put more faith in you than I did in my own husband, and now I'm going to bloody well *pay*.'

'Woof woof!'

'Oh shut up, Jennifer!' Lily snapped as she arose from her seat. 'Now, listen to me, Faith.'

'No! I *won't*! I'm never listening to you *again*!'

'Woof woof!' And now Lily was coming towards me, picking her way in her stockinged feet over the sea of strewn magazines.

'Faith! There's something . . .'

'Oh, get lost!' I said. 'Just leave me alone, Lily. I don't want to know! You're just so awful, Lily – *awful*. You're so vengeful, and you're so shallow. And you're a crashing snob!'

'I am *not* a snob!'

'Yes you *are*! I mean, you won't even fly Qantas because you think it's non-U.'

'That's not fair! But listen to me –'

'And you're so self-obsessed. *Moi!* – that's you to a tee. It's not *Om, Om, Om* you chant before that shrine of yours, is it – but *Me, Me, Me*! And as for all that astrological rubbish of yours, what a load of pants. Except that your own star sign suits you, doesn't it? Because you're a Scorpio, Lily, and there's always been a sting in your tail. Because you really *hurt* people. You know that? You cause a lot of unnecessary pain. Yes, Lily, you don't care how much you damage others, do you, as long as you always come first. And you're so competitive – *Moi!* should be sponsored by Winalot! I mean, you –' Lily's face, which had hitherto expressed a blend of contrition and anxiety, suddenly registered utter shock. For as she advanced towards me, she missed the bit of blank carpet she was aiming for and stepped on a magazine. Suddenly she was flipped into the air with a flash of gold knickers before landing, head first, and with a sickening thud, onto the gleaming white marble hearth.

'Christ! Lily! *Lily*!'

'Woof! Woof!' Jennifer Aniston had thrown herself off the sofa and was sniffing Lily's prostrate form.

'Oh *God*!' I gasped, panic rising in my breast. 'Oh God,'

414

I breathed, slapping her hands. 'Oh God, Lily,' I repeated impotently, 'oh God, Lily – Lily! Please *speak*!' I felt in vain for a pulse, then ran to the phone and dialled 999.

'It's my friend,' I said, 'she's slipped on a glossy magazine, hit her head and I think . . .' – I could feel my breath coming in ragged little gasps – '. . . I think she's dead.'

The next five minutes were the longest of my life as I waited with Lily's motionless form. Then at last I heard the approaching siren; then there were blue lights spinning across the walls and ceiling, strobing her lifeless face. As we sped through the backstreets of Chelsea in the ambulance, I could hear the twelve booming bongs of Big Ben. And suddenly, through the darkened windows I saw the fireworks exploding like stars.

'It's midnight,' said the paramedic. I nodded dumbly and gave him a bleak smile. 'Oh well, out with the old and all that,' he added. 'May I wish you a Happy New Year!'

January

'Happy New Year,' said a staff nurse to me politely. I gave her a watery smile. Then I looked at Lily, unconscious beside me – she'd been out for nearly three hours.

'Please, God,' I prayed, 'let her get better. I'll do *anything* if you let her get well. I'll go to Mass on a regular basis, I'll give all my spare cash to the poor, I'll even be godmother to Andie's baby, but please, please *don't* let her die.' Lily's life seemed to hang by a thread or, more accurately, by four trailing wires attached to two monitors, which beeped quietly away to one side.

The nurse unhooked Lily's chart from the end of the bed, then ticked it twice.

'Any change?' I enquired anxiously. Lips pursed, she shook her head. As I gazed at Lily's dormant face I mentally reviewed the last three hours: our drive to the Chelsea and Westminster, the stretchered dash into A and E, the beams of light shone into Lily's eyes, the prodding and tapping of knees. The alarming mention of a brain scan, and finally, her move to the Admissions ward on the fourth floor.

By now I was shattered by stress and by wakefulness, and my bladder was fit to burst so I asked the nurse if she'd stay with Lily while I quickly nipped to the loo. I ran down the corridor, then sprinted back, fearful to the point of semi-hysteria that she might die while I was out of the room. As I sped across the pale blue lino, I was aware of the faint aroma of antiseptic and of colourful pictures on the walls, of the sound of distant snoring, and the soft trill of a telephone.

And now, as I approached Lily's curtained-off bed, I could hear the sister's voice.

'Perrier?' I heard her say. She sounded bemused.

'Ye-es . . . Perr-i-er . . .' I heard Lily groan. 'Perri-e-r . . .' she repeated faintly. I ripped the curtains aside.

'Do you want some water, Lily?' the nurse asked. 'Is that it?' She tipped some into a beaker and held it to her cracked lips, but still Lily's eyes remained closed.

'Perr-i-er . . .' Lily muttered again. 'Want . . . Perr-i-er.'

'Yes, I'm giving you some water, here you are.'

'No, *Perrier*,' she repeated peremptorily. The nurse looked at me and shrugged.

'You'd think ordinary water would do, wouldn't you? All right, Lily – still or sparkling?'

'No, not water – *Perrier*!' Lily shrieked, and suddenly I knew.

'It's Laurent Perrier she wants!' I exclaimed. 'It's her favourite brand of champagne. Lily,' I said, grabbing her hand. 'Do you want some Laurent Perrier? I'll go and get some for you if you like. I'll get you a bottle. I'll get you a magnum if you'll only wake up. Lily, Lily – can you hear me?' I added desperately. 'It's Faith. Do you know who I am?' Lily's eyelids fluttered for a few seconds, blinked twice, then opened wide.

'O-oh!' she groaned as her pupils gradually focused on me, then she raised her left hand to her bandaged head. 'O-oh,' she murmured again. She shut her eyes, then suddenly opened them wide, as though startled. 'Oh Christ, Faith, I've really cocked up.'

'Lily!' I shrieked, clasping her hand. 'Oh Lily, thank God you're all right. I'm sorry I shouted at you,' I added. 'It's my fault you banged your head.'

'No, *I'm* sorry,' she croaked as, assisted by the nurse and by me, she slowly sat up. 'It's all my fault,' she added blearily, 'I got everything wrong.'

'But if I hadn't yelled at you, you wouldn't have fallen. You slipped on a copy of *Vogue*.'

'*Vogue*!' she groaned, rolling her eyes. 'Wouldn't you know it! I'll bloody well sue. But Faith, there's something I've got to tell you,' she added anxiously.

'It doesn't matter,' I said.

'Yes, it does,' she insisted. 'But the trouble is I can't remember what it was. All I know is that it's terribly important, but I – oh! I've got it!' she said.

'Honestly, Lily, let's just forget it, shall we?'

'No,' she said. 'You see . . .'

'I'm really not bothered,' I reiterated. 'Honestly, I'm just *so* relieved you're OK.'

'But it's about . . . her,' she whispered.

'Who?'

'Madame Ovary. *Andie*,' she explained.

'What about her?' Lily inhaled slowly, then looked at me.

'She isn't pregnant,' she announced.

'I'm sorry?'

'Andie isn't pregnant,' she repeated.

'You what?'

'There is no mini-ciabatta in the Aga, darling.'

'There isn't?' I said faintly. 'Oh.' And then, because I was so shocked, I simply said, 'Oh,' again. 'But how do you know?'

'Because three weeks ago I was at a bash at the Savoy. I went into the Ladies, and there was Andie, trying to get Tampax out of the machine.'

'Ah,' I said weakly, 'I see. Well, maybe she was getting them for someone else.'

'Pretty unlikely, I'd say. And she looked slightly embarrassed when she realised that she'd been seen.'

'And are you *sure* it was her?'

'Oh, yes. I've never met her, but I know what she looks like. It *was* her,' she insisted.

'And you think she's not pregnant?' I said faintly.

'Yes. That's what I was trying to tell you last night.'

'But hang on, Lily,' I said, my heart thumping. 'Why the hell didn't you *tell* me *before*?'

'Why didn't I tell you before?' she echoed as she gazed

mournfully into the distance. 'Because I'm a prize bitch, that's why.'

'You knew about this in mid-December?' She nodded guiltily. 'And you said nothing?' She nodded again. 'You kept *quiet*?'

'I'm sorry, Faith,' she whispered as she fiddled with her hospital wristband. 'I should have said.'

'*Yes*!' I exclaimed hotly. 'You *should*.'

'But I kidded myself that it wouldn't make much difference to you, because I told myself you were with Jos.'

'But Lily, you knew I wasn't really happy with him.'

'Yes,' she mumbled, 'I did.'

'And you knew I wanted to be with Peter.'

'I know,' she stuttered. 'It's true.'

'And you knew that the only reason I couldn't be with him was because of Andie's baby.'

'Yes,' she whimpered. 'You're right.'

'Oh, Lily,' I said, 'I don't understand how you could do something so mean and low.' By now her huge brown eyes were brimming with tears.

'I'm sorry, Faith,' she said, grabbing my hand. 'But I was so livid with Peter. It was only when you told me about the lovely reference he gave me that I realised my *awful* mistake. So I tried to tell you about Andie, but you wouldn't listen, and then I had my Freudian slip.'

'So Andie's not pregnant,' I said again. A wave of euphoria swept over me, and my anger evaporated like steam. 'You're alive!' I exclaimed softly. 'And Andie's not having my baby. So there *is* a God', I said wonderingly. And then, at last, I burst into tears.

'I'm sorry,' said Lily. Her brow was pleated with anxiety and her chin was dimpled with distress. 'I'm truly sorry,' she said again as two fat tears coursed down her cheeks. She handed me a tissue, and then took one herself. 'You see I was totally convinced about Peter, I was furious, I was . . .'

'Obsessed.'

'I was filled with loathing for him,' she confessed.

'Lily, you'd been festering.'

'Yes. But you know my career means *everything* to me.'

'So you were determined to punish Peter for an imagined slight, but instead you ended up punishing me. Oh, Lily,' I said miserably. 'You've done so much harm.'

'Yes,' she sniffed. 'I know. I'd do anything to put it right, Faith, but I really don't know how.'

'I do,' I said suddenly as I pressed another tissue to my eyes. I swallowed my tears, then glanced at the clock, which by now said half past four. 'I want you to ring Peter,' I said. 'I want you to call him right now and tell him what you've just told me.'

'At this time?' she said nervously.

'Yes! It doesn't matter, he'll want to know.'

'But I haven't got my mobile phone.'

'There's a hospital phone,' I pointed out.

'Oh, all right then,' she sniffed. 'Go and get it.' So I wheeled the trolley phone to her bedside, plugged it in, and fed in some ten pence coins. Then I dialled Peter's mobile number and passed the handset to Lily. She took a deep breath, then spoke.

'Peter,' she said quietly, 'it's Lily. Yes, I know it's the middle of the night. But, look, no, no, no, please, please wait – I think there's something you ought to know . . .' The conversation took no more than a minute, then she handed the receiver to me.

'Faith,' said Peter, his voice cracking with emotion and fatigue. 'Faith?'

'Yes, darling?' I wept.

'I'm coming home. Just give me forty-eight hours.'

'Happy New Year!' said my local newsagent two days later.

'And an extremely Happy New Year to you!' I replied as I picked up a copy of the *Mail*.

'Got yourself another dog then?' he asked, looking at Jennifer Aniston.

'No, I'm just puppysitting while her mum's in hospital.'

'Oh dear, I hope it's not serious,' he added.

'No,' I replied. 'It's not. On the other hand,' I said judiciously, 'there's a chance it might develop into something serious.'

'Will she be in hospital long, then?' he enquired solicitously.

'Just as long as she can,' I replied. The man looked at me quizzically, but I didn't have time to explain. The fact is Lily's refusing to leave hospital. I'd guessed the reason why.

'I've still got this . . . headache,' she said to the handsome consultant neurologist, Mr Walker, when I went to see her later. The nurse gave her a suspicious smile.

'Well, we've done all the tests, Lily,' Mr Walker replied as he checked her temperature. 'All you had was a severe concussion, but now I think you can be discharged.'

'Oh, no,' she said, slightly panic-stricken. 'I'm sure I need a little more observation. Can't I stay one more night?'

'But you've already been here three.'

'Oh, please.'

'Well . . . as you're in a private bed, I suppose so,' he conceded, 'but then tomorrow you'll have to go home.'

'But what if I have a relapse?' she suggested brightly.

'Lily, you're going to be fine.'

'But I might have sustained permanent brain damage,' she went on cheerfully.

'That's very unlikely,' he said.

'Well, can I come back as an out-patient?' she added desperately as he prepared to leave.

'I don't think that'll be necessary.'

'But I'll need regular check-ups,' she said as he parted the curtains.

'All right,' he conceded. 'I'll see you just once more.'

'Perhaps you could examine me over dinner?' she suggested happily. 'At my place – it's just off the King's Road.'

'Oh,' he said as the penny dropped. 'Well, tempting though that is, I'll have to think about it – medical ethics and all that. By the way,' he went on, indicating the Louis Vuitton canine carrier I'd smuggled in with me at Lily's request. 'I'm sure you know that dogs are not allowed.' She gave him a guilty smile.

'I know,' she said as she unzipped the bag. 'But she's only visiting, aren't you darling? She's helping me to get better,' she added as she removed Jennifer, grunting, from her bag.

'My mother has a Shih Tzu,' said Mr Walker suddenly.

'No!' exclaimed Lily, clearly thrilled.

'She's been shown at Crufts, actually,' he added.

'Really?' she said, incandescent with joy. 'I was thinking of entering Jennifer. Her Kennel Club name is Wicked Fantasy – her father was best of breed. But aren't they just adorable?' she added enthusiastically as Jennifer gave him a goitrous stare.

'Um . . . yes,' he conceded reluctantly. 'If you like that kind of thing. But I don't think you'll be entering her this year,' he added judiciously, 'because I'm sure you're aware that she's pregnant.' Lily's beautifully manicured hands flew up to her mouth, then she stared, dumbfounded, at her dog.

'My mother used to breed them,' Mr Walker explained. 'So I'm pretty sure.' He prodded Jennifer, who obligingly rolled over, and now, as the floor-length curtain of blonde hair parted, we could see a distinct swelling round her middle. 'She's due in a month, I'd say. Did you have her covered?' he added.

'Oh yes, she's got comprehensive life insurance.'

'No, I mean, did you have her mated?' he said.

'No,' said Lily. 'I didn't. Jennifer!' she added sharply. 'How could you! You little slut!' She looked at me. 'It couldn't possibly be Graham, could it?'

'Not a snowball's chance in hell.'

'It must have happened when she got out in December,' she explained, rolling her huge eyes. 'She'd gone all the way down the King's Road. Oh yes, Miss Jennifer Aniston,' she added wagging an admonitory finger, 'you clearly went all the way. God knows what they'll look like,' she went on with an appalled expression on her face. 'I doubt Jennifer managed to find herself the canine equivalent of Brad Pitt. Oh God,' she whined, 'they're going to be mongrels.'

'Cross-breeds,' I corrected her crisply. 'And there's nothing wrong with that.'

'But they might look hideous,' she said. I maintained a diplomatic silence. 'They might be incredibly *ugly* dogs, Faith. On the other hand . . .' she went on excitedly, seeming to glimpse the possibilities of the situation, 'I could put her into the magazine. Yes!' she added eagerly as she reached for her mobile phone. 'I can see it now. Jennifer – naked and pregnant, on the cover of *Moi!* I mean, if Demi Moore can do it, then why shouldn't Jennifer Aniston? We'll do it in April, we'll make the entire issue a dog special – we could call it *Dogue*. I'll get someone really fab to take the pictures,' she added eagerly as she reached for the phone and dialled. 'Hello, Polly? Listen, it's Lily here. I want you to book me John Swannell.'

'Don't over-exert yourself,' warned Mr Walker benignly. 'I'll check on you after lunch, OK?'

'Oh yes!' she said with a beatific smile. 'You can check on me *any* time. Oh, Faith,' she said as Mr Walker retreated, 'don't you think he's divine?' I nodded. He was certainly very good-looking, and he seemed rather nice. 'And to think,' she went on happily, 'that it's all thanks to my crack on the head that I've got to meet that heavenly man! Now, how's Peter?' she added. 'What's going on there?'

'He's coming home tomorrow,' I replied.

'Have you got any luxury lingerie?' she asked anxiously.

'I don't think I'll need it,' I said with a smile.

The following morning I bounded out of bed at three thirty, showered, then squished on my lovely new scent, *C'est La Vie*!, then got to work at four fifteen feeling excited and happy. 'Turned out nice,' I said to myself cheerfully as I studied the satellite charts.

'And so we have a *glorious* day ahead of us,' I said ecstatically as I began my eight thirty bulletin.

'What's she talking about? It's freezing.'

'The temperature's rising nicely now.'

'Bollocks – it's minus two!'

'Although there's a sixty per cent chance of rain.'

'Eight, seven . . .'

'But then what's a bit of water?'

'Six, five . . .'

'And the point about rain, of course.'

'Two, one . . .'

'Is that without it we wouldn't get rainbows, would we?'

'Is she taking hard drugs?'

'So dress up warmly, take a brolly just in case, and have a wonderful day.'

'Zero.'

'Thanks, Faith,' said Terry as Tatiana simpered beside him on the sofa. 'What a sunny soul you are.' I smiled. 'And now,' he said, turning to the autocue, 'the important, but thorny issue of fluoride in our drinking water. Should local authorities be able to compel water companies to add this controversial chemical to our wombat liberal Clinton face cream . . .' Terry stopped, then squinted into the camera, confusion written all over his face. 'Framework privatisation, neuroscience, badger hemlines . . . birdie . . .' he tried again, then paused, his eyes searching in vain for some meaning in the bizarre conglomeration of words as they scrolled down the screen. 'Breast size,' he continued slowly as he ran a nervous finger round his collar. 'Confidential taxpayer commitment, Livingstone pavement hairspray . . .' I stared at him as he squirmed on the pastel-toned sofa, his face aflame.

'What the fuck's going on?' I heard Darryl hiss in my earpiece. 'What are you up to, Lisa?'

'Pink granny helicopter bucket *Eastenders* . . .'

'It's not my fault,' she whined. 'The texts seem to have got all mixed up.'

And now, ignoring the mayhem in the gallery, I suddenly looked at Tatiana. She had this funny little smile on her face.

'Oh dear, Terry,' she interjected soothingly. 'You seem to be having problems there.'

'Well, I –'

'At your age it's probably your eyesight,' she said with impudent pseudo-concern. 'You really should get it checked out. But now let's go straight on to the next item, viewers, and a radical new approach to public transport. Joining me now is the Mayor of London, Ken Livingstone, to talk about new plans for funding the tube. Good morning, Ken,' she said with an ingratiating smile. 'Welcome to AM-UK!'

I ran upstairs to my desk and phoned Sophie.

'Did you see Terry?' I gasped.

'Yes!' she giggled. 'What a scream! I *almost* felt sorry for him,' she added. 'But have you seen the *Daily Mail*?'

'No. What's in it?'

'Me!' I grabbed a copy from the planning desk, quickly flicked through it and there was a huge photo of Sophie in a smart trouser suit, beneath the heading 'DYKE'S DELIGHT!' *Sophie Walsh, recently sacked from AM-UK! after revelations about her private life, has been bought by the BBC in a deal worth £200,000 a year. At the specific directive of Director General, Greg Dyke, the self-confessed lesbian is to front a new TV version of* The Moral Maze *on BBC1. Critics are already hailing her as Jeremy Paxman's heir apparent.*

'Sophie!' I exclaimed. 'You're a star!'

'You helped me, Faith,' she said.

'No, Terry and Tatiana did that.'

'Yes,' she giggled. 'I guess they did. No more psychic grannies,' she said happily. 'No more roller-blading cats. No more doctored autocues, and no more three a.m. starts. And at last my sister has finally reported Jos to the Child Support Agency.'

'Hurrah!'

'And how about you, Faith? Are you OK? I thought you looked rather happy just now.' I fiddled with my wedding ring.

'Oh, I'm terribly happy,' I said.

Peter and I hadn't told the children that he was moving back in. We wanted it to be a surprise. My parents had taken them snow-boarding for a week; when they got back, they'd find him at home. So, on the fifth, I sat in the sitting room with Graham, waiting for Peter to arrive. There was a bottle of champagne chilling in the fridge, along with the ingredients for a seafood risotto – his favourite dish. Now I signed the heart-strewn card for our wedding anniversary the next day. It was the sixth, the feast of Epiphany, the Christmas decorations would have to come down. We'd had enough bad luck over the past year, I reflected, and I didn't want to risk any more. So now, while I waited for Peter, I took the fairy off the top of the tree. Then I began to unravel the tinsel and unhooked the spangly baubles and glittering stars. Then suddenly Graham ran barking to the door as we heard the click of a key in the lock.

'Peter!' My arms went round his neck, and his went round my waist. 'Peter!' I said as Graham jumped up, whimpering with happiness, to lick his ear. 'Oh, Peter!' I said again. He took off his coat, grabbed my hand and led me upstairs.

'Oh, Faith!' he said as our limbs entwined in the candlelit silence of our room. 'Oh, Faith,' he murmured again. 'Oh, Faith, we nearly threw it away.'

'I know.'

'We got ourselves in such a . . . mess.'

'Yes,' I said as I stroked his hair, 'we did, but we're all right now.' We lay in bed for half an hour afterwards. Graham had jumped up and was lying blissfully between us, his head resting on his paws.

'I love you,' I said as I stroked his silky ears.

'I love you too,' said Peter.

'Mummy and Daddy *both* love you,' I said. Graham heaved a contented sigh. Now we got dressed and went downstairs and Peter opened the champagne. I started cooking the risotto, and as I stirred the rice we discussed the events of the last few days.

'You have stopped the decree absolute, haven't you?' he asked me.

'Yes, of course I have. I phoned Rory Cheetham-Stabb's office two days ago and left a message on his voice-mail.'

'And what happens to the decree nisi?'

'Nothing. But in due course we can just write to the court asking them to dismiss our petition.'

'Oiliver's left Fenton & Friend,' said Peter as he set the table.

'What a relief.'

'It is. Though I seem to have maligned him more than was strictly necessary. I thought that nasty little press campaign was his doing because he'd got wind of my takeover plans. I never guessed it could be Lily, because I knew she'd never do anything which might hurt you.'

'Ah, but she'd persuaded herself that you were the anti-Christ, darling, and that what she was doing was all for my good. She'd kidded herself that I deserved to be liberated from my dull suburban life with you.'

'Well, for a while you were liberated from it.'

'Yes, but then I wanted it back. I like being dull and sub-urban,' I added as I kissed him, 'as long as I can be dull and suburban with you. Do you forgive Lily?' I asked him as I turned up the heat.

'Yes,' he said thoughtfully. 'I do. She told me that she was truly sorry, so that's good enough for me.'

'But what about Andie?' I went on as I poured in more stock. 'Did she throw things?'

'No. She wasn't in a position to be nasty, because she knew the game was up.'

'Was she ever really pregnant?'

'No, but she thought she was. She'd missed two periods, so she was firmly convinced she was up the duff. She didn't actually lie to me about it – it was a phantom pregnancy, I suppose.'

'But I thought she'd done a test?'

'Yes, but she was so excited at the thought of being pregnant, she didn't read the leaflet properly and got it wrong. And when in December she realised she wasn't expecting, she couldn't bring herself to tell me the truth. I would have found out soon enough, so Lily's disclosure just speeded things up.'

By now the risotto was ready, and we'd had the champagne and were feeling slightly tipsy and very relaxed. Peter washed the salad and made a French dressing and we opened a bottle of good Sancerre. And as we sat in the kitchen, talking and eating, I looked at Peter's face in the flickering candlelight and thought, I love you *so* much. I'll never love any man as I love you. I nearly lost you, but now you're back.

'We'll move house,' Peter said. 'Shall we do that?'

'Yes. Let's.'

'A fresh start.'

'Mmm.'

'This is our new chapter, Faith. This is our *real* new beginning.'

'And our happy ending.'

'I think it is. Oh Faith, we're so, so lucky,' he added as he put down his fork. 'I mean, my God, I had a narrow escape.'

'You certainly did,' I breathed.

'I didn't want to have to do the decent thing again,' he exclaimed with a good-natured laugh.

'Sorry?'

'I didn't want to have to do the decent thing again,' he repeated. 'With Andie.'

'What do you mean – *again*?' He looked at me non-comprehendingly.

'Faith, you know perfectly well.'

'No,' I said quietly. 'I don't.'

'Yes, you do,' he insisted as I felt my heart contract. 'Look, it's all absolutely fine now, darling, but as you know, I'd done the decent thing once, when I was twenty. I didn't want to have to do it twice.'

'What are you suggesting?' I asked as I felt blood suffuse my face.

'I'm not suggesting anything. I'm saying.'

'What?'

'Oh Faith,' he said wearily. 'We've been through so much. Let's just give each other a break.'

'No,' I insisted as I fiddled with my glass. 'You've just hinted at something not very . . . nice.'

'Look, darling,' he said, 'we both know that you were pregnant when we got married, but to be honest I couldn't

428

care less. We made it work, and we've been pretty happy, so let's just leave it at that.'

'I don't want to leave it at that, because I consider your remark rather unchivalrous.'

'Well, I'm sorry, but the fact is, it's true.'

'We got married because we were in love, Peter.'

'Yes,' he said wearily. 'We did. But the main reason we got married, if you care to remember, was because you were three months gone. Now, please can we change the subject, because my little joke has obviously misfired.'

'So it was a joke, was it?' I said hotly. 'Well, as Freud says, "There is no such thing as a joke", Peter, and it's now crystal clear to me that you've held this against me all these years.'

'Well, I obviously wasn't *planning* on marrying at twenty, Faith, but I wasn't going to leave you in the lurch.'

'Oh, that's really *kind* of you,' I said sarcastically. 'And I suppose you think I should be grateful?'

'No, I *don't* think that,' he replied.

'Well, I really don't like you bringing this up and implying that I trapped you, and that you just did the decent thing, even if you did, because I don't think it's necessary to mention it on this day of all days after we've had such a hard year, and we were getting back together again and it was all looking so good.'

'It still *is*!'

'But you're clearly blaming me, just because I didn't like taking my pill because it made me feel sick. I've made my sacrifices too, you know, including not getting my degree, and bringing up the children, and not having much money, and I don't know why you have to mention it now after all this time.'

'I suppose because Andie's pseudo-pregnancy brought it all back for me.'

'But I feel very insulted by what you said there, Peter, and I've got some very negative feelings coming up. After all, these things happen, don't they, they happen every day of the year, and I didn't do it deliberately or anything, but it's just that

429

I think you're in the wrong to say something so obviously wounding.'

'Just forget it, will you,' he said as he cleared the plates. 'I didn't realise I'd hit a nerve.'

'Of course you've hit a nerve, because here you are accusing me of being sneaky and dishonourable and trying to ensnare you, and maybe, yes – maybe *that's* why you had your affair, to punish me, because you'd secretly resented it all these years. But as you *well* know, Peter, it takes two to tango and I didn't exactly have an immaculate conception, and I really don't like you saying that, because I've been through an awful lot too.'

'Well, maybe *you* wanted an affair,' he said. 'Or maybe we *both* wanted one.' I stared at him. Then looked away. 'Maybe we both wanted a little change,' I heard him say. 'Isn't that what you wanted too, Faith?'

'Yes,' I croaked. 'I did. I *did*,' I whispered. 'I'd been wondering, for quite a long time, what *if* . . . ?'

'So had I. And we found out. But "what if?" didn't make us happy, did it?'

'No,' I murmured. 'It didn't.'

'And are we happy now?' My anger had vanished.

'Oh yes,' I said tearfully. 'We *are*. I'm so happy,' I added as he drew me to him.

'So am I,' he said. 'I'm happy because I have Faith. So please would you stop being cross, darling?' I nodded. 'Because we're together again. We're together again,' he repeated as his arms went round me. 'Not for ever,' he added. I looked at him. 'But just on a permanent basis. You know, maybe, in an odd way, Lily did us a favour,' he added as he held me close.

'Yes.' I smiled. 'Maybe she did.'

At three thirty the next morning, the alarm pipped twice and I slipped out of bed; Peter groaned slightly, then rolled over again. It's as though nothing has changed, I thought as I gazed at his sleeping form. It's as though the intervening year hasn't happened, as though it was just a strange dream. Today is our wedding anniversary, I reflected as I showered and dressed.

Today we've been married for sixteen years. I left the card on my pillow for him to find, then hugged Graham and went down to the waiting cab.

When I got into work I smiled cheerfully at my colleagues as they sat hunched over their terminals. I had my usual double espresso, then turned on my computer, with its rainbow screensaver. Here's my rainbow, I thought to myself. It was here all the time. And the thing about rainbows, I now remembered, is that you can only see them when you have your back to the sun. I'm happy again, I thought as I looked at the newspapers. I can see clearly now.

I glanced at the front page of *The Times* which, to my surprise, carried a small piece about Lily. *New Improved* Moi! it announced approvingly. *Lily Jago, editor of* Moi! *has called on all women's magazines to have their covers printed on matt paper, after her near-fatal accident last week when she slipped on a copy of* Vogue. 'Moi! *will be leading the way in introducing non-slip covers,' she said. From next month* Moi! *will be the very first non-glossy glossy, but will lose none of its natural shine.* I smiled, then turned over the page. I found myself staring at a photo of Rory Cheetham-Stabb. *Celebrity Divorce Lawyer Censured*, said the headline. I scanned the piece. *Rory Cheetham-Stabb . . . Rottweiler reputation . . . Accused of professional misconduct.* Why? What on earth had he done? *Allegedly having sex with a number of his female clients.* Oh God. *William Thompson complained to the Law Society that Cheetham-Stabb's affair with his wife was one thing, but charging for the time spent in flagrante with her was quite another.* Now I flicked through the other papers – the tabloids had gone to town. 'LAWYER SCREWS CLIENTS SHOCK!' announced the Sun ironically, whilst Mr Thompson was quoted as saying that since he was footing the bill for the divorce he objected to being 'screwed twice over'. There was to be a hearing at the Law Society today, the paper explained. I found myself feeling sorry for Cheetham-Stabb, but on the other hand I wasn't surprised. I mean, why else would he think of us all as 'his' wives?

When I got up at lunchtime, I phoned Peter. He'd seen the piece.

'Poor guy,' he said. 'Did he make any advances to you?'

'I'm sorry to say that he didn't.'

'Oh, how disappointing, darling, never mind. But Faith,' he said, 'have you checked that he's *definitely* cancelled the application for the decree absolute?'

'I'm sure he would have done it,' I said. 'He's very efficient.'

'That may be, but I think you should call his assistant and make sure.'

'OK,' I said. 'I'll do it now.' So I phoned Rory Cheetham-Stabb's secretary. She said that Cheetham-Stabb was out.

'He's having rather a – busy day,' she explained tactfully.

'Of course,' I said. So I asked if there was anyone else who could help, and she explained that there was another solicitor who knew about my case, but he'd just gone to lunch.

'You see,' I said, 'I just want to check that Mr Cheetham-Stabb carried out my instructions about my decree absolute.'

'Well, I'm sure he would have done,' she said. 'But I'm afraid the only person who can help you is Mr Blake, and he won't be back until half past two.' So I took Graham for a walk, then did some tidying up. I put the rest of Peter's clothes back into our wardrobe, and hung up his coat in the hall. I filled the dishwasher and put in the last of the Finish rinse aid I'd won twelve months before. And now I took our wedding photo out of the drawer, polished it, and put it back in its old place. And I made a mental note to get Lily's lovely sunburst mirror repaired. The sun had come back into our lives, I realised. It was shining for us again. By now it was two thirty, so I telephoned Mr Blake.

'You see, I've been reconciled with my husband,' I explained. 'So three days ago I left a message for Mr Cheetham-Stabb asking him to cancel the application for the decree absolute which I imagine must be coming up quite soon.'

'Let me see when it was due. Your decree nisi was pronounced on November the twenty-second,' he explained, 'so six weeks and one day from then – plus three public holidays – brings us up to January the . . . sixth.'

'January the sixth?' I repeated. 'But that's today.'

'Er, yes,' he said. 'That's right.'

'Well then, obviously I really need to make sure that Mr Cheetham-Stabb has stopped the decree absolute. That's what I'm ringing to check.' I heard the rustle of papers as Mr Blake went through the file.

'To be honest, I can't see a note here saying that he has done that. In fact, looking at the documents I'm fairly sure that he hasn't.'

'What?'

'The answer is no.'

'He hasn't done it?'

'I'm afraid not, Mrs Smith.'

'But I don't understand,' I said weakly. 'I left a message on his voice-mail three days ago instructing him to cancel the application straight away.'

'Well, I'm awfully sorry Mrs Smith, but it looks as though that hasn't happened. It's very, *very* unusual for anyone to cancel a decree absolute, and in any case Mr Cheetham-Stabb has had rather a lot on his plate.'

'Yes,' I said, 'I know. But this was incredibly *important*,' I added. 'You see my husband and I no longer want to get divorced.'

'Well, I'm awfully sorry,' he repeated as I began to panic. 'But the application has already gone through. It was lodged with the court this morning.'

'Then we must get it stopped.'

'But we can't. You see they process them very quickly. I'm afraid your divorce will be stamped decree absolute by the end of today.'

'But I don't *want* that,' I insisted desperately. 'I don't *want* to get divorced!'

'Well, I regret to say it's too late.'

'Too late? No! It can't be! Let me tell you, I've been married for a very long time, Mr Blake, and I intend to stay that way.'

'Look,' he said awkwardly. 'I don't wish to be unhelpful, but there's absolutely nothing you can do.'

'But I –'

'I'm sorry, Mrs Smith. I really am. You'll have to take this up with Mr Cheetham-Stabb, when he's back, but I have to go to a meeting now.'

I clutched the phone as the line went dead, staring wildly into space. Oh, God, oh *God*. We didn't *want* to get divorced. We wanted to stay married for the rest of our lives. I phoned Peter and told him the news.

'Oh fuck!' he said. 'This is a disaster! I'll sue Cheetham-Stabb for misconduct, too.'

'But what are we going to *do*, Peter?' I wailed. 'Our divorce goes through today.'

'Phone Karen,' he said. 'Ask her. She's always given us good advice.' So I rang her.

'How awful,' she said. 'Cheetham-Stabb should have done it straight away. Especially as he knew the decree absolute was imminent.'

'Mr Blake said there was nothing we could do,' I explained as tears pricked the backs of my eyes. I glanced at our wedding photo. The minutes were ticking away.

'There is *one* thing you can try,' she said, 'as a last resort. You could go to First Avenue House.'

'What's that?'

'It's the building which houses the Principal Registry in which all the divorce papers are stamped. It's a long shot,' she added ruefully, 'but on the other hand you've got nothing to lose. It's at forty-two High Holborn,' she said. 'Go there right now, ask one of the clerks to dig out your file, and maybe, with luck, it won't have been stamped. But you'll have to hurry,' she urged me, 'because the building closes at half past four.' I looked at the clock – oh God, oh *God* – it was already five to three. I thanked her and phoned Peter back.

'Can you get there now?' I asked Peter.

'No – I'm in a meeting from three until four.'

'You'll have to cancel it, this is urgent.'

'Impossible – it's with the chairman, Jack Price. But I can

434

leave straight after that,' he added. 'You'd better get a taxi,' he said.

'I can't risk getting stuck in heavy traffic, I'll get the tube. Meet me at Chancery Lane underground at ten past four.' I ran out of the house, adrenaline pumped and overwrought. Luckily a train came within two minutes, but every time it stopped in a tunnel, I'd panic and look at my watch. By three forty I was at Victoria, by three fifty at Oxford Circus. But I'd forgotten how long the interchange was from the Victoria to the Central line. And of course the crowds were heaving, and of *course* the escalators were down. So by the time I got to Chancery Lane tube it was four fifteen. Peter was standing there, looking distressed.

'Come on!' he said. 'I think it's this way.' So we turned left and passed the red-bricked Prudential building and headed towards St Giles. I couldn't find number forty-two anywhere, it was almost dark, but then I spotted number two hundred and thirty-six.

'Peter, this is wrong!' I said. 'The numbers are too high. It must be the other way.' So we sped back towards the tube, half walking, half running down the street. We passed United House, and Rymans, and the arched entrance to Gray's Inn. And here was Alliance House, but we couldn't see number forty-two. So we suddenly stopped, in case it was on the other side of the road.

'Excuse me . . .' I turned. Looking at me enquiringly was an elderly woman. She must have been eighty or more. She was tiny, white-haired and slightly bent, and she was gazing at me with a slightly confused smile.

'Excuse me,' she said again. 'But don't I *know* you?'

'No, I –'

'You look so familiar, I'm sure I *do*.'

'No honestly, you don't and in fact I'm in a real hurry, you see . . .'

'Oh, I've got it!' she exclaimed. 'You're that girl on the TV!' I sighed and nodded. 'Well, I just want to say . . .' I braced myself for her to tell me how useless I was, like that chap who'd spotted me in Tesco's that time. 'I just want to say how much I *like* you,' she went on. 'You really make my day. Yes, you really make my day,' she repeated happily as she laid her frail hand on my arm. I looked at it; beneath the papery skin I could see a delta of pale blue veins. 'Yes,' she repeated beatifically, 'your lovely weather forecasts really cheer me up.'

'Well, that's terribly nice of you,' I said, 'but I'm afraid I can't chat, you see –'

'And you know, you've especially cheered me up recently because my husband died three weeks ago.'

'Oh.'

'Well, we're sorry,' said Peter. 'That's awfully sad.'

'Yes, it was sad,' she said. 'It was very sad, and . . .' There were tears standing in her eyes. 'We were married for sixty years,' she explained. 'We got married at twenty, you see. It's not like today.' She was removing a paper hankie from her sleeve. 'Everyone gets married so *late*. Sixty years,' she repeated wistfully as she pressed the tissue to her eyes.

'That's wonderful,' I said. 'But you see we –'

'And do you know what the secret is?' I shook my head. 'It's love. I always told my husband how much I loved him. Every day I'd say to him, "I love you, Harry. I'll always love you." And do you know, I always did. I hope you don't mind me telling you that,' she added, 'but it's just that I feel I know you, in a way.'

'Oh no, I don't mind at all,' I said as I felt my throat begin to ache. 'And I'm so sorry you've been bereaved, but the thing is –'

'Are you two married?'

'Yes,' said Peter. She nodded.

'I thought so. You look like you're in love.' I smiled.

'We are,' Peter said. 'But you see we've just got to dash to First Avenue House by four thirty otherwise we'll be getting divorced, so I don't want you to think us rude, but I'm afraid we've got to go.'

'Oh, I understand,' she said. 'Don't let me keep you. Don't let me keep you, my dears. Good luck,' she added. 'It's made my day. Meeting you. I hope you have sixty years together as well.' Now as we turned away from her and began to run down the street, we saw the building at last.

'*There* it is!' I said. 'There it is! Come on!' At that precise moment we heard two deep, sonorous chimes from above. We went on, as if to our execution, aware that the half-hour had struck. And now, here we were, standing outside First Avenue House. The massive oak doors were shut.

'We've missed it,' I murmured. Peter nodded. 'We're too late, Peter. We're too late. We're *divorced*,' I added, shaking my head. 'We never meant this to happen.'

'No.'

'We're divorced,' I repeated tearfully as we stood there in impotent despair. Peter looked at me; his face was grey.

'Oh Christ,' he whispered. And now a terrible gloom descended upon us as we turned and walked back the way we'd come. Silence gripped us for a minute. Then Peter reached into his pocket and pulled out a red envelope.

'It's an anniversary card,' he said bleakly. 'Perhaps it's not appropriate now. We're divorced,' he added, disbelievingly. He looked as traumatised as I felt. 'But on the other hand,' he went on as he put his arm round my shoulder, 'on the other hand, we're not splitting up. Yes, we may, technically, be divorced, Faith, but we're still together.'

'Oh, yes, that's right. We are.'

'In fact, we've never been *more* together, have we?'

'No,' I said, 'we haven't.'

'And I mean, what is marriage, anyway,' he added expansively, 'but a piece of paper?'

'Of course.'

'I mean, loads of people live together.'

'That's true.'

'So we can just cohabit, darling, can't we?'

'Yes,' I sniffed. 'We can.' By now I was starting to cheer up a little as we strolled down the street. And above us, rising into the inky sky was a perfect, silver full moon. What was it Lily's horoscope had predicted? That by the time of the January full

437

moon I'd discover why one particular person held an undying appeal. And that toe-reading woman had told me that I would definitely get divorced. And now I had.

'We'll cohabit, darling,' Peter repeated as his arm went round my waist. 'But, then again, you know what we *could* do?' he continued cheerfully.

'No. What's that?'

'Well, it's obvious. We could get married again.'

'Mmm.'

'I mean, Elizabeth Taylor did it, didn't she? Why not remarry your ex? Why don't we just do that, darling, and nip down to the register office? Or would you like a church wedding again?'

'Well . . .'

'Oh no, we can't,' he added, 'I was forgetting – Catholics aren't allowed to remarry in church. On the other hand,' he went on animatedly, 'they might make an exception for us, as divorcees who are marrying each other again. Shall we look into that, darling? I could write to the Pope.'

'Mmm . . .'

'It would be rather *nice* to have another wedding, wouldn't it?' he continued. 'I really like that idea. Do you think Lily will want to be bridesmaid again? And what do you think I should wear? Graham could be an usher. He's got a lot of sheepdog, so he'd do it well. He could wear a nice white ribbon through his collar – the kids would love it – oh yes, I can see it now. And we could have a really swanky reception this time, in a smart hotel. With a jazz band,' he went on dreamily. 'And real champagne, of course. And the good thing is we'd get lots of presents. Yes, Faith, we could have a bit of a do. I mean, wouldn't you like that, Faith? A really nice wedding? And of course a *fabulous* honeymoon. Come on darling, you've gone rather quiet, tell me what you think.' I looked up at him and smiled.

'Peter,' I said carefully. 'It sounds lovely. And I'm very honoured, of course. But isn't it a bit, you know – premature?'

'Premature?'

'You see, darling, I really don't think we should rush into anything. After all – marriage is a *very* big step!'